The Believers

The Believers

JANICE HOLT GILES

With an Introduction by
CECILIA MACHESKI

THE UNIVERSITY PRESS OF KENTUCKY

This edition published in 1989 by The University Press of Kentucky
Introduction copyright © 1989 by The University Press of Kentucky

Scholarly publisher for the Commonwealth,
serving Bellarmine College, Berea College, Centre
College of Kentucky, Eastern Kentucky University,
The Filson Club, Georgetown College, Kentucky
Historical Society, Kentucky State University,
Morehead State University, Murray State University,
Northern Kentucky University, Transylvania University,
University of Kentucky, University of Louisville,
and Western Kentucky University.

Editorial and Sales Offices: Lexington, Kentucky 40506-0336

Giles, Janice Holt.
    The believers.

    1. Shakers—History—19th century—Fiction.
I. Title.
PS3513.I4628B4 1989   813'.54   88-27901
ISBN 0-8131-1681-3
ISBN 0-8131-0189-1 (pbk.)

To Buddy, who in the line of duty ran afoul of
a "Shaker" bird, and to Ann and Steve
Because of all our fun

INTRODUCTION

"In the West . . . the gathering will be great." So said Mother Ann Lee in predicting the rise and success of her utopian community, the United Society of Believers in the Second Coming of Christ, better known today as the Shakers. Janice Holt Giles's historical novel *The Believers* is set in Kentucky in the early nineteenth century at a time when Ann Lee's prophecy seemed to be reaching fulfillment. *The Believers* opens in 1800, marks the first appearance of Shaker "scouts" from New York in 1807, and concludes in 1812 as converts dissatisfied with the life of the community were leaving the settlement and the Kentucky legislature passed a decree to permit immediate divorce to parties disenchanted with their spouses' Shaker convictions.

Giles's choice of the Shaker community as a setting and the emergence of Shaker beliefs as a theme are not firsts in American literature. Nor, in fact, are they uncommon or unlikely choices, particularly for American women writers. Giles's novel, published in 1957, comes more than a century after Catherine Sedgwick's *Redwood: A Tale* (1824) and the anonymously published short story "The Shaker Lovers" (1852). In the twentieth century the most successful fiction about the Shakers included *Susanna and Sue* (1909) by Kate Douglas Wiggins (better known as the author of *Rebecca of Sunnybrook Farm*), *The Way of Peace* (1910) by Margaret Deland, and *Dancing Saints* (1943) by Ann George Leslie. While these writers have been neglected by history, at least one writer of Shaker stories remains well known to readers today: Nathaniel Hawthorne contributed two short stories, "The Shaker Bridal" and "The Canterbury Pilgrims" (1838) to the Shaker legacy.

The modern visitor to Pleasant Hill or South Union, Hancock or Sabbathday Lake or Canterbury, attracted by the beauty and peacefulness of the village museums, often longs to people the barns and meeting houses, kitchens and sewing rooms with living Shakers. Since time and history have made this impossible, we must turn to fiction to hear something like those voices. Unfortunately the Shakers themselves did not write novels, although they have left a record of their lives in the words of their hymns, diaries, letters, and tracts. Many of these, however, are not easily accessible to the general reader, and it is for him or her that novels like *The Believers* fill a need. Combining history and imagination, Giles and the other novelists recreate the daily life of the Shakers in fictional form, thus offering an enjoyable way for everyone curious about Shaker life to learn more while reading a novel of adventure and romance.

This group of fictions, then, is clearly *about* and not *by* Shakers. Thus it is not surprising that the stories often remain outside the spiritual experience of the Believers and focus on the routine events of the communities, just as many visitors to Shaker sites today are more interested in the furniture and architecture than in the spiritual heritage. And while the various authors provide a range of attitudes about the community, none of these fictions really allows the Shaker dream to prevail. "The Shaker Lovers," for instance, startles us with its bitter denunciation of the elders, portraying them as greedy and lecherous, as thinly disguised hypocrites. *Dancing Saints*, perhaps the most sympathetic, must nevertheless take the young hero, Orville, who trained as an architect with the Shakers, out of the village and back into the world as the novel concludes. Both *Susanna and Sue* and *The Way of Peace* present the Shakers as gentle and well-meaning, but each heroine in the end decides to return to her duties in the world, counting motherhood too highly to sacrifice it for religious convictions.

The Shaker novel that allows a character to transcend social and family customs and expectations, to commit herself fully to the Society, or to present the Society as progressive and prosperous, is not among these texts, although the recent *A Maggot* by John Fowles offers a more ambitious literary use of Shaker material. Fowles constructs his tale with more sympathy for Ann Lee and the ideas she espoused than did the earlier writers. But if we are looking for Shaker propaganda, we will not find it in Giles. We will find instead something of the distrust and prejudice with which the Shakers were met by the "World's People," and, at the same time, the often wistful record of visits to the villages by those who wished to stay but lacked the courage or single-mindedness necessary to abandon their outside lives in exchange for lives devoted to God. *The Believers* is typical of the general trend in having its heroine finally reject the Shaker way of life. But Giles is more original in selecting a western community, rather than a New England one, as her setting, and in rooting the plot firmly in the history of Kentucky. She works hard to create authentic regional language for her characters and to frame the Shaker section of the story with well-researched background about the settling of the western territories.

But to appreciate Giles's story, we should first ask some broad questions about her choice of material. What has been the continuing appeal of Shaker material to such a wide range of American writers, over such an extended period of our history? And what has been the particular appeal to women writers?

First, we must expect that a community based on the principle of celibacy will always interest the human mind, especially in our post-Freudian age. This doctrine, after all, raises many questions about marriage, the family, male and female relationships, and of course, human sexuality. While these have always been the themes of fiction, I suggest that the special emphasis on celibacy in the Shaker manifesto provided writers—particularly women—with the opportunity to explore what we might call today an alternative life style. The Shaker prohibition against sex built a platform from which the writer could expound upon and get perspective on the problems that lack of celibacy so frequently posed for women in the days before reliable contraception—frequent child-bearing and the poverty that often derived from it. A community in which sexual tensions had at least theoretically been reduced was the ideal vantage point for reflecting on the violence that so often occurred within marriages troubled by hardship, poverty, and lack of education. Shaker communism posed (again at least in theory) the viability of communities based on gender separation, of child-rearing outside the nuclear family, of equal education for girls and boys, of freedom from sexual tension and from the demand for adherence to fashion, and, most important perhaps, the model of a political structure based on equality of the sexes. Is it any wonder that American writers, like museum visitors today, found much that was appealing, and much that was threatening, in the doctrine of the Believers? It is worth noting, too, that while few writers leave their characters to retire in Hancock or Union, they have gone so far as to bring them—and us—into the village. For that, at least, they merit recognition.

Second, in trying to understand the appeal of the Shakers we should remember that the analysis of a communistic society, whether utopian or distopian, has been a topic of interest to American writers from our beginnings. The new nation hosted many experimental groups—not only the Shakers but the Amish, the Quakers, the Zoarites, the Mennonites, Amana, Oneida, Bethel, Aurora—from the original pilgrim parents to the more recent "Moonies." A fictional account of the Shakers is thus another way of working toward a definition of our national identity. For Giles, writing in the era stained by the cold war and the hearings dominated by Senator McCarthy, the notion of writing about the communistic Shakers may have taken on contemporary meaning. One can only guess how much her portrait of the evangelical Richard McNemar was colored by McCarthy's red paintbrush. For while we today can admire the Believers as a group that advocated pacifism and preached racial and sexual equality, much of the fiction suggests that they can also be seen as a band of fanatics who threatened that most basic of human rights, reproductive choice. For women, the dogma of celibacy could be a great sacrifice of all the traditional female roles or, more radically, a greatly liberating device, freeing women, in much the same way reliable contraception has done, to work at a greater variety of tasks and to share with men the full life of the community. With so much controversy surrounding the Shaker doctrines, it is not surprising that novelists were attracted to them, for the fictional mode offered an ideal place for exploring many sides of the issues. Where women, in particular, might have hesitated to speak out directly on topics of a sexual nature, as writers they were able, through their plots and characters, to make their voices heard.

Thus celibacy served as a focal point for the writers' political interests. From the literary point of view, moreover, lack of consummation provided a very convenient plot structure. Since many of the novels are romantic, the writers could use the doctrine to allow her male and female characters to develop a relationship on neutral ground while they remain in the community. A closer look at some of the plots reveals how the technique works.

The Shaker plot is similar from novel to novel. An individual or a married couple approach a Shaker village or the Shakers approach them. The World's People experiment with Shaker life for a time, giving the reader a chance to see the inside of the village and to share with the newcomer the process of learning Shaker ways. The heroine or hero or both face a crisis; they must eventually make a decision about remaining in the community and taking permanent vows, or signing the covenant, or leaving. The individual has either gained respect and trust for the Shakers or has learned to see them as charlatans and fanatics. In most of the stories, one partner stays (usually the man) and the other leaves. Usually, too, the reader's sympathy is with the character who leaves, for that character has come to represent some kind of choice for freedom and individuality over the "repressive" forces of community living. Those who stay with the Shakers are perceived as somehow left to die, for they have cut themselves off from the natural processes of family and reproduction.

In a way, the entry to the village follows an ancient mythological pattern, that of the hero's descent into the underworld. Perhaps this Shaker experience is the American equivalent of that quest. The novels take us on a voyage to a land where the spirit is primary, where no one is hungry, to a utopia of practical ideas, hard work, and people who present rather Blake-like images—sexless and unhampered by the responsibilities of family. But like Ulysses and Aeneas, the American travelers clutch their golden boughs tightly, cling to their democratic notions, and reascend to the real world. That these returning travelers are mostly women is in some sense curious, for Shaker beliefs began with a woman and her response to the agony of childbirth and unhappy marriage. Perhaps it was Ann Lee's practical side that appealed in the past as it does today—the plea for a clean work environment and healthful living quarters, for practical ways of accomplishing tedious work, for a life that allowed time for spiritual reflection. The novels reveal a respect for these values but argue further that the price is too dear if it includes a rejection of motherhood and sexuality. The men, curiously, find this sacrifice more acceptable, though they are not the ones to suffer the agonies of childbirth and to carry the emotional and physical burden of rearing a family as the women do. Perhaps a closer look at *The Believers* will help us understand why Mother Ann Lee's utopia is represented in women's fiction as, in reality, a man's world.

The Believers is set in Kentucky in the early nineteenth century around the lives of the daughters and sons of the first generation of settlers. The narrative voice is first person, as Rebecca Fowler, who marries her childhood sweetheart, Richard Cooper, tells of their early years together as farmers and settlers on land belonging to Richard's father. (Giles thus continues stories begun in two earlier novels: that of Rebecca's mother, *Hannah Fowler*, and that of Richard's parents, *The Kentuckians*.) With the loss of Rebecca's first child in a stillbirth, Richard turns to God with questions. At the same time, the Shakers arrive in Kentucky as if called upon to provide answers. Richard soon persuades Rebecca to give up the farm and move west with the Believers. Reluctantly but dutifully she agrees.

On one level the novel is about the size and shape of westward expansion and what this aspect of Manifest Destiny meant on the human scale. Rebecca must leave her parents when she marries. She and her sister Janie both leave home with the knowledge that they may never see their parents again, for distances are vast when means of travel are limited. The "natural order" dictates that Rebecca create her own family, but this fails when her baby is born dead. Then Richard attempts to reconstruct the family by joining the Shakers, who constitute their community into "artificial" families. But as the plot develops we see his scheme too fail, as "natural law" calls parents to their ailing children and women to their men despite the dictates of separation pronounced by the elders.

Through Richard's choice we are brought into the Shaker community as novitiates. But because Rebecca narrates, we view daily life mainly through the eyes of the women. Giles creates realistic narrative, based, she claims, on diaries and documents culled from Shaker archives. Yet Giles, of course, looks at the belief system of the Shakers in the light of her own day, a day in which anti-red smear tactics might have frightened anyone from making a more positive statement about a communistic society. She warns us that we may be inclined to romanticize the Shakers by focusing too much attention on their artifacts and not paying sufficient attention to their religious and philosophical views.

Much like Margaret Atwood's *The Handmaid's Tale*, *The Believers* pivots on the issue of reproductive rights and sexual choice. Both novels are women's books in the special way they build a distopian society in which women's bodies and men's and women's sexual desires are regulated by public policy to the extent that politics and reproduction are identical. Giles's Shaker world is one in which the law mandates celibacy. Atwood's is one in which women are selected or identified for breeding purposes and cruelly "mated" with the men of the self-appointed aristocracy, while other women are cast in the role of the Wife or Prostitute. No woman is allowed to fill more than one role. Atwood's world is close to nightmare, however, while Giles's is less harsh, a world in which utopia has, sadly, gone wrong. Yet despite the differences in their respective visions, both writers may be read as feminists in that their texts privilege the power inherent in women to control society by their ability to reproduce, and both represent the political structure as one very much afraid of that power. While men's novels often make war the shaper of fates, women's novels like these offer the message that women are more important than military might. By the end of both novels, women have rejected the rules by which others had tried to regulate them and have returned to a more "natural" order.

Yet neither novel is a simplistic propaganda tool, and Giles in particular gives both sides a fair hearing. Her narrator, Rebecca, must struggle with her decisions about Richard and about her duty as a woman. And Giles is careful to create a strong female friendship between her heroine and Permilla, another woman brought to the Shakers by her husband's wishes. Permilla is beautiful, kind, and intelligent, and thus when she chooses to remain with the Shakers we see that the Society did offer refuge to many who needed it. Permilla finds the rule of celibacy a welcome respite from the demands of frequent child-bearing and the company of an unloving and often brutal husband. Her humor and strength prove adequate protection against any austerity the Shaker life requires of her. In contrast, other characters, such as Sabrina, brought up from childhood within the Shaker village, lack the stamina and courage that Permilla's life outside has given her and meet less happy ends. Giles even introduces a black family, slaves who have followed Richard and Rebecca from their farm into the Shaker village. While her portrayal of these characters is unfortunately tainted by the stereotypes of romantic fiction like *Gone With the Wind*, Giles does at least suggest that the Shakers were true to their principles in accepting blacks into the community on an equal footing with whites.

The Believers, then, offers the modern reader a well documented picture of daily life in a Shaker community in Kentucky in the early nineteenth century. It tells us about both the idealistic aspirations of the disciples of Mother Ann Lee and the disappointments of those who eventually left her fold. For those who come today to visit the meeting houses in the villages, who sample the herbs and admire the forthright design of the Shaker chairs, the graceful but utilitarian work of the oval boxes, Giles's tale can add a further dimension. For *The Believers* reminds us that the village we visit was not raised without struggle, that the simplicity of which the Shakers were so justly proud emerged not only from their hands but from their hearts as well. And those hearts, as Rebecca Cooper tells us, often found the gift of simplicity an awesome burden. In reading *The Believers* we come to appreciate the lives of the women and men who once dwelt in these comely buildings, sang the hymns and moved through the dances, and dedicated their lives to creating a better world. Finally, Janice Holt Giles offers an appealing fiction that helps us understand our own fascination with the Shakers. Her story renews, at least for the moment, the fading voices of Mother Ann Lee's children.

CECILIA MACHESKI

F O R E W O R D

AROUND 1800, a small fire was lit on the Gasper River in south-central Kentucky. It caught from the passionate zeal of two brothers, itinerant preachers from Tennessee, and quickly, with the heat, the rapidity and the intensity of a forest fire, it spread over all of the state, throughout Tennessee and on into much of the rest of the south. It was called "The Great Revival."

Such preaching, such passion and such zeal in religion had not before been experienced, and people were caught up in its emotional raptures, taken with the jerks and shakes, dancing like dervishes, speaking in unknown tongues, weeping, wailing, barking like animals, crawling, rolling, going into trances. So great was the interest, so fast the spread, that within two years crowds of ten, fifteen, twenty thousand were gathering for these revival experiences. It created schisms in established churches and created new denominations, and it left its mark so that even today, in the hill country of both Kentucky and Tennessee, there are strange, emotional sects whose religion is most strongly characterized by the emotions and raptures of the revival practices.

Hearing about this great revival "in the west" the queer, celibate group calling themselves The United Society of Believers in Christ's Second Coming, more commonly known as "Shakers," determined that this was the land seen in vision by their great leader and founder, Mother Ann Lee. They sent their missionary teams into the country and made converts. Eventually two communities were founded in Kentucky. One was located near Harrodsburg on Shawnee Run. It was called Pleasant Hill. The other was situated on the Gasper River, south and west of Bowling Green. Its name was South Union. This book concerns the latter.

All of the central characters are fictional, but Brother Benjamin, Brother Rankin, Sister Molly, the missionaries, are quite real. From journals, diaries, biographies, and from study of the actual location of the village, I have tried to recover the daily life as it was lived there. Most of the incidents which are worked into the plot have their origin in actual happenings. Not all of them occurred at South Union, but they did occur in some Shaker village, at some time in its history, to some person.

When the last ten Shakers left South Union, in the 1920's, the land and buildings were sold to the Bond Brothers, and for years it was run as a stock farm. More recently the Benedictine Order has bought several of the buildings, still as sturdy, as stout and as beautiful as they ever were, and a boys' school has been established there. It is a strange coincidence that what was begun as an experiment in communal living should again today be another experiment, though of a different nature, in communal living.

I have had great respect for the Shakers. They were a gentle, dedicated, innocent people, though in their dedication and innocence they perpetrated great wrongs because of their fanaticism. That is what this book is about.

The
Believers

CHAPTER I

MY NAME was Rebecca Fowler. I grew up in Lincoln County on the Hanging Fork of Dick's River. I was the third child, the second daughter, of Hannah and Matthias Fowler, being born to them in the spring of seventeen hundred and eighty-three.

Richard always said I was a handsome woman. I do not know about that, but it is true that I am tall, though not as tall as my mother, and strongly built, as she was, with her same dark hair and eyes. Great physical endurance came to me from her also, and if it is true that I have always had a very level way of looking at things, that, too, came from her, for I never knew her not to be sensible and wise.

The home on the Hanging Fork was a pleasant one, with enough of the world's goods for comfort, and with friends and neighbors settled all about. There was an older sister, Jane, who was very like my father, with fair skin and reddish-brown hair, and there were three brothers, one older than I, two younger.

We were put to tasks very early. When I was as young as five, I did my stint of the winter knitting, and I could turn the big spinning wheel to fill a spindle as evenly as my mother before I was ten. I learned to weave, to help with the stock, to work in the garden patch, and to take my portion of the care of the house, all at a very tender age. I count it excellent training for any woman.

My mother and father were strict with us, but not stern. They expected and exacted obedience, but I have always thought that discipline commenced early surrounds a child with safe limits for his growing up. We had as many pleasures as the times accorded. We went occasionally to spend the day with neighbors. We went to corn huskings and barn raisings, and to quilting bees. We were taken sometimes to the county seat town, and once, even, my father took us the long journey to Lexington. It was a marvel for our young eyes to see, the city. And always, after the church was organized, we went to meeting, for both my mother and my father were faithful Presbyterians.

And we had more schooling than most young ones of our station. A traveling Englishman stayed with us two winters. He was studying the ways of the birds and the animals of our country, and he carried a great lot of books with him. He also painted many of the things he studied. He was a fine gentleman and he taught us in return for his bed and board, even my mother and father learning under him. He read to us from his books and taught us from them. He was thorough in his teaching, too, so that we can all write a fine hand and have some understanding of rhetoric, grammar, literature, geography and history.

I remember how he read to us at night, all of us gathered around, and the wonder it was to hear him. He read from Shakespeare and from Plato and Plutarch and from Spenser. He could make the written words come alive as if the people themselves were speaking. My mother, who ever had a longing for learning, said it was Providence that had brought him our way. It may have been.

Among our neighbors were David and Bethia Cooper, who lived only ten miles away on the headwaters of the Green River. When we went there we usually took the night and I loved to go. When the supper was over and the fire logs were burning brightly, sometimes David could be persuaded to tell of the old times in the country, when Kentucky was yet a part of Virginia and he, young and lighthearted, one of the Long Hunters. But we young ones found it hard to believe that our settled and prosperous lands had once been a wilderness and that the only trails had been those made by the Indians.

I especially loved to hear him tell about the trader, Johnnie Vann, who had been his friend, and sometimes I would steal out to the graves back of the house where Johnnie Vann and his little Indian son were buried and still kept green and neat by David, and think of Johnnie Vann and his Delaware wife, and of the night their son had died here in David's house. David and Bethia had called their oldest boy Johnnie, in memory of the trader, for David said, "He saved my life and Bethia and I owe everything we have to him."

David was a better manager than my father and it was only natural that his lands should increase, his holdings prosper, and their home be larger and richer than ours. I loved to wander through its big, airy rooms with the furniture David had brought from the East. Bethia loved color and beauty and the floors were strewn with bright, gay rugs of her own making, and the beds were spread with piece-work quilts.

I have ever had a liking for beauty and color myself, and sometimes, I own, I wished our mother had been more like Bethia. My mother thought first of the service to which an article was to be put, its usefulness and durability. "Will it last?" she always asked. I could never see but that a gay, bright rug on the floor was just as lasting as a drab one. Impatiently she would say, "I've more to do with my hands than dye goods for making rugs." Our rugs were made of cast-off clothing, faded, worn and ugly, but of a quality to last forever. Once I wanted to piece a quilt for the bed in which Janie and I slept. "Yore coverlid is good yit," my mother said, "put yer hands to work on somethin' needful."

There were only boys in the Cooper family . . . seven of them. Johnnie, the oldest, was two years older than Janie, and it was always Johnnie that Janie liked and followed after. He was gay and fun-loving, as she was herself, but he was often unkind to both of us, teasing and tormenting us. It was Richard I liked best, who like myself was a third child, being but two years older than I. When Johnnie was unkind, Richard would comfort us, find some new thing to share with us, make up to us as best he could for Johnnie's carelessness.

He knew where the biggest pawpaws grew, and the juiciest blackberries, and the finest hazel nuts. He never seemed to mind having a little girl at his heels, as Johnnie did, and he never teased. He was, in truth, a sober lad, not given to laughing much. Johnnie looked like his father, who could have passed for an Indian he was so dark, but Richard took after Bethia. As a little boy his hair was golden, though it reddened by the time he was grown. His eyes were a deep blue, and his skin, from his childhood, had a flush of color on the cheeks as if it had been rubbed there.

He was a serious boy, but he was kindly, able, good and loyal. He was stubborn, though. He could set his head as doggedly as an ox on the home trail, and once he had it set no amount of threatening, or wheedling or sensible pleading could change it.

Once we were there in the deep of winter. It came on to snow after we had reached the Coopers' place and there was nothing to do but wait over a few days until it had melted somewhat. Richard had a line of traps set in the river. He ran them every evening. "Richard," his father said, when the snow had been falling heavily all day, "you'd best let your traps go today."

Richard was bundling himself into his clothes. He shook his head. "I can't do that, Pa. There might be some animal caught would suffer through the night."

"Better that than for you to get frostbit," David said shortly.

But Richard shook his head again and Bethia laughed. "You just as well leave him go, David. His head is set."

"It's not so set I can't change it, if I'm so minded," his father said.

Richard looked at him and David looked back at Richard. There was no defiance in Richard's look. There was simply the determination to do what he felt was his duty. And it was David who looked away first. "Go ahead, then, if you're bound to act foolish."

"Let me go with you, Richard," I begged.

Johnnie laughed. "You . . . a girl . . . strike out in those drifts?"

But Richard saw I truly wanted to go and help. He didn't laugh. "You can go if you want," he said. "I can break trail and you can follow after."

My mother protested, but my father said, "With Richard, no harm can come to her." So I was allowed to go.

It was cold, the wind blowing a spume of snow into our faces, biting through our heavy wraps, and we sank deep into the drift with every step. But Richard bent into it and I followed, putting my feet where he had stepped.

We reached the river finally and I was so cold my hands and feet had no feeling. Richard had to break the ice to feel under it for the traps. There was nothing in the first one . . . nothing in the second. We followed on down the river but there was nothing at all in any of the traps, but patiently and stubbornly Richard broke the ice at each place, plunging his hand into the cold water, dragging up the trap, looking at it, rebaiting it, and just as patiently setting it back in the water. He let me help with the baits.

There were ten traps to see to, and where another might have given up after the first half dozen, Richard plodded on, I at his heels, until the last trap had been looked after. He never once complained or said it hadn't been worth it. They were his traps. He was responsible for them.

When he had finished, without a word to me, he turned back toward home. My teeth were chattering and I felt as if my face was frozen. I could barely stagger along to stay in his tracks. Once I fell and Richard looked around. "Here," he said, taking off his mittens, "hold these over your face. There's frostbite on your cheek."

"Your hands will get bitten," I said.

"I'll put 'em in my pockets."

Oh, the comfort of those mittens, still warm from his hands, held against my frozen face. And, oh, the comfort of that straight-backed, small figure, plunging through the snow, sure of its destination, dogged in its persistence.

Back at the house as we thawed ourselves at the fire David said, "You could of saved yourself the trouble, couldn't you? There wasn't a thing in the traps."

Richard held his hands to the fire and rubbed them. "But there might of been," he said.

One other time when we were children I saw the evidence of his will and determination. It was summer and the Coopers were at our home this time. Late in the evening we had been sent to bring the cows from the upper pasture. The upper pasture ran straight up the side of the steep hill which was at the back of our house. It was not fenced except across the top of the hill, and there were many cliffs and sheer bluffs. The cows wandered up and down the hillside by the paths they had worn avoiding the steeper places. A cow of ours was due to freshen and when we found the others at the foot of the hill, Bessie was not among them.

"She's wandered up the hillside," Richard said, "they'll do that, searching out a place that's hid off to drop their calves."

"Well, let's take this bunch on back to the barn," Johnnie said impatiently, "and let Tice worry about Bessie."

"She might of come to harm," Richard said.

"Well, she ain't yore cow, is she?"

But Richard was already looking up the hillside, already thinking as near as he could with a cow's mind, to where Bessie might have hidden out. He started off. "You and the girls take the rest of 'em in," he told Johnnie, "and I'll seek out this one."

That suited Johnnie fine, but instead of going with him and Jane, I followed Richard. "It's liable to be rough," he warned me.

"If it's not too rough for you," I told him, "it won't be too rough for me."

"Suit yourself," he said, "but take care and don't turn your foot on these stones."

With unerring instinct he searched out all the worst places. We scratched our way through briar thickets, up and down cliffs, into shallow caves and rockhouses. Our hands and faces were scratched and I had skinned a big place on one of my knees and torn my frock. That worried me more than the scratches and skinned place. Mama wasn't going to like that torn place in my dress.

The sun had been sinking when we had started after the cows and before long it was getting dusky dark. I wanted to turn back. They would be worried about us at the house if dark came on and we hadn't come home, and besides it looked as if Bessie had picked herself a place we weren't going to be able to find. But I dared not say any of these things to Richard. He would only have sent me home and stayed on himself. Patiently he kept on and I found I could do nothing but scramble along behind him.

It was to my credit, though, that we finally found her. I suddenly remembered a little ravine that cut down past the spring, with a dark and hidden cave in its narrowest part. "Richard," I said, excited at having remembered it, "I think I know where she is!"

"Where?"

"In the ravine behind the spring!"

He set off at once, so rapidly I could barely keep up. And she *was* there, still tired from her labor, the calf so newborn it was not yet dry. We stood and looked at it and Richard turned to me and smiled. "Ain't nothing in this world so sightly as a new-dropped calf, is there?"

Gently he picked it up, Bessie nuzzling him uneasily, and he carried it to the barn, while Bessie and I followed contentedly. That calf was a heavy load for a ten-year-old boy, too.

We found my father and David at the barn, readying themselves to set out and look for us. "Well, what do you know?" my father said, his smile warm and gentle. "You found her, did you?"

"We found her," Richard said, giving the calf over to him. "Ain't it a pretty one? It would of been a pity for the wolves to get it."

"It would, now, fer a fact, though me an' yer pa was gittin' ready to start searchin' ourselves."

"For you younguns as much as for the cow," David said. "My sakes, Richard, you're tore to bits . . . an' Becky, too. Get on in the house an' let the womenfolks see to you."

My nervy feelings over my torn dress were unfounded, though. My

[5]

mother did not say a word. She only got out the ointment and salved our scratches and skinned places. "You done good," she told us, finally, which was high praise from my mother.

I looked proudly at Richard, but he didn't so much as glance at me. "The wolves might of got it enduring the night," he said.

By the time I was sixteen, Richard was my acknowledged suitor. He came regularly on Sundays to go to church with us, stayed for dinner, talked with my father, helped with the chores. "Fine lover *he* is," Janie used to say, tossing her red hair, "never makes a chance to be with you alone. You'd think he was courting the whole family."

"He suits me," I always answered. And he did.

I do not know why I was drawn to him, for he was quiet, earnest, not gifted with the power of expression. But no one ever knows why love comes. It may have been his faithfulness, his kindness, his steadiness. It may have been, too, because his eyes had such a depth I often felt swimmy-headed looking into them . . . or because his young shoulders were so square, or because his hands were so broad and beautifully formed. I only know for certain that there was no one else for me, and that I had only to look upon him to feel tender and soft and loving toward him, bending near him with a yearning to touch him, always.

I had faith that when the time came he would speak out, but I doubted if he would speak to me first. That would not be his way, I knew. And it worked out exactly as I had known it would. In the fall of that year he spoke to my father, but not in secret . . . he spoke out before us all. "I reckon," he said slowly, "you have guessed that I would like Rebecca to be my wife."

"You've taken long enough to make up your mind," Janie said tartly.

Richard looked at her levelly. "I have not taken all this time to make up my mind," he said, "for my mind has ever been made up. But a man cannot speak until he knows what his prospects are, and he cannot marry until he sees the way to realize them."

My father nodded approvingly. "You've spoke to yer pa, I reckon."

"I've spoken to him and my mother, and they are both pleased. Pa has offered to set us up with two hundred acres of land . . . in the river bottoms." He turned to me. "You mind the place where I used to set my traps? Along there, he says. The land is rich and good and a man could do well with it. He is giving us, also, Sampson, Cassie, and their girl, Jency."

I was not surprised. David Cooper could well afford to give each of his boys as they grew up two hundred acres and still have plenty left for himself. He had bought land until he owned, at a rough guess, near ten thousand acres all up and down the Green River valley. And in slaves he owned some twenty, counting the little ones. In our times and country he was counted a wealthy man.

Sampson, whom he offered to us, was a strong black, young yet and with many years of work in him. He was not overly bright, but he could follow orders. Cassie was his wife and Jency his daughter. Cassie, I knew, had been trained well in the house, but Jency I could have done without. She was only a child yet, but she was flighty and giggly and I doubted she would ever have much worth. But David would never separate a family, so with Sampson and Cassie, we must take Jency.

"This is the way I see it," Richard went on. "With winter coming on, I can turn to building the house. With Sampson to help we should get it finished by the turn of the year. Then we could throw up a log house for the blacks and some barns. It has been my thought we could get married in the early spring, if all goes well."

It was September. I had turned sixteen that spring. My heart gave a leap at the thought of being married to Richard by the time I was seventeen. In my confusion I dropped the poker with which I was jogging up the fire and it made a great clatter on the hearth.

"Sounds sensible to me," my father said, but he turned to look at my mother.

She was watching me. Her face wore an odd look, one I had never seen on it before, of puzzlement and tenderness and, it may be, regret. "She's awful young yet," she said, her voice so low we could barely hear her.

Richard looked at me. "I can wait, then."

"No . . . oh, no," Mama said, "they's no need of that. Hit's jist . . . jist . . ." and she laughed a little, embarrassed. "I reckon I warn't ready fer it yit. Seems like she's jist a little youngun, yit, to me." She looked across at my father. "You recollect when she was birthed?"

My father smiled at her. "I ain't likely to fergit it. You never even waited till I got back with Jane Manifee that time."

Jane Manifee had taken care of my mother at the birth of each of us. She had been like another mother to us to the day of her death. Papa laughed and told Richard, "When Janie an' Samuel was birthed I was that skeert I got Jane Manifee in here a week afore time. But Hannah, there, she wouldn't have it when Becky was due. Said they was time. Waited till I had to ride lickety-split to git Jane, an' then when we walked in through the door, there she set, this new little youngun done birthed an' swaddled in her lap."

Mama smiled. "All Tice said was, like he said ever' time, 'I'm glad hit's over with.'"

"I allus was," Papa said.

"Yes. An' now this 'un, our second girl child is of a age to wed herself. But," she brightened, "I *will* say this, Richard, had I searched out the world I couldn't of picked nobody I'd of wanted for her no more than you. I c'n trust her to you."

They left us alone, then. By that time we had what we proudly called a "settin' room," which meant no one had to sleep in it. Papa and Mama went to their own room after Papa had shaken Richard's hand and Mama had kissed him. Janie's nose was put out, I think, over me being spoken for ahead of her, but she was nice that night. She told Richard, "You've been like a brother all our lives, and it won't change things much, you being Rebecca's man."

And she hugged me tight. "It's going to be awful lonesome around here with you gone, Becky," she said, and I saw the glisten of tears in her eyes. Then she shook her hair back. "But I've no doubts we'll make out, and," she added slyly, "I'll likely be going to a home of my own ere long, too, and maybe sooner than you at that, what with Richard wanting everything so perfect before you can be wed."

I laughed, for it did not matter to me. All that mattered was that Richard had spoken and we were betrothed. It was the first time in my life I had ever felt shy with Richard, but I didn't know what to say, and besides I had a feeling he should be the one to speak first, which he did, finally. "You're willing, are you?" he said, looking at me from the corner of his eyes.

It came over me that maybe he should have learned whether I was willing or not before speaking to my father, and I was near laughing, but all I said was, "I'm willing."

Being ever a quiet man and an earnest one, he did not make much of his feelings. He said only, in so low a voice I could barely hear him, "Since I was a little boy, I have known."

"And since I was a little girl," I told him.

Willing, he had asked. I had tagged at his heels all my life and I would have followed him to the ends of the earth itself. I was more than willing. I was eager and glad and ready. To me it seemed only the most natural thing in the world that the sober, quiet little boy I had loved since I could remember should be the one I should make out the rest of my life with. It was as if I had spent my girlhood in the way my life must go.

We talked, then, of the future and of Richard's plans, for I had none. Whatever Richard wanted was what I wanted, too. I listened and agreed. He was ever the leader and I the follower.

With his great sense of propriety, being left alone did not mean he could make love to me. Not to the day we were married did he ever so much as touch me, saving once in awhile to take my hand. It would not have been seemly to him. Instead we sat and talked until he decided it was time he must go. His leavetaking was no different than ever, except that his face wore a look of content and pleasure and he smiled at me more warmly. "I'll be here next Sunday," he said.

"I'll be looking for you," I told him.

I stood in the door and listened to the beat of his horse's feet going down the long slope to the creek, then, all my joy swelling up in me, I turned and whirled a dozen times around the room, my skirts billowing and my hair flying out. I was going to marry Richard. He had spoken.

He had plans for us. He loved me, and I loved him. I could wait till the wedding for his arms and his mouth and his body, but the thought of them sent me dancing with bubbles in my throat and a deep singing in my heart. I was going to be Richard Cooper's wife, live with him, know him intimately, bear his children and raise them up. Oh, I could wait, and would, but there was nothing to keep me from thinking about it, from dancing about it, from dreaming about it.

When my excitement quietened down I banked the fire and went to bed. But I was a long time going to sleep. I could not help pretending that Janie, who lay so still beside me, was Richard and the very thought of him so near to me, warm and sleeping beside me, made me feverish with a mixture of embarrassment and happiness. I vowed I would be a good wife to him. I vowed I would help and tend and care for him till death did us part.

In a way, I made my marriage vows that night.

CHAPTER II

RICHARD'S PLANS had a way of working out. It may have been because he made them so carefully and exactly, or it may have been his determination to make them work. In either case, he and Sampson built our house that fall and winter. Each Sunday when he came he told me how much they had got done, and twice I rode over with him to look at the house. I made no suggestions about it. Richard was sensible and every idea he had for it suited me fine.

He built a frame house. There were still, of course, many log houses, and many folks still built them. Some liked them better, and they are quick and easy to put up. And there's this to say for them—they stand stout and square to all kinds of weather if they're built well at all. But the chinking inside is forever crumbling, and say what you will, wood borers and other insects have a way of infesting the logs in time. You're always brushing small, crawly things off the beds and out of the kettles and pots. My mother made nothing of them, nor would I have, had that been what Richard wanted.

But the old way of building a home of logs was no longer necessary. There were planing mills in the country and our house was made of oak sills and gleaming, golden poplar siding. It had three rooms—a sitting room and a bedroom at the front, and a kitchen across the back. The rooms were large and airy, as they were in Richard's father's house, and in my mind I planned to make the same kind of bright, gay rugs for the floors that Bethia used.

My father, who was handy with tools, made us a bedstead, and all winter my mother and I worked at the loom, making sheets and pillow covers. Bethia promised me a piece-work quilt and a feather mattress. Janie thought more of my clothing. She fretted that it was so difficult to get silks and satins in our part of the country. "She ought have at least one silk dress," she fussed at my mother. "Every girl should be married in silk."

"I warn't," Mama said, shortly.

"No," Janie retorted, "I've heard that story often enough. How you had two dresses to your name and you were married in your second-best."

"Well, I was married," Mama said, "an' that was good enough fer me."

My father and mother were married in the old fort . . . Logan's fort, which is now the county seat town, and Benjamin Logan himself read their lines for them. Mama had told of it, how she and Papa had decided one day and how, within the hour, they had gone to Benjamin Logan and he had married them, and how she hadn't bothered to change her dress, which was spotted with the morning's churning; and how within another hour they had been on their way here to Papa's place on the Hanging Fork. Oh, Mama had many things she could tell, when she was of a mind to. She was captured once by the Indians, too.

"Times have changed since then," Janie went on. "This isn't the wilderness any longer. Papa should order Becky some silk for her wedding dress."

Mama looked at me. "Do you want a silk wedding dress, Becky?"

It truly didn't matter to me and I could say so. "A new white muslin would do just as well, Mama."

Janie sniffed. "Oh, she never cares about how things look! A new white muslin, just like she's had every summer of her life! Well, when I get married Papa can just make up his mind to get silk for me. I *won't* be married in white muslin."

The day of our wedding was bright and sunny, as April days so often are in our country. I did not wish to shirk any of my usual chores on my last day at home, so I roused as early as common and did the milking. The sun was not yet up, but the day had come and the air was clean and fresh. The hillside back of the house was showing green already with little new leaves unfolding on the bushes and trees and there was a white mist of wild plum blooms and dogwood blossoms scattered all over the hill. Down by the creek there was a little skift of fog, but it was already smoking away. I knew it was going to be a fine day.

It was queer that I felt no great excitement. Perhaps I had thought about this day too long. There had been a whole winter to think of it. As best I can remember I only felt a gladness that the day would be fair, and a deep satisfaction that it had finally come. I could think calmly enough of standing beside Richard and making my vows, and I sternly did not allow my thoughts to go beyond that moment.

I think neither of us was nervous about the ceremony. The main room had been scoured and cleaned until it shone and Janie had made our brothers go up on the hillside and gather great armloads of the white blooms. She had banked them about the fireplace, where we were to stand, and I never saw anything more lovely in my life. It was as if a part of the clean spring woods had been brought into the house—and Janie made a little bouquet of plum blossoms for me to carry. I pressed it in our Bible and I kept it a long time, until it dried and crumbled, fragrant to the last with the memory of Janie's hands arranging it and giving it to me at the final moment.

And I was married in silk after all. Janie had her way and Papa made a special trip to Louisville to get the material. It was a deep brown, glossy and ribbed, with little bows of velvet stitched on the skirt. Janie had wanted it to be white or pale blue, but I knew that light colors would not be serviceable. There was a strong sense of Mama's practicalness in me and I wanted the dress to be one that would last me for church and special times for many years.

We were married by a young Presbyterian preacher who sometimes came into our part of the country. Richard had taken a great liking to him, for his earnestness and his zeal. He came from Tennessee and his name was John Rankin. He had a deep, solemn voice, and he gave to the ceremony something of that same solemnity.

The house was crowded with friends and neighbors and once the wedding was over it became very noisy and gay. Mama had been cooking for days and neighbors had been helping. The long trestle table we used for eating was set out under the trees and it was loaded until it groaned with good things spread upon it. Papa had seen to it that there was plenty of the good whiskey he made, and there was much laughing and joking and teasing. I saw Richard's face turn red more than once, and to tell the truth my own felt hot and flushed often. The jokes at a wedding feast aren't calculated to spare the feelings of a new-wedded couple.

Finally we were allowed to leave, accompanied by all the young folks of the neighborhood. It was the custom then for the young men to ride swiftly on ahead, racing for the prize of the bottle of Black Betty. They flew past us, circled around us, yelling and whooping in high spirits. And we were not spared the shivaree that night. Beating on pans and kettles and iron bars, whistling and singing, they serenaded us until Richard let them in. We had not gone to bed. There was no use, for we knew what to expect, and we were determined not to be caught in our nightclothes. I think they were a little dashed to find our light burning and us still dressed. The fun was in getting a couple out of a warm bed.

We fed them and they stayed on until morning, for they had brought a fiddler with them and nothing would do but they must dance away for hours. Neither Richard nor I danced, but we watched and sometimes looked longingly at each other, wishing it would end. The ways of a country are set, however, and one must abide by them. It was not until day was breaking that we were left alone, married now and free, by all the laws and the proprieties, to turn to each other.

I have tried to find the right words to set down what it was like being married to Richard those first few months. I turn them over in my mind, all of the ones I know, and none of them suit or fit, and I wish for new ones to tell of it.

It was fire, burning with a clean, clear flame, forking and leaping between us. It was joy, bubbling in my throat, swelling my heart, singing through my whole being with a loud, lovely song. It was pride, in belonging and possessing, lifting my head cloudward. It was good, with the solid goodness of health and wholeness and vigor. It was sweet, with a sweetness that melted and softened and flowed. It was peace, lying as quietly as a prayer on my soul. It was a time as nearly perfect as is ever given to mortal beings.

We worked, and there's no denying it was hard work. David had put all that land to pasture, so there was little clearing to be done, but the plowing of those matted and tangled grass roots wracked Richard's muscles day after day.

He would often come into the house at night too tired to rest, or to lie still upon the bed. "Let me rub your shoulders," I pled with him.

"I misdoubt it'll do any good," he said wryly. "They feel like they'd knotted up on me."

But he stripped to the waist and I put oil on my hands and rubbed his back and his neck and the sore shoulder muscles. I could feel the knots easing under my hands. Surprised, he told me, "Why, it does help!"

It was my habit, after that, to rub his shoulders every night for him. They were smooth, hard-muscled shoulders, broad, and tanned even through his linen shirt, and in the palms of my hands I could feel their life and strength. A man's shoulders are his noblest feature, to my mind, and often as I rubbed them I felt a surging pride in my husband's. They could bend to the hardest work and they could turn to me in the gentlest embrace. To be held in a man's arms, to feel their fierce, demanding strength close about her, is a woman's high privilege, and I never felt Richard's arms about me without a pure gladness flashing all through me. They were often about me in those days.

I had my own share of the work to do—the house to keep, Cassie and Jency to manage, the cow to tend, the chickens, the garden patch, the clothing to stitch and mend, the washing and ironing to oversee, the cooking for us all, and the redding up. However well trained a Negro may be, the duty and responsibility lies with the mistress. I wanted our house to be well and thriftily run.

Little by little we made ourselves a home there on the Green River, with the hills at our back and the valley stretching away in front, the clean, emerald water of the river always sounding in our ears.

It did not ever seem strange to me, for I had been there so often as a child. When, now, I went with Richard up and down the river to the fields it was no more than I had always done, following him to the river to fish or to run his traps. It had a familiarity almost as known to me as the banks of the Hanging Fork. No . . . I was never homesick. My new life was too happy and I took too seriously my new duties as a wife. I smile now to remember how important I felt, giving orders to Cassie, brushing Jency out of the way.

I had much to learn about managing blacks. We did not have them on the Hanging Fork. Not that my father and mother had any feeling about owning them. They were simply not prosperous enough. I was glad, when the responsibility for Cassie and Jency fell on my shoulders, to have Bethia not very far away to advise me.

Richard's mother was a small woman. She had grown stout, bearing seven sons, but she was wonderfully light on her feet still, and swift in all her ways. She was quick to laugh and trim in her dress. Her only vanity, so far as I ever knew, lay in her hair, which grew bountifully thick and glossy and even yet remained a rich auburn, with very little gray in it. She dressed it neatly and her caps were smaller than those of most women of the day. I think she did not like to cover too much of her hair.

About Cassie and Jency she told me, "Cassie is pretty well trained, Becky, but she'll never take the lead. Tell her what to do, and at first show her how you want it done. Then she'll always do it your way. You can't expect her to see what's to be done the way you do, however. But if you give her regular tasks, she'll do them to suit you, I think. She's not given to complainin' much, and she's stout and able, commonly. Jency . . . I don't know what to make of that one. She's of an age to commence trainin', but she's so flighty I've despaired of her. She'd as soon tell a lie as the truth, and you can't put a bit of dependence in her. The only things I ever found her good for were chores that take no thinkin' or skill. She can be sent for water to the spring and she'll not bring the bucket back more than half empty. She can bring in firewood. She can tend a youngun, if she puts her mind to it. She can sweep the yard, or bring in the wash. But you can't trust her to do one livin' thing that takes any mind put to it. If you set her to ironin', she'll either scorch ever'thing or let the irons get so cold they won't take the wrinkles out. If you put her to reddin' up the kitchen, she's as likely as not to spend the day blowin' bubbles in the suds of the dishwater. I don't know. I reckon she was just born flighty—too natural to learn. But maybe you can teach her. I never had the time."

She was a burden to me, too, but she was Cassie's daughter and Richard's way was like his father's. He would never have dreamed of separating a family. Sampson, Cassie and Jency went together. She was ten, I think, at that time. She had a high, giggly laugh which was her answer to everything. "I do' know'm," she would say, when asked about something, and then she would laugh and roll her eyes. She usually didn't know, either—where she had put the turkey wing we used to brush the hearth, where she had put the bowl of soft soap, where she had laid away my fresh-ironed caps. She drove me to distraction a dozen times a day with her shiftlessness, and she was forever about, underfoot, singing or giggling in that silly way she had.

She loved colorful things and she would occupy herself by the hour with a knot of ribbon or a bright bird's feather, sticking them in her kinky hair or tying them into her buttonholes. She seemed happy enough, but I doubted if she had the mind to be unhappy. As far as I could see there was nothing to do but follow Bethia's way with her—give her small outside chores to do that would relieve Cassie and me.

From the first she loved Janie, and I would have been glad to give her to Janie, for she might have done something with her. It was impossible, of course. Cassie would have grieved for her though she was only ten miles away.

Janie came often to my house. She rode over nearly every Sunday. She was restless, I think, after I'd gone from home. She and my mother had always drawn sparks from each other. Mama loved Janie dearly. She was her first-born. But Janie was willful, and she had ever wanted her own way. Mama used to say that she had never seen a young one so hard to thwart and control, but it was not her way to allow any child of hers to manage *her*.

When we were little, Janie had to be punished often, and she was sullen and sulky in her punishment. I was easier bent to Mama's will for I was more like her, and it came natural for me to see the reason of her wants. Janie thought that Mama favored me over her, but it was the other way around. Janie was always Mama's dearest love. It was only that I was more tractable and gave her less trouble.

Restlessness lay in Janie's soul, though, and ever had. If she had been a boy she would have left home early to adventure in the world. Being a woman, however, she was tied to the pattern of a woman's life, and it chafed and rubbed at her tediously.

Jency used to watch for Janie's coming on Sunday, and when she came in sight she used to run to meet her, laughing happily and trotting like a little black dog alongside the horse. Janie usually brought her some small thing—a pretty stone, a little sweet cake, a new bit of ribbon, a branch of flowers she'd picked along the way. Whatever it was Jency treasured it, and she would follow Janie and me around until, in distraction, I would send her away. She sulked, then, and was unhappy, and I was too tender-hearted to enjoy seeing her unhappy.

I early learned that if Janie set her to some task she would work willingly. Janie would take a roundabout way of teaching her, never losing patience with her. "Spread the ruffles of a cap *this* way, Jency, one little piece at a time, and test the iron carefully. See how beautifully it irons, then? Try it now. And see if you can't do one whole ruffle without a wrinkle." And Jency would bend over the board, her tongue bitten between her teeth as she tried very hard to do what Janie had told her.

If I told her the same thing she only giggled and said, "Yessum," and then, slack-handed, went right ahead and ironed a dozen wrinkles into the simplest piece. "I don't know why," I told Janie, "she does better for you."

"She likes me better," Janie said. "I've got the time to bring her little presents and pay more attention to her. You're busy with a hundred other things."

There is nothing more untrue than the saying that children, dogs, and very simple people, like blacks, know instinctively when they are loved. They do not see beneath the surface, that is all. Any hand that pats them is a kind one. Janie did not love Jency. She was amused by her. She might have been able to train her better, but her moods would have been quick and changeable, and where Jency never knew the feel of the whip with me, Janie would have striped her without thinking twice.

Aside from her restlessness at home, Janie was trying to decide between two of the young men of the county. It was my own wish that she and Johnnie, Richard's brother, might find favor in each other's eyes, but that was a futile wish and I knew it. They couldn't be together five minutes without quarreling. Janie said Johnnie was too fly-by-night and unsettled. Johnnie said Janie was too vain and foolish.

But either of the two young men courting her would have taken her to live in the remoter parts of the county. Both were presentable, it was true, both steady and dependable, but I doubted if Janie would be very happy with either. For one thing she liked people too much to enjoy being buried on a farm in the back country. Our own place on the Hanging Fork was too back-country to suit her and it was in the middle of a well populated section compared to some other places.

One Sunday when she came I knew something had happened to please and excite her. She could hardly wait for the chance to tell me and she fidgeted all through dinner. When Richard finally left to go to his father's on some errand, she fairly burst out, "Mr. Leavitt from Lexington has been visiting at home the past three days!"

"Who's Mr. Leavitt?" I asked.

"*John* Leavitt!"

I remembered, then. He was a lawyer in the city and a member of the General Assembly from Fayette County. He was counted an important person and a man of influence, for there was hardly an issue of the Kentucky Gazette which did not carry his name in some connection. "How come him in these parts?" I asked.

"He's trying to untangle one of those everlasting lawsuits over a piece of land. Some client of his claims to own that piece over the ridge back of our place. He had to see it, and he wanted to talk to Papa about it. Papa offered him to stay with us till his business was finished. He's not married, Becky."

"And he had eyes for you, I reckon." I laughed.

Janie laughed, too. "Seems as if he did."

"Is he still there?"

"No, he went back to town yesterday. I wouldn't be here today if he hadn't."

"No," I said, "you probably wouldn't. What age man is he?"

"Well, he's not a boy, if that's what you mean."

"I know he's not a boy. He wouldn't have got as far as he has in public life if he was a boy. But is he old?"

Janie put her head to one side and studied. "He'd be old according to your standards, I reckon. I don't know what age he is, but I'd think him to be around forty."

"That's old," I said immediately. "Janie, you don't want to marry an *old* man. How could you learn to love him?"

"Oh, love . . ." Janie said, flouncing. "What does love have to do with it?"

"You'll find out mighty quick if you wed a man without it."

"I'll chance it," she said. "Becky, he's a member of the General Assembly already. He has told me that he intends to stand for Congress and be sent to Washington. Think of living in Washington, Becky! And even if he never goes to Washington, I'd live in Lexington. In the city. I'd have a fine home and servants and fine dresses. I'd go out among the rich, and be rich myself."

"And maybe you wouldn't be a speck happier than you are right now."

"Oh, yes, I would. Happiness don't mean to me what it does to you, Becky. *You're* happy here on the river with Richard, doing just what you've done all your life. I'd die here. I want to travel and have money and live finely."

It troubled me, but I knew there was truth in what she said. We were of different natures. Mine was simple, asking only for simple things. I asked for nothing better than what I had, Richard and this home on the river, and in time, children. Janie had always dreamed, had always loved finery, had ever been impatient of the poky ways of the back country. What troubled me most, however, was the fear that this was youth and curiosity and venturesomeness, that she was mettlesome in much the same way a young, high-spirited horse is mettlesome. I was afraid that life and time would drag at her, in the end. "You talk," I said, "as if he had already spoken out. Has he?"

"No. But he asked Papa if he could call again."

"You think he'll want to marry you? There must be ladies in Lexington have set their caps for him."

"I'm not afraid of that. And if I make up my mind I want him, he'll offer marriage."

I didn't much doubt it. Janie had such a way of getting what she wanted that it might well be true she could have Mr. Leavitt if she decided she wanted him. But I couldn't quite understand Mr. Leavitt's interest in a girl from the country. Janie was pretty and gay and clever, but we were plain people. Of course there was no aristocracy in Kentucky, saving as people had made a name for themselves in the days of its settlement and early statehood, but many prominent people had come into the state of late, settled in Lexington or Louisville, and were rapidly becoming the leaders, overruling the older folks who had established the country. Mr. Leavitt was himself one of them. "Well," I said, "I hope you'll think about it a time before you make up your mind. What does Mama think of him?"

"Oh, Mama mistrusts anyone from the city. And she says he's too old, of course. She's forgot Papa was nearly forty when they got married. She'd rather see me in a log cabin out in some wilderness tract, naturally. She fussed at Papa for letting him come again. Much good it would do her. If I want to see him again, I'll see him, no matter what she or Papa say."

"You wouldn't slip out and see him?"

"Of course I would, if I was so minded and had to."

I would never have been so daring. "Suppose they caught you?"

"What could they do? I'm grown up, Becky. Mama can't whip me any more, or tie me in the corner as she used to do. All she *could* do would be to give me a tongue-lashing, and that would slide off me like water off a duck's back. But they won't try to stop me. Mama will fuss and Papa will go right on letting Mr. Leavitt come. You'll see."

And that was about the way it worked out. Mama did fuss, but not in front of Mr. Leavitt, and Papa did continue allowing him to call.

Richard and I were there one Saturday evening when he came. He was a short, spare man, not much taller than Jane, and his hair was growing thin on top of his head. But he was nicer than I'd expected. He had the easy manners that people with learning often have, and he was dressed richly but without pretention. He talked well and not boastfully. He rode a good horse and his hands were white and well cared for. It was easy to see he had never done any hard work with them. Or if he had it was so long in the past it didn't show.

That he admired Janie was plain to see. Even when he was talking his eyes would follow her about the room, or if she was sitting still, listening, he would glance at her now and then, and smile. She would smile back, as if they had a secret understanding and were only going through the formalities of courtship because it was proper. And that may well have been true.

That he came every week for a month, I knew, for Janie didn't visit me on those Sundays. But she brought him with her, finally, to tell of their betrothal. I felt flustered, having to serve him dinner, thinking him used to fine ways, but he set us all at ease, as he could. He knew land values, that was certain, and he walked with Richard over the farm. "It's a good place," he said when they returned, "one of the best I've seen in these parts. And you're a good farmer, Richard."

When he told us his intentions, after dinner, Janie sat with her eyes cast down, proper and prim as he talked. "It has been difficult," he said, "to persuade Miss Jane to leave her home. She seems much attached to it, and to this country. But I have managed to make her see the advantages of the city, and she has done me the honor to consent to be my wife."

Janie slanted a look at me from under her lashes and there was no hiding the spark of mischief in her eyes. I could have laughed outright. Janie attached to her home and the country? Nothing could have been more false. She would leave both gladly and eagerly. But I saw the picture of modesty and reluctance she had held up to him . . . the picture of a dutiful daughter, attached to her parents and home.

"I have spoken to her father," Mr. Leavitt went on, "and after some consideration he has given his consent, too." He frankly told us that a man in politics needed a wife, but he needed exactly the right kind of wife. "It is my good fortune," he said, "to have found in Miss Jane a woman I can cherish and who will at the same time grace my home."

I thought it sounded a little pompous, but it was evident that both he and Janie knew precisely what was involved, and what they both wanted. He needed a beautiful, gracious wife to further his political ambitions, to be the hostess of his home, and Janie was pretty, graceful and quick to learn. Janie wanted exactly the kind of life he could offer her and was willing to learn. There was some unscrupulousness in them both. "Have you set a date for the wedding?" I asked.

"I think," Mr. Leavitt said, a little ponderously—he could not help speaking occasionally like a man before the jury—"that is for Miss Jane to decide, though," he added, smiling fondly at Janie, "it could not be too soon for me, naturally."

Janie smiled just as fondly back at him. "There's time enough," she said.

If each of them wanted something more than love from the other, they managed a good pretense of hiding it. Between themselves they doubtless laid their plans. But before us, and others, they appeared a man and woman in love.

"I am not," Janie told me later, "going to be married in haste and without style. I need a year to choose and make the clothes I want. I'm going to make Papa take me to Louisville to buy dress stuffs this fall, and during the winter I can stitch them up. Next May, I think, will be soon enough."

She whirled around on her toes, much as I had done the night Richard had spoken for me, but for a different reason. "Oh, Becky, everything I want is coming to pass. Think! A fine home in Lexington, and servants and a carriage, and silks and satins, and parties and excitement . . . and maybe Washington in a year or two!" She settled down by the fire and stared dreamily into it. "Mr. Leavitt is going to busy himself with building our home . . . brick, Becky, think of that! He has a nice lot on Main Street. We've already decided on the plans and he is going to Philadelphia to select our furnishings—silver and china and rugs and the best furniture. He tells me we shall have to entertain often and that our home must be fine." She stretched her arms and shivered with delight. "I am so pleased I could shout and sing."

And I could not help being pleased for her, though it grieved me to think of her being as far away as Lexington and I had a feeling she would not return often to visit us. Not that she would ever be snobbish about her country relations . . . no. But I thought she would simply be so caught up in the flurry and busyness of her new life that she would rarely have time to come home.

"What is Mr. Leavitt's religion?" I asked. I don't know what prompted me to ask that question, save that a great revival of faith had been sweeping across Kentucky and religion had become a vital thing in every household.

Janie shrugged. "I haven't asked. I think he has no faith."

As I have said, my father and mother were faithful and strict Presbyterians, and we had been reared in that faith. Richard's family, too, were Presbyterian, and it had been one of the good things of our life that we went to church together when there was meeting. I felt as if Janie were taking one more step away from us all. "What about your own church?"

"It doesn't matter. Religion is a tedious thing to me. I can well do without it. But I expect we shall attend whatever church is most fashionable. I would like that, because it would be helpful in meeting the best people, and it would be a place to wear my prettiest clothes."

I shook my head. "You were raised as strict as I about church."

"And bored to death by all of it . . . a country church, the women in dark, unstylish dresses and bonnets, and country preachers, like John Rankin, as gloomy as the Old Testament prophets . . . dry as dust. I'll be glad to be rid of it."

Oh, there was little doubt Janie had been misput all her life. I knew she had ever found meeting tedious, and that she had been hard put to sit still through a service, but she had never said before she would be glad to be rid of it. "Don't talk so," I said, shivering, "something bad might happen to you."

She laughed. "I'll chance it."

I wouldn't have . . . not for the world. I would have been afraid the Lord would strike me down.

CHAPTER III

THAT WAS in the fall after Richard and I had been married in April. On one point my mind had been set at ease. I thought Mr. Leavitt would be kind to Janie. He might expect much of her, even demand it, but I thought he would be patient and, in general, good to her. His own plans would require it, but beyond that, I thought he was deeply attracted to her, felt for her an affectionate love much like that of a parent for a willful, high-spirited child. He humored her, gave in to her whims, petted her and spoiled her.

It was just as well, though, that I had other things to occupy my mind. I was fertile and had conceived readily and my first child was on the way. A woman's first child takes a lot of her dreams and thoughts.

My mother smiled when I told her, but she also sighed. "A woman's way ain't the easiest in the world, Becky, as you'll find out. You're commencin' early to learn."

"But I'm glad," I told her. "It's what I want."

She nodded. "An' I'm glad fer you. Hit's the joyousest thing, though the hurtin'est, to bear a youngun. You want I should come do fer you?"

"Of course I want you to come!"

"I thought, mebbe, Bethia bein' so close you'd as soon have her."

She was pleased, I knew. It showed in her face. She was a woman of sallow, dark skin, with heavy eyebrows that sometimes made her look a little fierce. And she could be fierce. She had killed an Indian once, not without tenderness in her heart for him, but she did it, and she could always do what had to be done. It was only by killing the Indian that she could escape him and return to my father and her home.

But I had not said I wanted her merely to please her. I did want her. I could not imagine birthing a young one without her beside me, strong and quiet and knowing what to do. I had grown up with her big, loving heart and I knew exactly how wide and open it was.

Janie had taken with a chill a day or two before and she was sitting by the fire, drinking down some tea Mama had made for her. "I'm glad," she said, looking over the cup at me and laughing, "all I've got is a chill and not what Becky's got stirring inside of her."

"You keep your chill, then," I said, teasing with her, "and I'll keep what I got. I got mine pleasurably, leastways."

"Both of you hush that kind of talk," Mama said, "it ain't fitten."

Janie made a small face at me, but we hushed. Mama had very strong ideas of what was fit and what wasn't, and she wasn't beyond giving us both a good shaking if we didn't mind, grown women though we were.

"As fer you, miss," Mama went on, "yore time will come."

"Not if I can help it, it won't," Janie said. "I've got no intentions of ruining my figure and raising up a bunch of little snotty-nosed younguns to mess up the house and take my time."

Mama looked at Janie and I thought for a moment she would give her the back of her hand. "You'll not go against the will of the Lord, I'm thinkin'," she said.

Janie buried her face in the cup of tea, but I heard her mutter, "The will of the Lord can be got around." Mama, being a little hard of hearing, didn't hear her, and I was glad she didn't. She would have been horrified.

The time of waiting for a child goes both slow and fast. I was healthy and well and not bothered with any ill feelings. In the beginning it made no difference, save in my thoughts and plans. I could do my part of the work as well as ever. But as the time passed and I grew heavy and awkward, the hours slowed down, and I had to turn more and more of the work over to Cassie.

The last months coming during the winter, though, made it easier for me to be resigned to staying in the house so much of the time. And I found that Jency was of more use to me than before. No one had told her, so far as I knew, of my condition, but apparently it fascinated her. She stayed close beside me much of the time, and she was quick to run for a ball of yarn that escaped me, or to poke up the fire to keep me from bending, or to bring me a cup of fresh water. I remembered that Bethia had told me she could be trusted to tend a young one, as far as watching over it was concerned, and I thought I could see how she might be very useful to me in time. One day she said to me, a little shyly, "It a comin' purty soon?"

I saw no reason for not telling her. "The middle of January."

She was sitting on the floor at my feet, holding her hands for me to wind a ball of yarn off the hank. She had black, shiny skin which stretched tightly across the bones of her face, and her eyes were extremely large, the whites almost blue so that when she rolled them, as she frequently did, the whole pupil was lost. Her hair, fuzzy and wiry, usually stuck up in wild disorder all over her head. Cassie sometimes braided it and tied it in small pigtails, and when she did, they, too, stuck up at odd angles like little horns. But she was a slender, graceful child. She bit her lip when I answered her, then ducked her head, giggling. "Reckon I kin hold it some?"

"Keep the yarn tight," I warned her, "or it will tangle. Would you like to hold it some?"

"Yessum."

I decided to take this opportunity to talk seriously to her and I finished winding up the ball and laid it aside. "Well, then, you'll have to show me I can put some dependence in you, Jency. You can't go flitting off after butterflies and flowers when you're tending a baby."

"Oh, no'm . . . I *wouldn't!*"

"You do now. When you're sent for water or firewood. And you slack the sweeping and bedmaking."

She hung her head. "Yessum. I don't love to do them kind of things. I likes younguns, though."

I can hear myself now, preaching to her. "But things have to be done whether we like to do them or not, Jency. You're not too young to understand that. When you're put to a task, do it as well as you can, and don't leave until it's done. If you can do that, by the time the baby comes I'll know I can trust you with it. You could help me a lot, then, for a baby needs a lot of tending."

She grinned from ear to ear and giggled excitedly. "If I does my chores, you mean I kin he'p with it?"

I nodded.

She jumped to her feet and hopped dizzily about on one foot. "You ain't never seed sich sweepin' an' reddin' as I aim to do, Miss Becky. You jist see!" She grabbed the hearth brush and commenced raising such a dust in the ashes that the room was filled with it and I nearly choked. "Jency!" I yelled at her, "put that brush down!"

"But I'm aimin' to commence, Miss Becky."

"You've been shown a hundred times how to brush a hearth, gently and easily, so as not to raise a dust. Now, do it right."

To my surprise she did it right, patiently and easily. And for the rest of the time before the baby came she continued to surprise me. She worked hard, and while much of what she did wasn't well done, she tried and that was more than she'd ever done before.

"Whut come over that youngun?" Cassie said to me one day, wonderingly. "I ain't ever seed her willin' to do sich a heap of work."

Cassie was a fat woman, her flesh firm and well attached to her, but like Bethia, she was light and quick on her feet. She was very black, also, pure Negro, as was Sampson. I told her Jency was trying to prove she could be trusted with the baby. Cassie laughed. "Mought be jist whut she kin do best, Miss Becky, an' be a big he'p to us. Hit was a good idee you had."

We hadn't thought, my mother and I, but that I'd have an easy time a birthing. "Not that any of it's easy," she told me, "but you're built right fer it." And I had no fear.

She came a week beforehand and we had a pleasant time together. I felt quiet and drowsy, perfectly content to sit by the fire. Cassie did most of the work and Mama sat and knitted and talked beside me. Often we spoke of Janie. "She's workin' all the time on her clothes," Mama told me. "She made yer pa take her to Louisville, an' she got a sight of goods there. Taken a sight of money, too—but he paid it over 'thout sayin' nothin'. Said he reckoned a man ort to give his girl what she wanted once in her lifetime, an' she'd soon be gone away from us." Mama sniffed. "I'd of curbed her bit a little, had it been me."

I said nothing, for Mama hadn't been able to curb her bit about going to Louisville, and she well knew what would happen when Janie got there. She went on. "She's got the most goods I ever seen all at one time in my life. They's a worsted fer a little jacket an' skirt, an' cassimeres an' laces an' fine muslins, an' somethin' she calls mousseline de soie fer nice, an' a silk with little gold threads all through it. That's fer the weddin', she says. She aims to have a dozen new dresses, she says, with bonnets an' slippers to match. Hit's took ever' penny we got, I don't doubt."

"Oh, now, Mama," I said, "Papa's got some put by, I know."

"Which he aimed to buy some blooded horses with," she said, wistfully.

I did feel a pang at Papa having to give up his dream of some fine horses to buy Janie's wedding clothes, but there was no use saying so. "What about her linens?" I asked.

"Home-wove ain't good enough for her," Mama said scornfully. "She says not to bother. Says Mr. Leavitt'll git their'n in Philadelphy. I never heared of such," she went on angrily, "a girl gettin' wed 'thout her portion of bedsheets an' feather ticks an' quilts an' spreads. I'd of been glad to do 'em for her, but never mind, she says."

"Well, Mama," I said, trying to comfort her, "times change and folks are all different. In your day . . ."

"In my day," Mama interrupted, "a woman went to her man with whatever she had, an' I hadn't no fine linens it's true. But what I had was fer my house, kittles an' seeds an' sich. I never give a thought to what I was goin' to put on my back."

"But you and Papa gave me what I needed for my house," I reminded her.

"So we did, an' glad to do it, fer you was sensible about yer wants." She sighed. "I reckon you're right . . . times change an' folks are different. But I'd feel a sight easier about Jane if she was more like the rest of us."

"She can't help being different."

"No, I reckon not. But I don't know where she gits it from. Not from me, she don't. I know that. An' I don't know in what way I mistaught her."

It never occurred to my mother that she herself had come adventuring into Kentucky. She had been with her father, it's true, but nevertheless, she had come. And my father had come from the Holston country, with restlessness in his feet. It did not occur to Mama that Janie came by her venturesomeness naturally.

The ways of the young, I suppose, are ever strange to the old, and each new generation must set up for itself. My father and mother had taken up land in the wilderness, had lived for a time in a lean-to shelter until they built their own home, with their own hands, of logs felled in their own woods. Richard and I had been given our land, and though he and Sampson had put up the house, it was built of boards, and I had Cassie and Jency to help me. There were no woods on our place, for Richard's father had cleared them off.

Now Janie would go to the city to live, and her home would be fine brick, and she would have a house full of servants to run it. Nothing stands still. You can't stay in the wilderness forever, and to each must come his own adventure.

I was taken in the night. I have often wondered why babies must so often begin their hard travail into the world during the hours of the night, and what it is that moves a child, after so long a sleep, to stir and stretch and start its journey. It must be that a woman asleep is quiet and that when its time comes, a child takes advantage of the quietness, nothing to hinder it, and says, "It's time I left this nest of darkness."

However that may be, it was deep in the night when I wakened with the first pains. I asked Richard to call Mama and she came at once. She sent Richard out of the room and then she satisfied herself that all was well. She told Richard, "You jist as well git some sleep in there in my bed, an' go on with yer plans fer the mornin'. Hit'll be up in the day afore I have need of you, likely."

Troubled and worried, as all men are at such a time, I suspect, he did so. Day came and wore on and the pain grew and grew. My mother had had her children in the old-fashioned way, staying up and walking until the child was ready, then kneeling for the birth. But we knew better than that by my time, and I was in the bed the entire time.

I was not worried when midday came and the child had not been born, but I was growing tired. I wanted to rest. "The only way you c'n rest," Mama said, "is to keep on tryin', Becky. Don't give down, now."

The hours of the afternoon passed and I did not know such pain could be borne. But even in the midst of it I could read the worry in Mama's face. "Something's gone wrong, hasn't it? It should have been here by now."

She wiped my face with a cold cloth. "Hit's takin' longer'n we thought, yes, but I d'know as they's e'er thing went wrong. Jist keep a tryin', Becky."

She had sent for Bethia sometime during the day, and they did everything they knew to do. I heard Mama tell Bethia once, "I wish Jane Manifee was a livin' an' here to take over."

"I wish so, too," Bethia said.

They had put an axe under the bed to cut the pains. They had rubbed me with hot oil. They had given me hot things to drink. They had tickled my nose with a feather to make me sneeze, which had almost killed me but had done no good. Nothing did any good. The child was taking its own time and nothing could hurry it.

In some fashion another night passed. I remember that Richard paced the floor in the sitting room, coming now and then to look in the door, and that Mama talked with him in whispers. Richard was like a stranger to me. Everyone was a stranger. The only things I knew were my body and the terrible pain. I remember the candle flickering and the sickly smell of burning tallow, and shadows of people passing, but they meant nothing to me. There was only the constant pain and the effort to be rid of it, and at last the wish, even, to die to be rid of it.

In the afternoon of the second day the child was born at last—or rather it was torn from me by Mama in desperation. It never drew a breath of life. But I didn't know that for a day or two. When the pain was over and I was blessedly at peace, I slept and slept and slept, waking only to be fed by Mama, Richard, or Bethia, and then to sleep again. But finally there was a day when I waked, was no longer worn and drowsy, and wanted my baby.

It was Mama who had to tell me. "Hit never lived, Becky. They warn't nothin' we could do, fer it had been dead a time an' a time. Likely all of yer last month a carryin' it, hit hadn't been a livin'. That's what give you sich a bad time. Hit warn't no livin' youngun to give you any help."

A great desolation settled over me and a kind of cold sweat broke out in the palms of my hands. "I want Richard," I told Mama. "I want to see Richard."

"He's right out back," she said, "he ain't been more'n hollerin' distance from the house since you was took. I'll git him."

He came immediately and sat beside me on the bed, gathering me into his arms. I broke into wild crying. "Don't grieve so," he said, smoothing my hair and rubbing his cheek against my face, "don't grieve." He held me until the worst of my crying was over. "It was for the best, no doubt."

"How could it be for the best," I said, "how could it ever be for the best for a little young one not to live?"

"I don't know," he said quietly, "but if that's the way the Lord willed it, it's not for us to question."

I drew away from him and rested again on the pillow, looking at him. Richard's faith was always strong and never confused. It should have comforted me, but it somehow didn't. I searched his good, strong face, with the ruddy color in the cheeks, the clear, untroubled blue of the eyes, the square jutted jaw, and I could only turn my head from side to side and weep again. "Was it a boy?"

"It was a boy . . . and perfectly formed."

"But without life."

"But without life. He looked like a little wax doll."

"You've buried him?"

"That same day. We decided it was best."

"I wish I could have seen him."

[25]

"We thought it would grieve you more."

It would have, of course, and they had been right. "I don't understand," I said, trying to choke my weeping, "I just don't understand. We'd counted on him so, and planned for him, and wanted him. Why should God do this to us?"

"How can we know?" Richard said calmly. "It may be He must test us first before trusting us."

Oh, I had no patience with that! And yet it was part of what I had been taught. The ways of the Lord are inscrutable. Whom the Lord loveth he chasteneth. The will of the Lord discerns the paths of men. It was the only way to look at it, the only sensible and comforting way, but I did not understand it, or it may be I *would* not understand it. "There'll be others," Richard said, taking my hand, "there'll be others. I have faith we'll be trusted to raise a young one or two."

And *that* was my only comfort. We were young and there *would* be others.

I was weak and ill for a month, but eventually I began to stir around and slowly my strength came back to me. I think it was not so much that my body recovered slowly, as my spirit. It took time for it to heal. But times does take care of all things, and work to do, duties and chores help it along.

You grieve for a little lost one, of course. But the need to see to food and clean clothes and a clean house gradually ease the grief. And then losing a young one was common in our time. There were few women who had not lost several. I sometimes think there are as many young ones buried in this country as have been raised up in it. If they come into the world sound and whole, they're apt to sicken while still young, with the summer complaint or the cold plague, and seems as if nothing can pull them through. My own mother raised five of us, but she lost three. Bethia raised seven, and lost three. That was the way of it. But I never got over wishing it had lived at least a little while.

And an odd thing happened to Jency. Mama told me that when they knew the baby was dead she had run off to the woods and stayed all day, and they could hear her wailing clear to the house. When she came back she took up all her old ways again. She became, if possible, even more flighty than common, so that no dependence at all could be put in her, and she giggled oftener and played more constantly. I suppose inside that woolly, kinky head of hers she saw no reason to do otherwise, now that there would be no baby for her to help tend.

I asked her one day to help me put away the small garments that had been made for the baby. She backed off, her hands clutched behind her, her eyes rolling. "No'm," she said, "I do' wanna tetch them things, Miss Becky. They's daid."

They were dead. But I prayed they might live again.

CHAPTER IV

"WHO," I said to Janie one day, as the time for her wedding drew nearer, "are you going to get to marry you and Mr. Leavitt?"

She shrugged impatiently. "I *wish* the wedding could be in Lexington. But I suppose Mama and Papa would have a conniption if I so much as mentioned it. I don't know. When is Preacher Rankin coming for the funeral?"

In those days we could not have a funeral during the winter months. The roads were little more than trails and it was impossible for the preachers to travel over them during the mud and thaws of winter and early spring. So we had the custom of burying our dead, but of having the funeral whenever the preacher could get around to us. Our baby's funeral had had thus to wait. "Richard sent word to him that we'd like him to come in April if he could. I reckon you know he's settled on the Gasper River down in Logan County, now."

"I'd heard it, yes. Papa named it, I think." Janie was sewing on a fine linen shift and she stopped to think and bite her thumb. "I wonder if April would suit Mr. Leavitt. We could have the wedding while Preacher Rankin is in this part of the country."

A wedding and a funeral. It struck me that preachers had much to do with the joining and the ending of life. "I didn't think you liked Preacher Rankin," I said.

"I don't . . . as a preacher. But he makes a good appearance, and he would give tone to the wedding. He's got learning and he don't chew tobacco and he wears decent dress." She nodded her head. "Yes, that's probably best. I'll send word to Mr. Leavitt as soon as possible."

"There's talk," I went on, "that Mr. Rankin has seceded from the Presbyterians and has come under the influence of the New Lights."

"I know. It makes no difference so long as he can marry us and makes a decent appearance. What happened down there in Logan County, anyhow? I've heard Papa talking of it."

"Oh, they've been having those big revivals down there—at sacramental meeting. A man passing our way the other day said they were aiming to have another big one this summer. He said it was past believing the things that go on . . . folks come under the influence of the spirit and take with the jerks and talk in tongues, and dance and shout. *He* said the preachers say it's the greatest spiritual awakening the country has ever known and it's spreading all over Tennessee and the rest of Kentucky. It sounds a marvel, don't it?"

"Sounds foolish to me. But what could you expect of that outlandish part of the country? Rogue's Harbor," she said contemptuously.

That was what everybody called Logan County, because it was so sparsely settled and every kind of mean, thievish, lawbreaking sort of person ran there for hiding out. It went odd that the very county named for Benjamin Logan, whom Papa and David Cooper thought was the finest man in the country, should be such a nest of outlaws. But that's the way it was. It had a bad name and there was no denying it.

"It would be something to see, wouldn't it," I said, "hundreds of folks under the spirit at one time? They say the preaching goes on all day, and folks come from everywhere around and stay during the whole four days of the meeting, and the singing and shouting lasts till up in the night. Richard kind of wants to go."

Janie sniffed. "Richard would. Maybe he'd come under the influence, too."

"Oh, no," I laughed. "Richard's too good a Presbyterian."

"So was Preacher Rankin."

"Well, Richard's different from Preacher Rankin."

"Not much. He's awful preacherish, seems to me."

It was true Richard's faith was strict, and he was sober about religion, but I knew in what ways he wasn't preacherish, so I could laugh at that idea of Janie's. I was almost certain that even then I was carrying again inside me the evidence of Richard's lack of too much sternness. But I hadn't told Janie or my mother. I don't know why. I think it was a superstitious fear that I'd best not talk of it too soon. They say, some women, that to make a garment or tell the news before the stir of life is bad luck. I'd done it before, running to Mama almost as soon as I'd known, and I *had* had bad luck. I didn't want to risk it again.

Before Janie had time to send word to Mr. Leavitt, however, we had news from Preacher Rankin that it would be the middle of May before he would be in Lincoln County. They were building a new church on Gasper River and he couldn't get away. We all talked it over and Richard and I decided to wait until after Janie's wedding for the funeral sermon. It would be a sad time and there was no use clouding her happiness with our sorrow. So Janie set the fifteenth day of May for her wedding, and we decided on the seventeenth for the funeral. She would be gone away by then and there would be nothing to sadden her new life.

It is a lovely month, May . . . perhaps the gentlest, tenderest month of the year in our country. It is then that the thrush, each morning and evening, sings a fluty, bubbling song. It is then that the rye grass in the meadows grows tall and thick, greener than a piece of dyed velvet and as soft to touch. It is then that the skies turn a deep blue, dark and down-bending, drifty sometimes with woolly white clouds. It is then that the trees bloom, the locust and crabapple and the tulip poplars, and the air is heavy with scent and bees drone drunkenly making their honey. It is then that the little frogs start their clamor at the waters' edge, and the whippoorwill clucks his nightly call. It is the time of newborn things, leaves, buds, blossoms, grass, lambs and calves. It is the time of planting, when the sun is gold and warm and the earth is soft to the plow.

Janie's wedding came on a Friday. Richard had his corn and oats all in, and Cassie and Jency and I had most of the garden planted. I remember how Jency made little hills over the squash with her hands, piling up the warm earth and patting it into place, crooning some nameless tune to herself all the while, and how when a great black and gold butterfly crossed the row she scattered all the careful little hills trying to catch it. Cassie stood with her hands on her hips and eyed the ruined hills. "Now look whut she gone went an' done! Jency, you come back, you heah me!" But Jency was over the paling fence and in the edge of the woods, only a high trilling echo to tell her path.

I was provoked. "Cassie, *what* are we going to do with her?"

Cassie shook her head and started methodically making up the hills again. "I dunno, Miss Becky. I dunno whut git into that chile. Seem lak her haid jist ain't turned right. I gits hopeless, times."

I got hopeless, too. It wasn't so much that we needed Jency's help. We did very well without her. It was my feeling of responsibility for her. I felt if she weren't properly trained no good could ever come of her, nor would she ever be very happy. I believed as strongly as my mother that hands should be turned to work to be happy hands, and to this day nothing has disproved that belief in me.

But I did not know how to put Jency's hands to work. I hoped that when she knew there would be another child she would once again reform. Only time could tell, though.

Preacher Rankin came the day before the wedding, but we did not immediately see him. He went directly to my father's house. The wedding was to be at noon. Janie said all fashionable weddings were held at noon.

Mr. Leavitt stayed in town and was to ride out that morning. Their home was not yet finished, so he had taken rooms for them at an inn in Lexington. They were to go there first, where Janie could see the new house for herself, and then Mr. Leavitt was taking her with him to Philadelphia to choose furnishings. He had made one or two trips already, but he thought Janie would enjoy going and she could select her own curtains and rugs. She was pleased. I thought it would be a very rough trip for a bride, but she was excited by the whole idea. Mostly, though, she was eager to see Philadelphia. "I hope," she said, "my dresses won't look back-country."

"How can they?" I asked. I was helping her to dress. It seemed to me they were all very splendid.

She settled the beautiful blue dress, threaded with gold, about her waist. "Well, I made them from drawings I saw in Louisville, and they're supposed to be the latest styles, but it's hard to get the exact drape from drawings. I can tell better when I see how the women are dressed in Philadelphia. And I can make any alterations necessary."

As it had been for my own wedding, the house was spotless and shining, with flowers placed about the room. I missed the gathering of neighbors, though. Janie had had her way. She did not want our country friends and though Mama and Papa had been dismayed, they had given in to her. "Just the family," she said, "and of course the Coopers, since they're part of the family, too, now."

"But why, Janie?" Mama had said. "Folks'll think it's quare."

"Let them think it. This is my wedding and I don't aim to have a house full of crude, ignorant people, making jokes and heehawing and spitting tobacco juice and swilling whiskey. I want it quiet and decent."

Janie had never been to a fashionable wedding in her life and where she got the ideas for one, I don't know. Perhaps Mr. Leavitt told her, or perhaps she saw pictures in the books in Louisville. But she took some of the goods of her dress and made a wreath of little flowers to wear in her hair, and she had lace mitts for her hands and carried a small nosegay of early roses.

Mr. Leavitt looked very fine, too, in his new blue coat with the brass buttons and his pale tan trousers, and Preacher Rankin somehow managed always to keep his black decent and fresh.

But it was so quiet a wedding that it seemed hardly a wedding at all. Besides us, there were only the Coopers, and not all of them. Johnnie wouldn't come. He laughed when he was invited. "Do you want me to dance at your wedding, Janie?" he'd asked.

She had turned a deep red and had been angry. "No," she said, shortly, "and don't come. You'd only disgrace us all by drinking too much." Which was hardly fair of her, seeing that Johnnie was as temperate a young man as any.

"You needn't worry," he told her, "I don't aim to come."

Janie had flounced off, but it had bothered her more than she owned. She had been disturbed over it for several hours, though she had denied it. "I can do without Johnnie Cooper at my wedding," she'd said.

We sat in rows, subdued, all in our best, the boys clean-scrubbed with their hair slicked down and you could have heard a deep breath during the ceremony.

Like most lawyers, Mr. Leavitt's voice was firm and clear-sounding. I had a giggly moment when it seemed to me he had the bearing of a man in court. I half expected to see him turn and start pacing the floor and commence a peroration. But he stood with great dignity beside Janie and made the proper responses, and when the ceremony was over he did a thing which I had never seen done before. He turned to Janie and in front of us all put his arms around her and kissed her. It was no quick and flustered smack either. I saw Richard's foot shuffle and I knew he was embarrassed clear to his toes. Then Papa cleared his throat and we all crowded around to offer our good wishes.

When I saw the table I knew Janie had had a hand in the food, too. There was ham and biscuits, pressed chicken and sauce, and tiny cakes I knew Mama would never have bothered with. Instead of Papa's good whiskey there was wine, which Mr. Leavitt had sent. He lifted his glass before he took a sip, and inclined his head toward Janie . . . "To my wife," he said, and we all felt clumsy and awkward, not knowing what to do. It went the strangest to us.

They left at once, as soon as Janie had changed. Mama stood in the door, her arms folded across her chest the way I've seen her stand a thousand times, and watched as they rode down the slope to the road. "There," she said finally and, I think, a little bitterly, "goes my firstborn youngun. I misdoubt I'll ever see much of her again."

"Oh, now, Mama," I said, trying to comfort her, "she's just going to Lexington. She'll come home to visit often."

She shook her head. "It ain't the miles she's goin', Becky. She could go to New York an' come back when she pleased. Hit's her ways I'm a thinkin' of. She's shakin' the dust of the old place off her feet. She'll not be wishin' to come, an' that's what grieves me."

To some extent I felt it, too . . . but I had faith that Janie wasn't all fluff and style, and while I didn't think she would come often, I did not believe she would entirely forsake her people. "She'll come," I said, "you'll see."

The house felt empty after they had gone, but we set to work redding up, as Bethia said, "to take up the slack." But we had no more than got started when Johnnie rode up. I was never more surprised in my life, for he *was* drunk . . . and it took Papa, David and Richard all to handle him. He was roaring and shooting all over the place, scaring Mama and Bethia out of their wits. They got him off his horse finally, and then Richard did the only thing there was to do—knocked him unconscious. They put him to bed in Janie's room.

We took Preacher Rankin home with us. I had a sight of work to do before Sunday, which was the day of the funeral. A funeral is like a wedding in one way. Folks come from miles around, and some, good friends, would have to be housed and fed.

We'd sent the word the service was to begin at nine o'clock and by sunrise the wagons and horses had commenced gathering. There was a considerable crowd. Some came from love of our folks and us, but many came for the pleasure of gathering together.

Richard had laid the baby in the little grassy plot back of his father's . . . where Johnnie Vann, the Indian trader, and his son were buried, and where Bethia's little ones had been laid. "Would you have wanted him put some place else?" he'd asked me later.

"No. That's near and we might as well make of it a family burying ground."

"That's the way I figured it," he'd said.

Looking over the crowd, I reckoned there was about three hundred. Preacher Rankin commenced quiet and slow, as was his way, talking about the shortness of life and how man is cut down like grass. He spoke of the pure soul that had departed and of how, instead of grieving, we should rejoice, for it would never know the sins and sorrows of this world . . . that it had but rejoined its Maker in heaven and was even now clad in raiments of light in everlasting peace and happiness. All of that I knew, but I could not help thinking that by now it would have been fat and soft, maybe able to lift its head, look about, smile a little. And the breasts which had never nourished it, and which had given me so much trouble drying, ached with a hunger for it, clad not in raiments of light but in the clothes I had made for it. It was a sad time for me, and it would have been sadder had I not now known for certain that a new little one was on the way. It is hard to put off the feelings of the flesh.

Then Mr. Rankin began to put more fervor into his sermon, which went queer to me, for he had ever been a sober, orthodox man, given to great solemnity in the pulpit. He was a man of learning and it had been his delights to expound the text, word by word. I had never known him to raise his voice before. Now it was as if an inner fire had been lighted in him. He exhorted and he thundered and he preached with great zeal and physical manifestations of power. He seemed to grow taller and mightier before our eyes, and his face grew red and the sweat streamed down his face. There were times when tears joined the sweat and made the grooves of his face a channel for the rivulets.

He spoke of the fallen state of man and of the necessity for repentance and redemption. And he said the only way to salvation was for the lost world to confess its sins and forsake them, to take up the cross and follow Christ in regeneration. "The coming of the Lord is at hand," he shouted, and his deep voice was like a trumpet sounding, "and the hounds of hell are at your heels! Repent . . . repent . . . repent!"

This—repentance—was the burden of his message. The crowd, seated on the grass, swayed and moved uneasily. None among us were without sin and it was a troublous message to hear. But there were no manifestations of the spirit among us, for the ways of the revival had not yet reached our part of the country and we were bound by the older, quieter ways of the church. Our lack of response moved Preacher Rankin to shout at us that our hearts were hardened in sin, that we were a thankless generation, and he likened us to the people of olden times who offered up their sacrifices to the idols of gold. "You think only of your flocks and your lands and your vineyards," he accused, "when it is your everlasting soul that is in peril. Now, before it is too late, give thought to the state of your soul!"

He preached for three hours, laboring mightily, and when he had finished, the coat on his back was wet with his sweat.

We walked, silently for the most part, down the hill, some of the people, Mr. Rankin among them, stopping at David and Bethia's, some going on to our place. We seemed none of us to know what to say. "Well, I d'know," Papa said finally, "hit goes the quarest to me to hear Preacher Rankin takin' on so. An' I don't know as I'm all that big of a sinner. Hit don't set good on my stummick to be told I'm unregenerate."

"Maybe we all are," Richard said thoughtfully. "Maybe we are and don't know it."

But Papa was still growling. "I d'know as I've fell from grace. I do the best I kin. Go to meetin' when they's e'er'n to go to . . . treat my neighbors kindly, an' me an' Hannah allus has prayers ever' day."

"What if that isn't enough?" Richard asked. "Paul said 'faith without works is dead.'"

"Well, how's a body to show his works? I ain't aimin' to git out shoutin' an' jerkin' an' dancin' like some I've heared of."

"Maybe," Richard went on, "until we do we don't know what it's like to be filled with the spirit."

I looked at Richard and felt a little stirring of disquiet. Preacher Rankin, I thought, had got home to him some place and troubled him. It wasn't like him to give countenance to the strange goings-on of the revivals otherwise.

"Now, Richard," Papa said, "you know all that ain't called fer."

"I don't know. I don't know what's called for and what isn't, but I reckon Preacher Rankin does and I'm aiming to ask him if there's a chance."

There was a chance, for in the afternoon Mr. Rankin came down to our place. He did not preach again, for many of the people had gone home, but he talked quietly to a few of us. He told us of the many things that had happened on Gasper River. "Never," he said, "have I witnessed the like of it. I have said, and you have heard me, that when I first began to minister to the people of Gasper River I had not seen so cold a group to religion. They were steeped in sin and they had hardened their hearts to any ministry. I saw no evidence of any seriousness of a religious nature among them. That has changed. A fire has caught among them and it is spreading to the utmost ends of this country. People come from everywhere to our meetings, and many come under the conviction of the spirit."

Mr. Rankin was a small man, neat in figure and face, never, as we had formerly known him, given to this fire of which he spoke and which we had witnessed in his preaching that morning. "What," Richard asked, "was the starting of it?"

[33]

"Two brothers came from Tennessee two summers ago to preach at the sacramental meeting. I had never seen or heard such preaching, and I marveled at the response of the congregation. They were moved to strange utterances and manifestations, and the two men preached with such conviction and labor that at the end of their sermons they were exhausted. I, myself," he went on, "had a visitation most strange to me at the time. I had prepared my sermon carefully, as was my wont, but when I got up to preach in my own turn, the message which poured from my lips was not one of my own thinking or making. I hardly knew what I said, the origin being so manifestly divine. I became simply the mouth-piece of the Lord, and He spoke through me as never before. I found myself weeping and exhorting and shouting, which I had ever considered an indignity in the pulpit before. And I was overcome with joy and strange emotional feelings."

Richard listened carefully, pondering what Mr. Rankin was saying. "What do you make of such feelings?"

"The joy of the Lord," Mr. Rankin said at once, "oh, the ecstasy of it!"

"You did not feel, then, that you had been swayed by the other preachers?"

"Perhaps . . . to some extent, yes. But it was *meant* I should be swayed, Richard. It was *meant* the fire should be lit."

Richard was silent a moment and then he said, a little hesitantly, "You have left the church, we hear."

"I have entered a new ministry. I have seen the plain error of my former convictions."

"What, now," Richard asked, "is your position on predestination and the election of saints?"

"Error," Mr. Rankin said firmly, "pure error. Only by repentance, confession and taking up the cross can salvation be assured. I labored many years under that error, and mistakenly I taught it and preached it. But I thank the Lord my eyes have been opened to the truth."

Richard shook his head. That he was troubled was plain to see. And because he was troubled, it troubled me. For myself the ways of the church were sufficient. I had no questions about them. But something was stirring in Richard, making him question and examine. It made me feel uneasy. "We've heard," he said, "that folks go into trances at your meetings, take the jerks, roll and dance, shout and speak in tongues unknown to men, see visions and prophecy."

"It is true."

"What do you make of it?"

"It is the spirit of the Lord at work. In these latter days He is stirring up the people, charging them with new zeal and joy. I make it that He is trying, before His second coming, to bring the faithful into the fold."

Richard moved restlessly. "Would a man be damned, then, if he did not believe?"

Mr. Rankin was positive about this. "He would be. Having heard, having witnessed, I can see nothing but his eternal punishment if he hardened his heart."

"But what if he hasn't heard or witnessed?"

"It is there to be heard and to be witnessed. It is open and free to all. Come," Mr. Rankin said, "come to the next meeting. It will be held the first week in July. Come and see for yourself—and I have faith you will be convinced."

Richard looked at me. I did not now want to go. I had been curious before and would have liked to witness the spectacle, to see and hear the strange happenings. But Richard's uneasiness had altered that. It was as if I had stepped onto a quivering bog and knew not where to place my foot next. I felt confused that Richard's concern should be serious. When he looked at me, I said nothing. I was constrained to silence before Mr. Rankin. Also, I little doubted what I thought or wanted would weigh much. Finally Richard said, "Well . . . we *might* come."

And I knew we would go. Mr. Rankin had always had a strong influence on Richard. He had ever liked and respected him. In my hearing he had said more than once, "John Rankin is a sound man." He leaned now toward following wherever he led, through that liking and respect.

"Good," Mr. Rankin said, "good! You will see, as I have seen, and your heart will be opened, as mine has been."

So it was that we set our feet upon the road that led us finally all the way to the Believers. A wedding, a funeral, and Richard's trust in one man changed the whole course of our lives.

CHAPTER V

A GREAT CROWD had already gathered when we arrived at the Gasper River meeting grounds. I had never before, save in the city of Lexington, seen so many people together. Wagons and carts were placed all around the grounds, like framework. People had come from far and near, prepared for the four days of meeting, with bedding to roll out on the ground or lay in their wagons, and food to last out the time. Each wagon or cart made the center of a small camp. We ourselves had come thus prepared.

I do not recall that we had discussed any further the question of going to the meeting. I had been certain we would go, and apparently Richard had been aware of my certainty. Several days beforehand he had said,

"We'd best take the wagon, I reckon. It would come in handy for sleeping."

"Yes," I had agreed.

"I'll have Sampson put in some fresh straw."

Cassie and I had then set to work to prepare food and to make ready a box of pots and kettles for cooking. She and Sampson were to stay behind to see to things. I took Jency for whatever help she might be.

We were four days on the way. At first she had been greatly excited. She had sat in the straw in the back of the wagon, bouncing happily when we hit a rough place, her big eyes round at each new sight, her giggle sounding often. Sometimes she crawled over the endboard and ran along beside the wagon, picking a flower or two, singing to herself, or simply dancing along, glad of the sun and the open road.

But along toward evening when we had been several hours in country new to her she became quiet, and looking back, once, I saw her watching the road down which we had come. Turning, she saw me looking at her. "Ain't we 'bout there, Miss Becky?"

"No, Jency," I shook my head, "it will be three more days before we're there."

Her eyes widened and she drew in her breath, but she said nothing more.

On the second day she continued very quiet. Thinking she was homesick I tried to interest her in the unfamiliar countryside. "Look, Jency, at the rocks in that cliff. And see how the ferns grow down the side of it."

"Yessum."

There was no giggling or singing or dancing along the road that day. She had eyes only for the way we had come. When we stopped for the night she began crying. "Miss Becky, I wants to go home."

"You can't go home, now, Jency. It's too far. We'll be there pretty soon."

"Yessum. But I is skeered we's goin' so fur we ain't never gonna git back home."

Richard laughed at her. "This isn't very far, Jency."

She looked at him from between her fingers. "Seem powerful fur to me."

"That's because you've never traveled before."

She broke into a wail. "An' I wish I ain't ever commenced travelin'! How we gonna git back?"

"The same way we've come. With this team and wagon and right down this trail. Don't you think I know how to take us home again?"

"Yessuh."

"Well, what are you cryin' about?"

"I'd jist feel better to commence startin' back right now, 'fore we gits any further."

"Well, you can't," Richard told her, shortly, "so you just help Miss Becky and forget about it."

Her forlorn little face touched me and I thought to comfort her, when Richard had taken the horses to water, by telling her about the new child. "In January," I told her, "just like the other one."

Morosely she sighed. "An' jist like the other'n, hit'll be daid."

"Don't say that, Jency!"

"No'm," she said docilely, "but bad luck is bad luck, an' you commences havin' it with younguns an' hit won't leave off."

She had voiced my own inner fears and I was sharp with her. "Gather the firewood," I told her, "and keep still."

But when, on the fourth day, we reached the camping ground and she saw that we had actually been heading toward some place where there were other people, and not, as I suspect she thought, toward the edge of time, her interest quickened and she became lively again.

There were far too many people to be accommodated in the new meeting house, so the preaching services were to be held in the open. Two platforms had been built, one at either end of a long open space, with woods coming up on all sides. This made it handy for the families with children. Small ones could be put to bed in the wagons which ringed round the space, and mothers, knowing they were safe nearby, could continue to listen to the sermons.

It was a common sight to see them sitting on logs or wagon tongues, a baby at their breasts, their attention still focused upon the preacher holding forth, or handing out corn pones to the older ones, their ears still hearing the sermon.

We drove roundabout, looking for a place not too crowded by neighbors. Richard had the same idea as all the others—a place near the meadow, but shaded from the sun and heat. We found one, finally, though another wagon was drawn up too near to suit Richard, and there were several children in the family. I counted three small ones, not knowing if that was all.

A woman was cooking the evening meal as we drove in, but she turned from the fire to look at us, and the children lined up and stared. She made a quick motion and they scattered, but from various vantage points, behind the wagon, the trunk of a tree, they continued to stare. When we had pulled up and Richard had set to unhitching the team, the woman set her pots off the fire and came toward us. Feeling stiff from sitting all day I was clumsily trying to climb down over the wheel. Jency had already bounced out the back and was hopping, first on one foot then on the other, looking at the great open meadow with the platforms.

"Here," the woman said, laughing at my awkwardness, "let me give you a hand." That was Permilla. My first memory of her is of her lending me a hand. Almost my last one was the same.

I took the hand she offered and, laughing at my own awkwardness, jumped to the ground. "Gits a body in the legs, don't it," she said, "ridin'. Now a horse, hit'll git you a different place, but I'll take a horse any day to settin' too long in a wagon."

She was a woman as tall as my mother, which meant she was a little taller than I, and in all my life I have never seen a woman more naturally beautiful. She stood straight and easy, not overburdened with flesh, but not angular in any way. It was as if nature had given her exactly the proportions she needed for grace and use. I once read from a book by a man with some knowledge of beauty that the perfect proportions for a woman's body was an equal division into thirds. From her shoulders to her waist, from her waist to her knees, and from her knees to her ankles should be the same. If you looked at Permilla's body you saw at once that she had been endowed with such proportions. Her bosom was generous, her hips likewise, and her waist, tied around with her apron, was neat.

If you looked at her face you saw a skin like new cream, unwrinkled yet by time, smooth, rich and deep in texture. No feature was prominent, each exactly right, blending into the next to make a perfect whole . . . the nose, the brow, the chin and mouth, nobly made.

Her eyes were blue, the deep blue of the summer sky, fringed by long, upcurling lashes, and her hair swept back from her forehead in close waves, gathered into a knot on her neck. It was as golden as sun-ripened corn. She did not wear a cap and it did not occur to me to wonder why. "You all come fur?" she asked.

"From Lincoln County," I told her.

"Hit was wearisome, I'd reckon."

I agreed. "Four days on the way."

"We're from hereabouts. We could of rid over a horseback, but Thomas, that's my man, said we'd have need of the wagon fer campin'."

"Have you been to the meetings before?" I asked.

She shook her head. "No, but they's been sich a talk of 'em we allowed we'd come an' see fer ourselves. So I jist packed up the younguns an' come on."

"How many children do you have?"

"Jist the three you seen a peerin' at you. We live so fur in the woods they're like woodsy things theirselves. I'm mortified at their manners."

"You needn't be. Children are naturally curious."

"Well," she said, laughing a little, "a body cain't expect 'em to do smart when they ain't ever had the chance. Whyn't you all jist eat yer supper with us this evenin'? Hit's nigh ready an' I'll bound you're too fashed to cook."

I was tired, but I doubted if Richard would want to eat with strangers. "We'll make out," I told her, "but I thank you anyway."

"Make nothin' of it," she said.

Richard had finished feeding the horses and came around the end of

[38]

the wagon. He hesitated, seeing me talking to a strange woman. Seeing him, Permilla laughed. "My name is Permilla Bennett," she said; "we're camped right next. My man is Thomas Bennett. I jist been tryin' to talk yer woman into takin' supper with us, seein' you've had a long drive."

Richard told her who we were, and as I expected demurred at having supper with them. "We wouldn't want to trouble you," he said.

"Hit wouldn't be no trouble," she told him. "If Thomas'd jist come on, hit'd be ready soon." She shaded her eyes with her hand and looked out across the meadow, then she started laughing. "Speakin' of the devil," she said, "here he comes right now." She waited until he was within hailing distance then she called to him. "Thomas! Oh, Thomas, come over here an' make the acquaintance of the Coopers."

I couldn't have been more surprised. A man as old as my father came shambling toward us, thin, gaunt, straggly-whiskered, bent in the shoulders, with lank, greasy hair falling about his ears from under a flop-brimmed hat. My amazement must have shown, for Permilla said dryly, "My man is some older'n me."

Later, when I knew her better, she told me something of her past . . . how she'd been raised on a poor place in the woods, how little she'd ever had, and how when Thomas came along, old as he was, she'd taken him to get away from her home where a stepmother had made her life almost unbearable. I had my doubts that she'd bettered herself as far as poverty went, but I reckoned that unless a man actually mistreated you, it was more agreeable to be beholding to him than to a stepmother.

Thomas spoke pleasantly to Richard and made a small bow to him. "They're aimin' to take supper with us," Permilla told him.

"Only," Richard insisted firmly, "if we can bring our part."

"That's agreeable," Thomas said.

"It'll be the only part fit to eat if I don't git back to that fire," Permilla said, laughing.

Thomas offered to show Richard about the meeting ground and they started off together. Permilla called after them, "Don't you be long, now. What vittles we got is nigh ready."

"We'll be back soon," Thomas told her.

Permilla and I then set to work with the meal. The children gathered about. They looked to be all of one age, four, five years old. It was hard to tell. "Are two of them twins?" I asked.

When she laughed Permilla had a way of throwing her head back. It was the prettiest sight to see. "No," she said, "but they mought as well be. Ain't but ten months betwixt any of 'em. That'n," she pointed to the girl, "is Nancy. She's six. Matthew an' Aaron is both five. An'," she added, "they'll be another'n come spring."

"I reckon they're a right smart trouble so close together that way," I said.

"They've like to drove me out of my wits, times. But a body makes out. Hit's this new 'un I wisht I was shut of, though. Seems like I jist cain't git up no enthusiasm fer no more. I thought to avoid against it, an' I done right well fer a spell, as you c'n see, but you cain't hold even a old man off forever." She sighed and then laughed. "Oh, well . . . it ain't the worst could happen, I reckon."

I was a little embarrassed by her open way of talking, and ordinarily I would have been pretty shocked. But you could tell she meant nothing but one woman's talk to another by it, and remembering Thomas I couldn't actually blame her.

That meal together was the beginning, for during the entire time of the meeting, the whole four days, we all ate together as one big family, Permilla and I sharing the work as if we had known each other always. She did her work as quickly and easily as I, and we found no awkwardness in working together. If I made bread, Permilla fried meat, and if I stored leftover food afterward, she washed up. There was no need of deciding. We seemed like four hands on one body, to know how to give and take together.

The first preaching service began the next morning, and four different preachers took turns throughout the day. There was a stop at midday for the people to eat and rest awhile, then the preaching was resumed. At the end of the day I felt a disappointment, for it had seemed much like an all-day meeting in our own church. There had been no evidence of excitement. I mentioned it at supper. "They say," Permilla told me, "hit's the night meetin's that sets 'em off. Likely they'll git goin' this evenin'."

She was right. Pine torches had been lighted and placed near the east platform, for the preachers would take turns only from the one platform during the evening. As night came on and the darkness fell over the woods and the meadow and the pine torches cast a smoking, red glow over the faces of the people, it seemed to inspire the preachers.

At first they preached in short turns, each giving way to another fairly soon, and there was almost as much singing as there was preaching, the preacher stopping short to break into song. The songs were strange to me, sung much faster than the sober, serious hymns of the church, but some of the people must have known them, for they joined in the singing readily enough. There was a swaying amongst the people as they sang, and a clapping of hands, and some shouting of "Glory!" occasionally, but it was not until a preacher who had not taken any turn during the day rose and came forward that we saw an expectant and excited look upon their faces. This was the man they had come to hear, evidently . . . the man they had been waiting for. "Who is he?" I whispered to Permilla. We had stayed on the edge of the crowd, purposely, so that we might see better.

"One of them brothers from Tennessee . . . I don't know which'n."

We were standing, for the crowd was on its feet now.

The man, tall, spare, with a dark face and bushy eyebrows, stared out over them in complete silence for a moment. Then, like a gun pointing, he leveled his arm at them and shouted, "Ye are doomed! And the fires of hell await you!" A moan went up from the crowd, and somewhere among them a woman screamed. "Ye are doomed," he repeated. His voice was deep and full and carried to the woods on all sides.

I have often pondered the effect of a voice. The best preachers are always those with good, deep voices. It matters not how little he has to say, so long as he has the voice of authority. He can move, sway, control a crowd, so long as he speaks with certainty and in full, rounded tones. Nor does it avail a man to have much to say if he must say it in weak, limping inflections. This man spoke with authority. His voice sounded like the voice of doom itself, like a trumpet sounding a call, and even to me who expected not to be moved, it brought a shiver of apprehension.

I do not know how long he preached. All sense of time was lost, for within fifteen minutes of his first words we saw what Mr. Rankin had promised. We saw people throw up their hands, spin and whirl round and round, fall to the ground and lie still as death. We saw them carried off as stiff as corpses, and laid where they would not be trampled.

We saw one woman, standing not far from us, taken with the jerks. It began with her head, with a snapping and jerking of her neck which looked to me as if it would break, and it spread to her arms and hands, then to her entire body, until she was like to come unjointed. A man standing beside her, her husband we took him to be, tried to guard her from those who crowded around, and led her finally, toward the platform and the preacher.

We saw people milling in a kind of slow dance which sometimes increased until they were spinning wildly. And then we began to hear the strange, unintelligible sounds of people speaking in tongues. I felt dazed and confused, not knowing where to look, felt strange in a strange place.

Richard nudged me. "Let's go around the edge and get near the front. I can't hear the preacher now with so much noise going on."

I told Permilla and she and Thomas followed as we wound our way through the edge of the crowd. "What do you make of it?" she asked, on my heels.

"I don't know," I told her honestly. "I never saw anything like it before."

"If it's the spirit workin'," she said, "like the preachers say, hit's takin' awful quare ways, ain't it?"

But I knew nothing of the workings of the spirit. I had been reared to believe I was a child of the covenant, my parents having me baptized before I could remember. I had never doubted that by predestination and sanctification I was among those elected to be saved. To be moved by the spirit was something entirely foreign to my way of thinking. But suppose Mr. Rankin and this preacher are right, I thought. Suppose all I have been taught *is* error? Mr. Rankin said he had seen the error of his ways. And he was a preacher. It made me feel very uneasy.

We found a place near the platform, for so many people had fallen out that room had been made. Kneeling in the trodden grass immediately in front of the platform were those who had come forward, weeping, shouting, dancing, to pray and to be prayed for. The preacher stood over them, exhorting, singing praises, praying mightily.

That Richard was moved I could tell, for he stood leaning forward, eagerly intent upon all that happened, listening, and his face worked as things the preacher said were pounded home to him. "He's got the power," I heard him mutter, "he's really got the power."

I was growing very tired of standing, but I still was interested. Then Richard suddenly made a move forward. "I'm going up for prayers," he said.

Fearfully I looked around at Permilla and Thomas. "I'm going with him," I told them.

"We'll go, too," she said, and the four of us made our way to the kneeling group in front of the platform.

I must confess that after a time on my knees I sank into the grass and sat there, hearing the sounds all about me, aware of the crowds milling, but feeling only gratitude to be sitting down finally. Richard, more hardy then I, never left his knees and that he was laboring hard under prayer was plain to see. The sweat ran down his face and his lips moved, though his voice was lost in the other sounds. Permilla soon sat beside me, and Thomas beside her. They were, like me, still more curious than moved.

It surprised me to be touched on the shoulder. "Ah, Rebecca. You and Richard have come, then." It was Mr. Rankin. I motioned toward Richard, and Mr. Rankin went to lay his hand on his shoulder, and bend over him. "Keep in the labor, Richard," he admonished, "keep in the labor. You will be rewarded."

A long shudder ran through Richard's body and he slumped forward. I was frightened and reached for him, but Mr. Rankin warded me off. "It is the first sign," he told me. "Leave him alone." He knelt beside Richard and lifted his own voice in prayer and praise.

But no further sign was manifested to Richard that night. Finally, weary beyond measure, we went back to the camp and parted quietly with Thomas and Permilla. "I feel," Richard said, lying beside me, "as limp as a baby, as soft and drained of strength."

Jency, on a straw pallet under the wagon, whimpered. "I cain't sleep, Miss Becky. They's makin' sich a racket a body cain't sleep. How long they gonna keep it up?"

"I have no idea," I told her. "You'll just have to stick your head under the straw, I guess."

She must have done so, for I heard no more from her. I myself had no trouble getting to sleep, though there was no lessening in the noise, and for all I know the meeting may have lasted all night.

Not on the second evening, nor the third, was there any further sign given to Richard, though each evening he went forward and labored. Permilla and Thomas and I went with him.

Before the last evening, as we sat at supper, Richard spoke out. "I have the conviction, but I am not granted the vision," he said.

Thomas looked at him. "You think they're preachin' true, do you?"

"I know it. My last doubt is gone. But for some reason the manifestation is denied me."

"Mebbe hit'll come tonight," Permilla said.

"I pray it will." He turned to me. "Rebecca, we cannot go back to the error of our old ways."

I had foreseen this ever since Mr. Rankin had talked to him, but I said, "I don't know what you mean."

"We must withdraw from a church which preaches error."

"What will we do?" I saw the little meeting house, built of logs but framed over in recent years, in which we had gathered with our families and friends all our lives, and I felt an immeasurable homesickness for it. I wished we had never come to Gasper River.

"I don't know," Richard said, "but it will be revealed to us."

To some extent I understood what was working in Richard . . . doubt, first, then fear and conviction. I did not understand all that was happening, but that something was happening I knew full well. All his beliefs were being upset. I did not yet know how much, nor did I comprehend at all where it would lead. But that there was no turning back for him I knew.

Mr. Rankin preached that night. He had been preaching during the daytime, leaving the nights for the two brothers. But they had worn themselves out and he took the turn. I don't know how much that had to do with Richard's breaking through, but that it had something to do with it, I am convinced. When it was Mr. Rankin, whom he loved and trusted, who stood before him and told him he was doomed, when it was Mr. Rankin who offered salvation through confession and repentance, he was suddenly freed of the last bond. And I saw my husband, commonly so quiet and sober a man, turned into a spinning, jerking, whirling person, laughing and weeping at the same time, joy spread over his face, breaking into shouts that meant nothing to me, for they were in a language I did not understand.

Mr. Rankin saw Richard's transport and came down from the platform, to shout praises himself, though I think Richard never knew he was there. "What shall I do?" I asked him. "I'm afraid he'll be hurt."

"Leave him alone," Mr. Rankin said. "When he is quieter you can take him to your camp. Thank God the spirit has made itself known to him."

But I didn't know whether to thank God or not. Mostly I only felt bewilderment to see Richard so taken. And then, whether he caught it from Richard or himself came under the power I do not know, but soon after Richard's manifestation, Thomas began to jerk and speak in tongues. Permilla, after one amazed look, drew away and left him alone, as she had heard Mr. Rankin advise me. "If that don't beat the world," she said to me, watching in astonishment. "I'd never of dreamt it of Thomas."

"Hush," I told her, "we'd better pray ourselves."

"You pray," Permilla said. "I'm done prayed out."

But she stayed beside me until such time as we thought Richard and Thomas could be led away. Respectfully the crowd parted to let us pass. Any person who came under the power was treated as if he had been visited by angels. Some reached out to touch the two men, hoping, it may be, to draw from them something of the same visitation.

Richard slept like a child all night. I think he never knew we had come to the wagon, or that I had settled him comfortably in the straw. He was like a person walking in dreams, peacefully following where I led him, doing what he was told. He never spoke one word to me, and when I knew, finally, by his deep, even breathing that he had fallen asleep, I could compose myself. It had been a wearying, confused time and I was glad of the comfort of the bed. I wept a little at discovering this stranger in my husband, but not overly much. He was still Richard, and my husband, and I was by his side.

The meeting was over.

But we did not start home immediately. "I'm going to talk to Brother Rankin," Richard told me, even before we had eaten breakfast the next morning.

It was the first time he had spoken of him thus. In this new faith all men were brothers, and spoke so to each other. He went off and I watched him go, full of apprehension for what might now occur. Jency came creeping out from under the wagon, bits of straw sticking in her hair. "Whur Mister Richard goin'? Ain't we goin' home today?"

"I don't know," I told her. "He's gone to talk to Mr. Rankin."

"Miss Becky," she said, "he gonna keep us down here fer good. We ain't ever gonna go home." She started crying. "I wants to go home. I wants my mammy. I got no likin' fer this place."

I felt both impatience and pity for her. "We'll go home," I assured her. "Probably we'll start today. Mister Richard only wants to talk a little while with Mr. Rankin. You'll see your mother again very soon. Now, go on and get some water, like a good girl."

She wiped her eyes with her dress tail, but her face was still woebegone. "He not like he wuz, Mister Richard ain't. He done changed."

He had, indeed, but I forebore to say so. "Go on and do your chores, Jency. I promise you we'll go home."

"How you knows it?" she asked doubtfully.

"Oh, use your head, child," I said. "We've got a farm and a house, and Cassie and Sampson to see to. There's no way we *can* stay here."

Her face brightened. "Yessum. Hit's the truth, ain't it? We got things to do at home."

I smiled at the idea of Jency having things to do anywhere, but if it had consoled her I was glad.

I joined Permilla at the breakfast fire. "When are you and Thomas leaving?"

She shrugged. "There's nary a bit of tellin'. He's done went with Richard . . . to talk to that preacher. Hit don't matter so much with us . . . we jist got a day's travel an' we'll be home. But I reckon you'd like to git movin'."

"I would," I admitted.

The men had not come by the time breakfast was ready, so we fed the children and then, reluctantly, ate also. We redded up the cook things and packed, saving out a little food for the men, then there was nothing to do but wait.

It was the middle of the morning when they came, both looking very serious and earnest. Neither Permilla nor I asked any questions. We fed them, then both men turned to hitching up their teams. "Well," I told Permilla, "I reckon this is goodbye."

"I reckon it is," she said, clasping my hand. "But likely we'll meet again next meetin' time."

"I expect so."

She suddenly threw both arms about me. "Rebecca, take keer of yerself. Fer I've a fondness for you I've not felt for many before."

Thomas had his team ready first and they wheeled out of the space which for four days had been a home to us. Permilla waved, the children waved, and Thomas ducked his head in a farewell nod. "They're good folks," Richard said, "and honest. It'll be good to have them for neighbors."

Thus I had the first intimation of what was to come, but it was not until we were on the road, past the crowds, that Richard told me what he had decided. "I aim," he said, "to sell out on the Green and buy down here."

I tried to take this in, but it came too suddenly. "You mean to sell our place? That was given to us? That we've worked so hard to get started?"

Slowly he nodded his head. "I've spoken to Brother Rankin about it. I want to be closer to where he is. We would be, now, amongst a worldly people, not in sympathy with us. It's best, he thinks, and so do I, for us to join forces all together here. Those of us, that is, that have come under the spirit."

But I had not come under the spirit, and I would not be among worldly people not in sympathy with me. I would be among my own folks. I would not be joining forces with anyone. I would be a stranger in a strange land. I looked about me at the country, like and yet different from what I was used to. I could not, somehow, believe Richard meant for us to live in this unfamiliar land. It made no sense to me. We had been born and reared in Lincoln County. There wasn't a family we hadn't known since childhood, or who hadn't come, strangers, and been taken into the settlement. Here we would be the strangers. And Logan County, of all places— the hiding place of criminals and lawbreakers.

Wildly I thought of my mother, and how I could have run weeping into her strong and comforting arms, sought refuge there from this foolish scheme taking form in Richard's mind. But almost as soon as this feeling stormed over me, it passed. I was a woman. I was married. This was my husband. And soon there would be a child. A married woman, with duties and responsibilities, does not run weeping to find refuge in her mother's arms. That is past with her girlhood. Her strength and refuge must be in her husband.

Richard was speaking again. "Brother Rankin knows of a good farm handy to his. He says it can be bought. It's not as big as the Green River farm, so the difference ought to be enough to allow a man to get a good start."

"What," I said suddenly, "what if David won't let you sell the place?"

"He gave it to me outright. He made it over with a deed. There's nothing he can do about it if I want to sell."

"He won't like it, though."

"Maybe not, at first. But I'll pick careful who I sell to, and in time maybe he won't mind."

Privately I thought he would always mind. The land had been his own. To have strangers, no matter how congenial, at home right in his own front yard would never be to his liking, I was certain. But I knew also that nothing could swerve Richard. Hadn't I, all my life, seen his stubbornness and known it? It was no more than could be expected of a man who never had any trouble deciding what he should do, once he had seen his duty. "How soon," I asked, "do you figure on making the move?"

"Not for a while. We'll get the harvest in first. Sell sometime after that, buy and get moved before time for breaking ground next spring."

For the first time since we had married I felt resentment toward Richard. He had not asked once whether I wanted to make this move. He hadn't even indicated he wanted to make it. He had simply gone, highhandedly, to Mr. Rankin and decided it.

Of course he had not actually consulted me about our home in the first place. His father had given him the land, and he had decided on the house. But at least he had talked with me about it, had told me everything he planned. A man must, naturally, take the lead, make the decisions, and it is a woman's place to follow. But when it came to uprooting a woman's whole life, it seemed to me he might have talked it over first. I said nothing, however. It would have done no good, and it might have done great harm. "What about Cassie and Sampson and Jency?" I asked.

Richard looked at me, surprised. "Why, we'll bring them with us. I'll need Sampson more than ever."

Jency had probably been listening all this time, for she broke into loud wails. "I done tole you, Miss Becky! I done tole you! We ain't a goin' home atall!"

Richard turned around. "Jency, you hush, before I stop the team and get a switch to you. We're going home right now."

"But we ain't gonna stay there. You done say so. You done say we's movin' to this godforsaken country."

Richard grew very stern. "I don't want ever to hear you say such a thing again, Jency. Instead of being godforsaken, this country has been blessed of the Lord. His will has been revealed here and he has made his intentions known. We are moving to the promised land."

Jency was easily frightened of Richard. His way with the blacks was always just, but it was often very strict. She snubbed her sobs, but I heard her mutter, "Doan look lak no promised land to me."

Richard heard the mutter but I think he did not catch her words, for all he said was, "That'll be enough, now, Jency."

We rode on in quiet for a time. Then I said, "Are Thomas and Permilla going to sell and move to Gasper River, too? You said they'd be our neighbors."

"Yes. They'll have the land right next to ours."

I wondered if Permilla was learning, even as I, of the change in store for her. I could even smile at the thought that she, unlike myself, might even now be giving Thomas a piece of her mind. But from what she had told me of their hill farm, I thought the move would vastly improve their circumstances, and it might be she would welcome it gladly.

That was my comfort, however, that Permilla would be my door neighbor. If I had to give up my home, leave my people, go to a strange land to live—with Permilla close by, something, at least, would be gained. I hugged this comfort to me all during the time which followed.

And the thought crossed my mind, too, that my baby would be born in its own and rightful place. I was glad for that.

CHAPTER VI

THAT OUR FAMILIES would disapprove of Richard's decision was to be expected, but Richard lost no time telling his father what he intended to do. He was never one to shirk a duty because it was unpleasant, and he sought David out the next Sunday after we had got home.

I shall never forget the scene which followed. David and Bethia were so shocked that at first they didn't believe it; then when he took it in, realized what Richard had said, David stormed out at him so angry he was white around the mouth and trembling. He shouted and argued and pled until he was hoarse. None of it moved Richard one whit. "By grannies, boy," David told him, shaking his fist at him, "if I'd known you could be so addle-pated and reckless, I'd never of given you that land in the first place. I thought you was steady and to be trusted. I thought it would suit and please you. I aimed to help you get a start."

"You did," Richard told him, "and I wouldn't want you to think I'm unthankful, for I'm not. It was a big help. But a man has got to do what he thinks is right."

"Right!" David shouted at him. "How can it be right for you to sell the land and go traipsin' off to Gasper River? What's right about it?"

"My belief. I'm sorry to go against you, but I've got to follow my convictions."

"Convictions, hell!" David yelled. "It's just a parcel of damn foolishness. That preacher . . . I'd like to take a horsewhip to him!"

Richard said nothing. Bethia was sitting by the window, her mouth quivering at the quarrel between them, not knowing what to say, or whether to say anything, and I felt torn in two halves, listening. I didn't want to go to Gasper River. I didn't want to give up our place on the Green. I didn't want, now that I had time to reflect, any part of this strange new faith. But deep down inside of me I knew Richard would never give over his decision. If necessary he would leave his father and mother and never see them again. If necessary, I was afraid, he would even leave me.

David went on, more calmly. "Now, listen to me, Richard. You been raised in a good settlement, amongst good folks, and you been raised in a proper church. *Why* ain't that good enough for you?"

Richard shook his head. "Because I have seen the truth."

"The truth! There's a hundred different kinds of truth . . . the Methodists got one, the Baptists got another, and every religion thinks it's got still another. If you'd of just went over to any of them, I wouldn't open my mouth. But you got to go traipsin' off to Logan County and join up with a bunch of jerkin', dancin', crazy folks. What kind of truth is that?"

"The only truth."

David had come up against Richard's stubbornness too often to have any real hope he could change him, but he kept trying. "I don't aim to have just anybody settled in my front yard," he warned Richard. "That piece of land was mine . . . and I ain't thinkin' much of the idea of havin' some shiftless, no-good settler on it, though," he said, "I deeded it to you and you can sell to whoever you please, I reckon."

"I aim to pick careful," Richard told him. "The folks'll be of the kind you won't mind."

"Humph," David said.

Bethia was crying by then. "Richard, I don't understand you. I don't know what to make of it."

"Well, Ma," he told her, weary now of the talk and storm, "just put it down to my ways. I go by what I believe, and if it leads me to part from here, there's nothing I can do about it."

"You'll be so far away!"

"It ain't really so far. We can come and go."

"It'll be you doin' the comin' and goin', then," David said, sourly. "I ain't aimin' to set foot in that lawless land." And they never did, and there was forever after a strain between them and Richard.

It was like Richard not to put it on me to tell my folks, either. The very first Sunday we took the day with them he named it to them. And I think if he had said he was going to take me across the waters to live my mother could not have been more dismayed. The look on her face changed from disbelief to horror and then to grief almost more swiftly than I can write it. "You ain't!" she said, finally.

"Yes, ma'am."

Mama looked sadly at me. "You aim to take my girl, the only one that's left to me, off all that piece from me."

Richard tried to be gentle. "That's the way it has to be, Hannah. I wish it was closer, but it's on the Gasper River and nowhere else. We can't move the river or the folks. We can only go where they are."

Like David she cried, Why, and once more Richard tried to explain. But it was hopeless. There was no understanding except from those who had seen and heard and none of our people had done either. It was like trying to explain God, or the feeling one has in the spring of the year, or the gladness in one's heart filled with love. Words don't really explain. They just tell. It's the only way folks have of telling, but it's a poor way sometimes. If hearts could only speak to hearts it would be better, but hearts can only beat and ache and break.

Cassie and Sampson took it quietly, although Cassie told me once it grieved her. "I'd thought to spend the rest of my days in this place," she said. "I doan rightly known whut's come over Mister Richard to take us all off to that outlandish country. Hit ain't goin' to seem natural, Miss Becky."

"No," I agreed, "it won't seem natural to any of us for a while, Cassie. But your work will be just what it's always been, and Mister Richard and I will take care of you just as we have always done. There's nothing for you to worry about."

"No'm. I ain't wearied. I jist cain't git used to it, is all."

Jency wouldn't speak of it. It was as if she had deliberately put it from her mind. She flitted about as always, singing, dancing, chasing butterflies. I thought perhaps the change would affect her least of all. There are butterflies to chase anywhere in the world.

[49]

We went about our work as usual. Sampson and Richard worked in the fields and Cassie and I kept up our chores, but there was always in the back of my mind the move soon to be upon us. I kept thinking of packing, of things to take and things to sell or leave or give away. I couldn't settle happily to any task for the necessity of thinking of the new ones lying ahead. There was a sadness to everything I did, for when a move hangs over a body, there's little heart for work. There's the knowing it isn't to last, and all my pride and feeling of joy in our home was lost. Instead, each day I was telling goodbye to the house, the farm, the river and the hills. It was foolish of me, keeping the hurt so alive, but there seemed no way I could help it. It lived with me every hour of every day, hung there like a heavy cloud, haunted me like a ghost come to abide with us.

And it was worse when Mama came. Her long, dark face reminded me, piercing me like a sword, of the time when she would no longer be able to ride over for the day, and there would be months, maybe years between the times we could be together. She never ceased grieving over it, but one thing she did understand . . . a woman has to go where her man goes. She did not question that. She only grieved that Richard's faith had changed and he must go.

There were three things which brightened my days—the remembrance of Permilla, the thought of the new child, and Janie's letters.

Janie had not been back since her wedding, but she wrote fairly often. Her letters were long and full of what she had been doing. Sometimes they were written to Mama, sometimes they were written to me, but they were always meant to be shared. They were sent by courier to the county seat and there was always someone coming our way to bring them out.

It took me out of myself to read that their house had been finished and they were settling into it . . . that the real lace curtains and red velvet draperies she had bought in Philadelphia had come and were being hung . . . that Mr. Leavitt had bought a young yellow girl for her, to be her maid . . . that in addition she had a good cook and another black to help the cook . . . that she had a boy to drive her out, and a new carriage to be driven in . . . that she had been to a ball and had worn her new evening dress and that she had danced until her slippers were worn through.

She told us nothing of how she felt. Always she spoke of what she was doing, where she was going, what she was wearing, but she seemed gay, excited, happy. "She don't say," Mama said once, "if she's commenced a youngun yit."

"She wouldn't say in a letter, Mama."

"No, I reckon she wouldn't. An' I misdoubt she'd send fer me at all. She'd likely be ashamed of her country relations."

"Oh, now, Mama."

Mama looked at me very directly, her dark eyes sharp and keen. "She would, you know." Then she shook her head. "Hit goes the quarest to me . . . her livin' in the city like rich folks. Hit don't seem natural fer one of my younguns."

It didn't seem very natural to me, either, though I didn't say so. But Kentucky had been built by people bettering themselves, and Janie had taken her own way to what she thought was better. Mama would never understand it and there was no use talking about it.

She guessed sooner than I expected that I was bearing another child. I didn't feel as well with this one as I had with the first, but that could have been laid to my worry over the move. What Mama's eyes were quick to see was the first swelling of bosom, long before the thickening and widening of waist. "You're in the family way again, ain't you?" she said one day.

"Yes."

"I hope," she said, "hit'll be birthed afore you have to leave out. You had sich a time with the other'n I'd hate fer you to be off somewheres I couldn't have the keer of you."

"It will be. In January, like before."

Mama's face brightened. "Likely," she said, "hit'll go fine this time. A woman sometimes loses the first 'un an' then does good with all the rest."

I knew that was true. Many women did lose their first and then have no more trouble. But Jency's prophecy had never really left my thoughts. And I had a fear of what she had said. It troubled me and kept me from being wholly happy about the child.

And I was right to be afraid, for this child never even came to term. In October, three full months before it was due, it was born, with never a chance to live. It was another boy, and I could not even find tears to weep this time. It seemed as if I had known it all along. The only thing I felt about it was a deep despair and hopelessness and I lay in the bed in a kind of dumb listlessness, without the heart to try for strength to rouse myself.

Richard had set his mouth in a grim line. "It's a punishment, Becky," he said one day when he had brought my dinner to me and was sitting beside me. "It's a punishment for the way we've been living. The Lord don't aim for us to have young ones till we've set ourselves right with him."

Hope is a strange thing and it springs from strange sources, sometimes even from despair. After he had gone I lay there and thought about what he had said. Something was wrong, and maybe he was right about it. I thought of my queer feelings at the meeting last summer, of how I had held back and disliked it and distrusted it. Maybe it was I who had to be chastened. Surely Richard, who had been given the light to see and the gift to speak, surely Richard was in grace. But I, with my doubts and confusion, who had made no effort to lay hold upon Richard's truth, perhaps it was I who was drawing the frown of the Lord upon us. I thought much about it, lying still in my bed those days of recovery, with Mama coming and going quietly, seeing to me and the house, grieving in her own way both for me and for the child.

And suddenly it seemed to me certain that Richard was right and we must hurry to make this move to Gasper River . . . that there was no time to be lost. I would put aside my doubts. I would believe as Richard and Mr. Rankin believed. I would pray and I would be humble and surely the wrath of the Lord would be averted. I was in a frenzy now to go immediately. I would conceive again, quickly, as before, and it must not happen until we were among the fold of those saved and I myself had received the truth. Another child would be doomed unless we made haste.

I sent for Richard. He came, anxious, afraid that I had taken worse. "You're poorly?" he asked immediately.

"No. I wanted to talk with you about something. Have you got the time?"

"Depends on how long it takes. We're gathering the corn. Couldn't it wait till supper?"

"No . . . I want to tell you right now, while it's clear in my mind. Richard, could we leave here sooner than you'd planned?"

He drew up a chair to the side of the bed, and seeing he meant to stay I propped myself upon pillows. "I don't know," he said. "There's a heap of things to be done. I didn't allow you was in any hurry to get moved. Facts is, I figured you didn't like the idea too good, and was kind of dreading it."

"I was. I haven't wanted to make this move. It has seemed foolish and ill-considered to me." And then I told him how my thoughts had run and I was almost feverish in my eagerness to convince him. "I know now," I told him, "that you were led . . . it was meant to be . . . and that I have been holding us back. I want us to hurry . . . hurry before there's another doomed young one on the way."

Richard's face lightened joyously, his mouth quivered and his eyes blinked away a sudden wetness. He raised his arms and tightened his fists exultantly. "I've been praying for you to be convicted. It's been my prayer night and day ever since we came back from Gasper River. I couldn't help knowing you didn't fully believe, and it has laid a burden of sorrow on me. Now my prayers are answered." He rose and shoved the chair back. "We'll go. We'll go as soon as ever we can get ready. Sampson can finish gathering in the crops and I'll see to selling the place."

"How soon do you think?"

He thought about it, counting over what had to be done. "Before Christmas," he said, finally.

I suppose my face showed my disappointment.

"You needn't to worry," he said, divining my thoughts, "I'll not . . ." but he broke off what he meant to say, for not even married folks talked openly of their relations. But I knew what he had in mind. There wouldn't be any chance for another child to start until we were on Gasper River. I nodded to show my understanding, and he bent down and kissed me, smoothed my hair back, smiled at me.

I felt closer to him than I had since we had come home from the meeting. I felt as if I had once more laid my hand in his, to go any journey with him, leading any place. I felt as if once again I was beside my husband, and that he was no longer a stranger in his ways or in his thoughts to me. It was a good and comforting feeling.

Now my strength and heart and will returned with a bound and I looked forward to the days ahead with eagerness and even with joy.

In the end it was all accomplished, though not without bitterness. David hated so to see the land sold outside the family that he wanted to buy it from Richard himself. But Richard would not have it. "I can't take your money for what you've given me," he told his father, "and I have need of the money to buy the land on Gasper River."

"If I'm fool enough to pay it," David said, "I don't see what difference it makes."

"I do," Richard said shortly, and in anger David stalked out of the house.

It was one of the Worthington boys who bought the place. They'd been neighbors from the first and grudgingly David admitted that if someone else was to have it, one of the Worthingtons suited him all right.

Richard sent word to Mr. Rankin to buy the Gasper River farm and we sorted and packed and made ready to leave. There were two wagons full, and Richard drove one, Sampson the other. We took one cow and calf and David and Papa between them bought the rest of the stock.

There was a small log house on the new farm, and though I knew it would be crowded for a time, Richard had promised to build as soon as he could, so I took all the house things.

We set out on a Wednesday morning. Mama and Papa had come to help us and had stayed on for our leaving. Bethia came down and brought food for the journey, but David wouldn't come. I would have left with a heavy and grieving heart if it hadn't been that I was full of the feeling that we were turning toward the Promised Land. But in spite of that feeling I wept a little, looking back, seeing Mama's tall figure standing in the doorway, knowing how sad she was; seeing Papa, looking old and a little bent, not knowing whenever we would meet again, and seeing Bethia, her apron to her eyes. Richard quoted the Scriptures to me, trying to comfort me . . . "There is no man that hath left house, or father, or mother, or wife, or children, or lands, for my sake, and the gospel's, but he shall receive an hundredfold . . . and in the world to come eternal life."

"I know," I said, wiping away my tears, "I know . . . but it is hard, just the same."

[53]

Sampson was sullen and Cassie sat in the second wagon with her shawl drawn over her head, her heavy shoulders drooped and rounded, moaning constantly. They were not being separated, except from the rest of the blacks David owned, but you would have thought they were being sold down the river. "Ain't no good gonna come of it," Cassie kept muttering, "jist mark whut I says . . . ain't no good gonna come of it."

Richard bade her be quiet.

Jency, who was driving the cow and calf, took it the least hard. I had expected her to wail every mile of the way, but she danced along beside the wagon, singing and giggling as usual. She's so silly, I decided, that she's probably forgotten she ever went to Gasper River with us.

She wasn't very good at driving the cow, for she flitted constantly from one side of the road to the other, picking up little stones, clutching them for a while and then discarding them, picking dried weeds and switching the seed buds off, so that the cow was left mostly to go along as she wished. Often Richard had to hand me the lines and get out and prod her along. "That Jency," he grumbled, "I don't see how as sensible a woman as Cassie ever bred such a nitwit of a youngun."

I laughed. "There's sure not much of Cassie in her. She took mostly after Sampson."

"Sampson's dull," Richard agreed, "but he's not foolish. Jency's just plain light-headed."

The countryside was bleak and wintry, though it was not overly cold. Nothing can look so barren as trees and hills stripped down to their bare bones by winter, and meadows which are so thick and green in summer can stretch brown and dead-looking when the grass has been bitten by frost.

As heavily laden as we were, and burdened with the slow-moving cow and calf, we were a week on the way, and though I had never seen it, I knew too well how cramped and ugly a log cabin can be. There were many in our country, with whole families living in one or two rooms. I knew it meant living and keeping the house in one room for us, for the back room would have to be given over to Cassie and Sampson until we could build a place for them. It meant sitting and cooking and eating and sleeping, all in one room, and I dreaded it.

Finally Richard said, on the seventh day, "This is the beginning of our land," and I looked about with more interest.

It lay level to rolling, bush and weed grown, but not unpromising. "Is it good land?" I asked.

"Brother Rankin says it's as good as any to be found hereabouts."

"But is the land in these parts good?"

Richard nodded. "As good or better than up our way. The house is on that little creek flowing there."

Well, I thought, water would be handy anyhow. But I wouldn't have worried about that. Kentuckians always built handy to water. It was the first thing they thought about when picking a house site. "How far?" I asked.

"Just around that bend, and off the road about half a mile."

We came to the bend and turned off on a rough track that led to the right. "I don't see the house," I said.

"It's over that little rise."

Then I saw smoke. "Richard," I said, grabbing his arm, "there's smoke coming from the chimney!"

"Well, what do you say! Brother Rankin has doubtless gone over and started a fire to warm the place up for us."

"He knew we were coming today?"

"I sent him word, yes."

But it was not Mr. Rankin who had been so thoughtful. When we drove up to the door, it flew open and Permilla came running out, her beautiful face breaking into a smile. "Welcome," she cried, "welcome, Rebecca!"

Like a child glad to see its mother, in haste and joy, I tumbled out of the wagon and ran straight into her arms. "Oh, I'm so glad to see you," I said, "Permilla, I'm so *glad* you're here."

CHAPTER VII

THERE IS NO USE recalling all that happened in the years which followed before the Believers came. It is enough to say that we worked hard, Richard constantly improving the farm until it was a fine property. He loved a blooded horse and he built up his stock until he had a good breed, which he often took into Indiana to sell and trade. But he ever had a liking for all stock, and we had a fine herd of cattle and a goodly flock of sheep. We prospered. "To those who believe," Richard was fond of saying, "shall be given an hundredfold." It appeared to be so.

In time he and Thomas Bennett, Brother Rankin and Sampson, and other men of the settlement, built us a good, stout house, larger and finer than the one on Green River. Though to say we had ever left the Green wasn't strictly true. It flowed to the north of us, out of sight, a much wider, statelier stream. But we were still in Green River country, though the smaller streams of Gasper, Muddy and Red took its place as our main watercourses.

I liked knowing it was there, though. In the first years it gave me a feeling of home and sometimes when we traveled that way and I stood on its banks and looked down upon its emerald waters, remembering they had flowed past our old place, it was as if touching the home earth had softened and blessed them and if I knelt and put my hand in the water it was like laying it on the old land.

But I was not often homesick. In the beginning I missed my father and mother. That was only natural, but marriage ever separates a child from its parents. The way of all young things, birds, animals, children, is forward, away from the old home, and in time I ceased to feel a great loss.

I had come to Gasper River finally, willingly and eagerly, and I had found a peace there which comforted me in most things. And then Permilla, whose home was only a mile away, came to be as close to me as my sister, my mother, my whole family, except for Richard. There was rarely a day we were not together, sharing our work, our trials, and our joys. She was never just a friend. From the first she was more than that—loving, helpful, tender, laughing, always present when I needed her, always loyal, always devoted. And I think I meant as much to her.

During those six years she bore two more fat, healthy children, and they had to take the place of my own, for I did not conceive again.

It was a grief to me, and to Richard, but Brother Rankin told us, "The Lord may have other plans for you. He may be preparing you for some great mission. It is His will that for now you should have no children, and while no one may know the purposes of the Lord, they will be revealed in time."

This we accepted ourselves and believed. And we set aside our troubled thoughts and laid off our grief. I had none of the feeling of despair I had had before. I had none of the feeling of sin and punishment, for I had a deep and abiding faith that we had come into the fold and that the will of God would be worked in us. And I never lost hope.

In meeting I felt a happiness to be in the right way, though as I have said, it was never given to me to see the full vision. There were others who were denied the gift, Permilla among them, and when we talked about it we agreed that to some was given the ecstasy and to some the quiet presence, and we were those who had been visited in stillness. We did not question it, or allow it to trouble us, nor did we strive for more than was manifested to us. "Hit's no use," Permilla said, "I jist don't feel no call to shout or roll or dance, an' as fer speakin' in tongues I couldn't if I tried."

I felt no call either. Brother Rankin did not condemn us for it. It was he who told us that the gift worked in stillness as well as in song and commotion.

I sent a letter to my father and mother as often as I could, and several times each year one came from them. I missed Janie's letters, because it was more difficult for word to come from her to us now, but Mama sent on many which came to her.

Janie was out of sympathy with me, anyhow. She had been horrified at first and then impatient with our move. She could in no way understand it. "Have they lost their minds?" she asked in a letter to Mama. And in another letter she said, "I hold Richard to task for this. He was ever a stubborn, pigheaded man and Rebecca is too willing to follow where he leads. Everyone with intelligence knows this wave of revivalism that is sweeping the country is only among the ignorant and foolish who can be easily swayed by their emotions."

Maybe . . . it *was* emotional, of course. But who is to say that emotion must have no place in true religion?

There was one memorable time, when we had been on Gasper River some three years, when, suddenly and without warning, Janie and Mr. Leavitt paid us a brief visit. They did not even take the night, for we were still crowded into the little cabin, though the foundations were laid for the new house. Janie looked very out of place there, in her dark silk gown, with her fur mantle drawn about her shoulders, her plumed hat atop her pretty red hair and her slippers dainty on the floor. I felt drab and dark and ugly beside her, for she had caught me at the washing, in a soiled and water-soaked dress, with my hair straggling.

Mr. Leavitt had business in Bowling Green, she said, and she had taken the opportunity to come along and see for herself how I was making out. It would have been hard to convince her that we were doing well, though we were. The house had had to wait until Richard improved the land and the stock. She looked about her and shrugged closer into her fine clothes. "I don't see how you stand it," she said.

"It won't always be this way," I told her. "Richard has begun our house, and he has a good start on the land."

"One day of it would be more than I would enjoy."

"There is a happiness you don't understand, Janie."

"And I don't want to understand it," she retorted, "if it brings a body to this."

I turned the talk to her own life and she became merry and gay again, telling now of things she enjoyed. Mr. Leavitt had stood for Congress and had been elected. They were going to Washington soon. She looked forward to it eagerly. "Mr. Leavitt has taken rooms for us at the best inn," she said.

"How will you occupy yourself while he is about his business?" I asked her.

She laughed happily, throwing her head back and shaking the plumes on her bonnet. "The way I occupy myself all the time . . . at teas and parties and balls. Time never hangs heavy on my hands, Becky."

She talked on about Washington and the society there, Mr. Leavitt's importance, his friendships with the great figures in public life. It sounded fine. She had been to see Papa and Mama on that same trip and she told me about them. "Just the same," she said, "they're just the same. They'll never change."

"Except to grow older," I said.

"Yes, of course. But Mama is still stout and able. Papa seems to be a little feebler and the boys do most of the work, but he says he's in good health."

"I wish I could see them," I said, wistfully.

"Why don't you? Make Richard take you for a visit."

"Someday," I said, "we plan to go, someday."

In some ways it was like having a stranger in my home. This fashionable young woman did not seem like the sister with whom I had grown up and with whom I had slept every night of my life until Richard and I were married. I could not conceive that we had ever fought over the cover, or snuggled under it together for warmth . . . or that we had shared the chore of milking on early, misty mornings . . . that we had listened together to Mr. Foster, the Englishman, and learned together under him, though even as I felt the strangeness I could hear Janie's voice solemnly reciting after him, "Gallia est omnis divisa in partes tres," and then throwing down the Latin text, yelling, "Oh, who cares about how Gaul was divided! The only Latin I'm interested in is 'Amo, amas, amat!' " It had shocked Mr. Foster profoundly. "Jane," he had said sternly, "Latin is the root of all civilized tongues. A proper understanding of it is necessary to be an educated person."

"Well, I wish it had took root in Rome and stayed there," she had muttered sullenly.

"Taken," Mr. Foster had corrected her automatically.

"All right, taken," but she had picked up the text and set to work again. However impatient she became she did wish to have learning.

Looking at her now I thought how little her background showed on her. She might always have worn silk and been familiar with the ways of cities and the great figures of the day. Mr. Foster had taught better than he knew.

At the last, when Mr. Leavitt had called for her and she had risen to leave, something of my sister returned. "Did you know," she said, "that Johnnie Cooper is in the city now? He's freighting goods to Louisville. They say he is doing well."

I hadn't heard it. "I'm glad," I said; "do you ever see him?"

"Why would I see him?" she said, laughing. "A senator's wife see a freighter?" Then she put her arms about me. "Becky, if there's ever need, if there's ever trouble . . . well, don't forget my home can be yours."

It was my turn to laugh, though feeling warmed by her affection. "I've got Richard," I told her.

"Yes . . . of course," she said. She gathered her skirts about her. And she swept out the door holding them high from the mud and wet of the dooryard.

And I did have Richard, a happier, lighter-hearted, more joyous Richard. He was near the man he most trusted, Brother Rankin, among the people who had been given the light. He counted it a blessing and he never ceased to be thankful that we had been found worthy to belong. It made everything he did a glad task, ran all through his entire life and mine. He laughed oftener, though he prayed much too, he was faithful in every way to his convictions, and that knowledge gave him a daily, living zeal.

Settled all about us were the people of Brother Rankin's congregation, who were, with us, like members of one big family. In the midst of a lawless land we were undisturbed, at peace with ourselves and the world. As I had come to know Brother Rankin better, I had come to love him almost as much as Richard did. He was the saintliest man I have ever known, and I do not except good Brother Benjamin who came later. There was no guile in him, or sin. The whole congregation revered him and adored him. He had only to speak gently, and we were ashamed of any guilt. It accounted in large part for our lack of discord. With such a shepherd, how could the flock stray? I have often wondered how it would have been had not the Believers come among us.

They came, though . . . in October of eighteen hundred and seven. I will remember the day. It was the seventeenth of the month, and as fine a day as autumn ever sent, the sun warm and bright and the air clean and fresh. Permilla and Cassie and I had been doing the wash. Permilla had got in the way of bringing her things over to our place, for the summer had been droughty and their water was low.

Jency was minding her young ones. She was growing up, now, but she was still flighty, still giggled constantly, sang as much as ever, and went dreamy-eyed over the sight of a bird, a flower or a butterfly. She did love children, though . . . there was no doubt of that, and she was a good hand with them.

Back of our house, on a little rise of land, was a grove of cedar trees, thick and dense, the ground beneath them laid over with their dried and fallen needles. In the middle of the grove was a small hut, an old lean-to, built, it may be, by the first settler on that piece of land. Jency loved the cedar grove and the little hut. "Hit's like a cave," she told me, "that a body kin hide away in."

She often took Permilla's young ones there and, like a child herself, played house with them. I had seen it, swept and brushed, and set about with broken bits of kettles and dishes, and I had given Jency cookies and biscuits with meat between them for their play-house dinners. She had Permilla's children there this day, and we were free of the care of them.

The wash place was down at the creek and Cassie had rubbed out all the white things. Permilla and I had brought them to the house to hang and were taking joy in the whiteness of the clothes, the bright, warm day, and our own pleasant company, when Permilla shaded her eyes with her hand. "Appears like we're aimin' to have company, Becky. They's three men a comin' up the land."

I whirled around and looked for myself. They were strangers, so I smoothed my hair and took off my wet apron and told Permilla, "I'd best see what they want."

"I'll jist keep on hangin' the clothes," she said, nodding.

[59]

I went to meet them at the front porch and that was my first sight of Issachar Bates, Richard McNemar and Matthew Houston. They were men of good appearance, clothed decently and soberly, though they had the dust of the road on them. They'd mistaken our place for Brother Rankin's. I set them right and gave them water to drink and they set off back down the lane. "What did they want?" Permilla asked.

"They were looking for Brother Rankin," I told her. "I didn't ask their business and they didn't say."

I thought no more of it until Richard came home that evening. "There's three preachers visiting at Brother Rankin's," he told me.

Preachers were always welcome at his house and I made nothing of it. But Richard went on. "They're from Union Village, up in Ohio."

That stirred me a little for we'd heard of Union Village and the United Society of Believers there, Shakers they were called, and we'd heard, too, they had got a foothold at Shawnee Run in Kentucky. "Are they aiming to hold a meeting here?" I asked.

"They have a wish to, but Brother Rankin said he couldn't hardly find it in himself to give them the meeting house for their services."

"I don't blame him," I said. "We've got no need for the Believers in our midst. How did they take it?"

"Pleasantly. They aren't argufying men."

That was all that was said about it at the time, but the next day we learned that John Sloss had offered them the use of his house for their meeting. "Are you going?" I asked Richard.

He nodded. "Brother Rankin is going. I reckon we will, too."

It was a strange message we heard that night, Richard McNemar doing the talking. In all my life I have never known a man more forceful, more powerful in his speech. He had a pleasant manner, but he was a scholar and he knew how to talk to folks. There was something that drew you to him and you sat still and listened, fearing to miss a word.

He told us about the Believers, and about Mother Ann, their founder. He told us how she had come under the fire of the spirit when she was yet a young woman in England, and of her persecutions there, and how she had lived through them unharmed as if the love of God had stood between her and her tormentors. And how, when she had been in prison she had been visited with visions and a revelation, that she was to lead the way in a new faith.

When she came out of prison her face so shone with her visitation that her friends were convinced and were willing to follow her. They believed, as she did, that the Christ had appeared in her, that his second coming had been made through her, and from that day she was called Mother.

In her vision she had seen a new land waiting for the gospel, and she had seen the faces of a new people. She knew this new land must be America, and she had worked without ceasing to get a little band of her followers to come with her across the waters.

Richard McNemar told us of their settlement at Watervliet, in New York State, and of the revival of the spirit there, and how Mother Ann and her brother, William, had journeyed through the country roundabout, preaching and teaching and bringing the people out of the error of their ways. He told how she had visited in Harvard and recognized the faces she had seen in her vision, and knew henceforth she had been led aright.

He told of her persecutions in Massachusetts, how she had been driven hither and yon and had been imprisoned again, but how it had never lessened her faith nor her good works, and of the clustering of folks about her, in New Lebanon and Harvard and at Watervliet.

He told of the miracles she had done, like the healing of the sick, and the time she had seen angels standing about the mast of the ship they crossed in, during a bad storm, and had comforted the captain and the crew with her knowledge the ship would not go down. And how, soon after she had seen the angels, the leak in the ship had stopped.

He told, then, how in her latter years she had seen another vision of a great work to be done—"In the West," she had said, "where the gathering will be great."

"For years," Richard McNemar said, "it had not seemed possible, and Mother Ann died. The men she had appointed her bishops on earth served their time and died. But now, our revival in this country here has pointed the way."

He was, himself, from the western country and had been a Presbyterian preacher in Ohio when the first missionaries of the Believers had come into the country. "It was revealed to me," he told us, "they had the truth, and I confessed and joined them, and all my congregation with me."

That had been several years before and Union Village had been the result. Now they had come to the Gasper River country, he said, bringing the good news. "It is well," he said, "to go to the source of the spring, for everyone knows the revival had its birth here on Gasper River."

That was the beginning of it. They held their meetings nightly in the homes of the brethren, and we always went. They preached and held their queer exercises, a kind of dancing back and forth with much shaking of their hands and arms. "Be joyful," Mother Ann had told her followers, "labor in singing and dancing."

"Why should the tongue," Richard McNemar said, "which is the most unruly member of the body, be the only chosen instrument of worship? God has also created the hands and the feet, and enabled them to perform their functions in the service of the body. And shall these faculties, or indeed any of the powers and faculties of man, which God has given to be devoted to his service, be active in man's service, or in the service of sin, and yet be idle in the service of God? God requires the faithful improvement of every created talent."

And again he told us, quoting the Scriptures, "And Miriam, the prophetess, the sister of Aaron, took a timbrel in her hand; and all the women went out after her, with timbrels and dances." And again, "There-fore they shall come and sing in the height of Zion, and shall flow to-gether to the goodness of the Lord: then shall the virgin rejoice in the dance, both young men and old together; for I will turn their mourning into joy, and will comfort them and make them rejoice from their sorrow."

They sang sweet songs, but strange to us. One I have ever loved was Father James' song:

> *In yonder valley there grows sweet union*
> *Let us arise and drink our fill.*
> *The winter's past and the spring appears,*
> *The turtle dove is in our land.*
> *In yonder valley there grows sweet union,*
> *Let us arise and drink our fill.*

They explained their shaking exercises to us, quoting many passages of Scriptures. "Thus saith the Lord of hosts, Yet once, it is a little while, and I will shake the heavens, and the earth, and the sea, and the dry land. And I will shake all nations."

"Shake out the evil and the error," Richard McNemar said, "shake all sin and wrongdoing away," and when he said it and shook his hands down-ward it was as if you could see the error shaking free of him.

But Brother Rankin was not easily convinced. The dancing, singing and shaking did not appear strange to us. We were used to the manifestations of the spirit in our own meetings. Brother Rankin wanted to know, how-ever, what they believed. "Do you believe in the Bible?" he asked.

"We believe in the Bible," Richard McNemar said, "but we do not believe it was God's final revelation to man. God was never beholden to letters as the only means of revealing His will. He continues to reveal Himself in people and places, and the testimonies of Mother Ann are proof of that."

"Do you believe in original sin?"

"We do not. We believe God is too merciful and too fair-minded to condemn all of mankind because of the sin of Adam, and we believe in the perfectibility of man himself. We believe he is God's instrument on earth."

"Do you believe in the Trinity?"

"How could we believe in such an absurdity as a three-sided male God in the universe? When all of nature proves that male and female are the correct order? We believe that the spirit of God is given alike to men and women, and that it comes from both a father and mother element in him."

"Do you believe in the Immaculate Conception?"

"No. For if Christ were God how could He set an example for man? And how could He die? The spirit of God lived in Christ, and it lived again in Mother Ann, but neither of them partook of the nature of God."

"Do you believe in the resurrection?"

"Of the spirit, but not of the body. The spirit is separated from the body at death, and while the body moulders, the spirit is freed for eternal life, to go ever onward to new truths and new light. Death is of the body and it is the beginning of the spiritual adventure."

"On what is your theology based?"

"We preach," Richard McNemar said, "four principal things—confession of sin, celibacy, withdrawal from the world, and common ownership of property."

Those were hard things for us to understand. Confession of sin we could have sympathy for. That went natural to us. We practiced it ourselves to some extent. "Why," Brother Rankin asked, "must the laity be celibate? Has not God commanded all created things to be fruitful and multiply?"

"In the times and seasons appointed by the Creator and established by the laws of nature," Richard McNemar answered him. "In all of creation only man disregards these laws of nature. Alone of all the animals he is guilty of lust and the pleasures of lust."

"Do you, then, condemn marriage?"

"Not among the world's people, no. But among God's people it cannot be countenanced."

"Were you ever married?"

"I was. And I set aside my wife to attain the perfection of the flesh. Only those that deny themselves and take up the cross against the propensities of that nature are justly entitled to eat of the Tree of Life and live forever. Man disobeyed God in the Garden of Eden," he went on, "and the sin by which all evil came into the world was the sin of sex. Among Believers that sin must be eradicated."

We who listened were gathered together in families, husbands and wives and children, and we heard him in stunned silence. I remember the hand of fear which clutched at my heart as I watched Richard, leaning forward on his chair, chin propped in his hand, drinking in the words of this compelling, powerful man. If Richard came under this man's influence, would he, then, set me aside?

"Are you never tempted?" someone asked.

"At first I was. I am but a man and the flesh is hard to overcome. But I can say in truth that I have conquered the temptation now."

"What," another asked, "would happen to the world if all people came under this conviction? Would not the human race die out?"

Richard McNemar laughed. "Would that be so bad a thing? Would it not then be freed for the great adventure of the spirit?"

"Was Mother Ann married?" my own Richard asked.

"She was. And she bore four children which all died in infancy. It was owing to their deaths that she first became convinced that lust between man and woman, even in married life, was a sin. She put away her husband and lived out her life in celibacy."

There was great confusion among us as they continued to stay on and to preach their strange new gospel. Permilla and I talked about it. "What do you think of it?" she asked.

"I don't know," I confessed, as once before I had done when Richard had come under the influence of the revivalists. "It goes so queer to me."

"That idee," she said, "of puttin' aside husbands an' wives, Becky . . . hit won't work."

"It seems to have worked for some."

"Fer some, mebbe . . . an' fer a while . . . but they's too many that's full-fleshed an' couldn't hold to it."

Richard could, though, I was afraid. Richard could do whatever he came to think was right, and by all the signs, by his quietness, his brooding over what he had heard, his constant talks with Brother Rankin, I knew it was affecting him. And since that night when Richard McNemar had talked of the sin of lust, he had not turned to me.

I was filled with fear. I could in no way believe that what we felt was lust. It was natural, right, joyful. I did not want to be put aside. I went through those days with a troubled mind and heart, and my great hope lay in Brother Rankin. Richard, I thought, would never follow where Brother Rankin held back.

The meetings continued and we continued to go. It was explained to us why it was necessary to withdraw from the world, in order that perfectibility might be attained, and that an example might be set to the world. It was explained to us why a common ownership of property was necessary. "We believe," Richard McNemar said, "that there can be no church in complete order according to the law of Christ without a joint ownership, joint interest and union, in which all members have an equal right and privilege according to their calling and needs, in things spiritual and temporal." He read to us from the Covenant which the Society had drawn up many years ago.

"Does that mean," my Richard asked him, "that everyone who joins the Believers must give up his property?"

Richard McNemar folded the paper from which he had been reading. "No. You can hold title to your property if you like. You don't need to deed it over to the church. Many do, who want to dedicate themselves and come into full membership. But you don't have to. You do have to put all your earnings, all your income and crops into a common fund, and you cannot be paid for your labor for the church."

"How, then, is a man to live?"

"All live equally and alike, provided for according to their needs by the common fund. None has more than the rest, unless he be sick or old . . . none goes in want, and all must work." And then he quoted that saying of Mother Ann's which came to be so familiar to us all, "Put your hands to work and your hearts to God."

The first convert was John McComb, who, I think, made his confession to Matthew Houston. We talked about it at home, Richard and I. "Do you believe the others will follow?" I asked him.

He was troubled. "I don't know."

I felt I had to know what was in his mind. "If Brother Rankin goes in, will you?"

He leaned his head in his hands. "I don't know . . . I don't know."

"Richard," I said, speaking out plainly, "this thing they believe . . . these things . . . they aren't natural. It isn't the way folks were meant to live . . . none working for himself, but for all. Husbands and wives living apart . . . it goes against everything we hold to be good and right."

He dropped his hands and looked at me. "How sure are we it's good and right? If what they say is true, then Mother Ann's way is the only right way and the only good way. We've had no young ones, and maybe that's the sign it was wrong to . . . to . . ."

I felt hot and angry. "Are you ashamed of living with me as a husband?"

He stirred restlessly. "Not ashamed, no. For a man can know no shame when he knows no error. But if he comes under the truth . . ."

"Is that why you've not touched me these last two weeks?"

His eyes wouldn't lift to meet mine. "I had to think about it."

"And what about me?"

He looked at me, then. "I'd not wish to give you hurt . . . but how can a body go against their convictions?"

I felt wild. Whichever way I turned seemed to have but the one end . . . Richard's convictions. "But this withdrawing from the world? And living apart? How can it be done? There's no place to withdraw to!"

"They tell that if enough are converted here it'll be a mission for a time, and we can go ahead and live as we've been used to doing. Except for putting together our profits and labor. Each family to its own place until we are gathered in order."

"What does that mean?"

"Well, in time they'll make a place here where all can live together, out of the world. It's called being gathered in order."

"You," I said bitterly, "have learned a heap about it, haven't you?"

"Yes. I meant to. I wanted to know all I could about it."

"You're going in, then."

"Becky . . . I've said I don't know."

"If I don't go in with you, what will you do? Set me aside just the same?" In my unhappiness I could not help dealing him hurt.

Richard's face grew red. "Mr. McNemar said as long as a man and wife lived in the closeness of one house it wasn't to be expected, hardly, they could keep apart. Said they'd have to practice it and come to it little by little."

I looked at his face, so beloved all my life. He was twenty-six, now. The ruddy, high color in his cheeks had faded a little, browned over by sun and wind and rain, and a few weather lines had wrinkled around the corners of his eyes. It would be a long time before he had many lines, though, for his skin was not thin and it would never sag and fold as some men's did.

He had been happy during our years on Gasper River and it showed in his face. I have called him sober, but it was not soberness which showed now in his face so much as quietness and peace. He would never be a lighthearted man, such as his brother Johnnie, for he had too much sense of duty and too great a feeling for responsibility, but he was not a dour man, and in our years with Brother Rankin his face had lightened, staying strong, but appearing less set.

I studied it, thinking how known it was to me—its shape, which my hands carried the feeling of in their palms with no need to touch for remembrance, from having touched so often.

I looked at the broad, strong shoulders, not showing yet any bend from burdens carried, still straight and thick. My eyes traveled on down the arms, stout as oak to lift and heft, or to clasp, rough and demanding in sudden passion, around my waist . . . and to his hands, square, broad, useful, gentle to any animal and to me, to soothe in pain or love. This was the man they wanted me to put aside?

At that moment I hated the Shakers and I wished with all my heart those three men had never come to Gasper River. We had done well enough without them, been happy without them, lived in peace without them, and then they'd come, stirring up trouble and strife. My hatred flared up and I grew angry. I would not *let* them take Richard away from me. "We've had enough practicing for now," I said suddenly, going to him and putting my arms about his neck, drawing his face down against mine. "Two weeks has been a long, long time, Richard."

At first he stood rigid, unyielding to me . . . but then as the warmth of my body, its whole length pressed against him, flowed into him, he raised his arms and tightened them about me. He laid his mouth on mine, hard, as if hungry and thirsty for it, and then he swung me off my feet, and without a word carried me into the next room, broad daylight though it was.

He *could* not, I thought, in fierce exultation, put this away . . . this that was the best of him and me . . . surely not even Richard, stubborn, determined, surely not even he could put this that lay between us away.

CHAPTER VIII

I SHOULD HAVE known better, of course. I had too much experience with his ways not to know that not only he could, but he would, if he thought it was right. And he came to think it right.

It was only two days later that he told me of his conviction. We were eating supper. I had already laid out our clothes to go to the meeting and had to hurry a little to set out the meal. Richard walked about, waiting, and I thought it made him restless having to wait to eat. He was ever one to want food right off when his stomach demanded it. "I'll have it ready," I told him, "in a minute."

He didn't answer . . . just kept on with his pacing. When we sat down and he'd said the blessing, he took food on his plate, but he did not touch it. Instead he said bluntly and plainly, "Rebecca, I've made up my mind. I'm going to join up with them."

"With the Shakers?" I said, like an idiot, for it was plain who he meant.

"With the Shakers."

I leaned back in my chair feeling cold and hot at the same time, with a queer trembling set up inside of me, afraid, deeply afraid, a sinking coming over me so that I thought I would faint away. It made me sick and I felt as if the few bites I had taken were going to rise up in my throat. "No," I managed to say, past the woolly dryness and nausea. "No, Richard."

"Yes." He broke off a piece of corn pone and buttered it, then sat staring at it, crumbling it between his fingers.

I watched the bread break into small pieces, shredded under his fingers, and it came over me that that was what he was doing to us . . . breaking us into little pieces. And suddenly a swift anger took hold of me and I stood, hanging on to the edge of the table, my body shaking as if I had an ague. "You'll not!" I yelled at him, and my voice was more a scream torn from me than a voice. I had never spoken so to him before, but I could not bear this thing he wanted to do. "You'll not do it," I shouted, hitting the table with my fist, making the dishes clatter. "They won't have you without me. They won't take a husband without his wife, or a wife without her husband. I heard them say so! And I'll *not* go in with you! Do you hear, Richard? I'll not do this thing!"

He put his hands up over his face and I could see how white he'd got. His hands were trembling, too. His mouth moved, but no words came. I stood and watched him, almost hating him for what he was willing to do. Finally he took his hands down. "I hoped I wouldn't have to say this." He stood up, too, then. "I didn't want to say it. But there's a way they'll take me. If I provide for you, so's you'll not come to want . . . if I leave . . ."

All my anger drained out of me, and my knees sagged so that I had to reach for a chair or fall. "You would do that?" I said, and all I could manage was a whisper.

He looked at me, pleadingly. "I don't want to."

"But you would . . . you would, wouldn't you?"

He locked his hands in front of him and raised them and a kind of shudder ran over him. "I'd *have* to! Don't you see, Becky? I'd *have* to!"

A sword piercing me could not have hurt worse. It seemed to me as if a deep breath would tear the walls of my chest and the pain would go flowing down my sides, like blood from the heart itself. Hot tears scalded my eyes. "Richard . . . ?"

"Don't," he said, turning away, "don't. Do you think it's easy for me?"

No . . . to do him justice, I didn't think it was easy. I had seen him get up from our bed, pace the floor, groan in his labor to see the truth, pray without ceasing through the hours. That afternoon I had tempted him, I had seen him turn away when he was spent, white-faced, angry, at me, at himself, and I had heard him mutter, "The woman Thou gavest me . . ."

No, I didn't think it was easy. But I did think it was wrong. "God made us the way we are, Richard," I pled, "male and female created He them. He intended men and women to join together, to live together, to have children . . ."

I stopped, knowing the moment I had said the word that I, myself, had condemned us. "But we have no children," Richard said, "and that's just it. It wouldn't be so hard to think it right if we had, or ever could have . . . and it's been plainly shown to us . . . the Bible says, 'in season and for the procreation of young.' There is no season for us, Becky. For us it is lust, and for us it is sin."

And I knew there would never be any shaking him.

Janie wrote to me. "Why did you do it? Why didn't you hold out against him?"

My parents wrote to me, "Why?"

Richard's folks wrote to me, "Why? What sense does it make?"

The only sense it made was that I had to go where Richard went. What else could I do? It was his conviction that the Believers had the final, the ultimate truth. It made him willing to set me aside. It was my conviction that nothing should part me from my husband. I might have to live apart from him, but I would be where he was, where I could see him, could, in some measure, watch over him.

That night, before meeting began, we, with Brother Rankin and two others, made confession to Richard McNemar. They made theirs joyously. I made mine in sorrow and pain. They had few sins to confess, but Brother McNemar, seeing my sadness, drew from me my own hurt and grief. He was gentle, but he was firm. "You must do this willingly, Sister Rebecca."

"I am willing."

"For whose sake, Richard's or your own?"

"For the sake of us both."

"But you do not believe?"

This was a confession and I could not lie. "No."

There was a moment of silence and then his voice came, very firm. "We can admit you to partial membership, Sister Rebecca, only if you are willing to try to believe. Are you willing?"

I had to go where Richard went. "I will try," I said, and I knew I *must* try.

Brother McNemar smiled at me. "That will be enough. We can't admit you or Richard to the Church Order, but you can come into the Novitiate. In time, when your efforts have borne fruit, and I have faith they will, you can come into the Church Family."

I did not know what he meant, what the terms he used meant, and I thought perhaps Richard would be unhappy over the limitation, but he was not. Instead he was pleased with me. "It will come," he said, "and we will be within the fold at any rate."

We joined in the exercises for the first time that night, publicly making it known we had confessed and been received. I was awkward and self-conscious, but Richard and Brother Rankin went forth as if they had always been accustomed to the slow shuffling step and the shaking. There was great rejoicing and weeping and singing, and Brother Rankin received the gift of tongues and sang and spoke in them.

There was no joy in me, but at least I had won a little peace. Many another wife or husband had to make that same choice I made, and to some a peace was given, and later, even joy . . . to some it was never given. Permilla was one of those, but then she never wanted peace, nor the kind of joy the Shakers knew.

She went in, for Thomas would have set her aside, but he had so little with which to endow her that with five children she hadn't much choice. "I'd let the old fool go," she told me in disgust, "if it warn't fer the younguns. But they'd have a hard way to go with jist me to do for 'em, no more'n he could pervide. This way they'll not go hungry, an' they'll do as good as the next 'uns." She laughed. "Hit won't misput me none not to have him botherin' me, I c'n tell you that. Hit'll be a relief. But I've got no likin' fer livin' amongst 'em so close. How is it they're aimin' to manage, Becky?"

The three missionaries had been among us a month, and twenty-three people had been converted. The last night before they left they had called us together and given us instructions. As best I could I explained it to Permilla, who evidently hadn't listened to a word. "We're to go on living on our places the way we do now, families together. But the men are to work for the common good, and everything they raise and sell or make in any way is to be put in a common fund. Brother Rankin is to be the head of us for a time, but they'll send down from Union Village somebody to preach and see to things from time to time. In time, as soon as it can be worked out, we'll be gathered in order."

"An' that," Permilla said, "is what I mainly don't understand."

I understood it all too well. When that happened, when we were gathered in order, it meant that families would be broken up. We would leave our homes, a community would be established, and we would go to live in Shaker families within the community. It would be here, on Gasper River, for Brother Rankin had given his farm as a start, and doubtless his home would be one of the houses used. But no longer would husbands and wives and children be a family. The Shakers classified their people into three main families . . . the Novitiate, in which Richard and I, Permilla and Thomas, any other married couples not dedicating both their property and themselves, would belong. There was the Junior Order . . . the unmarried people not yet ready for full membership, for one reason or another, and there was the Church Family, those who had committed themselves and all they owned to the church, never expecting to live outside its folds again, and had made full dedication. Brother Rankin had gone at once into full membership. Few of the rest of us could, or even wanted to, though it was I who held Richard back. He was ready. I, because of my unbelief, was not.

"What do they aim to do about the blacks?" Permilla asked.

"They go in with us," I told her, "but until we are gathered they will stay with us. Things won't change much for them until the gathering, then Richard intends to free them and if they want to leave, they can. Brother Rankin says there are enough blacks among us that we'll have a Black Family in the community for them if they want to stay on."

"Is that a rulin'? That you got to set 'em free?"

"No. You can keep them if you want. But not to serve you, of course. They'd have to work for the community. And when we're gathered, the Believers are the ones responsible for them, not the owner."

"Humph," Permilla said. "Hit appears to me they've hit on a awful good scheme to git their hands on a heap of property, one way or the other. You don't *have* to give 'em yer land, but if you don't, you cain't git into the middle of the church, an' I misdoubt anybody *not* deedin' over their property'll ever git very fur with 'em. An' you don't *have* to give up yer blacks, but you mought as well. You cain't git the use of 'em. They're a smart bunch, you ask me."

Many believed that of the Shakers, but from the start I didn't. I didn't think they cared about accumulating land or property. They wanted and had to have enough of it to make a place for their people, and it is true that they got their start in every village they set up in our part of the country, at Shawnee Run, on Gasper River, and at Union in Ohio, by the gift of land from converts. But I gave them credit for wanting to put in practice what they believed . . . that in union lay their hope, to withdraw from the world and to live as they saw best, in purity and peace.

I didn't believe then, and I don't now, that they had any intentions of growing wealthy and strong, that they wanted to own great tracts of land, that they wanted to run things. Mostly they wanted enough to raise what their communities needed. Mostly they traded and sold to as good an advantage as they could, for the sake of the community. And who, in the long run, owned the land and the stock and the buildings? No person ever had anything of his own among the Shakers . . . the community owned everything. The trustees acted for the community and I have seen their books of strict accounting.

It was the jealous-hearted, who couldn't bear to see the good farms, and blooded stock, and stout shops, and houses and mills, and the shrewdness of the trustees who traded so well, that never gave over the notion they were grasping and mean and leeching at heart.

But it felt strange to me to be defending them to Permilla, for I had been sorely hurt by them. I had to say what I believed, though. She looked at me oddly. "You ain't really been swung over, have you?"

I shook my head.

"I wouldn't of thought it . . . you bein' so foolish over Richard the way you are. I d'know as I could of did it, had it been me."

And I said what I always said, "What else could I do?"

She shrugged. "Nothin', I reckon. Though as young as you are I jist mought of left him go. Got me another man." She laughed.

"Follow your own advice," I told her, laughing, too.

"With five younguns? Don't think I never thought of it, though." She talked brashly, always, and I thought nothing of it. "What," she said, then, "are they aimin' to do with the younguns when the gatherin' takes place?"

I was afraid to tell her, for had they been mine I would have been heartbroken. I was silent so long she asked me again, impatiently. So I told her. "The least ones will be in a Nursery, and the others will be in the School Family . . . with teachers to look after them."

"They ain't to live with their own folks?"

"No."

She thought about it. "I reckon you could see 'em, though, if you taken a notion."

"I'd think so." I didn't actually know, for having none we had not asked about it. We only knew what Brother Rankin had said of the ordering of things.

"Well," she said, finally, "as long as they ain't took plumb outen my sight, I d'know but what it'll be a relief to me to have 'em off my hands. They're a sight of trouble, times."

I would have given anything to be so troubled . . . but mothers who had small children under their feet all day often grumbled about their care.

"It's so," I told her, "they can teach them properly and bring them up in Shaker ways."

Permilla put both her hands on her hips and threw her head back to laugh. "If they c'n make Shakers outen mine, they're welcome to do it. But I misdoubt they'll git very fur. They're too lively a batch. Them boys is goin' to give *somebody* a hard time, you mark my words."

It was not that Permilla was hard, for she was not. It was that she had been raised poor, brought up cruelly, wed early to a man older than her father, and while Thomas had never mistreated her, he'd never done much in the way of providing. They'd had an easier time here on Gasper River than any place they'd lived, and that was because Brother Rankin would see none of his flock in want and every man had lent a hand. I was certain that Thomas was joining the Shakers more because he thought it would be an easy way for him than for any other reason. He would have his family taken care of, anyhow. He knew he would have to work, but he must have believed he wouldn't have to work very hard. Permilla said so at any rate. "He's aimin' on takin' it easy an' lettin' the others have the keer of what's rightfully his'n to tend." She had few illusions left about Thomas.

There were many changes in our way of living, though outwardly it seemed much the same. Most of the converts were from Brother Rankin's congregation, living close about, and it made it easy for him to oversee things, putting all the crops together, portioning out each family's share, holding meeting and keeping us banded together.

I couldn't help thinking how some fared so well under this new plan, and others of us had to do with less. There were Thomas and Permilla, for instance, though I never begrudged her anything that came her way for she deserved it, whose portion was larger than they were used to, because of the size of their family.

There was young Robert Jewett and his wife, Annie. Robert was a smart, able young man, just beginning to get a good start. His crops had done well. They all went into the common barns, and he and Annie took less than they would have had, and Annie complained endlessly. She loved finery and she had her own plans of what to do with Robert's earnings. They were denied her.

There was Henry Akins, as lazy and shiftless a man as Thomas Bennett, but younger, with a brood of little ones. He and Lacey profited greatly, and the children had more to eat than ever before in their lives.

There was William Steel, a good, managing man with a fine property. Amanda had fought him every step of the way into the Society, but she had finally given in, as I had done. She felt bitter and hard about it, and she lived in hopes that by the time of the gathering in order she could persuade William differently. I thought she had as little chance as I with Richard. They had lost four of the five children born to them, and the little boy spared to them was the apple of their eye. They were foolish about him, doted on him, spoiled and petted him, and I would have done the same in their place.

There were David and Nancy Brown, good, fine people, devout and among the few who both had gone, equally ready, into full membership. Without regret they had deeded everything they owned to the church. I wondered how Lucien, their boy, a lad of about fifteen then, felt about losing his birthright. He was a handsome boy, tall, upright, winsome in every way, deserving of the best a father and mother could give him. I thought it a poor best they were serving him, but it was none of my affair.

From the start Brother Rankin depended much on David and Nancy, on Richard and on William Steel, for help in administering the community's business. They all had good properties, knew how to make them pay. He asked their counsel often, they spent much time with him, they took over part of the leadership from him.

We had our meetings, and as the news got about, people of the world came often to watch them. None were ever turned away, though many of them laughed, poked fun, even tried to disturb the exercises, aped them, making mock of them. Brother Rankin preached two sermons, one for Believers, and one for the world. There were some converts made, but not many.

Our own home was a strange place to me for a time. Richard moved into the spare bedroom. He said it was best and I knew it was, though I had determined never again to tempt him against his will. I even made myself leave off touching him for fear he would think I was putting temptation in his way, though there were times when my hands reached for him out of habit, twisted over remembering the feeling of his face and shoulders. Even handling his clothing, washing it, ironing it, became a torture of remembrance for me and often, if alone, I buried my face in his shirt, just to feel something which had touched him, been worn next to him.

The missionaries had said it wasn't to be expected perfect continence could be practiced until we were gathered in. But what they said about it meant nothing to Richard, and I knew it. He had his own convictions, and he had set himself to achieve it at once.

It was hard. It was even hard for Richard, for it goes unnatural to set aside the habits of years. More than once I saw his own hand reach toward me . . . more than once I saw him look longingly at me, and hoped . . . but he was ever able to conquer himself, to turn brusquely and stride out of the house, out of the sight of me.

Many were the nights, in that wide and lonely bed, heavy hearted and miserable, I wept until the pillow was wet. And many were the nights Richard went, after supper, to Brother Rankin's, staying late, hoping to return after I'd gone to sleep. I never had. I always heard him come in, heard his restlessness, wished he had less determination, more frailty, would come, finally, into my bed again. But I might as well have wished for the moon. He held to it . . . and little by little it became easier.

That others let it make little difference in their ways was soon to be seen. Permilla, for instance, grew big with child that first year. She told me, "I wish they'd of gathered us in straight off! 'Pears like knowin' he's to be gathered an' denied has jist set Thomas off!"

I could not help laughing. It sounded so like Thomas.

"Oh, well," she said, laughing with me, "hit'll jist be another'n fer them to have the keer of once they git us settled. I don't know's it's e'er thing for me to lose sleep over."

She bore children easily and quickly, and they were always fat, healthy, bouncy with energy. I envied her. My own grief now was not so much for the two I had lost, as for those I would never have. I had never entirely given up hope. I had to, now. I had to accept it . . . I would never have a child of my own.

It was a year and a half before they sent Brother Benjamin to us to be our leader. Brother Rankin did well, but every Shaker village was under someone sent from the East. David Darrow, at Union Village in Ohio, was the head of all of us in the western country. He'd been sent from the Mother Colony at New Lebanon in New York State, and there were several more had been sent to help him, Brother Benjamin among them.

He was a little man and still young when he came to us, just past thirty. His full name was Benjamin Seth Youngs, and what he lacked in size he made up for in zeal and will and shrewdness. He was like a whirlwind to make things go. He came in May of eighteen hundred nine, and though the time had not yet come for our gathering, we felt wonderfully bound together by his presence.

He lived at Brother Rankin's, but the first year he was with us he traveled much on missions . . . in Indiana, Ohio, and other places. He was always coming and going, always ready to preach and exhort, and he knew more about the Shakers than any other man among them, I do believe. It was he who had written the book called "The Testimonies of Christ's Second Appearing," which we called Mother Ann's Testimonies. He read from it to us, often. Our meetings became livelier, more joyous, quicker-spirited, and there were many more conversions.

He had an able mind for the practical, too, and started us building, in preparation for being gathered. First must come a Meetinghouse, and with great zeal the men worked on it most of one spring and summer. It was built of planed lumber and painted white. Then, because there were so many children, a School House must be built. Larger, more conveniently located barns were built, and more land was bought. "We cannot be gathered," he told us, "until we can support ourselves. We must have at least a thousand acres and proper houses must be supplied for the families."

Brother Rankin's house would serve for one. The McComb place, which adjoined, would serve for another. Cabins could be built for the blacks, and there was a big, barny building which could be made into a house for the School Family. But a new house had to be built for the Church Family.

I well remember how queer it looked to me when the sides had been raised and the plan of it was seen. There were two front doors, one for the men, one for the women. There was a great center hall with two stairways rising up from it, one for the men, one for the women. And upstairs the men had their own side for sleeping and keeping their things, and the women had theirs.

On the third floor was the large meeting room, where the Family could have its own exercises and services. For while Shakers met in the Meetinghouse for services together on Sunday and other special occasions, each Family had its own daily services in its own house. "Is that," I asked Richard, "the way the other houses will be divided off?"

"That's the way all Shaker houses are planned," he told me. "Of course at first, till new ones can be built, we'll have to make out the best we can. But in time every Family will have its own house built like this one."

Of course the Meetinghouse should have prepared me. There were two front doors there, and it even had two gates in the picket fence, one for the men, the other for the women. And inside we sat on separate sides of the room. I couldn't help thinking that the Shakers didn't put much trust in human nature. They took every caution to keep folks well apart. I didn't know as I blamed them with the most of us, and I could see how they might have to take care till folks were ready for full membership, but it did seem to me they might have trusted the Church Family a little more. I said so to Richard. He shook his head. "It's not that they don't trust them. It's just that they believe in separation."

That seemed so foolish to me that I said, more tartly than I meant to, it may be, "Then why don't they just set up different villages for them? Why keep the men and women together at all? Why not a village for the men and another village for the women, instead of two doors, two stairways, two gates? They might as well separate good while they're at it!"

Richard looked at me in astonishment. "Why, there's women's work and men's work to be done! How could men do the cooking and washing and tending the young ones and keeping the houses?"

"Well, it's nice," I said shortly, "to know we're good for *something*." My temper passing I went on to say, "They're just asking for trouble, Richard. Those separate doors and separate stairs and separate gates aren't going to keep folks from doing what comes natural to them. They wouldn't even be needed for people like Brother Rankin or Brother Benjamin or even you. But they'll be a mighty poor bar for any that are really tempted. Matter of fact, they'll just add to the temptation. There'll never be a time some of those men commence climbing their own stairs but what they won't be put in mind of climbing the other, and maybe put in mind of how to slip and do it. And every time some of those women go through that separate door, they'll know clean to their fingertips what man's going through the other one. Some will plot to time it just right. Oh, there's more ways of killing a cat than by choking it to death on butter, Richard, and there'll be some to find them . . . and everything that reminds them of being separate will just edge them on."

Richard looked sadly at me. "Oh, ye of little faith," he quoted at me. "Maybe," I said, "maybe . . . but it's just common sense I'm talking."

"Well," he said sharply, "it's worked in the colonies in the East, for a good many years, too."

"How well has it worked? How much backsliding has there been?"

He didn't know, and of course nothing I said was of any great importance to him anyway. He believed what he believed and nothing could change him. Not that I was trying to. It only seemed to me vastly impractical, this business of separation without separation. It was like asking for cake when there wasn't even any bread. That was my mother in me, I guess. She could always go straight to the heart of a thing, see its flaws, recognize its imperfections. Like her, I could not help doing the same thing, and common sense told me this was a flaw.

Another thing I had been pondering came to my mind and I spoke of it. "How," I said, "if there's not to be any marrying or bearing of young, do they intend to keep going? In time the Society'll die out of itself."

But Richard had an answer for that. "There'll always be converts to bring children in."

I started laughing. "So the Shakers, too pure to bear children, are going to depend on the sinful world to provide young ones for them!"

Richard looked at me severely. "Rebecca . . ." he had long since quit calling me Becky, "you talk as if you weren't a Shaker yourself."

Oh, I wasn't . . . I wasn't. No matter what I had confessed or promised to try to believe, I was not. But I could not help it. It was my way to think things through and doubts arose I could not put down. It seemed to me the Shakers asked you never to think, simply to believe. I could not believe, and I was used to thinking.

We had been sitting by the fire, the day's work done. Richard was tired and he had slipped off his boots. The harvest was nearly over, but he had worked hard all during the time. The barns were full and the men felt fine about the good crops. I was knitting. It was a mild evening and we had but a small fire. The room was dimly lit by it and the light of the one candle we had burning. At about the same time we both noticed that the light in the room had grown very strong. Richard glanced around. "What's making it so light in here?"

Immediately I saw that the light was coming from the outside. I ran to the window. "It's the big barn, Richard! It's afire!"

He grabbed his coat but forgot his boots and in his stocking feet ran out of the house. I threw on my shawl and ran after him. Outside there was a great blaze streaking up into the sky and we could hear the crackling of the flames from where we were. It was the main barn, the newest and biggest one, on Brother Rankin's place. We ran down the road, other people joining us, and we could hear the shouts of the men who had already reached the fire.

Richard ran too fast for me. He could always run with the speed of a hare, but I caught up with Permilla and Thomas. Thomas was puffing and panting. "They'll never save it," he said, between puffs, "hit's gone fer shore."

He was slow and Permilla and I ran on ahead. We came to the edge of the crowd gathered about. The men who had been dashing around, trying to put the fire out, looked black and scorched, and they coughed from the smoke and blinked the streams of water from their eyes. Even where we stood, the great heat of the blaze set our faces to burning. Brother Rankin stood near, weeping and wringing his hands. Brother Benjamin stood beside him, agitated but trying to bring order into the confusion. Finally he raised his hands and made a trumpet of them. "It's no use, men. It's too far gone. Let it go. Let it burn. I don't want anyone to be hurt."

There was actually nothing to do but let it go. There wasn't enough water in the whole creek to put it out, or enough of the men to draw it up and carry it. As the men heard him and passed the message along they fell back from the heat and smoke into the crowd. Brother Benjamin's shoulders slumped. "This is the work of the devil, John," he said to Brother Rankin. "Someone of the world set this blaze. They picked the largest barn, the one that held the most grain, the one that would do us the most hurt if lost."

In the light of the flames I saw him raise his face and lift his arms, and plainly I heard him say, "Oh, Lord, even as Mother Ann, Thy servants are persecuted. Forgive them, for they know not what they do, and give us, Thy servants, the strength of our Mother to endure."

It was our first experience of persecution.

CHAPTER IX

SOME OF THE PEOPLE felt bitter about the burning of the barn, but in meeting Brother Benjamin admonished them. "We do not return violence with violence. Instead we shall set about rebuilding the barn at once."

It was true. Shakers did not believe in violence of any kind. They would not go to war, and in the time I was at South Union I never knew of a teacher striking even the most rebellious school child. Richard McNemar had told us how, when they had been driven from Harvard, beaten as they walked along the road, the brethren had tried to take the whip upon their own shoulders when it fell on one near them. It was a gentle, tender, loving side of them.

Anyway, though we suspected, even knew the barn had been deliberately set, there was no way of proving it. But it had hurt us badly. They had chosen well how to damage us the most, for the barn had been full of corn and wheat and oats, and the loss of so much of our crops gave us a very lean winter. In order to eat we had to kill stock we intended to sell, and even so there were times when we ate very sparingly. Those with children fared better, for, properly, Brother Benjamin decided the children must not go hungry. Poor little Brother Benjamin denied himself so zealously that he seemed little more than a feather in the wind, but it was a feather constantly heartening us. "We must not hang our harps on the willows," he said.

Whatever the world found in us to condemn, none could help but admire the courage of our people that winter. The barn was rebuilt, work on the house for the Church Family went right on, and instead of spending our small funds on ourselves, it was decided to buy more land with them. We ate mush and milk when the meat ran out, and sometimes not enough of that, but the work was never neglected and the plans were not altered. "Part of this new piece of land we are buying," Brother Benjamin said, "has many sugar trees on it. We will establish a sugar camp there in January. And on the creek we will build a sawmill. A brick kiln must be built, for the next buildings must be made of brick for stoutness and permanence."

We ever feared that the Meetinghouse would be burned after that, and it was decided to build a new one as soon as possible, of brick. We did all those things in which we were counseled and led. Richard grew lean before my eyes, but his strength increased so that he never seemed to tire.

There was some falling off of the members that winter, but not much. I recall that John and Viney Parks, an elderly couple, left us, Viney saying spitefully, "I may burn in hell, but I'll shore do it on a full stummick!"

Brother Benjamin let them go, giving them back what they had brought, a sore-backed nag, a feather tick and a rocking chair. He smiled wryly when they went away, Viney riding the nag, John walking beside it. "I doubt," he said, "Viney's stomach will be filled very soon."

They returned within the month, begging to be taken in again. It wasn't, they found, so easy to fill their stomachs in the world, either.

The time of our gathering was in September. My Journals begin in that month. I do not now know why I was minded to keep one. It may have been to ease my troubled heart. Or it may have been because journal-keeping was so common among the Believers I caught the infection. I have forgotten the reason, and it does not much matter now. But here they are, old, brown-backed, and here is the date of the first entry, September 10, 1811. It says:

We were this day gathered into order. Richard and I are assigned to Brother Rankin's old home with the others of the Novitiate. Already we are called the East Family because the house lies east of the Church Family Dwelling.

With us in this house are Permilla and Thomas, Henry and Lacey Akins, Robert and Annie Jewett, William and Amanda Steel, John and Viney Parks, and others. Set over us as spiritual leaders are Brother Samuel Eades and Sister Susan Robinson. As temporal leaders we have Samuel Shannon and Priscilla Stewart. Richard is appointed a deacon to have charge of the work of the men. No deaconess is appointed. Sister Priscilla will have charge of the work of the women herself. I suppose they do not think any of us worthy yet. I am appointed to the washhouse for my first duty. This is the hardest duty we have, and I think it is to chasten my unbelieving spirit. It does not matter. I am able and stout to work and what Sister Priscilla does not know is that washing has ever been a pleasure to me.

Sent to us to be over the entire village along with Brother Benjamin are Joseph Allen and the sisters, Molly Goodrich and Mercy Pickett. They are all from the East. They appear to be godly and trustworthy.

Our home is to be torn down so that the lumber may be used in the village. The land remains in our name, but its use is given to the Society. We have been required to hand in an inventory of everything brought with us and given to the Society, so that should we ever decide to leave, what is rightfully ours may be given back to us. We were not required to sign the Covenant, since we are not yet admitted to full membership, but we did sign an agreement that we came willingly and donated both ourselves and our property to the further use of the Believers. We had also to sign that we had paid in full all debts and obligations and that there was no call upon us by the world.

Our furnishings have been distributed where they were needed. The bed in which I am to sleep is not my own. I have nothing of my own any longer, except the clothing which I wear, and except for a change even that has been taken for use with others who had less. We are allowed two dresses each, two shifts, two caps and two bonnets.

Permilla, Lacey, Amanda, Annie Jewett and poor old Viney Parks are in the room with me. A wall was torn cut between two rooms to make this large bedroom which we share. There is another, larger bedroom which houses eight women. Across the hall is a similar arrangement for the men. Permilla has set out her belongings next to mine. It all seems very strange to me.

Those written words cannot in any way tell what I felt the day we moved out of our home. I had long since resigned myself, as best I could, for resignation does not come easy to me. But no one can know until the time comes how he is going to feel when parted from all that is familiar to him, when he goes into a life so new that there is nothing about it known or apprehended. It is a desolate feeling. It would be desolate enough to go hand in hand with one's husband, but there would at least be the comfort of knowing he stood beside you. Instead of that comfort, there was the certain knowledge that never again would Richard stand beside me . . . that so long as we lived he was no longer my husband. He was a man of the Shakers, and my thoughts were supposed never to linger on him, nor my ways to be joined with his.

Cassie, Sampson and Jency went with us. Richard called them into the house the night before the removal. He had made out papers of manumission to give to them. He explained to them what we were going to do. "But you need not go with us," he told them. "Those papers I have just given you set you free. You can go where you will—or you can come with us if you'd rather."

Sampson, who was dull in the head, looked at the paper as if it might turn on him and bite. "Whur we go, Mister Richard, do we go off by ourselfs?"

"Anywhere you please."

Cassie folded her paper. "I ain't aimin' to go nowhurs. I goin' with Miss Becky. I been give to her, an' I s'pose to tend her. An' that's whut I aims to do. Sampson, you aims to do the same."

Then Richard explained that they would never work for us again, that their work would be assigned to them in the village. "Don't make no difference to me," Cassie said firmly, "I goin' whur Miss Becky is at."

Jency, whom I had tried without success to teach to read, was examining her paper, laughing when she came across a letter she recognized. "That 'un's a gee," she giggled, "an' that 'un's a ess." She came swaying out into the firelight, finally, the paper rolled into a thin strip, tied into one of her braids. "Jency!" I said to her, "take that paper out of your hair this minute. Give it to Cassie to keep for you."

"We s'pose to keep 'em?" Cassie asked, looked bewildered. "Whur we keep 'em at?"

Richard gave up. "I'll keep them for you. But remember, if you ever want to leave, all you have to do is ask for your paper and you can go."

In great relief Cassie and Sampson handed back their papers, sighing to be rid of them. Jency held on to hers, however. "Hit's mine," she said. "It's yours," Richard told her, "but not to play with. This is a legal paper, and someday you may want it very badly."

"I wants it now," she said, sulkily.

"What for?"

"Hit's purty . . . all white an' crackly. I likes it."

"Give it here, Jency," Richard said, but she tore it out of her hair suddenly, crumpled it in her hand and ran giggling from the room. Cassie started after her. "Oh, leave her alone," Richard said. "If she loses it or destroys it, I can have another one made out."

For days Jency wore the paper, torn now into many pieces, in her short, wiry braids. Ever so often she would reach up and tweek a braid, listen to the paper crackle, and giggle. She was a woman in body now, and it was a very handsome body she had. She had finally bloomed out and was full-breasted, narrow-waisted and slim-hipped, and she walked with a kind of swaying swift grace that reminded me of a flower bending before the wind. She had been a woman for a good many years, her health having begun early on her. But mentally she had never passed childhood, and there were times when I thought it was a very early childhood at that. I doubt if she had the mind of Permilla's six-year-old. So far she had been kept under Cassie's firm hand and my watchful eyes. I hoped Sister Priscilla would have the good sense to keep her close to Cassie's side.

Permilla and I went to our beds that night in different moods. She was gay, glad to be shut of Thomas finally, glad, even, to have her children off her hands. She stretched and yawned and curled up like a cat, comfortable and easy in her mind. "This ain't goin' to be bad, Becky."

I barely heard her. The strange room, the presence of the other women, the narrow, hard bed, the plain, straight chest which I shared with Permilla and Annie Jewett, each of us having only one drawer for our belongings, and above all else the knowledge that across the hall Richard lay in the men's room, filled me with a sadness which made me want to weep. I held back the tears with difficulty, but I was too proud to let the others know how I felt. Softly Permilla whispered after the candle had been snuffed. "You all right, Becky?"

"I'm all right."

"You ain't grievin' none?"

"Some," I admitted, "but it's all right."

She reached out her hand, warm, gentle, loving, and took mine. "I ain't Richard, Becky, but I'm still right alongside of you."

I couldn't have answered without giving way, but I squeezed her hand and held on to it. She continued to whisper, chuckling a little over whether the baby would give trouble during the night. The smallest children had been put in care of several of the Negro women with Nancy Brown in charge. Jency was among them. Sister Priscilla had not done what I had hoped she would, kept Jency by Cassie's side. Jency was to be in the Nursery . . . Cassie in the kitchen. But Jency *was* good with young ones, and Cassie would at least sleep in the same place with her. "Cassie and Jency will see to the baby," I told Permilla. "Jency loves the baby."

"Oh, I ain't a wearyin'. She sleeps good, mostly. But they's times she gits woken up an' they ain't e'er thing to do but take her up an' rock her till she goes off again."

"Jency will rock her."

"Yes."

Permilla was to go to her several times a day to let her nurse, but otherwise she was to leave her to the care of the others. Permilla's work duty was in the dairy. She knew nothing about it for she had never owned more than one cow at a time, and while she knew how to strain up milk, set it to turn and churn it, she had never worked with large amounts, nor known how to care for crocks and tubs and settling vats. She had never made cheese. "Hit's a good thing," she said, laughing softly, and in the dark I thought how her eyes crinkled when she laughed, "hit's a good thing they's to be somebody over me, fer I'd likely turn out a cheese would curdle the stummick of a cow itself."

"You'll learn," I told her.

"I reckon."

At the Family Meeting that evening, when our work duties had been read off to us, we had been told that they would be shifted each month, and that unless sickness prevented, each of us would be expected to take a turn at everything to be done. There was a duty for making beds and sweeping the chambers. There was one for cooking, and some of the blacks had been told off for redding up the kitchen. There was a duty in the washhouse, and for ironing, for the women did the washing and ironing for the men of the Family, too. There were duties for spinning and weaving and sewing. For the present we had all to wear the clothes we brought with us, but as new ones would be made, they would be all alike, for none was to have finery and none was to have richer stuff than any other, and none was to be dressed differently. Annie Jewett, who loved pretty things, had asked in Meeting, "Are the colors to be all the same?"

Sister Priscilla had said, "No. You can pick your own color, so long as it is a color we can dye ourselves."

The choice of colors was wider than you'd think, for we all knew how to dye and we could produce a bright, pretty blue, a deep, dark red, a nice brown, purple, yellow and green. We were to buy nothing, however, we could make for ourselves. This meant there would be no silk, no cottons, no patterned fabrics. And it meant no pretties of any kind, no fripperies, such as Annie so dearly loved. She had sulked frowningly, and muttered, "I'll wager they'll be as ugly as sin."

Permilla had nudged her and whispered, "Pick red, Annie, an' leave off yer shift. Hit'll show yer hips good enough."

Annie had giggled and Sister Priscilla had peered sternly at her.

Thinking of it, I smiled. Annie had been very quiet, though, when we had been shepherded to our room. She had knelt obediently beside her bed for evening prayers, but she had slipped under the covers without a word to anyone and turned on her side away from the light. Our beds were in a long row down the wall, with only a little space between them. Mine was at the end, Permilla's next, then came Annie, Amanda, Lacey and Viney.

There had been some whispering among the others, as between Permilla and me, but when she and I had stopped, the room was very quiet. We had not been supposed to talk after prayers, but I think only the actual presence of Sister Priscilla would have kept us from it that first night. It was all too new and strange to us and more than human frailty could withstand not to talk a little to each other.

In the quiet, now, I heard a sniffle and then a choked sob, and then as if she had held it back as long as she could, Annie gave way to a fit of weeping. Permilla was beside her in a moment and I was not much longer reaching her bed. She was shaking with her, crying and her hands were cold to touch. "I wish I was home," she said, between gasps for her breath, "Oh, I wish I was home. I don't care if I go to hell for it, I'd rather to, than to be here in this Shaker house!"

"Sh-sh-sh," Permilla warned her, picking her up in her arms and rocking with her back and forth, "sh-sh-sh, Annie. You'll have Sister Priscilla in here amongst us."

Annie only wept the harder. "I don't care . . . I don't care about her nor none of 'em. I just wish I was home. I want Robert and my baby. I've not ever slept away from my baby before. Why can't we keep our younguns beside us?"

Permilla kept patting and rocking her, smoothing her hair, and talking softly. "I don't know, honey. Mebbe Becky kin tell you, but it don't make no more sense to me than it does to you. They jist got their rules, I reckon, an' we got to abide by 'em. Yore youngun will be all right, though, same as mine. Don't grieve fer it so."

I thought Annie was more homesick than anything else . . . the way a child away from home is at night, the way we all were right now. I gave her credit for loving her young one, but I'd known her to complain of him and even neglect him when he bothered too much, and I'd even seen her smack him, as little as he was, if he didn't hush whimpering. But I guessed a woman could feel bothered and fretted with a young one without losing any part of her love for it, and I felt sorry for Annie now.

Then my pity for Annie spread to all the others, parted from their children as well as their men, and I wondered how many were crying in the dark. I guessed that only the ones who'd never been married took any great content in this gathering into order, or those who were widowed and had nothing to lose. Their loneliness in the world was ended. Their lives would be richer. Ours, we could not help feeling, were robbed of something good, and though we had been told, and had tried to believe it, that we had gained eternity, we felt poorer for the gain.

Under Permilla's mothering hands Annie became quieter.

There were footsteps in the hall and we all scurried like guilty children to our beds. The door was opened and Sister Priscilla stood there, holding her candle up, peering in at us. "I thought I heard talking in here."

She was a scrawny woman, tall and thin-lipped, gray-eyed, gray-haired and gray-faced. She even dressed in gray. She wore steel-rimmed spectacles over which she peered when she needed to look closely at anyone. They seemed forever perched on the end of her nose, and she was always having to push them back in place.

"Yes, ma'am," Permilla said. "Annie had a pain in her stummick. We was tryin' to decide whe'er we ort to call somebody or not." She lied cheerfully.

Sister Priscilla went to Annie's bed and laid her hand on her forehead. "You're not hot," she said.

"No, ma'am. I feel better now," Annie told her.

"Maybe I'd better give you a physic."

"No'm. It was just something I eat, likely. It's passed on, now."

"Has anyone else felt any discomfort?" Sister Priscilla eyed us sternly.

Amanda spoke up immediately. "I did—but it wasn't as sharp as Sister Annie's."

"Sister Rebecca?"

"Yes, ma'am. A little." I could lie, too.

"Sister Lacey?" Lacey looked frightened but she nodded her head. "Yessum."

"Sister Viney?"

"Yessum . . . a mite."

Sister Priscilla looked at all of us. I don't know whether she believed us or not, but out of Permilla's eye I caught a look of triumph. We had a loyal group . . . this was its first test and no one had backed down. We had all stood together. "Humph," Sister Priscilla said, balancing her spectacles. "Are any of you in pain, now?"

In a chorus we all said we were not.

"Very well, but I think we had better have prayer together again."

Permilla rolled her eyes up, but obediently we all got out of bed and knelt while Sister Priscilla led in prayer. I never thought much of Sister Priscilla's prayers. She always told the Lord exactly what to do, and when she told Him now to forgive us and to save us from our sins, I guessed that she knew we had all lied to her. There was no way she could prove it, though.

She kept us on our knees a quarter of an hour, then left us without another word. When her footsteps had faded down the hall and we had heard the other door close, Permilla snorted, "Prissy Priscilla!"

Everyone laughed, and from that time on, in private, she was known among us as Prissy. It was not right, perhaps, but even now I am not ashamed of it. Permilla had given us a handhold on something humanly warm, and when Sister Priscilla scolded, or lectured, or talked severely to us, we had only, behind a hand, to mouth her name for all of us to laugh quietly inside and to feel banded together. And there were times when we needed to laugh and to feel bound together.

●

C H A P T E R   X

I DID NOT SLEEP well and wakened early, before the rising bell had rung. The windows of the room were still dark, but there was a twittering and cheeping of birds outside that told that daylight would soon be breaking. A rooster crowed down in the fowl yard and in a moment another one crowed and then another until finally dozens had joined in. There was a world of difference in the sounds they made. Some were deep and long-drawn, the full voice of an old rooster, practiced and experienced . . . some were shorter, shriller, but able to sustain the lengthy final note . . . some were high and scratchy, broken off, the way a young boy's voice will break during its changing time. These were the young ones, just learning to crow. But however different they were in sound, they were all alike in their lustiness. You had to give them credit for trying.

I had slept too fitfully ever to lose consciousness of where I was, so I felt no confusion upon waking. I lay and listened to the sounds of the other women. Permilla, turned toward me, breathed quietly. Someone farther down was snoring and I guessed that Lacey or Viney had got turned on her back. Annie breathed a little heavily, as though she might be taking a catarrh in her head, but I knew it was because of her weeping the night before. Amanda, like Permilla, was quiet.

Here we all were, I thought, brought together into this room. We had all been neighbors for several years and we had all been members of Brother Rankin's congregation. We knew as much about each other as neighbors usually know. We knew that Annie was a pretty, flighty little thing, early married, brought among us by Robert who had grown up in our midst, that she loved pretty things, wasn't a very good housekeeper, was tempery, but quickly over it.

We knew that Lacey Akins was fat, lazy, shiftless, had borne effortlessly ten children in ten years, was a dull woman, almost stupid, blind to dirt and filth in her home or on her person. Almost the first thing the Shakers had done with her and Henry and their whole brood of young

[85]

ones was to order them to the creek to bathe. But it had ever taken someone watchful to see that they came to Meeting clean.

We knew that Viney Parks was old, gossipy, sharp-tongued, but spry, clean and proud even in the days when she and John had been so poor they'd slept on a straw pallet on the floor. Being Believers had brought them up in the world, so far as creature comforts went, but Viney never owned it. And no more had John who sometimes grumbled, "We was free in them days, leastways, to do as we pleased."

We all knew that Amanda Steel was a speckless, spotless woman about her house, that she had a pinched, unchanging look on her face, but that she could work hard and uncomplainingly . . . that she did for William and her young one all any woman could do for her family, that she was miserly with William's money and made it stretch far. She had never liked giving over their portion to the community. She could not bear to see the handling of her affairs turned over to someone else.

Then there was Permilla whom everyone knew to be as good as she was beautiful, unconscious of her beauty, kind to all, laughing quickly and easily, a little bawdy in her humor, but not overly so. Her sympathies were quick and her heart was big. She felt no enmity toward anyone, ever. She was easygoing, tender and generous.

And there was myself. What they knew of me and thought of me I did not know, except I was certain of Permilla's love. They ought to have been able to say I was a good hand at work, that I kept a clean house, that I tended Richard as best I could, saw to the blacks, carried my load as was given me to carry, helped with the sick, and was given to reading the few books that had come my way. But I did not know. The way we see ourselves is often not the way others see us.

Here we were, now, all set aside, to labor for each other, for none of us could accumulate for ourselves. Our duty was plain and clear . . . to worship in joy and purity . . . to work with willingness and equity. I wondered how we would make out.

The rising bell rang, clanging across the yard, sounding and echoing through the whole house. It brought us all up at once, sitting in our beds. "What time is it?" Annie asked, peering about the dim room.

"Four-thirty," I told her. "You recollect, don't you, the bell is to ring at four-thirty until October, then it's to be changed to five for the winter."

Permilla stretched, ruffled her hair and wiggled her shoulders. "What was it they told us to do first?"

"Pray," Amanda said, shortly.

We got out of our beds and knelt. We were to pray silently for whatever length of time we wished. But since only fifteen minutes was allowed us in which to dress, it could not be for very long.

One by one we rose, placed chairs at the foot of the beds, laid the pillows on the chairs and stripped back the covers to air. It was not our duty to make the beds. We dressed hurriedly, afraid of being late this first morning. Each of us put on a change of underthings, and a fresh dress. The clothing we had worn into the community was to be washed before being worn again. We laid our soiled things in a heap on my bed. The others hurried out, each to report to his own duty.

My own duty required that I gather up the soiled clothing in the room, go along the hall and gather it from the other bedroom, and take it to the washhouse. Then I must return for the soiled clothing of the men, which had been collected and laid in neat bundles outside their door.

Brother Rankin's house had been a large one, and changes had been made in it to accommodate a Shaker family of separated men and women. There had been one stairway already, and another at the back of the hall had been built. The men were to use it. The dining room had been made larger, and two doors had been cut into it, the left one for the men, the right one for the women. There was no sitting room left in the house, for it was not needed. It had been turned into the spinning and sewing room. The attic above the bedrooms had been built up higher and a large room had been made of it for our Family Meetings.

There were no men in the house as I went about my work, for their duties all lay outside. I did not see Richard, though I could not help looking for him. He must, I thought, be overseeing some work in the fields. I would see him at breakfast, I knew, but it was an hour and a half before the breakfast bell would ring. This was to give us all time to get our work well started, and to give the women on kitchen duty time to prepare the meal.

Permilla had gone to the dairy and Annie and Viney, who had duty for cleaning our bedroom, were at work, sweeping and dusting, making the beds. There was no disorder to clean, for we had been admonished never to leave anything lying about. This emphasis upon neatness and cleanliness came straight from Mother Ann, who had said, "Be neat and industrious; have a place for everything and keep it there; keep your clothing clean and decent; see that your house is kept clean and orderly and your victuals are prepared in good order. Be neat and clean and keep the fear of God in all your goings forth."

In the kitchen, as I went back and forth taking the clothing to the washhouse, I saw Sister Priscilla overseeing the cooking. Lacey was there from our room and I thought, laughing inside me, how little help she would be for a time. Cassie was bumbling about, muttering under her breath, slicing meat. "Whut you doin', Miss Becky?" she asked, when I passed through the second time.

"It's my turn in the washhouse," I told her.

"You give me them clo'es," she said, "just give 'em right here. You ain't no call to be packin' dirty clo'es backards an' forrards."

"Cassie," Sister Priscilla called out, "Sister Rebecca has the wash duty this month. Your duty is here in the kitchen."

"But I'se washed Miss Becky's clo'es ever since I been give to her."

"Not any more, Cassie," I told her, drawing the armful of soiled clothing away. "Remember what Mister Richard told you."

"Mister Richard done tole me I'se free."

Sister Priscilla came around the big table in the middle of the room. "So you are, Cassie. You are entirely free and you can leave the village if you like. But as long as you stay here you will do the work assigned to you. And you will *not* wait on Sister Rebecca any more."

Cassie stared at her and her big mouth puckered. Her lower lip pushed out stubbornly. "I was give to Miss Becky, an' I ain't aimin' to leave her, an' I aim to he'p her the best I kin, an' you ain't got no say-so about it."

Sister Priscilla's lips set in a thin line. Hurriedly I put the clothes on the floor. "Cassie," I said as sternly as I could, "Mister Richard and I both told you that things would be different here. I have to take my turn at all the chores and you can't help me. You have to do whatever work is assigned to you. Right now you're to work in the kitchen. Now, you mind what I say and do it well, like you've been taught. And you mind what Sister Priscilla tells you, you hear?"

Cassie looked at me pleadingly. I shook my head. "Yessum," she said finally, grudgingly giving in. She understood me. She was used to being told by me. She would obey, though she didn't like it.

I was sorry to have trouble on the first morning, and I wished Sister Priscilla had been able to manage her. But she was from the East and she had had no experience with blacks. I hated to have to tell Cassie to mind her. I know it looked as if I were taking over, but I was afraid Cassie would rebel. Even so, Sister Priscilla said, "This will have to be reported."

"She'll mind, now," I said. "She's just not used to doing for others."

"It was explained to her."

I could have shaken her. Explaining once isn't enough for a Negro. You have to explain again and again, tell them over and over, show them, be patient with them. And of course the last thing Sister Priscilla could understand was the kind of loyalty one's own blacks feel. "Well, report me, then," I said, more sharply than I should have, perhaps. "Cassie was only doing what she's been trained all her life to do."

"Very well," Sister Priscilla said, agreeing suddenly. "You will see Sister Susan immediately after breakfast."

Sister Susan was the spiritual leader and all confessions of the women had to be made to her. I wondered as I went out the door what I was going to confess. That I hadn't trained Cassie properly? That I hadn't explained the new way of living? Sister Susan was from the East, too. How could she understand the workings of Cassie's mind any more than Sister Priscilla had done. I decided that it must be told simply as it had happened, and that in some way I must protect Cassie from the accusation of disobedience and impudence.

By the time the breakfast bell rang we had sorted the clothing and the water in the tubs was hot enough to put the white things to soak. We left them to go to breakfast, going in as we had been instructed, through the right hand door.

Special tables had been built . . . long, trestle tables. The men ate on their side of the room, the women on theirs and no conversation was allowed at all. When we went in, we were to kneel by our chairs for silent prayer. Then we were served. The tables were set so that a complete meal was put in front of each group of four. There was no need to pass the bowls, or to ask for anything out of reach.

On that first morning I could not pray, for all my thoughts were of Richard. I had seen him among the men, filing into the room and my mind was full of him. I could not put the thoughts of him away and concentrate on prayer, save to ask, beggingly, that he should be kept safe and protected.

Before my eyes, closed as they were, there stayed the sight of his hair, brown, thick, curled close to his head, and its texture under my hands was a disturbing memory. After nearly four years of never touching him, how could the memory still be so strong? And his shoulders, big under the jacket he wore, squared heavily from his neck . . . how could I remember so well their smoothness to touch, and their strength to hold? I had not seen his face, for his back was turned, but as I tried to wrench my thoughts away from him, its remembered shape and look rose before me, and my mouth trembled threateningly.

I rose from my knees and though I had determined not to look his way, my eyes flew immediately to search him out. He looked up at me, meeting my look, and he smiled. I drew my chair under me quickly. I had need of its support, for my knees went suddenly weak, and a great anguish filled me. Oh, Richard, Richard, my heart cried . . . how can this be right for us? How can we never again touch or talk? For the Shaker rule was that there must always be a third person present when a man and a woman talked. Richard would never break it, I knew.

I thought I had already suffered all the hurt possible over this thing we were doing, but so deep a sense of loss, so awful a sense of despair overcame me at that moment that sick waves of nausea boiled up in me and the very smell of the food was repulsive. This was the way it was going to be, day after day after day. I prayed then. I had wanted to be where I could see Richard. I prayed that I would have the strength to continue seeing him. I prayed that the soreness and longing might pass. I prayed that I might be given a joy in worship which would remove this physical ache from me.

I took only the smallest helpings of food, for another rule was that nothing must be left on our plates, and I knew I could not eat more than a few bites. They were like straw in my mouth.

Permilla nudged me. "Look at Thomas," she whispered out of the corner of her mouth. "He's all broke out in sweat. He's likely havin' to work harder'n he expected."

Sister Priscilla rapped sharply on the table, eying Permilla over her spectacles. Permilla sighed, and on the outgoing breath I heard a faint "Prissy!"

When the meal was finished we knelt again for silent prayer and then we filed slowly out to go back to our tasks. Sister Priscilla caught up with Permilla in the hallway. "Sister Permilla, you will see Sister Susan before going back to the dairy. Wait outside the door until she has finished hearing Sister Rebecca."

"Why have I got to see Sister Susan?" Permilla asked, her eyes wide with innocence.

"You were talking in the dining room."

"How do you know I was talkin'?"

"I saw your lips moving."

"I was prayin'."

For a moment Sister Priscilla was caught flat-footed. Her mouth dropped open and her spectacles slid wildly down her nose. She could not possibly have heard what Permilla said, so there was no way she could dispute her. Except finally to ask me, "Was she praying?"

Without a moment's hesitation I said, "She may have been. I didn't hear what she was saying."

A flaw in the Shaker organization from the first was too many rules, too much rigidity. It made us all band together against authority. Inevitably, when caught between loyalty to each other and loyalty to the elders and eldresses, we chose each other. We lied, as a matter of course, as children will do when found out and faced with punishment. There was nothing for Sister Priscilla to do but settle her spectacles, say, "Humph," doubtfully and tell Permilla she could go to her work.

I made my way to Sister Susan's room, which she shared with four other women. They were at their tasks, so she was alone. She was a small, frail woman, given to much ecstasy in Meeting, given to much prayer in private. She had a countenance of singular innocence, for she had been born into the Shakers and had never known any other life. Not for her had been the sorrows of parting with husband or children. She was well versed in all the Shaker beliefs and it was she who most often quoted Mother Ann to us. She was elderly now, and almost white-haired. "Come in," she called, when I knocked.

"Sister Priscilla has told me to report to you what happened in the kitchen this morning," I told her.

"Yes," she answered, "she has told me."

I repeated as simply as possible what had occurred, took the blame for it on my shoulders, asked patience with Cassie. There was not a grudging bone in Sister Susan's body, and she smiled at me when I had finished. "These things," she said, understandingly, "will work out in time. It may be that you have not labored hard enough to help Cassie understand our ways, but I think no other blame can be attached to you. You show no pride or arrogance of spirit."

I had, then, in conscience, to confess my impatience with Sister Priscilla, which was a graver matter. Sister Susan asked me to pray with her then and there, for patience of soul, for dutiful obedience, for chastening of spirit. I could and did willingly pray for those things. Only if they were learned could I hope for peace of mind. I felt I had to learn them.

In great earnestness Sister Susan prayed, too . . . and then she told me I could go. I felt relieved that she had not required that I make public confession at Meeting.

The rest of the morning passed quickly. At ten minutes before twelve the bell rang again for dinner. Afterwards we went back to our tasks. Supper was at six. But we were not free in the evenings, either. Some kind of service or meeting was planned for each of them. That first night, for instance, we were to meet for practice in the dance. There was a brief interval between supper and Meeting when we could go to our rooms, rest, talk together, order our few small affairs.

Permilla flopped on her bed. "I'm wore to a nub. If anybody," she said, raising on one elbow, "thinks workin' in that dairy is easy, jist wait till it's their turn. All them tubs an' vats to be lifted, all that bendin' an' stoopin'. An' a full day of it is too big a bargain, seems to me."

I was tired, too. There were about thirty of us in the Family, and a washing for that many people is fairly sizeable. I'd been bent over a tub most of the day. My back ached and my hands felt swollen and water-soaked. Amanda had drawn spinning duty, so she was the least tired of us all. Annie and Viney, after cleaning the bedroom, had been put to weeding in the fall garden. Annie complained her back was broken, and Viney was so tired her poor old face was white. "I ain't goin't to have much sperrit fer dancin'," she said.

I didn't think many of us would, not this first day anyhow, but only illness could excuse one from either duty or Meeting.

At seven-thirty we went up to the meeting room. There was nothing in it except some benches set all around the four walls. The floor space was needed for the exercises. Brother Benjamin had come over from the Church Family to lead us. He waited until we were all seated, and then he explained to us that crowded as we had been in our homes, with no place large enough to go through the formations of the dance properly, we were all awkward and stiff. He said that now we must go forth more quickly and freely to perform the exercises, more joyously and with more abandon. His way of teaching was to bring out six sisters and six brothers, to lead them through the dance so that we might see it.

In the beginning the Shaker songs were a mystery to me. Some of them had words, but many of them did not . . . they seemed only notes, and used to the hymns of the old church, as I was, many of the tunes sounded queer to me. They went up and down without much tune at all, and the rhythm was often broken right in the middle, from slow to fast, then back to slow again. That night, feeling I suppose that many of us were tired and dispirited, Brother Benjamin used Mother Ann's Lowly song for the dance. It had no words except "Lowly, lowly, lowly, low," over and over again.

Those of us watching sang, and the chosen ones went through the steps. They were the slow step and the shuffle. Anyone could do it. But what was a marvel to see was the formations Brother Benjamin taught. Like soldiers on drill the dancers moved, first in solid rank, men facing the women, passing, breaking and passing again, this time in twos or threes, next time all together, wheeling, turning, interweaving. I doubted I could ever learn it!

Of course I did, but not that first evening. We sang Lowly, Low, the dancers practiced. Then Brother Benjamin sent them to their seats and called out those of us who had been watching. I have ever had to guard against self-consciousness when performing before people, but I was so intent upon doing the formations right that I forgot all about myself. I did not want to be the cause of breaking up a set.

They say that in Mother Ann's day there was no set formation for the dance—that each whirled and turned according to his own impulse, that it was lively and free. But Mother Lucy Wright was head of the church now, and she laid great store by the proper steps and formations. She even sent missionary teachers to the villages to help them learn to dance properly. Brother Benjamin never needed to be taught, though. He knew every step and every formation, and he, himself, was a good teacher, patient, careful, watchful.

When we had labored under his teaching he sent us to be seated, and he read to us then from the Testimonies. Following which he broke into spontaneous song and led all who wished to follow into a quick and lively shaking dance. Shaking, too, must be done properly. It begins with a loose wrist, and a shaking of the hands, then it moves to the forearms, from there to the shoulders, and finally, in its full power, it takes hold of the entire body.

During the shaking exercise Sister Susan was visited with the gift of song in tongues, and since it is the Shaker way to recognize all gifts immediately, we stopped the dance and circled around her while she sang. Her face was alight with joy and the vision giving her the song, and Brother Benjamin, realizing at once that the song was beautiful, whipped out a notebook and took it down. It became one of our favorites, and I remember it well:

> O calvini criste I no vole,
> Calvini criste liste um,
> I no vole vinin ne viste,
> I no vole viste vum.

When the vision left her she was pale and weak. But she tried to tell us what she had seen. "I saw Mother Ann and Jesus, side by side, smiling, beckoning, approving. Oh, it was a vision of light and joy!"

We came to call her song the light and joy song, and since its rhythm was quick, we often used it for the lively dance.

We were dismissed with prayers and praise and went tiptoeing to our rooms. We had ever to walk softly . . . it was the rule. Walk softly, close doors softly, speak softly. I can see Permilla yet, lifting her foot, tempted just once to stamp it down with a great noise. But she never did.

As we passed from the meeting room in orderly file, I saw Annie Jewett, who walked ahead of me, brush softly against Robert, who somehow was near her, saw her hand touch his and saw him jerk as if a coal of fire had touched him, draw away. I did not blame her, though I would not have dared touch Richard so. But I knew what had made her touch him. We were supposed to report any such breaking of rules. I would have cut out my tongue before reporting it. Let them see for themselves what went on under their noses!

Bedtime was nine-thirty until October, when it would be moved up to nine. Most of us were too tired to talk after the candle was out that night. We lay quietly, and soon were asleep. Our first day in the Shaker village was ended. We had felt its pattern and its rhythm. We knew a little more, now, what to expect.

In her bed, quiet as the rest of us, Annie Jewett did not weep that night.

CHAPTER XI

MANY PEOPLE have never understood the way a Shaker village worked, thinking we all lived together helter-skelter and had no plan or organization to our affairs. Nothing could have been more wrong. If there has ever been an organization with more detail and care given to it, I have not heard of it. Everything that mortal could devise had been foreseen.

The Mother Colony was at New Lebanon, New York, though in Mother Ann's day it had been at Watervliet. Out of New Lebanon came every decision save those which affected a colony in its peculiar and daily worries. The Ministry of the Society was handed on through chosen successors . . . they were never elected. Mother Ann had appointed James Whittaker to be her successor, and she had gone further and named Joseph Meacham to follow Father James. The head Minister was a place to be held for life. It was, I guess, a little like the place of the pope of Rome.

The elders and eldresses were appointed by Mother Lucy, now the head of the Society, and in our day they came from the East, because all our colonies in the western country were new and it was thought we needed the guidance of those better trained. These appointments were for life, too, and only unseemly behavior could remove an elder or an eldress. Our leaders, Brother Benjamin, Brother Joseph Allen, Sister Molly Goodrich and Sister Mercy Pickett, had not yet been ordained. In time they became elders and eldresses, but not that first year.

A Journal had to be kept in every village and strict reports to New Lebanon had to be made. And nearly every year someone from the East was sent to teach and help us.

In the East, where their shops and industries were already working, each village had a group of folks called trustees, who handled the business of the village in the world. As yet we had no need for them, but Brother Benjamin was making such great plans for us that he expected us to have our own trustees six months to a year after our gathering. In our part of the country Brother Benjamin thought we would do well to raise pure-bred cattle, to make a good quality of whiskey, to make straw hats for sale, and especially he thought it would be profitable for us to develop a seed industry. Those were his plans for us.

Most of us were hand-minded; that is we had no talent for leadership, but since our leadership came from the East, that was nothing to worry about.

And we did not live together helter-skelter. Each Family had its own house. Those of us who belonged to the Novitiate, the class of formerly married ones not yet ready for full membership, were called the East Family, as I have said. Those in the Junior Order, never having been married, but for one reason or another not yet ready for full membership, were called the North Family. There was then the Black Family, the School Family, and the center and heart of every Shaker village, the Church Family. We early began to call their dwelling Center House.

Save for the School Family, which hadn't the time, each Family had its own portion of land. It raised its own crops, conducted its own affairs, sold and traded its own harvests, kept account of its own earnings, kept its own Journal, had its own Meetings.

It is true that when something important, like buying more land, or building a new structure, or setting up a mill or shop or industry, was decided upon, both labor and money could be called into use. Men would be taken from their regular Family chores and asked to help. Money would be asked from our Family treasuries. None of us minded. Only as the community prospered could we as Families prosper. We had the good of all at heart.

Once a week, on Sunday, the whole community met together for services in the Meetinghouse . . . unless it rained. We were so conscious of the need for thrift, so conscious of the value of property, that even if it were only a misty, damp day, we did not risk soiling the carpets in the Meetinghouse. We met in our Family rooms then.

Sometimes, if a special service had been planned, we met on a week night together. But otherwise we had our own work to do and the other Families had theirs . . . we had our own services, and they had theirs.

Those of us who drew duties outside the house came into more contact with the members of the other Families. For instance, I, at the wash-house, was with women from each of the others. Permilla, likewise, in the dairy was thrown with others. But if your duty was indoors you rarely, for the length of time of your duty, saw anyone save the members of your own Family. We came, thus, from seeing the same faces so constantly, to love the duties which took us outside the house, because we were at least thrown with women whom we did not see all the time. And inevitably we gossiped. The news from one Family was passed on to others, and we knew, generally, what was happening in the entire village.

Some of the gossip was just the irritable carping which came from knowing too well every habit of the women who slept in your room with you, or ate at your unit at table. I remember Permilla saying of Amanda, "She dresses the same way every morning! Every blessed morning, she puts on her shoes and stockings first. If she'd just once put on her dress first, it'd be a relief, but it'd shock me so I don't know as I could stand it."

And I remember my own irritation with the way poor old Viney Parks constantly cleared her throat. And all of us hated to hear Lacey Akins' heavy snores. Sister Priscilla's way of letting her spectacles slide down nearly to the end of her nose before pushing them back was a thing which grated on us, too. "I'm jist livin'," Permilla said, "fer the day they slide plumb off." Oh, yes . . . perfectibility is a very hard thing to achieve in the flesh.

There were also those who kept watch for every least rule broken, ran quickly to report it. Most of us did not do this. Instinctively we held together, but in any group so gathered there are some who find virtue in talebearing. Sister Susan was understanding of this and she often chided the tattler. But Sister Priscilla pounced on each sinner as if she relished the discovery of sin.

We learned early whom to watch . . . but in our own group in the bedroom we thought we were safe from tattling. We learned different there, too.

My Journal tells me that it was in December and I had the dairy duty. Cassie came to me one afternoon, troubled in heart. "Hit's Jency, Miss Becky. She ain't doin' right, I'se afeared. She makin' eyes at that big feller of Mister Steel's . . . that yaller boy, Clayton. You best go see her. Hit don't do no good fer me to talk to her."

Annie Jewett was on duty with me from our house. I told her I was going to run down to the Nursery and see Jency a moment. She nodded and I knew she would keep an eye on my cheese tub. "I won't be long," I told her.

Of course I was supposed to take the matter to Sister Priscilla or Sister Susan, but I hated to get Jency into trouble. Besides, I didn't think they would get anywhere talking to her, and, too, I still felt responsible for her.

Jency met me with giggles and a gladness which touched me. "Miss Becky! I ain't seed you hardly atall since we come here. I'se so glad you come."

"I can't stay," I told her. "How are you, Jency?"

"Jist fine," she said, rolling her eyes and giggling again. "I'se jist fine."

"Do you like it here in the Nursery?"

"Oh, yessum . . . I likes younguns, you knows that. I jist purely loves 'em."

It was the truth. She did love them, all sizes and ages, and her one virtue was that she could be depended on never to neglect them. Any child put in her care could be certain of receiving love and attention. Maybe it was a special gift given to her to offset her fickleness and flightiness in everything else. But whatever it was, she had a way with them and they always loved her in return.

I went straight to the point then. "What's this Cassie tells me about you making eyes at Clayton?"

"I ain't makin' no eyes at him."

"Cassie says you are."

Jency sniffed. "Oh, Mammy, she 'fraid of ever'body. She 'fraid fer me to stir outen the house of a night."

"You aren't supposed to stir out of the house at night, except to go to Meeting. You're supposed to stay right here with the children."

"I does. I ain't never leave these babies less'n hit's my turn to go to Meetin'."

"Do you go to Meeting?" The Blacks had their own meetings, just as the rest of us did.

"Yessum," she said, "I ain't ever missed. I likes Meetin'. All that dancin' an' singin' . . . hit's a heap of fun."

"It isn't supposed to be fun. You're supposed to be worshiping as you sing and dance."

"Oh, I does. I praises the Lord an' Mother Ann an' I shouts loud. I shouts louder'n any of 'em, Miss Becky. But it's fun, too, ain't it?"

It was not until years had passed that I realized the Shaker ecstasies in Meeting were indeed a great pleasure . . . that in some ways, indeed, they were very kin to the ecstasies of marriage and took the place of them. But at the moment I frowned at Jency and sternly reminded her again, "No, it's not fun. It's a labor to get good . . . to dance in the joy of the Lord . . . to shake out the evil."

[96]

"I shakes it out! I is a good shaker, Miss Becky."

I didn't doubt it. Knowing her lightness on foot, her dancing ways, I could guess that she would move through the exercises with grace and energy. "Is Clayton making eyes at you?" I asked her, then.

She giggled. "I reckon."

"Jency," I said very firmly, "if you want to marry Clayton you can . . . you are free and so is he. But if you get married you'll have to leave the village."

"Oh, we ain't studyin' on gittin' married."

"Then you'd better stay away from him. When do you see him, anyhow?"

She gave me a sly look. "I ain't seein' him, 'cept 'round an' about."

You couldn't get any closer to the truth than that. No matter how well you know a black, you *never* know them very well . . . but one thing you can be certain of. When they get that closed, set look on their faces, you'd just as well give up. It's a sign they put up, saying this far and no farther can you, a white-skinned person, come. There was nothing for me to do but rely on my old way of giving orders. "Jency, you be a good girl now. I don't want to hear any more of this nonsense about you. You leave Clayton alone."

"I'se bein' good," she protested.

"Well, see that you keep on. There'll be trouble if you get mixed up with Clayton."

Her eyes widened. "Whut kind of trouble?"

How could I tell her? I had never talked to her about the things between men and women, about being got pregnant, having children out of wedlock. I hoped Cassie had. Perhaps I should have, then and there, but it came hard to me to talk about such things with anyone, much less a black girl. So I took refuge in vagueness. "Trouble," I said, "that would make it go hard with you."

One of the babies in the next room cried just then and she went to see it. She came back with Annie's little boy on her hip. "Ain't he sweet?" she said, pushing his hair back from his forehead, laying her face against it. "He been asleep. Jisi woken up. He hungry, now. Miss Annie better come tend him purty soon."

I took the child and held him for a moment, felt his softness and fatness. The old hunger for one of my own was never far below the surface. Then I handed him back to Jency. "I've got to go. Now, you mind, Jency. Don't go gettin' into any foolishness."

"Yessum. You tell Miss Annie, do you see her, little Robert is woken up."

When I got back to the dairy I gave Annie Jency's message and she left immediately to go to him.

It was after supper that night, when we were in our rooms resting before Meeting, that Sister Priscilla came to the door. She did not come in. She stopped and stood in the doorway. "Sister Rebecca, will you come with me, please?"

When Sister Priscilla summoned you, it always meant trouble of some kind. "I suppose," I told Permilla, "she saw me slip down to the Nursery this afternoon."

Permilla laughed. "She's got eyes in the back of her head, old Prissy has. I don't know how she finds out so much."

A sort of closet at one end of the hall had been enlarged to make a small room where either Sister Susan or Sister Priscilla could see one of us privately. Sister Priscilla was already seated before the table which served them both as a desk. She looked at me sternly when I went in. "Your cap is awry."

I had been lying down and I hadn't thought to set my cap straight. I put it right under her watchful eye. "You are in the way," she said, "of letting your hair escape at the back. That is a show of vanity, Sister Rebecca. Do you take pride in those curls on your neck?"

This was so unjust that I felt my face warming, but there was never any use arguing with Sister Priscilla. Unbendingly she never saw anything but what she wished to see, nor ever listened to any verdict but her own judgments. My hair was heavy, black, curly, like my mother's. To get it all under the little white net caps we had to wear was an effort at best, and during a day's work some of the short curls in the back would slip their place in spite of me. I tried to watch it, but unless I kept it constantly in mind there were times when doubtless I did look unkempt. I tucked the curls up under my cap.

Sister Susan always asked you to sit down in her presence, but Prissy kept you standing. Power in the hands of some natures takes the form of petty tyranny. "It has been reported," she began then, "that you left the dairy this afternoon."

For others I would lie . . . for myself, never. "Yes, ma'am, I did. Cassie was bothered about Jency and I went down to the Nursery to talk to her a minute."

"You were gone exactly thirty minutes. What did you have to say to Jency that took so long?"

I had no intention of telling her the truth, so I said the first thing that came into my mind. "Oh, Jency had been sassy to Cassie and I had to scold her."

"You should have come to me or to Sister Susan," she said, when I had finished.

"I felt I could do more with her than either of you, Sister Priscilla," I said, and I tried to say it kindly.

"It was none of your business! It was entirely the affair of the leaders of this Family. When," she broke out suddenly and heatedly, "are you going to learn to leave these black people alone? When are you going to learn they no longer belong to you? That you can't influence and order them about?"

I kept my silence.

Prissy rubbed her thin hands together and they rustled like dried paper. "Did you go to the small barn, Sister Rebecca?"

"The small barn?" I said, wonderingly. "No, ma'am. Why would I go to the small barn?"

"I'm asking the questions," she snapped at me. Then she added, dryly, "Brother Richard's duty is with the calves in the small barn this month."

The implication was very plain. The calves were kept in the small barn, which was very near the Nursery. But I had not known Richard's duty, and even if I had known he was there I would not have sought him out. Not because I was too strong to, but because he was, and it would have done no good. "I did not know that," I said honestly. "Has it been reported that I went to the barn?"

"It does not matter what has been reported. I asked you if you went to the small barn."

"And I have told you that I did not. I have no proof of this and you will either have to believe it or not as you see fit—but I did *not* go to the barn!"

Sister Priscilla's eyes blazed up. "I think you must be made to suffer humiliation for this, Sister Rebecca. Your proud and arrogant spirit must be lowered before us all."

"Perhaps," I said, "but humiliation or no, I did not go to the barn. And there is another thing, Sister Priscilla. If you do not put Jency to work by Cassie's side, you will regret it."

"I am the judge of where people shall work, Sister Rebecca," she said, shortly, "and I do not think I shall regret any decision I make. When I want your advice I will ask for it. You may go now."

I was glad to go. The insinuation she had made had boiled inside of me, and I was positive she did not believe me. If, indeed, I must suffer humiliation, I could. It meant being accused of pride and arrogance before the Family Meeting, perhaps even in full Meeting, and it meant that all the members would cry "Woe, woe," at me and that I should be humbled before them. It was not an idea I relished, but at that moment I would have suffered it and more rather than sit quietly and listen to Prissy's sly insinuations.

I told Permilla about it that night after everyone was asleep. I was still angry and upset. "They's somebody tellin'," Permilla said. "She's a cute one, Prissy is, but she cain't see ever'thing she knows."

"Maybe she went to the dairy while I was gone."

"No. She couldn't of. She was in the spinnin' room where I was at. They's somebody tellin'. Who was on the duty with you?"

I named the women.

"Was Annie the only one from our Family?"

"Yes."

We were both silent, the same idea having struck us. "It wouldn't be Annie, would it, Permilla? We've all protected her too much."

"Sh-sh-sh . . . I'm a thinkin'."

After a time she spoke again. "You recollect when I slipped off an' spoke a minnit to Thomas? When Aaron was down with the catarrh in his head an' I wished fer Thomas to see him? I knowed Prissy wouldn't let me off to go, but I figured Richard'd let Thomas off a little spell. Prissy knowed about it 'fore nighttime." She laughed. "She acted like we'd gone up to the hayloft an' tumbled there." Then she sobered. "Annie was on the washhouse duty with me then."

It began to fit together . . . the other times we could think of when one of us had been reported. The time Amanda slipped down to see her children at the Schoolhouse . . . the time Lacey had drunk too much fresh wine and she'd dozed and slept through an afternoon while the others did her work for her. Annie had been present every time. "Hit's her, all right," Permilla said, "couldn't be nobody else. Hit all fits together too good."

"But why? Why would she tell? What is she expecting to gain?"

Permilla was quiet for a time, thinking. Then she said, "Hit appears to me she is gittin' on the good side of Prissy so's she kin git by with somethin' of her own."

We had all seen her brushing close to Robert in the dance and exercises. We had all felt pity for her and kept it to ourselves. But what else was in her mind? Suddenly I remembered she had to go to the Nursery several times a day. The small barn was very near, and on the way to the Nursery. I sat bolt upright in the bed. "Permilla, I'll bound you Robert's on the duty in the small barn with Richard. She's slipping to see him."

"Why, shore! Hit stands to reason. Whyn't we think of it before?"

But there was a further puzzle. Where was Richard when Annie met Robert in the barn? "Why, my sakes, Becky . . . he's likely off to the pasture with the calves, saltin' 'em, or movin' 'em from one place to another. They could easy rig up a signal that'd let Annie know if Richard was there or not." ·

"What'll we do?"

"Keep a eye on her. You're in the dairy with her. Make some excuse fer workin' next the door when she goes to the Nursery. See if they's e'er thing hangin' from the barn door, or winder. Likely it'll be somethin' like Robert's jacket or his kerchief. Jist keep a eye on her."

I did. But for a few days Annie went straight to the Nursery. Then one afternoon, when I had seen Richard herd a bunch of calves out of the door and off to the hill pasture, a rake used for heaping up the straw in their stalls was set against the door. Robert came out of the barn with the rake in his hand, stood watching Richard for a moment, then, as if it were the most natural thing in the world, he put the rake down, leaning it against the open door. I kept busy, but I watched Annie then. She was working at the far end of the dairy room, washing crocks and tubs. She heaved a big sigh when the last of them was done and wiped her hands on some sacking which hung close by. "Whew!" she said, "I got to get a breath of air."

I remembered, then, how often, every day, she went to stand in the door for a breath of air . . . and it December. She wandered slowly to the door, stopping along the way to peer into the vats, as if watching them. She opened the door, stood there a moment, then laughing, she pressed her bosom. "It's time for that youngun of mine to eat. I'm running over and spilling down my dress front. I'll not be gone long, if Prissy should happen in." Like the rest of us, she called her Prissy.

I made as if to get some fresh straining cloths from the press, which stood by the window, so I could watch. But Annie did not make the mistake of going straight to the barn. She went down the path to the Nursery. There was a stand of hazel bushes on one side, after she'd passed the barn, and I saw suddenly how easily she could slip through the hazel bushes to the back door of the barn. It may have been that she had done it every day I had watched. Neither had I thought of the rake as a signal. It may have been there each day I had watched, too. They had an almost perfect plan.

I went on with my share of the work. When Annie came back she was flushed, happy looking, as a woman is who has received love. Gaily she said, "That youngun of mine is sure growing." She laughed. "Tugs like a man."

The other sisters looked shocked, never having been married. I remember that Sister Sarah, a little wisp of a spinster from Center House, flushed to the roots of her hair. She became very busy of a sudden with pouring up some clabbered milk. And her hands shook as she poured, so that the milk spilled onto the floor. Annie peered at her and then said, cruelly, "What's the matter, Sister Sarah? Ain't no man ever tugged at yours, have they?"

Sister Sarah broke into tears. "How can you say such things? It isn't decent!"

Annie shrugged. "There's a lot that's not decent to folks like you."

She shook out her skirts. There was a wisp of hay clinging to the hem in the back. Silently I bent over and picked it off. "I'd leave off teasing Sister Sarah, if I were you, Annie," I said, holding the wisp of hay where she could see it. "Those hazel bushes must be awfully dry, to catch on your skirt the way they've done."

Her face whitened and her eyes widened. She put her hand over her mouth . . . then she brazened it out. "They are. They'd burn if there was the least blaze got to 'em."

Permilla and I talked again that night. We whispered because we knew

Annie wasn't sound asleep. Finally she sat up in bed. "If you all are whispering about me, you'd best come plain out with what you're saying."

"All right," I said, "come over here to my bed and we'll come plain out with it."

She came.

"Now, we know," Permilla told her, "what you've been up to. We ain't keerin' nothin' about it, except that if you don't want it to get to Prissy, you'd best keep yer mouth shut about what few things the rest of us does. We ain't none of us, leastways, doin' what you're doin'."

"I ain't told nothin'," Annie said, sullenly.

"Oh, yes, you have. Ever' time one of us gits reported, you've been around to see. Prissy, fer all she's sharp-eyed, cain't see ever' least thing. She's bein' told . . . an' you're the one doin' the tellin'. You are a low-down, sneakin' snake, Annie Jewett. They's things ever' woman in this room has seed with her own eyes, an' could of told long ago, but we never. We stood by you. Fer you to turn on us is about as Judasy a thing as I ever heared tell of. What made you?"

Annie began to cry. "I couldn't stand not seein' Robert all this time. I *had* to see him. I figured if I told on the rest, Prissy wouldn't ever guess anything about me. She'd think I was too good to."

Permilla sniffed. "You ain't got no more guts than a white-livered rat. Tellin' on folks that've stood by you."

Annie sobbed. "I just can't stand this being separated. And I *hate* living amongst all these women. I hate you, and Becky, and Amanda, and all the rest of you! I don't care how much trouble you get into!"

"You better keer . . . fer we c'n shore git you into a heap. You better commence keerin' a right smart, right now!"

Annie wiped her eyes and looked around the room. "Look at it! Look at the plainness and bareness! Not one thing pretty to lay your eyes on in the whole place. Look at those dresses hanging on their pegs! Look how ugly they are! I don't see how they could have thought up an uglier way to make women's clothes. I hate 'em! I hate 'em all!"

We had our new clothing by then, and I suppose they did appear very plain and drab to one who loved pretty, bright things. The sisters in the Church Family had decided that since time was short there would be only a few colors made up. They said it would take too long to make up dyes for more. There had been offered to us only blue, brown, and a red so dark it was almost black. I had picked a blue and a brown. Permilla had done likewise, and so had most of the other sisters. But Annie had chosen red for both her dresses.

The style of a Shaker woman's dress was simple and plain. There was a bodice, and a full skirt pleated onto the waistband. The skirts reached to the ground, of course. And because Shakers held the sight of a woman's bosom indecent, even in outline, we all wore white kerchiefs around our necks, brought forward and crossed over our breasts. I have thought more than once that they chose a very poor way for hiding the natural fullness of many women, for the white kerchiefs in some cases only added to the roundness and the richness of their figures. Permilla, for instance, could never be hidden by a kerchief, and I had some trouble myself.

The tears brimmed over again in Annie's eyes. "Well," I said, "it's just a waste of energy to hate it. You're here and as long as Robert stays, here you'll be. Seems to me you'd do better to get used to it."

"If I have my way," she said hotly, "both of us will be leaving here sooner than you'd think."

"Oh," Permilla said, "so that's yer game. Tryin' to persuade Robert to leave. Gittin' him to tumble you in the hay so's to git his lust up, in the hopes he'll get dissatisfied an' leave. I wouldn't put it past you to git in the family way on purpose, so's he'd have to take you off."

"I wish I could! I wish it was time to wean little Robert, so's my health would come back on me!"

"Oh, I ain't to say blamin' you none," Permilla said, laughing. "If Robert was mine I doubtless would do the same. But you'd have a hard time convincin' Prissy or Sister Susan, or Sister Molly over at Center House, you hadn't sinned jist the same."

"I ain't aimin' to try."

"I c'n see that."

"You won't tell, will you?" Annie asked this anxiously.

"Hit's what we ort to do, seein' as you've tattled on all the rest of us."

"I'll stop it. I'll not tell another thing."

"You'll take a vow to that?"

Annie raised her right hand. "I'll take a vow. Not another word will I tell."

"Prissy'll think it goes quare . . . you bein' so good to run to her."

"Let her think. If you'll not tell, I can make out."

"What do you say, Becky?"

It had never been in my mind to tell, but I thought Permilla had made enough use of the threat. For my part, I didn't care what Annie and Robert did. I only envied her the possibility of swaying Robert to go her way. "I'll not tell," I said, "*unless* something else is told on one of us."

"There'll not be," Annie said, "not from me. I've given you my promise."

I didn't think her promise was worth much, but I did think that the fear of being caught out with Robert and his being sent to the sugar camp or the new sawmill might stop her.

Permilla lay down and pulled the covers up. "Well, git on to bed, now. Prissy'll be stickin' her nose in the door in a minnit, or one of the others'll be wakin' up. Jist mind what we've said, now."

"I will."

A little forlornly Annie made her way back to her own bed. She'd been a tattletale and I thought it a thing to be despised in her. But I felt sorry for her. In her place, with a man not so strong in his conviction, I don't know but what I would have done what she was doing. Not the tattling . . . I would never have done that. But if Richard had signaled me from the barn I'd have gone so fast that my feet would have seemed to have wings.

The tears I shed when it was quiet in the room again were because there would never be a signal for me. In no way could I convince myself that there would be. Following in a man's pathway can lead you to a terribly lonely place, and I was there that night, and for many days and nights thereafter. That loneliness accounts for the spots on the pages of my Journal.

CHAPTER XII

I DO NOT KNOW what first awakened me, but out of deep sleep I was suddenly and immediately roused. I lay there, feeling uneasy, listening, not knowing what I had heard or what had roused me. The room was quiet, save for the breathing of the other women, and it was entirely dark, a patch of grayness showing at the windows only a little less dark than the room itself. But something, some feeling, some noise, some movement, had brought me awake.

Then I heard it again . . . a faint, small chattering of the windows in their frames. The wind, I thought—it's blowing up to rain. I slipped out of bed and went to the windows, looked out. The night was clear and cold, moonless, with a sky full of stars. The winter-stripped trees were as still as death, no wind stirring their bony limbs. But there is no sound like windows fretted in their fittings. I could not have been mistaken.

I laid my hand against a pane of glass. It was cold and still under my palm. But even as I held my hand against it, a tremor ran through it, the glass shook, the frame quivered, and there was that scrabbling sound, like a rat scratching behind the walls.

Then the floor beneath my bare feet trembled. The house, I thought frantically—the house is shaking all over! Frightened, I whirled around, and as I ran toward my bed the whole floor tilted so that I had a feeling of running downhill. The beds, on their rollers, began to slide toward that end of the room and I heard a thud as someone fell to the floor. It was Viney Parks, because she cried out at once, "Oh, my Lord! I've fell out of bed! Come help me, somebody. I've fell onto the floor!" And then her voice was smothered as if covers had been thrown over her head.

I don't recall ever in my life feeling so bewildered and confused. When the very floor under your feet starts shivering and tilting, when beds start rolling about, when windows clatter and there is no wind, it's as if spirits are walking the earth with giant treads, making a palsy in their wake. It's uncanny and ghostly, otherworldly and terrifying. Richard, I thought . . . I must find Richard quickly. The thought was instinctive. In danger, Richard had always been beside me. I started to the door.

Everyone was awake now and there was a hubbub and babel of voices. I heard footsteps running in the hall. "What's happening?" someone said, and "What's made the beds commence rollin'?" And then there was Viney's plaintive, smothered voice, "Somethin' has fell on me! I'm dyin'! Git this bed offen me . . . help, somebody, help!"

A semblance of reason returned to me as my hand reached the door knob. A light, I thought . . . I must make a light and help Viney.

The tremor passed and the house stood still again. I called out, "Everyone stay where you are. I'll find a candle and make a light."

I fumbled for the candle, found it, flew to the hall with it, thinking the quickest way to get a light would be from the coals in the fireplace downstairs. But Richard was in the hall, a lighted candle in his hand, dressed already, and to my frightened senses wonderfully calm and steady looking. In my terror I fled to him, and he held me tightly. "Are you all right?" he asked, struggling to hold his candle and to hold me, too. "Becky? Are you all right?"

Ah, the comfort of his arms about me again. In my relief I wept, shaking as if taken with an ague, and leaned my head against his chest, hearing the beat of his heart under my ear. I managed to say, between sobs, "I'm all right." I wished never to part from the strength of him and the sure, solid flesh which was once more warm against me. But almost immediately he remembered, and put me from him.

I swayed toward him, wanting to be held again, but he ran his eyes over me disapprovingly, "You're in your shift, Becky."

"I know. I was going for a light."

All about us there was noise and confusion, from the men's rooms, from the women's other bedrooms. "Here," he said, holding out his flame, "be quick and get back inside your room."

My hand was shaking so that I could hardly hold the wick to the flame. "What is it?" I whispered. "What's happening?"

"I don't know. No one knows."

"But what can it be?"

Impatiently he said, "I told you, nobody knows. Make haste with your light, now . . . and get back in your room. Put your clothes on. Get the other women dressed. Whatever it is, we must face it decently. Someone will come and tell you what to do."

But he *had* thought of me. He *had* been quick to ask if I had come to harm. That was something, I told myself, as I ran back to the room, fiercely glad for it. He still had a feeling for me. And though his eyes had disapproved my shift, they had also, surely, been remembering. There is no way memories can be wholly erased. For years he had known the body under that shift. He had put it away . . . but he *had* known it. Even redeemed saints must sometimes, and perhaps with secret pleasure, turn over their memories.

The bedroom was in wild disorder. All the beds had rolled into a mass. For easy cleaning in the rooms, our beds had been fitted with rollers which moved so smoothly that a child could have pushed them with one hand. Now they had rolled with the tilting floor, shoved up solid against the walls, most of them straight, but one or two awry and tilted. Viney's bed had turned on its side, as I had feared.

Permilla was standing in the middle of the room, Annie clutching her, white-faced and weeping. Amanda Steel was standing at the window. There was a shapeless hump in Lacey's bed, as if all the covers had been piled there, but it was alternately moaning and praying. I set the candle in its holder. "Amanda," I cried, "come see if Lacey is hurt! Permilla, help me find Viney."

Amanda turned swiftly from the window. "I'm not caring if Lacey is hurt or not. I'm going to see about my boy." She brushed past us and was out the door even as she spoke.

I grabbed Annie by the shoulders and shook her. "Hush up! Get into your clothes. Get dressed, right now!"

"It's a judgment," she moaned, shrinking away from my hand. "It's a judgment on Robert and me for sinning. It's the end of the world come."

"The Lord isn't going to end the world because you and Robert have sinned," I snapped at her. "Permilla, see if you can find Viney under those beds."

I snatched at the covers over Lacey and threw them back, quilt after quilt. She was on her knees, fat and huddled, her head sunk between her shoulders. "Have we done been kilt?" she said, blinking in the light. "Have we went to heaven?"

"Not yet," I said, and as frightened as I was I could not keep from laughing. "But if you'd stayed under those quilts much longer you'd have been there yourself pretty soon. Get your clothes on."

Permilla, who could never waken suddenly, was slow in her movements, still drowsy and unfrightened. I ran to help her as she struggled with Viney's bed.

As I ran toward her, Annie cried out, "Oh, my Lord! Look at those dresses on the wall!"

I glanced her way quickly. The dresses were swaying, as if a wind had blown through them, and then the floor began to tilt, this time in the other direction. The beds started to roll again. Permilla and I were caught between them and Viney's overturned bed and we braced ourselves to hold them back. Permilla leaned against Viney's bed, which did not slide, and slowly it righted itself under her hands. Viney was there, flat on the floor, protected by the covers and her pillow. Permilla and I peered at her, unable as yet to help her. Permilla said, turning to me, "I'd like it if somebody would tell me what's goin' on here. The house a quakin' and shakin', an' beds rollin' all over the place. Has the Shakers got even the dwellin's to shakin' out evil now?"

Quaking! Why hadn't I thought of it? I had heard of earthquakes in other parts of the world, but none had ever been known in Kentucky. This could only be an earthquake, though, making the house groan and tilt and shake so. And all my fear returned full force. The house could tumble around our heads and fall. The earth itself could split open and swallow us up. "It's an earthquake, Permilla!" I cried.

"Earthquake! Fer goodness' sake, what is a earthquake?"

"The earth shaking and trembling itself!"

Her eyes widened. "I never heared of sich."

"Well, you're in the middle of one now. Hold back hard on these beds till we can get Viney up from here."

We could hear people running in the halls, talking, and I knew the confusion in the rest of the house was as great as in our room. "Richard said for us all to get dressed and someone would come and tell us what to do."

Permilla chuckled. "Now, that's real thoughty of him. Reckon the house'll hold till they git around to tellin' us?"

That was exactly what I was afraid of, but I only shook my head. The tremor slowly passed, and we shoved the beds back. Viney lay as if she had been killed and I thought perhaps the side of the bed had hurt her badly. Permilla and I bent over her. "Viney," I called to her, "Viney . . . are you bad hurt?"

Her eyes opened. "I think my brains is busted out."

Quickly I ran my hand over her head. It was dark between the beds and I could not see her plainly, but when I held my hand to the light there was no blood. "You're not bleeding," I told her. "Here, let us help you up."

She was little and light and we lifted her without trouble. We laid her on the bed. She groaned, and then suddenly she sat straight up, pointing a finger at us. "Some joker," she said, angrily, "turned my bed over, an' me in it! Hit warn't no idee of a joke, to my mind, neither!"

Permilla threw her head back and laughed. "Now, which 'un of us you reckon it was, Viney?"

"Oh, Permilla," I said, "this is no time for jokes. Viney, if you're able, get up. It's an earthquake. Richard said for us to get dressed."

Like Permilla, Viney widened her eyes, and then as spry as a young lamb she scrambled off the bed and ran to the peg which held her clothing.

Permilla and I hurried to get into our own dresses. The door opened and Sister Susan stood there, looking very small and frail, but fully dressed, even to her cap. "Sisters," she said, her voice a little quavery, "Brother Benjamin has sent word that we are all to move downstairs. We are having an earthquake, and it will be safer on the lower floor."

"Hit'd be safer," Permilla said, dryly, "if we'd git plumb outen the house, seems to me."

Sister Susan shook her head. "Brother Benjamin says it would not be. A crack might open in the earth."

"What's to keep a crack from openin' an' swallerin' up the whole house?" Permilla wanted to know.

"We shall pray. Put out your light and go to the spinning room as soon as you are dressed."

"Humph," Permilla sniffed, "we'd best do more'n pray."

Sister Susan left and as we finished dressing, some of us faster than others, one by one we went downstairs. "I'll put the candle out," I told Permilla, when she and I were left alone. "You go ahead."

She went out the door. Something in me needing a moment alone kept me longer than I meant. I did not consciously pray, but I remember standing quietly in the now still room, wondering if we were all to meet our deaths among falling logs or splitting earth. I was afraid, but for some reason, since the second tremor, I was less afraid than I had been. This was a stout old log house. Unless the earth opened beneath it, perhaps it would stand.

It may have been one minute, it may have been five that I stood there, before I sniffed out the candle and groped my way across the dark room, into the dark hall, and down the dark stairs. I remember wondering why there was no light on the lower floor, not even a glow from the fireplace. It was as dark as our own bedroom and the halls. Someone brushed past me as I fumbled along, making my way to the big spinning room, someone in a hurry and breathing fast.

In the door of the spinning room I could see against the windows that people were clustered, and someone was praying . . . one of the men . . . Brother Samuel. They must all be kneeling by their chairs, I thought, and feeling for an empty one, I went to my own knees, but I could not think of what Brother Samuel was saying. I kept waiting for the tremor of the house to start again . . . kept thinking of those stout log walls, of how they would be strained and twisted, and might, perhaps, come crashing down around us.

When Brother Samuel had finished his prayer, another voice took it up, then another and another. Finally Sister Susan's slight voice, quivery, broken, took up the prayer. I wondered if we were to spend the rest of the night in praying. I wondered where Richard was . . . wished I was near him. If we're going to die, I thought, I'd like to die with my hand in his.

My eyes were closed, but against them there suddenly shown a light. Sister Susan's voice stopped, and she gasped. I opened my eyes. In the doorway, holding a candle aloft, stood Sister Priscilla. Her hair was disordered and she wore no cap. Her free hand fumbled with the loose strands of hair. "I cannot find my caps," she said, distractedly, "my caps are gone. Both of them are missing!"

I had never seen her without her cap before and I saw now that her hair was thin, almost balding in front. In great distress she kept pulling her back hair over the high, domed forehead. "My caps are gone," she said again, whimpering. "I can't find my caps!"

Every eye in the room was turned on her, every face showing astonishment. She must have entirely forgotten that the men would be gathered in the spinning room, too. She stood there in the doorway, clearly lighted by the candle in her hand, her face distraught and worried, looking oddly naked, almost shaven, without the fringe of hair which always bulged under her cap. I remember thinking that she must puff it toward the front when she put her cap on, since she was so nearly bald in front. Her hand kept worrying the shining, balding forehead. She was as nearly undone as I have ever seen any person, distracted, unthinking of her appearance.

Someone giggled . . . Permilla, of course. And then Sister Susan rose from her knees, slipped the kerchief off her neck and went to Prissy, tied it with her own hands about her head, patted it into place kindly, murmured to her and led her into the room to a chair. She took the candle from Sister Priscilla's hand. "Brother Benjamin said to have no fire of any kind . . . for fear of setting the house." She snuffed it out.

There was a rustle in the dark as people rose from their knees and settled into their chairs. Then in her sweet, quavering old voice Sister Susan started a song . . . Father James' song, "In yonder valley there grows sweet union . . ." and a kind of peace flowed over us all as we joined in and lifted up our voices. We sang on and on.

We sang and prayed the rest of the night. My Journal says that the first quake was felt a little after one o'clock in the morning. Brother Benjamin, who came from a family of clockmakers in Massachusetts, and whose love of clocks showed itself in the beautiful hall clock in Center House, had verified the time. There were several other quakes before the night was over, but none so severe as the first two. Each time there was a warning tremor, the chatter of the windows, and each time my stomach knotted and tightened, dreading the straining and groaning of the house, the tilting of the floors, but they did not follow. The tremors were slight and quickly over.

Someone in the Church Family rang the rising bell as usual, at five o'clock since the days of winter had set in, and as we stirred to go back to our rooms, a voice spoke from the doorway, in the dark. "I am Stephen Burke," it said. "I have come to tell you that the children in the School Family are safe . . . that they are undisturbed and have been quiet and unafraid during the night."

We could not see him, but we knew that he stood slender in the door, tall and unweighted with flesh, quiet, deep-voiced, gentle and kind. He was the head of the school, a young man not more than thirty years, not married, of great learning, of great love for children and great patience with them. He, too, had been sent to us from the East, to set in order the teaching of the children.

A sound, as of a small wind sighing down the chimney, whispered around the room . . . fathers and mothers breathing relief, and I remembered Amanda, wondered where she was. Brother Samuel lifted up his voice again in praise and thanksgiving for watchful care through the night. When he had finished we heard Stephen Burke's footsteps down the hall, and the door closing behind him.

There were those, long afterwards, remembering the first night of the earthquakes, who said they felt no cold during the long hours without a fire. They said they had felt too uplifted by the season of song and prayer to feel the cold. They said, instead, they had felt warmed as if a blazing fire had burned the entire time. None in our room said so. I myself had felt bitterly cold toward morning. Permilla said she had felt as if her bones had frozen to the marrow. Annie claimed her hands and feet had gone numb, and poor old Viney Parks had shivered until her teeth clacked in her head.

But we ever had a room Sister Priscilla called discontented and troublesome. It may be. And it may be we should have been separated. Had we been parted, perhaps, had we been thrown with others more dedicated, some of the things which happened to us all might have been averted. I do not know. It may just as well be that what happened would have occurred anyhow. Before all else we were wives and some of us were mothers. We were only hand-minded Shakers.

The order of the day was only slightly disturbed. We were told we could light a candle now, and back in our rooms, with light, we set our beds to rights, laid back the covers, put things straight. Amanda was among us, but no one asked her when she had returned. We asked, instead, if the children had been badly scared. "No," she said, "Brother Stephen had clustered them all about him in the main room, and he told them about earthquakes, how something inside of the earth rumbled and trembled, but mostly nothing very bad happened. He told it so good they were all ears, and as far as I could see, not one of them was the least bit scared."

"Was mine behavin' theirselves?" Permilla asked.

Amanda nodded. "Brother Stephen had your girl on his knees, and the last I saw of her, she had her thumb in her mouth, as contented as if he'd been her own mother."

Permilla laughed. "I reckon she'll suck that thumb till the day she's growed. I couldn't never break her of it. He's a good man," she added, "a awful good man, Brother Stephen."

"He must be," I said.

We turned to the task of tidying the room. Dresses had fallen from their pegs, bonnets and caps were lying about, chairs had been tipped over, and there was general confusion which we had to set to rights. Turning a chair up, Permilla began to chuckle, then she threw her head back and laughed until she shook. "What's funny?" Annie Jewett asked.

"Prissy," Permilla said, "did you ever seen anything funnier'n her bald head in the light of that candle?"

It made us all laugh, remembering, until I, wondering, said, "What could have happened to her caps?"

Permilla's eyes glinted with the tears of her laughter. "Well," she said, "if their room was in as big a mess as our'n, they're likely mixed up with the covers some place."

I had my first suspicion of what had happened, then. Permilla had said that too offhandedly, and while the caps would have fallen to the floor, perhaps, they couldn't have got mixed up with the covers on the beds. Besides, one, at least, her spare one, should have been in her drawer. I looked at Permilla. She deliberately winked at me, and I knew she had stolen them. I was more than a little aghast at her daring. It was she, of course, who had brushed past me in the dark, hurrying. How she had managed it, I couldn't imagine, but it had been a terrible, awful, complete humiliation of Sister Priscilla, and I was taken with a fit of giggling, remembering. It paid her in the most devastating coin at hand for the little pricks and burrs she had so constantly put in our way. It was wrong, of course . . . deeply wrong, but it was so rich a joke, so wonderfully funny, all I could do was stand helpless with laughter.

As we went downstairs I managed to whisper to Permilla, "How did you know she was bald-headed?"

"I seen her once, with her cap askew. Figgered she kept her back hair pushed up front. Warn't it wonderful?" She giggled noiselessly behind her hand, her shoulders shaking.

"Sh-sh-sh," I warned her. "Where did you put them?"

"I got 'em under my bodice. I aim to bury 'em today. She ain't ever goin' to find them caps."

The mystery of Sister Priscilla's caps was a seven-day wonder. Everyone searched for them. No one could imagine what had happened to them. She knew, finally, of course, when they never came to light, that someone had taken them, but there was no way in the world she could find out who had done it. The house had been too dark and confused. She could only, for days, peer suspiciously at all of us, over her spectacles, and cover her head as best she could with a kerchief until she made new caps.

There was something a little pitiful in her humiliation. Until she wore a cap again her head was not held so proudly. Nor did she walk quite so straightly. Instead she scurried a little, kept to her room, spoke very little, looked harried and distressed.

My conscience bothered me a little, but not very much, and besides I had another worry almost immediately. The blacks had been so terrified when the quakes first began that Brother Benjamin, remembering them tardily and going to reassure them, had found them scattered and many of them fled into the night. Jency was among those still missing when morning came.

Cassie came to me in the dairy, wringing her hands, weeping. "She's gone, Miss Becky. Jency's gone. Cain't nobody find her."

I did my best to comfort her. "Mister Richard will find her," I promised her. "He'll go right away and look for her. She can't be very far away, and he'll find her. Don't cry, Cassie, I promise you Mister Richard will search her out."

She sobbed, her fat face distorted with her grief, the tears making her black cheeks shine, her shoulders hunched and shaking. "She's so flighty, Miss Becky, ain't no tellin' whur she's went. Ain't no tellin' whur she's headed fur. He'll have to git started soon, if he's to look her out."

"He will," I said again. "I'll go right now and find him. How did she get away from you?"

"Miss Becky, how you goin' to hold on to a streak of lightnin'? How you goin' to ketch a flittin' bird? How you goin't to ca'm a quiverin' colt? She there one minnit, shakin', rollin' her eyes, prayin' amongst the rest of us . . . next minnit she gone, an' ever'body else stampedin' out the door behind her. Ever'body flyin' about . . . ever'body skeered to death, 'fraid the world shakin' to pieces . . . ever'body fleein', 'fraid of Gabriel's trump. How I know whur she gone . . . whut she do? I look for her . . . call her . . . seek her ever' place I knows. She jist gone, Miss Becky. She ain't liable to stop till she git back home."

"Where's home, Cassie?"

Cassie's hand flew to her mouth. "Only the Lawd knows whur that chile's home is at. Oh, hit's trouble, Miss Becky, hit's trouble has come upon us."

I hugged her and patted her and tried to calm her. "You go back to the washhouse, now, Cassie, and try to rest easy. We'll not stop until we find her. Stop crying, now . . . and go back to your work."

She had been shifted from the kitchen to the washhouse, and she had been happier out from under Prissy's foot. She went, bowed down, shaking her head, still wiping her eyes with her apron.

I wanted to go immediately to Richard, but I was learning the way that must be taken. Instead I went to Sister Susan, Prissy being for that day hidden in her room, and Sister Susan in charge. I asked for permission to go to Center House and report Jency's flight to Brother Benjamin. I thanked heaven it was Sister Susan in charge. "I will go with you myself," she said immediately.

At Center House, we had, first, to report the matter to Sister Molly Goodrich. She, as foresighted as Sister Susan, sent word for Brother Benjamin to come, and almost at once he was with us. I asked him to relieve Richard of his duty. I told him that only Richard would be able to find

Jency, and that unless she were found soon, she would come to harm in the cold and wet of the winter weather.

He agreed instantly that it was Richard's place to search for her, and promised to see that he was relieved of his duty. Eased of most of my troubled feeling, I went with Sister Susan back to our own house. I had done all I could do, and it was out of my hands now. I asked for permission to tell Cassie that Richard would be starting to look for Jency immediately. With great understanding, Sister Susan allowed it.

That day passed, and in the roundabout way gossip travels, we all knew by afternoon that several of the blacks were still missing. Richard, William Steel, and one other man were not among us at dinner. We knew they were searching.

It came to my ears during the afternoon that Brother Benjamin himself was with them, heading up the search. It also came to my ears that William Steel's yellow boy, Clayton, was among those missing. What ease I had felt, knowing the search was on, left me then, and a sort of frantic fear took hold of me. I worked on in the dairy, turning up cheese vats, molding butter, with my mind flying in all directions, trying to think where Jency could have gone . . . if Clayton was with her . . . where they would have hidden out if they were together.

Suddenly, like a picture held before my eyes, the little hut in the cedar grove on the hill back of our old house came to mind, and as surely as I knew my name, I knew Jency had made her way to the hut which she had loved so much, in which she had played house so often with Permilla's children. "Hit's like a little cave," she had said, "that a body kin hide away in."

I knew it must be I who went, now, to find her. If Clayton was there with her . . . it might be that if Clayton were there with her and it was I who found them, I could in some way protect them, keep them from the censure and anger of the village, from the penances and humiliation sure to follow.

I took off my apron and saying not a word to anyone, slipped out the door. This could not be done the Shaker way. It would have to be done my way, and I would have to take whatever consequences followed.

I hurried past the Nursery, into the woods, avoiding the road that ran through the village. I would be stopped there, if I were seen, and I would certainly be seen. It was shorter through the woods, anyhow. I would come out of them at the back of the old house, on the far side of the cedar grove.

Once into the woods, out of sight, I ran, stumbling on the uneven places, taking a direct course across the hollows and small hills, wading the little creeks which flowed in the bottoms of the ravines. I had a great fear, now, that the men might stumble onto the hut before I got there. I was sorry I had gone to Brother Benjamin, asked that Richard be sent. Richard would be judging and stern with Jency. My greatest wish, now, was to reach her before he did. Nothing would stand in the way of his reporting her in all her folly, if he ran across her and Clayton together, if indeed the whole party did not stumble over them and have full and immediate knowledge.

It was not more than three miles, the way I went, but I was out of breath, torn by the briars, wet, exhausted, when I started the slight climb up the back of the hill. I must go quietly, I remembered. I must not alarm her . . . make her run still farther.

But I need not have bothered. They were asleep, locked in each other's arms, Jency's wiry braids pillowed on Clayton's shoulder, both of them looking very young and very innocent. That they had not been so innocent was plainly evident, however. Even as I stood in the door, shocked in spite of myself, Clayton stirred and his hand strayed over Jency's satiny black thigh which showed from an edge of his shirt.

I stepped back from the door, thinking what to do. Call out, I told myself, but stand where they can see you. I heard a sigh, a long, deep, drawn-out sigh. Their sleep was almost over. Quickly I moved to the door, turned my back their way, and called, "Jency!"

There was the scrabble of movement inside the hut, a small squeak from Jency, and then, from habit I suppose, she answered me, "Yessum?"

"Get dressed quickly. Mister Richard and Mister William are searching for you and Clayton. Hurry. They may come any minute."

I heard them moving, the quick, scurrying movements of haste. "Hurry," I said.

Quicker than I would have thought, Jency was beside me, her eyes wide with fear. "Whut they do, Miss Becky? Whup us?"

I took her by the arm to keep her from flying away. "Clayton," I said, "go back into the woods. Hurry. Get back as fast as you can. Find a hollow tree. Hide in it and stay there until you're found, or until tomorrow. Tell that you ran into the woods, found this hollow tree, hid there, spent all the time there . . . say you slept. Can you remember that?"

He ducked his head. "Yessum. I run into the woods. Found me a holler tree. I been sleepin'."

"Don't you dare to mention Jency's name!"

"No'm."

"You have no idea where Jency went. You didn't know she had run away. You never saw her, or anyone else. You were by yourself."

"Yessum. I wuz by myself."

"No matter who questions you . . . no matter what they ask, you were by yourself . . . in the woods, in a hollow tree."

"Yessum." He grinned. "Mebbe I wuz, too, Miss Becky."

I felt shame that I had seen them, shame at the lies that must be told. I could have taken a whip to him, to both of them. Grimly I set my mouth. "You'd better make sure you don't forget it." I turned to Jency.

"And you, Jency, you came to the hut . . . you were scared, you remembered the lean-to. You thought you would be safe here."

Her eyes rolled until only the whites could be seen. "Yessum . . . an' that's the God's truth. I wuz skeered outen my skin!"

"But you never saw Clayton."

"No'm. I ain't seed Clayton."

It was sickening, telling them the lies they must later tell. I felt poisoned by my own guile. How did it come so easy to me to think of them? I wondered at my own facility. Somewhere, surely my own soul must be tarnished a little. I could have spewed up the food in my stomach. But I could see no other way. "Go on, Clayton," I told him. "We'll wait here until you're in the woods."

Without looking at Jency again he disappeared around the corner of the house. I wondered, then, if their souls were even kin to those in white bodies. Like animals, I thought, mating quickly, in heat, and as quickly done with. It was unjust of me, but I was too angry and disgusted.

I looked at Jency. It was no good talking to her. She knew now, and forever, what I had been too timid to tell her. I shouldn't have been, I thought. I should have spoken plainly. But it was too late, and I could only hope that the seed of their heat would not take root. Bitterly I feared it would. It would be just their fate, I thought. And I wondered if Jency had any idea what might happen to her. Would she know? Would she, in the far, dim recesses of her mind, know even the first symptoms? I had to warn her. "If your health misses next time, tell me," I said.

She slanted a quick glance at me. She knew, then. For some reason I felt reassured. She wasn't quite as ignorant as I had feared . . . nor quite as innocent. "You hear me, now, Jency. Don't go tryin' to lie about it if you miss your time. It won't do any good."

She shook her head so hard her braids flew out. "No'm. I ain't goin' to lie. I tell . . . but not Mammy. She kill me."

"If it happens, she'll know . . . and everyone else will know, in time. That's one thing you can't hide. But if you tell me first, maybe something can be managed."

She giggled. "Yessum. But it ain't happen, yit."

"Oh, it probably will, you little fool!" I took her shoulders and in my anger and frustration, shook her until her teeth chattered. "What got into you, anyhow? There's not but one end to such things, and you've got sense enough to know it. I *know* you've got that much sense!"

When I turned her loose she looked at me without resentment, her face beaming, a grin widening to her ears. "Yessum," she whispered. "But hit's like all the singin' an' the dancin' an' the shakin' all put together . . . hit's a pure liftin' outen yerself, ain't it? Why is it bad?"

I could have died right there, I felt so suddenly sick with my own longing, with my own envy, with my own pitiless renunciation. And I could have killed Jency for reminding me. I grabbed her arm. "Come on. We'll go by the road. You've caused enough trouble for one day."

For two weeks there were occasional earth tremors, sometimes at night, sometimes during the day. Some of them were faint, amounting to little more than a slight quivering, as if the earth had settled a little, some place in its inner parts. Some of them were heavier, setting the windows and the dishes in their cupboards to chattering, but not again did we have so violent a quake as the two on the first night.

Months later we learned that to the west of us a vast area of the earth's crust had settled deeply, and that the waters of the Ohio had boiled and rushed into the sunken land, forming a great lake, in which even the trees were drowned. We had no such violence in our parts, but still we walked warily, always a little uneasy, always fearing the next tremor. It was not a very peaceful time.

I remember that Brother Benjamin wrote in the Church Family Journal on the last night of December, "So quaked out the old year." And I heard him say, not too humorously, "It seems as if our little ball might be shaken to pieces very easily." It did so seem, indeed.

CHAPTER XIII

SINCE SHAKERS did not believe in violence, no punishment was meted out to the runaway blacks. Instead there was an understanding of their fear, and Brother Benjamin gently took upon himself the fault in not going to reassure them earlier to prevent their scattering.

They were all rounded up within a few days, came home sheepishly. Like panic-stricken children they had done what came natural to them . . . wild before their fear. No blame was attached to them, though I think William Steel lectured his boy, Clayton, rather severely.

By the grapevine of gossip I learned that he had not been questioned. His story was accepted . . . he had fled to the woods, hidden out in a hollow tree and stayed there until found. Richard and William ran across him the next day after I brought Jency home.

No blame was attached to me for going to look for Jency, when I explained how I had known where to find her. Instead I was praised for quick thinking. I did not tell Cassie what I had seen in the hut. I thought that until, and unless, it was necessary there was no use grieving her. She scolded Jency roundly, threatened to take a limb to her did she ever do such a thing again, and Jency, giggling, promised glibly never to run away again.

My humiliation, for arrogance with Sister Priscilla, was evidently forgotten in all the excitement of the days of the earthquakes. It was not mentioned again by her. Indeed, for weeks there was a new humility in her. The memory of her shame lived in her mind for a long time. It was not in her nature to remain sweet-tempered and charitable for very long, but at least for a time she was unnaturally quiet, distraught and less firm in her ways.

This served me well, for a messenger came during that time, bearing word that my father was ill and that if it were possible I should come home. My mother felt it might be his last illness. I asked permission to go, not knowing how it could be worked out, for we were not allowed to travel alone in the world. I wished that Richard might go with me, but I did not mention it. I doubted he would go, for fear it would look too much as if we wanted to be alone together. Some man, however, must make the journey with me, and since a man and a woman could never be alone together without a third person, another woman must be delegated to accompany us. I made no suggestions. I simply asked permission to go. Sister Priscilla, in her more kindly state of mind, was willing to present my request to the Center House officials.

They were saved the trouble of working out the details, however, for on the third day after my request had been made I was called from my duty. I had the kitchen duty that month and Prissy came, herself, to tell me, "Your sister is here and wishes to see you. You are to go to Center House immediately."

A great excitement boiled up in me at the thought that Janie was here, that I should see her again. In a Shaker village, so withdrawn from the world, it is easy to forget that one has a family outside. I must own that in the routine of the days, in my own preoccupation with myself in these new surroundings, I had not often thought of Janie. But now, knowing she was here, that I was going to see her and talk to her, all my memories of her swarmed over me and I felt trembly with anticipation.

I made certain my hair was neat, my cap straight, my kerchief correctly crossed, and I felt a secret gladness that I had on my blue dress, for it was more becoming in color than the brown. Janie might think my clothing queer-looking, but at least it was fresh, speckless, orderly, and not bedraggled and water-soaked from bending over a tub of suds as it had been the last time.

She was standing at the window when I went into the big room where guests were received, but, hearing me, she turned and we flew into each other's arms, holding tightly, patting, weeping a little, exclaiming over the strangeness, laughing as we wept. I held her off, finally, saying, "Let me look at you."

She was thinner, looking older, but she was still very beautiful, and her clothes were very grand. Her face was still eloquent of her feelings, but there were lines about her mouth which, when she was not smiling, showed strain and imperiousness. "I've come," she said, "to take you home with me. Mr. Leavitt is with me and we have the large carriage. You know that Papa is very sick?"

"Yes." I felt tremulous, a little unnerved by the idea of setting out from the quietness of our village, going once again into the world.

"I have spoken to your . . . what is he, an elder? The man who runs your village, anyhow. He seems disposed to give you permission to go with us."

"I'll have to talk with him, myself," I said.

"Well, hurry, then. We should be starting on."

I went for Sister Molly and Brother Benjamin. They came and talked with us, grave, sympathetic, understanding. Readily they agreed I should go with Janie. "When you are ready to return," they told me, "if no way is provided, send word to us and we shall come for you."

It was not customary, of course, for a member of the village to go into the world, and had I been a member of the Church Family it might not have been allowed. Full members were forever dedicated to the Society, and all worldly ties were broken. They were married to the Society, "leaving father and mother, brother and sister" behind. But, being a Novitiate, there were privileges which could be extended to me.

"May I see Richard to tell him?" I asked.

"We have sent for him," Brother Benjamin told me.

We sat in silence, then, until Richard came. Janie seemed lost in thought. Brother Benjamin and Sister Molly, having nothing more to say, said nothing. Silences were a part of our way of life. In meetings between brethren and sisters there was little small talk.

Sister Molly, who was a plump, brown little woman, given to cheerfulness and good humor, kept busy with her knitting. Her hands moved deftly with the yarn and the needles clicked rhythmically. No one could knit as rapidly and as smoothly as Sister Molly. Her stint during the winter months was a stocking each day, and this was in addition to the rest of the work she did. I do not recall ever seeing her hands idle, except in Meeting. She had no difficulty obeying Mother Ann's dictum, "Put your hands to work." The most familiar sight in Center House was Sister Molly's lap piled full of work, Sister Molly's hands forever busy.

When Richard came he sat across the room from Janie and me. He asked politely about Mr. Leavitt, and when Janie's errand was explained to him, he nodded gravely. "I am glad you think Sister Rebecca should go. She can be of comfort and aid to her mother."

Janie's mouth quirked when Richard called me Sister Rebecca, but she said nothing. "If there is word you wish to send to your own parents," Brother Benjamin said, "it can be done."

"Tell them," Richard said, looking at me, "that I am well and that I am happy."

Tell them, also, I thought bitterly, that he is dead to everything outside the Believers . . . dead to me and dead to them. "I will tell them," I said, and if my voice was brittle with dryness it was no more than I was feeling.

Richard left, then, without saying more. Oh, yes . . . at the door he did turn and say, "I am sorry your father is ill. I hope he may be sustained in peace and comfort."

It was like a crumb thrown from a full table. Janie's head went up proudly. "Our father has his own way of meeting trouble and sickness."

Richard bowed slightly and went out of the room.

Brother Benjamin then told me to see Brother Samuel, of our House, who would provide me with funds for the journey. "She will need no money," Janie said quickly.

"Nevertheless," Brother Benjamin said gently, "it is our duty to provide for her."

It took me only a little while to be ready to leave, I had so few possessions. Mr. Leavitt, who had waited in the carriage, spoke kindly to me and took my small box, stowed it away, and we drove off. The carriage was very handsome, roomy, and comfortable. A black drove the team of beautiful bays, and our speed down the road was wonderful to me. I looked back once, felt again a tremor of uneasiness to be leaving what had become so familiar to me. But it was good, too, to be beside Janie . . . to know I was going to see my father and mother again.

Janie broke our silence. "My God," she said, loosening her bonnet, throwing it on the seat beside her, "how can you stand it? So stuffy . . . so hideously ugly . . . so smirkingly pure!" And she mocked Richard's pious use of my name. I could not help flushing. "How can you bury yourself in that place, Becky?"

"You grow used to it," I said.

When Mr. Leavitt had finished his term in the Senate he had not run again. He and Janie had returned to Lexington where he was once more engaged in the practice of law. He was a judge, now, and a very respected and prominent citizen of the state. But he had grown very corpulent now, and his face had the color of pasty dough. The motion of the carriage seemed to weary him considerably and I thought he must not be well. I asked Janie when we stopped for food once. "No," she said, "he is not well. He has a shortness of breath that troubles him, and a weakness in his limbs. So small an exertion as climbing the stairs makes him trembly. But he makes light of such things."

"You should make him take more care, Janie," I said.

"You do not *make* Mr. Leavitt do anything, Becky," she said, "but it troubles me."

She had grown very fond of him, I could see. But I thought it was more the fondness one has for an indulgent father than the deep love that should exist between a husband and wife.

We were three days on the way, and then we came to the Hanging Fork. It had not changed at all, but I had changed so much that it seemed strange to think I had waded and fished and swam in this little creek. It was like going back in a dream to days almost forgotten. The horses slowly pulled us up the long slope to the house, the old part still showing the logs, silvered with weather, the new parts shining white beside them.

Mama stood in the door and a deep pain went through me, seeing her. It had been so long. She stood exactly as I had seen her stand a thousand times, her arms folded across her bosom, quiet, as steady as the house itself. All the strangeness left and I was a child again, come home, eager to be enfolded in her strong arms, eager to be held against all harm and hurt.

I stumbled out of the carriage and ran to her. She received me gladly, the tears flowing down her face, but her arms were just as tight as ever, just as strong. "I'm glad you've come," she said. Then she turned to Janie with the same dear welcome.

"How is Papa?" I asked, when we went inside.

"Porely."

"He's no better?" Janie asked quickly.

Mama shook her head. "He'll not git no better on this earth. His time has come. You'll want to see him, but make yerselves comfortable, first."

Janie laid off her wrap and bonnet. I took off my cape, and the bonnet we Shakers wore over our caps. Mama looked at my white netting cap, smiled at me. "Hit's good to see you, Becky. You got a good color." She turned to Janie. "Janie, you're a heap thinner. Ain't you feelin' peart?"

Impatiently Janie twisted her skirts around. "I feel all right. I want to see Papa."

Mama took us into their bedroom. I would not have known him. Of course it had been ten years . . . he was in his seventies now. But besides his age, sickness had emaciated him. He was gaunt almost to his bones, the covers barely disturbed by the thinness of his frame. His head looked skull-like on the pillow, his hair almost gone from its top. His cheeks were sunken and the skin of his face was gray, loose and sagging. His eyes were closed. Fearfully I watched the covers over his chest. They moved so little, so very slowly. A hurting like a knife slicing bare flesh went deep into my chest. Oh, I wished I had never left him . . . wished I had stayed on at home, never wed, never traveled into the strange ways Richard had led me. At that moment I wished I could turn back the years, see my father strong and laughing once more, hoisting me to his shoulder, riding me around the house like a horse, me clutching his hair and laughing and kicking his ribs. "Is he asleep?" Janie asked, and her voice sounded so choked I looked quickly at her. The tears were wet on her lashes.

Mama shook her head. "He's been like that two days now . . . not knowin' what's goin' on. Hit won't be much longer."

"But what's wrong?" I asked. "What has made him sick?"

"Somethin' inside of him, I reckon . . . an' his years. He's had a hurtin' in his chest fer several years. Never complained overly, but hit never has went clean away fer any spell of time."

Janie dropped her face into her hands and sobbed aloud. "I can't bear it!"

Mama smoothed her hair. "Hit's got to be borne, Janie. Hit's the way of life." Her voice was low, sad, but it was calm. I remembered how many times I had heard her say, what's got to be done, has got to be done. I myself had said it, I myself had taken comfort from it. It was as if Mama had a pact with fate . . . as if she said, what must be, will be, but nothing will ever defeat me.

"Is there anything we can do?" I asked.

"No. Ever'thing's been done. They ain't nothin' now but to keep watch to the end."

Neighbors had been kind, she told us. The settlement had grown and there were good friends on all sides. They had come, sat up, watched, helped with the work. Two of our brothers had left home, one to go to Pennsylvania, the other to go to Ohio. Mama had not sent for them, hardly knowing where to send. Our oldest brother, Samuel, was still at home. He looked tired and worn down. "He's hardly had a minnit's rest since yer pa was took," Mama said. "He's did the work, set up, an' slept as little as a human could an' keep goin'."

"He can sleep, now," Janie promised. "Becky and I will take our turn."

Mr. Leavitt stayed a little while, then he went on to Lexington. There was nothing he could do, and there was little room for him in the house. Janie hardly knew when he left. She turned out of her fancy gown, rummaged in our old room and found a dress she'd left behind long years ago, put it on, tied her hair back, rolled up her sleeves. "I'll do the milking tonight," she said.

Mama looked at her. "My sakes, Janie, if you don't look more like yerself than I've seed you since you went away," she laughed shakily, rubbed the woven stuff of the old dress. "I kept all the things you girls left."

"I thought you would have. You never threw anything away." Janie stretched her arms high over her head. "I feel like my old self!"

Suddenly I wanted to be rid of my Shaker garb. I turned eagerly to Mama. "Is there a dress of mine here, too?"

"In the same chest with Janie's."

Janie followed me into the room and sat on the bed while I undressed, threw off the netting cap, loosened my hair, felt it fall free and unhampered about my shoulders. "Now," she said, "you look natural."

We both laughed. It was good to slip into our old things again.

Papa lingered on for a week, though each day we thought would be his last. People came and went, bringing food, staying to sit up at night. Janie, Mama and I went about doing the work, falling easily into our old habits, and slowly all thought of my life in South Union faded, all remembrance of Richard, of the sisters and brethren faded, and the only reality was the routine of our days—the morning milking, the redding of the house, waiting on Papa, cooking, sitting, talking with neighbors. Time slipped back into an old groove, turned back into old ways, and I felt myself to be once more Rebecca Fowler with no past but the days spent in this house.

It was on the third day, I think, after Janie and I had come that Johnnie Cooper came. He brought a pudding baked by Bethia. And he brought word that she and David would be over the next morning, sooner if needed. Mama had only to send the word, he said. He had grown heavier, but he was still sinewy, hard-muscled, flat as he had always been. Mama made him welcome, bade him sit down, and he spoke pleasantly to me. "I didn't know you were here."

"We came several days ago, Janie and I."

"Janie?" His eyebrows shot up.

I nodded. "She and Mr. Leavitt brought me. She's at the barn, I think. A hen of Mama's stole her nest, right in the middle of winter, and has hatched out a batch of little chickens. Janie's tending them."

He asked about Richard. I told him as best I could, the question bringing back to my mind the Shakers and the village, and all that I had left there. "He's a fool," Johnnie said shortly. "He always was a pigheaded, stubborn fool. You ought to leave him. Leave him there where he's chose to go. No need for you to waste your life."

And for the first time in my life I did not feel hotly defensive of Richard. I just shook my head, making no reply.

I asked about our old place on the river. He told me about the Worthingtons, what they had done to the place, how they'd built onto the house, made a fine property of it. I was glad. "Would you want to ride over and see it?" he asked.

"No." And I did not. There was no use seeing it. It had not been home for too long a time.

He stood up, then, moved restlessly about the room. Mama was with Papa. "Well," he said, "I'll get on back."

It occurred to me he hadn't said why he was at home. I asked him. "Are you still in the freighting business?"

"In a way," he said, "but I'm freightin' down the river to New Orleans, now."

"Have you prospered?"

He smiled. "Better than I'd hoped. I've got a store in Louisville . . . one in Lexington, three boats for the river trade and a string of wagons. It's what I like, trading. Pa can't see it. Still thinks I should've stayed on the farm."

"No," I said, "the farm was too settled for you."

"That's what I tell him. But I come home for a little visit, when I can. The folks are getting old. I get to worrying about 'em."

I was glad he had prospered, and I could see how trading would be a thing that would appeal to him. He was sharp-witted, ever. It would tickle him to make a good trade. I looked at him, standing beside the fire, swarthy, black-haired, restless, and thought his father, David Cooper, must have looked a lot like that when he was a young man, come pioneering and hunting into the wilderness of Kentucky. I wondered that he couldn't understand Johnnie's restlessness better. Certainly he must have known the feeling of it himself. "I'm glad you've done well, Johnnie," I said. "You're married, are you?"

"No." He didn't explain any further . . . just said no, and let it go.

"Janie'll be sorry she's missed you. Why don't you go out to the barn and speak to her a minute?"

"I might," he said. "You let us know, now, will you?"

I promised and he left.

He came again, several times. And he and Janie seemed to get along more agreeably than I'd ever seen them. He still teased her a little, sometimes angering her . . . as when he teased her about all the parties and balls she went to. "There's nothing happens in Lexington," he told me, "you don't see Mrs. Leavitt's name in the newspaper."

"And why not?" she'd say, tossing her head.

"No reason why not. Especially seeing that Mr. Leavitt is such a prominent citizen."

Janie looked quickly at him when he said that, but he was poking the fire and didn't meet her eyes. She looked down at her old dress. "I look like going to a ball right now, don't I?" and she laughed.

"You look awful good to me," he said, shortly. Then he straightened up, threw the tongs down on the hearth with a clatter and walked out the door, saying not another word.

"Well, what in the world . . ." Janie said, then she laughed. "He's the same old Johnnie, isn't he? You never know what to expect."

He was indeed the same old Johnnie, for I understood now why he had drunk too much the day she was married. He loved Janie then, and he loved her now, and I thought it was likely that was why he had never married.

Papa died on a Sunday, without ever waking to know Janie and I had come. Once I thought maybe he had. His eyes opened and I thought perhaps he knew me. They seemed to focus, and then they watered, and his lips moved as if to say something, but the lids closed wearily again and his breathing labored. Mama came in, then, with hot bricks to put at his feet, which were always cold. She laid the warm-wrapped bricks in place, felt of them once more. "He's slow a dyin'."

Janie had sat up the night before, slept all the morning, and when Johnnie came in the afternoon, he'd persuaded her to let him catch up a horse for her and go for a ride. "It'd do you good," he'd told her.

Mama had urged her to go. "You need to git out," she said. "You been too close to the house. I'm afeared you'll sicken."

So Janie was not there at the last. Samuel was, and Mama and I. Bethia and David were there also. It was just at sundown, and Bethia was fixing us something to eat. David had gone to feed. Mama and Samuel and I were sitting there, not talking, just sitting as we had done all week. Papa sighed, took a deep breath, and let it out, and never took another one. We waited, for his breathing had become so slow it sometimes seemed minutes between breaths. But there wasn't any more. Mama went to the bed, touched his face, laid her palm against his cheek . . . then she bent and kissed him. "Goodbye, Tice," she said, and gently she pulled the covers over his head, straightened and walked out of the room, out of the house, up the hill at the back straight to its top . . . to the ridge meadow. Samuel and I watched her go. "You reckon I better go after her?" he said.

"No," I told him. "She's going to that place they always loved. You recollect she's told us they stood up there the day after they were married and picked out the place to build the house. Leave her be."

When Janie came in her face was as white as if she'd seen a ghost, and she'd been crying. She was still crying, in fact, almost blinded by the tears as she hurried, stumbling, through the sitting room and into our bedroom. I followed her, thinking she must somehow have heard. "Don't grieve so, Janie," I said, putting my arms around her. "It's like Mama says. It comes to all, and Papa is safe, now, never more to suffer or to want."

She was shaking with sobs, but she whirled around and looked at me wildly. "Is he gone?"

Without waiting for me to answer she brushed past me and into Papa's room. We heard her cry out, and when I went to her, she was lying on the floor beside the bed, the covers dragged from Papa, clutched in her hands. She had fainted dead away.

The time of a funeral is always a little unreal, dreamlike. People come and go, food is prepared and set before you, you eat, you do the things that are necessary, you sleep and you waken. David and Bethia and the other neighbors took all the burden of tasks off of us, and in some way the arrangements were made for the burial, the grave was dug, the coffin made. As in a trance you know these things are being done, that they must be done. Papa was to be laid in the ridge meadow, where the three little ones had been put as they died. And when everything was ready we climbed the steep hill, David, William Worthington, William Casey and others of his friends bearing him on their shoulders.

Mr. Leavitt was there, Janie leaning heavily on him as we climbed. But I walked with Mama and Samuel, and only Mama had breath enough at the end of the climb to speak. No one had needed to support her. She had leaned on neither Samuel nor me. "He'll rest easy here," she told us, "a lookin' down across the country he loved."

That night we sat about the fire, talking. David was sad at the passing of another friend. "They're all a goin'," he said, "the ones that took the risks an' opened up the country, settled it, made it safe for the ones to follow. Soon there'll be none of 'em left. Ben Logan's dead . . . Jim Harrod's dead . . . Dannel Boone has quit the country . . . all the old ones are either dead or left out. It'll be my time, soon."

"Don't say such," Bethia said, reaching out her hand to him.

He shook his shoulders as if shaking off his thoughts, smiled at her. "Well, Ma, I feel pretty lively. I'll likely be around a right smart spell."

"I should hope so!"

Mr. Leavitt had gone back to Lexington, leaving Janie. He was to come for her in another week. Janie wanted Mama to go to the city with her, make her home there. But Mama had no idea of doing so. "Samuel is to wed Mary Worthington in the spring," she said. "He aims to bring her here, an' he'll manage fer us. This is my place an' I'll never leave it."

Even Janie could see it was best. She turned to me. "You aren't going back to that Shaker town, are you, Becky? Now you're free of it, come home with me."

I was not tempted to go home with Janie. Her life in the city would never have suited me. But I cannot say, truthfully, that I was not tempted to stay with Mama. All the old ways had returned, in all their goodness, to tempt me. I knew I had only to say I wanted to stay and I would be welcome, freely, gladly, tenderly welcome. I thought of the paths my feet knew, across the meadow to the creek, down the creek to the old mill, up the ridge to the clearing, to and from the house to all the buildings, about the house from fire to table to bed.

It would have been peaceful to stay, but even as I thought, longingly, of the peace, I knew I would not stay, and I knew the peace would not last. Even as I thought of the familiar pathways, I remembered the flag-stone walks in the village, the twin stairways, the long room with the rows of beds, Permilla, Annie, Lacey and Viney and even Sister Priscilla. And I thought of Richard. I had gone a journey I could not turn back on. You cannot recover childhood, nor can you ever find your home in your past. I had followed Richard to South Union, and it was now my home. I shook my head. "I am not free of the Shakers, Janie. I must go back."

She was angry with me, but Mama smiled understandingly. She would have followed Papa there, and as long as he lived she would have remained where he was. She knew what I had to do.

[125]

CHAPTER XIV

I WENT STRAIGHT to Center House to tell Sister Molly I was back. I was received joyously and when I told that my father had died, there was a tender concern. "Would you wish," Sister Molly asked, "for us to call Richard so that you may tell him?"

I did not wish it. I would have given my hope of eternity, almost, to have had him beside me, as Mr. Leavitt had been beside Janie, even in estrangement, when Papa died. But he had not been, had not even suggested he might go with me . . . had stood apart and separated. What concern of his was it, now? I shook my head. "No. Brother Benjamin can tell him."

Gently Sister Molly said, then, "If you are weary from your journey, Rebecca, it can be arranged for you to take a day or two of rest before resuming your duties."

"No." What I wanted was to get back to work, to recover the sense of routine, to feel again the smoothness of habit. "I am not overly tired," I said.

"Then," she said, "let me tell you of a thing we have been discussing. Sit down, Rebecca, and listen." She pulled a chair forward for me. Eagerly she said, "You have more learning than is common among the women, Rebecca. Brother Benjamin and I have been talking—we think you should be relieved of your duties in East Family and put to teaching. The School group is growing so fast that another teacher is badly needed. Would you be willing?"

Would I be willing? We were not often asked that question, and it was so new an idea that I could not immediately think clearly about it. My first feeling was one of dismay, to be moved from the East Family to the School House. I did not much want to do that. "I don't know," I said, "as I'd like being moved from East Family. I've got used to it there."

"Oh, you wouldn't move for a while. There isn't room for you to live in the School Family right now. You would continue to sleep and eat with the East Family. But you would be relieved of work in the Family, and instead of being under the care of Sister Priscilla, you would be under the immediate supervision of Brother Stephen and Sister Drucie."

That I would welcome. But I felt timid about teaching. How did they know I could? Suppose I failed? What if they were wrong about me? "It's been a long time since I studied, Sister Molly," I said hesitantly, "I don't know if I can teach or not."

"We think you can," she said, smiling. "We think you will make an excellent teacher. Of all the women in the village, we think you are perhaps the most capable and certainly the most qualified."

No one, human as we are, can fail to feel a pride in being singled out, told such things. It was the only pride we Shakers took . . . the pride of competence, for certainly one chore was very like another in that there was neither hope nor intent of accumulating money, nor of power or individual treasures. There was only the pride of the spirit, of doing well what one was given to do, of giving a good accounting of one's abilities. That was present in us all. "What would I have to teach?" I asked.

"Brother Stephen will tell you. He has full charge of the teaching. I think it would be among the older girls, however."

I knew so little about the school that I truly did not know what subjects were taught. I felt some apprehension about teaching Latin, for instance, and I mentioned it. "Oh, we do not teach the languages," Sister Molly said. "We do not believe they are needful or practical. We want to give the children only a good grounding in rhetoric, reading, figuring, and some understanding of geography and history. We have questioned whether even history is essential, but Brother Stephen has held out firm that it is, so we continue it, for the time at least."

Once again the thought crossed my mind that the Shakers did not like you to think overly much. And perhaps they were right. Thinking often leads to doubt and unhappiness. Too many thinking Shakers might undermine their entire structure. "When would I begin my teaching duties?" I asked.

"If you don't feel you need to rest, tomorrow is as good a time as any."

It seemed to me I needed a little time, to look over the texts, to visit the school, watch the procedure, prepare myself, but apparently the thought did not occur to our good little eldress. I decided boldly to take the plunge. "Very well."

"Will you tell Sister Priscilla to see me immediately, then, Rebecca, so I may inform her? And at Meeting tonight we will announce your appointment. We are having a Union Meeting tonight because Brother McNemar is visiting, and he cannot stay until Sunday." Her round, firm-cheeked face beamed. "We have been blessed with great messages from him all week. I am so happy you have come home in time to hear him again, Rebecca. We have had a great visitation of the spirit under him."

I felt no great joy at the prospect of seeing or hearing Brother McNemar again. I could never forget that it was his missionary zeal which had brought us all within the fold of the Believers, and I was not convinced that we would not have been better off left alone. Sister Molly touched my arm. "Welcome home, Rebecca. It must have been trying to be away from the village."

I looked at her wonderingly. Never in her life had she lived outside a

Shaker village. It would, indeed, have been trying to her to be separated from what constituted her entire world.

It was almost time for the supper bell and I went straight to the kitchen to look out Sister Priscilla and give her Sister Molly's message. The moment I saw her I knew she had recovered much of her poise, that she had deliberately pushed the humiliation of her stolen caps into the back of her mind, pushed it so far that she would never allow it to disturb her again. She shoved her spectacles up, peered at me, and with never a word of welcome said, worriedly, "Now, what can she be wanting with me at this time of day? She knows the supper meal is cooking."

I gave her no idea of what was wanted, simply repeated that Sister Molly had said she was to come at once. She looked around impatiently. "Very well, but you will have to help out here in the kitchen. There's no use your going to dairy now, anyhow. It is within half an hour of mealtime."

When she had gone there was a scurrying from the other rooms, and a clustering about me. Permilla came, hurrying, from the spinning room. "I seen you walkin' over from Center House, an' I couldn't hardly wait to git to you." She hugged me tight and kissed me. "Lord, but we've missed you. You've been all right, have you?"

Oh, but it was good to see Permilla again! "All right," I told her; then there was Lacey and Viney to greet, and Amanda, all old friends now. Only Annie, in the dairy, was missing. Amanda was on kitchen duty and when I said we mustn't take the time to talk she sniffed. "Everything's ready. Prissy just don't like to give up things can run without her. It'll all be on the table when it's time. Did your father get better?"

Once again I told of his death, and they were sympathetic. Lacey, always easy to cry, wept and spoke sadly of the briefness of man's time. Viney clucked and opined that it was bad, but it came to all men. "I'm starin' the Grim Reaper in the face myself," she said.

"Oh, you'll live to be as old as Methuselah," Permilla told her. Then she looked thoughtfully at me. "I don't rightly know what yer feelin's are. Not ever keerin' overly fer my own pa, I don't to say feel it fer you, but I reckon you've been troubled, an' I'm sorry fer that." She was always honest, Permilla.

I was eager to hear the happenings during my absence, but there seemed a scarcity of news. Prissy was back to her old ways. The work shifts would be changed the next day and each one was anxious to know what he would draw. "Hit'll be my turn in the kitchen, I reckon," Permilla said, sighing, "an' Prissy'll be underfoot ever' blessed minnit."

I started to tell, then, that I was to begin teaching, but I thought better of it. There might be a change at the last minute. Best, I thought, to say nothing and let the announcement at Meeting tonight be the first they heard of it. Then it would be official. "I hear Brother McNemar is visiting," I said, instead.

"Yes, an' Union Meetin' ever' night," Viney said. "I've done danced till my bones hurt, an' listened till my ears is wore out. This'll be his last night, or I don't know as I could hold out."

"Sister Molly tells me there have been many gifts of visitations."

Permilla nodded solemnly. "Prissy was took with a whirling gift one night. Hit come to my mind she was shown' off in front of Brother Mc-Nemar, fer she whirled till her skirts flew up an' her legs showed."

"Not Prissy!"

They all affirmed it. "Prissy . . . yes, ma'am." Viney started chuckling. "You ort to seen her!"

Fervently I wished I might have. "Did Brother Benjamin stop the dance?"

"Oh, yes. He stopped it right off . . . to give her gift the proper room. An' she needed it, I will say."

"How long did it last?"

"Best part of a hour, I'd say," Viney went on. "Hit was a sight, now. She'd whirl an' float about, on her toes like, then she'd whizz right clean acrost the room, an' if they was anybody in the way, hit was jist too bad. Warn't no stoppin' her, neither. They said she was as stiff as a poker, till she fell all of a sudden in a trance, an' they laid her aside. When she come to, she claimed she'd saw a vision of heaven, all white an' gold an' shinin', an' said she couldn't hardly wait to take up her residence there."

"I cain't hardly wait, neither," Permilla said dryly. "I wish she was done there. But if she's *aimin'* to be there, I d'know as I keer to go."

Amanda now looked at the clock on the kitchen shelf. "It's time to dish up. The rest of you get out and let us make ready."

We set the food on the table just as the bell rang, and in ten minutes the brethren and sisters filed in. "You go on and eat," Amanda told me. "It isn't your turn in the kitchen yet."

Prissy came in with a flurry just as we knelt for prayers, and she looked at me directly when we rose and were seated. A feeling of triumph rose up in me. You, I thought to myself, have said your last say to me—you have sat in judgment on me for the last time. I am free of you! I think she hated it, the whole idea, for I had been a good victim for her acid tongue. I think she had set herself the chore of humbling me completely. It was now snatched away from her, and she looked at me disapprovingly, as if I had gone behind her back and played a trick on her. But I could hold my head high. I had not. This good thing had come without my help, but I reveled in its goodness.

Across the room Richard glanced my way, but no smile lit his face. He gave me, instead, a sober look, nodded in recognition, fell immediately to eating. Brother McNemar, I thought, has had his usual effect on him, making him ever more stern, ever more dutiful. He could not even let his mouth soften to my presence, or his eyes send me any message of sympathy or welcome.

[129]

Instead of hurt, I felt a hardening. Very well, I thought. Stiffen yourself, ice yourself over . . . you may as well. For the first time there stirred in me something of my own worth. I had more learning than Richard. I had been singled out by the elder of the village, and by the eldress, for a task which Richard could not have done. I felt its honor deeply, and I was glad. I would, I vowed fiercely, no longer live in Richard's shadow, yearning over him, longing for him. I had been set aside as a wife. So . . . I would make of myself an individual. I would think for myself and I would act for myself, being neither timid in the face of Richard's convictions, nor dutiful toward them. I would teach, and teaching I would study and learn, and I would make myself, not Rebecca Fowler again, but a new and more sturdy Rebecca Cooper. It was a vow I took, and one which I wrote in my Journal that night. And it marked a turning, an important turning, in me.

For the first time in my life I had been thought worthy of something which I, myself, could do, could perhaps do well, and which, perhaps, only I could do as well. All my childhood I had felt my mother's strength, been sheltered by it, and from it I had gone into Richard's strong keeping, into his strength of purpose and will. Now, for the first time, I was singled out . . . I, Rebecca. And I, Rebecca, was going to make the most of it.

It was during the rest period after supper that Sister Susan sought me out. "You are wanted at Center House," she said.

I thought it had to do with my new task and went hurriedly. But I was met by Sister Milly, who led me into the receiving room. Richard was there, with Brother McNemar and Brother Benjamin. They asked about my father, and they were properly sympathetic at the news of his death. "Your mother and father are well," I told Richard. "They sent you their good wishes."

He looked leaner and thinner to me. When you see someone day after day, the small changes which occur are not manifested to you. After even a brief absence you are able to see them differently. Richard looked almost gaunt, his cheekbones showing high and the line of his jaw more sharply drawn. "I am glad they are well," he said.

"Johnnie," I said, "is a merchant now, with a store in Lexington and another in Louisville, and he is also engaged in the river trade."

"Worldly traffic," he said, briefly dismissing Johnnie.

Brother McNemar took over the conversation, then. "We have sent for you, Sister, to discuss your readiness to come into full membership. Richard has a great wish to be completely dedicated. It depends, of course, on the progress of your understanding, and upon your willingness."

I looked at Richard, who was studying the carpet under his feet. "It would mean, also, wouldn't it, deeding our lands over to the church?"

"It would. No one in full membership may retain ownership of any property. Have you received the gift, yet? Are you ready and willing?"

One month earlier I would have been uncertain, torn between a wish to make Richard happy and my own disinclination. Even one day earlier it would have been true. But with a firmness which surprised me, I spoke out. "I am neither ready nor willing. I do not wish to part with our land yet, nor do I believe so strongly as to want full membership. I am sorry if this makes Richard unhappy, but I must go by my own feelings."

Richard looked up at me, then, and had we been alone I am certain he would have spoken angrily to me. His face flushed and his eyes narrowed. He held his tongue before the elders, however. Brother McNemar looked sorrowful. "I am sorry to hear you speak so. I had hoped that a few months of withdrawal would make you see the error of your ways . . . would bring you, repentant, into the Church Family. Where lies the lack, Sister?"

I thought about his question. "I do not know," I told him, then, honestly. "In my heart, I expect . . . in all of my nature. I have made some progress," I added truthfully, "but I feel a great reluctance to part with the last of our property . . . I feel . . ."

Brother McNemar smiled at me and shook his head. "So long, Rebecca, as you hold on to any material possessions, there will be this reluctance. A full and free dedication is the only possible way to enter into the kingdom."

I knew he was right. And I was not now terribly unhappy in the village. Even in so short a time I had grown accustomed to its ways. But it was true that within me there was still the need to know there was some place of my own. I did not consciously think, or even hope, that one day I might return to it, but the thought of the land, there, still in my name and Richard's, had always been comforting to me. I could not bring myself to part from it.

And I did not know whether I wanted to enter into the kingdom. There was an inner disquiet, not yet stilled, that this adventure was fragile and impermanent. It seemed, somehow, to be a dam set across the waters of life . . . and dams are sometimes broken, breeched, and waters, seeking the sea, will flood over them and have their way in the end. I shook my head, repeating, "I cannot consent."

Bitterly Richard looked at me. I was holding him back, and I knew now why he had thinned down. His heart was set on full membership. He wanted deeply to be a part of the Church Family, set apart, a little holy, more exalted, more trusted than the others. He could not bear not to be. "You are stubborn, Rebecca," he said.

I felt like shouting at him our old childhood saying, "Look who's calling the kettle black!" But I held my tongue. I doubt if ever in his life the thought crossed Richard's mind that he was stubborn himself. So certain was he, always, of the rightness of his convictions, that it would have been the last thing he could see in himself. I was denying him, almost for the first time, and he was disturbed and angry with me. I could not help it. I could give no other answer.

"Let us pray together," Brother McNemar said, and we went to our knees. Both he and Brother Benjamin prayed earnestly that I might be led to see the whole truth . . . that I might be received of the spirit, and by the spirit, into the full life. I barely heard them. In spite of my new-found courage, I had been deeply shaken to go against Richard. It went against every habit of my life, but I was determined to hold to it, until and unless these doubts I felt, so intangible as almost to be wordless, might be removed from me.

The Meeting bell rang as we rose from our knees, and I joined Sister Molly and Sister Mercy to go across the road to the Meetinghouse.

We sang and then Brother Benjamin read from the Testimonies, after which he announced my appointment to the School group. I heard it with relief. I had thought they might change their minds about it. But immediately Brother McNemar broke into song . . . "Whoever wants to be high, highest, Must first come down to low, lowest, And then ascend to high, highest, By keeping down to low, lowest." It was a song we had not heard before, and I knew it was meant as a warning to my pride.

It was no accident, either, I was sure, that Brother McNemar chose that night to instruct us further in the dance of blessing. We formed in squares, the men at one end of the room, the women at the other, and we moved in the slow shuffle step toward each other, weaving through the squares, our hands turned palm up, to receive the blessing of the spirit. I tried, but my palms felt as empty when the dance was finished as they had when it began. No blessing was vouchsafed me.

CHAPTER XV

WE HAD over one hundred children in the school at that time, all ages and all sizes. Some were the children of our families, some came from the neighboring settlements, being brought to board with us and to learn. Some were orphaned and placed with us for lack of a proper home.

The Schoolhouse was the pleasant white frame building constructed before we were gathered into order. The boys and girls were not taught together, of course. Brother Stephen had the task of teaching all the boys. There being more girls, there was another woman besides myself. She was Sister Drucie, of Center House, a plump, motherly widow, with no children of her own. She had been sent to us from Union Village in Ohio. It was she who greeted me when I entered the Schoolhouse early that morning. "Brother Stephen will be here soon," she said. "We will meet together to talk over your duties."

She showed me over the rooms, two downstairs, two up. "This one," she said, in the upstairs room to the left of the hall, "will be yours."

It was a spacious room, well lighted, with sturdy benches set toward the back, and a smaller group set well forward. I wondered at the separation, but said nothing. I would be told, I thought. The colors most often used by Shakers in their interiors are blue and white. All the classrooms were painted white, but the wainscoting and door and window frames were that beautiful, bright blue so beloved by them. There were the usual pegs around the walls, for even the children were taught to put things where they belonged, to be neat and tidy. There was a chair for me and a table . . . and that was the classroom.

We heard the door being softly closed downstairs. "There's Brother Stephen, now," Sister Drucie said. "We'd best go down. There isn't much time till the children will be coming in."

I had seen Stephen Burke often, in Meeting, coming and going about the grounds, for though he taught during the winter months, he took his turn at hand labor when not teaching. He lived with the School Family, however, so I had never spoken to him, beyond a greeting. I felt a little apprehensive now . . . a little timid, for I thought he might wish to examine me.

I have said that he was a tall man and slender, with a gentle, kindly manner. I think I had never observed more than that. Now, sitting in the room with him, listening to him, I saw that his eyes were brown, a very dark, liquid brown . . . that his hair was still luxuriant and thick, fair as a child's and waving back from his high forehead, curling about his ears. As his hands picked up one of the texts from his table, I saw that they were slender, tapering, and from the way he smoothed the cover of the book, probably sensitive to the feeling of things, the textures which they handled. He welcomed me warmly. "We have great need of you, Sister."

Hesitantly I explained how long it had been since I studied. But he waved that information aside. "The important thing is that you have studied. It will come back to you. You were grounded, were you not, in rhetoric, reading, writing, figures?"

"I was . . . and in Latin, geography and history. By Mr. Foster, an Englishman."

He leaned forward in his chair. "Not Emory Foster, the naturalist?"

"Yes, sir. He stayed in our home for over two years, studying the birds and animals around about."

"What a privilege!" Then he laughed. "I have no fear of your ability to teach, then."

Then he picked up the other books on his table, one by one. "These are the texts. Oh . . . we are beginning to use the Lancastrian system here.

We are very crowded, with not much help. It seems the best, as well as the most modern method."

I was ashamed that I had never heard of the Lancastrian system. I said so.

"You noticed how the classrooms are divided? A set of benches at the back, a few grouped together near your table?" he asked.

I nodded.

"Actually, you will teach only a small, select group of the older girls . . . the best of them. They are monitors, and it is they who will teach the others. We could never manage in any other way. But I have welcomed it, for I believe it to be the best system of teaching currently used. Now, this," and he settled forward, leaning his elbows on the table, "is the way it works. This morning, when the children have assembled, most of the pupils will be seated in the rear. They will study, aloud naturally, under the supervision of half of the monitors. You will be instructing the other half. In the afternoon, they will take charge of the teaching, and you will instruct those who were teaching this morning." This was plain and simple. I nodded to show my understanding. "What are the subjects?"

"I am coming to that. There is a shift of pupils in the morning and afternoon. It sounds complicated, but actually it is not. It is very reasonable. They rotate between Sister Drucie, who will instruct them in the practical arts of sewing, spinning, weaving, and she will also teach them some music, and you, who will instruct from the texts." He leaned back, smiling happily. He laid his hand on the stack of books. "Here are the texts in rhetoric, arithmetic, geography, history . . ." He smiled ruefully. "There are no texts for reading. But I have furnished some of my own books, from which you may choose. I hope," he said eagerly, "you have read Shakespeare . . . Spenser, John Donne?"

I laughed. "Shakespeare, yes . . . and Spenser's Faerie Queen. Mr. Foster carried with him a folio of Shakespeare, Spenser, the essays of Bacon . . . and the Bible."

"No better texts to be found!" Brother Stephen said emphatically, slapping his hand down on the table. "No better texts in the world. If you read those books aloud to your students they will forever have a love of literature."

I wondered about the hand training of the boys, since there was only Brother Stephen to teach them. "Oh, they get plenty of that on the farms," he said. "The actual experience is much better than any training I could give them. They help with the milking, feeding, care of the stock, and in the spring the older boys will be let out of school to help with the plowing and planting. Hand-minded, you know . . . hand-minded. The Shakers are a very practical people."

He rose. He had a way of moving very quickly. "You will find the children amenable, docile, willing. Love is the answer, Sister Rebecca. Children taught in love are loving children. But if there are problems, be sure to speak to me."

I gathered up the books, Sister Drucie helping stack them in my arms. "I'm glad to be shut of them," she said, laughing. "Teaching out of books goes hard with me."

Brother Stephen laughed with her. "But you are an excellent teacher, Drucie, in the things of the home."

It was evident that there was more freedom here than among the men and women in the other Families. The very nature of the task made it necessary, for there was no sharp division between the man's work and the woman's. Both were the same, and they called for a mutual support and concern. I felt like singing, I was so happy.

At my table I arranged the books, touching them lovingly. The texture of their covers came through my fingers, felt of knowledge and learning, felt of adventure opening up . . . and all my eagerness under Mr. Foster returned.

I laid open the first book under my hand . . . the text for rhetoric, laid it open at no particular place, and the first words I saw were the ones I had heard in Mr. Foster's voice so many times . . . "Rhetoric defines the rules which govern all prose compositions or speech designed to influence the judgment or the feelings of men, and therefore treats of all matters relating to beauty or forcefulness of style." It was as if I were twelve years old again, sitting at Mr. Foster's knee, this book in his hand, his eyes bent on its pages. "Rhetoric is divided into the following classifications: rhetoric, grammar, logic, prosody, diplomacy and literature." And on another page . . . "an adjective or a transitive verb is absolute when the adjective has no noun, or the verb no object . . . an example, 'Fortune favours the brave.'" I leafed on through the book, and there it all was, heard, learned, remembered. I set the rhetoric text aside.

Next lay a slender volume, bound in leather, darkened by time, worn by use. The corners were slick from handling, the back beginning to fray. It was a book much read, and therefore a book much loved, I thought. It was a book of poems . . . the poems, I saw, of John Donne. It opened of its own accord at one particular place, and the page was ragged from thumbing. Brother Stephen, I thought, loved either or both of these two poems. I read the one on the facing page first.

> If poisonous materials, and if that tree
> Whose fruit threw death on else immortal me,
> If lecherous goats, if serpents envious
> Cannot be damned, alas! why should I be?
> Why should intent or reason, born in me,
> Make sins, else equal, in me more heinous?
> And mercy being easy, and glorious
> To God, in His stern wrath why threatens He?

I read only that far, wondering, as I took them in, at Brother Stephen, a Shaker, loving such lines, wondering, as I realized the poet had said his words for me, too. "If serpents, envious, cannot be damned . . . why should I be?" So thought I. So had I questioned. So had I searched.

Hurriedly I closed the book. I did not, now, want to read more. But I knew I would read them all. I knew I must read them all, for here was a man of reason, a poet who sang of truth. I laid the book aside. I doubted that Brother Stephen had intended it to be taught. I thought it must be his personal volume, and that in some fashion it had got mixed in with the texts.

There was the noise of children gathering and Sister Drucie called up to me. "We open school with singing, Sister Rebecca. Will you come down and join us?"

Like small, good Shakers they were separated, little men and little women, each to his side of the room. Like small, good Shakers they knelt meekly and docilely, hands folded, heads bowed, through Brother Stephen's prayer, then with great decorum they sat while Sister Drucie found the key for the opening song, lifting their voices then, in a Shaker hymn of praise.

The voices of the younger children were high, sweet, a little wavering and sometimes off key. Mixed with theirs were the clearer, truer voices of the older girls, and the deeper, fuller voices of the older boys. There were Permilla's children, clean, neat, plump with their good food, red-faced with energy. There was Amanda Steel's boy, looking, I thought, very like Amanda, with his small, pointed face. There was Lucien Brown, manly already, handsome, open-countenanced. There were Lacey's young ones, and no amount of cleanliness could remove from them the stamp of their birth, the dull inexpressiveness of their faces, the flat, unperceiving look of their eyes.

There were many children I did not know; indeed most of them I had seen only in Union Meeting. One girl, older, almost grown, sat well forward, evidently a monitor given watch over the younger ones beside her. I had never seen her before. I wondered who she was. She was as round as a partridge, short, sitting little taller than her charges. Under her white cap her hair was brown, glossy with brushing and clean-shining, soft and silky-looking. Her face was pink with color and youth and good health, her mouth small, ripe and full. She glanced my way and I saw that her eyes were very large, darkly lashed, with winging brows curved over them, and as deeply blue as Richard's. She was a very pretty girl.

Brother Stephen asked me to stand and told the children I was a new teacher, that I would have charge of all the studies for the girls, while Sister Drucie would now teach them the arts of handwork. They stared at me, as children will, curiously and intently. I felt self-conscious before them, found difficulty remaining poised and calm. But I managed it, and then we were dismissed to go to the classrooms.

As the children filed out, Sister Drucie stopped the pretty girl. "Sister Rebecca," she said, "this is Sabrina Arnold, lately come with her father to South Union. She is one of the best students. You will come to rely on her very much."

The girl flushed and ducked in a small curtsey. I smiled at her and said I was happy to know her, and to know I could count on her. She flashed a lovely smile at me and then fled up the stairs.

The morning sped by, when I had learned how far in the texts Sister Drucie had gone. I had expected to feel timid, uneasy, uncertain. Instead, fortified perhaps by my own joy, there was neither fear nor uncertainty. As if led again by the voice and hand of Mr. Foster, I proceeded, sure of my knowledge, sure of myself, eager to share this joy and knowledge with the girls.

Once when I looked up Brother Stephen was standing in the door. I was reading aloud, the Ninety-fourth Sonnet of William Shakespeare, that one beginning, "They that have power to hurt and will do none . . ." when I saw him. My voice faltered for a moment and his picked up the lines from memory, continuing to the end . . . "The summer's flower is to the summer sweet, Though to itself it only live and die, But if that flower with base infection meet, The basest weed outbraves his dignity; For sweetest things turn sourest by their deeds; Lilies that fester smell far worse than weeds."

The eyes of the girls turned to him as he spoke the lines, widened as they turned back to me. When he had finished he smiled, made a small motion with his hand, and walked quickly away.

Set atremble by not knowing how long he may have listened to my reading, or my interpretation of the poems, I closed the book. The girls sighed. And Sabrina, Seth Arnold's daughter, said, "I wish we could study only poetry, Sister. You read it so nice."

"Poetry," I said, smiling at her sweet, upturned face, "is for your delight and edification. We cannot have all sweets, however, and you must be prepared in the other subjects."

I learned that, after all, I was not to take the dinner meal at East House. "There's no sense," Sister Drucie told me, "in you trudging over there just to eat and come back, when the meal is prepared in the School House. Take it with us."

It suited me as well.

In the afternoon I went over the same ground I had covered in the morning, with a different set of girls. But I somehow lacked the wish to read Shakespeare's sonnets with them. I missed the posy face of Sabrina. The afternoon girls seemed very dull after having her wide eyes upon me all morning. And, strangely, the summer flower sonnet made me feel uncomfortable.

I was still keyed up to the effort of the day when finally we dismissed school. We had Union Meeting again, the last one before Brother Mc-Nemar was to leave, and it was a prolonged and wearying one, to me. I took no joy in the exercises or the dance, my mind full of the day's work, my thoughts on the morrow. But it was a happy preoccupation.

In our room, finally, the candle snuffed out so Prissy could not see a light, keeping our voices to a whisper, Amanda and Permilla came and sat on my bed, asking about the school, about their own children. It was like Lacey, we thought, to go straight to bed, not thinking to ask about hers. Annie was quiet, under her covers, and asleep as we talked. Viney groaned over her bones, warning us they were aching till she doubted she'd move in the morning, but she was on her cot nimbly enough, at that. "Don't you'uns set up an' talk, now," she cautioned us, "till Prissy comes. She'll have us all out on our knees, an' I ain't wishin' to be on mine no more till mornin', if I c'n git on 'em, then!"

"We'll be quiet," we promised.

"Does mine mind his manners?" Amanda asked.

"He does," I told her. "He is smart in his ways, and a good boy."

"I've taught him to be so," she said, "but a body never knows how they'll do without their own mother to see to 'em."

"He's doing fine," I repeated, but I think she would have been happier had I told her he was drooping and frail without her. She was ever strong in her belief it was wrong for him to be parted from her.

Permilla chuckled over my report of hers. "I don't misdoubt it," she said, when I told her they were fat and bouncy, wiggly with their good health and high spirits. "They was ever a trouble to me."

"Aaron," I said, laughing, "had to sit in the corner with a fool's cap on his head for making spitballs."

"That's jist like him," she said. "Oh, they'll not come over many of their ways on that 'un, I'm thinkin'. My," she went on, "jist think of you a teachin', Becky. You like it?"

"I love it," I told her. "I love it more than anything I've ever done."

"Well, I allus knowed you was smart. Likely you'll be kept in the school the rest of yore days."

I hoped I would be. "You drew the kitchen duty for this month, didn't you?" She had waited table at supper.

"Oh, I knowed I would. Hit's the onliest one I've not had yit. 'Twas bound to be my lot this time. 'Twon't be long, though, till the garden work is on us. That's what I'm wishin' fer. I've allus loved a garden. An' to be outside . . . I cain't hardly wait."

Amanda slipped away to her end of the room and Permilla settled into her bed. It was quiet for a long time, and I thought Permilla had gone to sleep. I lay planning the lessons for the next day.

CHAPTER XVI

IT WAS A lovely spring that year.

I awoke each morning eager for the day, happy in my work, loving every moment of it. Relieved of duties in East House I spent the hour and a half before breakfast with my books, going over the lessons for the day. I loved the feeling of the pages under my hand, the crinkle of the paper as I turned them, the words which leapt up at me as I read.

Brother Stephen loaned me many books, out of which I did not assign lessons, but which, teaching me, added to the knowledge I could impart. And as I read, in a history of his, about the Gallic wars I wished the Shakers did not hold against the teaching of languages, for the Latin would have made it so much more vivid.

Occasionally, when the lessons went especially well, there was half an hour left over, and I used it to tell about other things, about the Greek city states, the wars, the beginnings of architecture and sculpture, of thought, of drama, of the rise and fall of the Roman Empire. I recalled much of what Mr. Foster had told, but I also learned many new things from Brother Stephen's books.

The girls listened dutifully, were interested, I think, but it was Sabrina who really learned, who wanted to learn, who asked the questions. Eyes fixed on me as I read or talked, wide, fascinated, she drank it all in. I would often see her breath catch in her throat at some beautiful phrase, see her eyes go dreamy as it lingered in her mind. She sought me out frequently to question further, she asked for the loan of the books, she read constantly in whatever time was spared to her after her tasks.

I think I realized, almost from the first, that actually I was teaching Sabrina. The others picked up, parrotlike, what was assigned to them, with little eagerness to do more. Beside Sabrina, who was like a colorful bird in a flock of drabs, they were dull and without spirit, no song to sing, no wings to stretch. I came to love her dearly.

One book I did not loan her . . . the book of John Donne's poetry. I returned it to Brother Stephen, but not before I had read every verse myself. Many of the poems were about love, many of them were marked heavily with ink markings, showing that Brother Stephen had read them, found them . . . what? I wondered. Over some of them my face warmed, knowing I was reading the words he had read, had even marked to be studied and reread. And the words stayed strangely with me . . . "First we loved well and faithfully, Yet knew not what we loved, nor why . . ."

And there was one titled "The Relique," which I learned by heart, not wishing to learn it but in some way compelled. I can still say it through to the end, and it now has had its meaning made clear to me. "When my grave is broken up . . . And he that digs it, spies a bracelet of bright hair about the bone, Will he not let us alone, And think that there a loving couple lies, Who thought that this device might be some way to make their souls, At the last busy day, Meet at this grave, and make a little stay."

When I handed the book to Brother Stephen he took it, rubbed the worn leather cover. "I thought I had lost it . . . left it in the woods some place. I am glad to recover it." He held it as if it were a treasure. "Have you read from it?"

"Yes. But I thought it was not meant to be one of the texts."

"Oh, no." He laughed. "No, John Donne would hardly be suitable for teaching in a Shaker school." He looked down at the book, ran his slender fingers over the cover again, tracing out the name. "He was a very great preacher, you know, and he was a very great poet."

It surprised me that he had been a preacher. My face must have shown it, for Brother Stephen said quickly, "He was the royal chaplain and the Dean of St. Paul's. Early in his life he seemed destined for a court career, but that was ruined for him by his marriage. It was King James I who insisted that he take holy orders and become a preacher."

"How did his marriage ruin his court career?" I asked.

"He was secretary to Sir Thomas Egerton, and secretly he married Sir Thomas' niece. When it became known, he was dismissed from his position and even imprisoned."

"What did he do?"

"He had been . . ." We were standing in my classroom. The pupils had gone for the day. Below we could hear Sister Drucie setting her room to rights, moving softly about. Brother Stephen motioned to my table. "Shall we sit down? Do you want to know about John Donne, Sister Rebecca?"

"Oh, yes . . . please . . ." and we sat at my table, forgetting, both of us that we were Shakers and that this kind of conversation was forbidden.

"He was born a Roman Catholic and he was educated at Oxford, but even as a young man he relinquished the Catholic faith and became an Anglican. He studied law in Lincoln's Inn, and went to sea with the second earl of Essex, against Spain. When he returned he was given the post as private secretary to the Baron of Ellesmere. But, as I have said, his love for Mary More, the baron's niece, and their secret marriage, resulted in his dismissal. He practiced law for a number of years, but he began to delve into philosophical thought, and his writings in opposition to the Catholic Church brought him to the notice of the king. Under the king's urging he became an Anglican priest. No more eloquent sermons were ever preached, and no finer poetry was ever written. He thought for himself. He was not bound by any other mind."

I was bold enough to say, "Is that why you like him, mark certain poems?"

"Yes. Because . . ." he hesitated, "a man's mind should be free." He rested his chin in his palm, stared out the window as if seeing faraway things. "There is a whole vast universe of thought waiting to be explored . . . by the poets, by philosophers, by logicians, by astronomers, and scientists, by essayists and theologians. There is the whole mystery of life! Have you ever thought, Rebecca," he said, dropping his hand and leaning forward eagerly, "of how little we know about everything? The world, the universe, the mind, the soul, this human being we call man? Do you realize that we are only beginning to think about such things? The Greeks . . . they began it, but in the endlessness of time that was only yesterday. There are so many answers yet unanswered."

A man's mind should be free . . . I repeated it to myself. It was like fresh rain spray blowing in one's face, clean, refreshing, exhilarating. It echoed and echoed in my own mind . . . a man's mind should be free! Oh, I did believe that! No mind should be bound and straitened by any other . . . to each should be open the far trails of reason. My hands fumbled my apron, the narrow, starched apron all Shaker women wore, and I was recalled and deadened by my remembrance. Minds were not free in Shakerism. And I was puzzled, then, by Brother Stephen. "How can you so believe," I asked, "when for Shakers everything is plainly answered?"

He looked at me, astonished. "But I am not a Shaker!"

I stammered in my own astonishment. "But you are here . . . you are among us . . . you were sent, they say, from the East, to teach in this school. . . ."

"Does that make me a Shaker?"

I spread my hands helplessly. "I didn't know. I presumed so."

He laughed. "I was brought here to teach, but I come from New York, not New Lebanon. I am required to conform to Shaker ways while here, but I am not even a Novitiate, nor likely to be one. I am not attracted to the theology of the Believers."

"Why? What is wrong with it?"

Instead of answering, he asked me a question. "Tell me, Rebecca, why are you a Shaker?"

It was the old question again. "Because my husband is one."

"You, yourself, are not in sympathy?"

His directness confused me, but I tried to be honest. "I have some doubts, yes."

He leaned forward. "Do you really believe, Rebecca, that Mother Ann was the second Christ? Do you really believe in the extreme emotionalism

[141]

of the singing and dancing exercises? Do you really believe in this with-drawal from the world? In the separation of men and women?"

"Do you?" I countered.

"No," he said shortly. "I believe that Mother Ann was a woman dis-appointed in her marriage, frigid by nature, repelled by sex . . . so she repudiated it. I believe she was given to fits of some kind, in which she thought she saw visions and dreamed dreams. Anyone who fasts and prays for days and nights on end is likely to see visions, if only spots before their eyes they can turn into visions. I don't believe for one moment she was the second Christ . . ."

"But I believe," I interrupted, "she *thought* she was."

"Perhaps," he said. "Maybe she was entirely honest. But that does not mean she was right. There is nothing easier for a highly wrought person to believe than the idea that God leads him. It is such a comforting ex-planation. And so much of religion is based in fear and superstition, Re-becca—fear of being damned, and superstition in the rites to appease a jealous God and secure salvation for eternity."

I hesitated, then asked, "Are you not religious at all, then?"

He smiled. "In my own way, I think I am. But few others would think so, perhaps." He flung his arms wide. "If you mean, do I believe in God . . . I do. But I do not believe that His nature can be fully known or comprehended. I do not believe that any church can say 'This is the truth and the only truth.' And the rites of the church, of almost any of them, are still very near paganism."

"But the visions and the gifts of the sisters and brethren? During the shaking exercises and the dances?"

He shrugged. "You can work yourself into almost any kind of frenzy if you have restrained every normal emotion, then turn it loose in an orgy of religious zeal."

"You think they are not real?"

"Oh, yes. But savages can beat drums and chant and dance until they have real gifts of tongues and visions, too. It is almost pure emotion."

"I have never had a vision or a gift," I said.

He gave me an amused look. "Do you want to have?"

I confessed that I could never forget my own sense of dignity, that sometimes the gifts of others embarrassed me.

"There," he said emphatically, "you have put your finger on it exactly. The reasonable man is inherently a man of dignity. How can he help being? Human dignity is invested with divine dignity."

"But Brother Benjamin is a reasonable man . . . and Richard McNemar is a reasonable man. They are both scholars."

"They may be learned without being reasonable. Neither of them is a reasonable man, actually. Religiously they have a blind spot. There, they are both emotional and as fearful and superstitious as the most ignorant savage. No, the more I see of Shakerism the less I like it. Man's mind and his spirit and his human dignity were meant for freedom. There is no place where freedom is so constrained as here . . . no place where it is exchanged so willingly for safety. And it will not work, Rebecca. This great adventure of theirs, this pure adventure of the spirit will not work. For by his very nature, man must seek his own destiny, not have it prescribed for him. Authority will kill the very thing it seeks to control. All dead civilizations prove that. The wind of the spirit will sweep through Shakerism, lift it aloft for a while, then bear the soul of it away on its wings. The life and the zeal will fade, and only the remembrance of a passing wind will remain."

His words sounded like the tolling of a bell, a tolling very familiar and I knew that my own intangible, inarticulate feeling of impermanence and fragility had been uttered for me. There was the ring of truth and reason in the words, and I knew they were so. "I wonder," I said, "that they were willing to have you here."

"There are few good teachers in the Society," he said. "There was almost the necessity for going outside. I have a good education. I know the system they wanted installed. I came well recommended."

"Why did you come?" It was an impertinent question, perhaps, but he had told me so much, so indiscreetly, so trustingly, that I thought it could not hurt to ask.

He shrugged his shoulders. "I don't really know. The adventure of it, perhaps. I had never seen this country and I had heard much about it. I was restless. I have ever been restless and of a wandering nature."

"Were you born in New York?"

"I was born in London. I learned John Donne at Oxford." He smiled, and the next words came with a rush. "I came to America, pulled by the same spirit of restlessness, the same feeling of adventure. It is a new world. I seem ever to be pushed and prodded on."

"Is that why you have never married?"

He looked at his hands, made a temple of his fingers. "Perhaps . . . or it may be that I have never found a woman to love. Or a love that could make me say, 'All other things to their destruction draw, Only our love hath no decay; This, no tomorrow hath, nor yesterday; Running, it never runs from us away, But truly keeps his first, last, everlasting day.'" His voice was very low as he said the lines, his eyes on his templed fingers. Then he lifted them. "But I think I have sought it all my life, and nothing less than that kind of love would serve. I have not wanted a love which ran away."

Neither had I—but it had run, willy-nilly.

Suddenly I stood, picked up my books. I did not want to hear him any longer. He stood, also, and looked down at me. "Will you feel the need to confess this to Sister Molly, Rebecca?"

Mutely I shook my head, and he laughed. "You are not a very good Shaker, Rebecca."

I felt shaken. "I try," I said.

"Why?" He blocked my passage through the door.

The sounds below in Sister Drucie's room had long since stopped. "Because I must," I said.

"Why must you?"

"I don't know," I cried, feeling tormented. "Let me pass, Brother Stephen."

Quickly he stood aside. "Of course. I have been rude. Forgive me. If you were truly happy . . ."

"If I were truly happy, what?" I asked, looking up at him. He seemed very tall above me.

"I would never have said a word."

"How can you know?"

"Because you think . . . and no one who thinks can be happy here."

"Then I shall quit thinking!"

"Ah," he said softly, "but you can't. And there's the rub . . ."

"Don't," I cried, almost weeping, and running I fled down the stairs, to the safety of the outdoors, the narrow stone walk, the strong, stout Shaker buildings. I drew a deep tremulous breath. I ought, I told myself, to report him. He should not be here among us with his heresies. But they were my own heresies! Beleaguered and not yet wishing to be with others, I hid my books in a bush and turned off to go to the fowl yard. I would help Viney feed the hens, I thought.

But I was drawn aside by the blooms in the orchard. The trees were full of blossoms on that fair May day. There was a sweet, heavy scent from them, a heady scent which made me close my eyes and breathe in deeply. The grass was soft and long. I could lie here, I thought, a little while . . . compose myself, put Brother Stephen's heresies from my mind, renew my . . . renew what? Faith? Had I any? Zeal? Belief? Comfort? Purity? Purpose? I sank into the long grass under an apple tree, stretched out, let my limbs lie flat and quiet, rested a moment.

I drowsed, but never went entirely to sleep, so that footsteps approaching roused me, and I sat up. It was Richard, and caught off guard, surprised at seeing me in the grass, he stopped short and spoke to me. "What are you doing here?"

Instead of answering I looked at him, seeing him as I would a stranger, as indeed he had almost become. He was very lean and brown, and he had let his beard grow during the winter and the covering of his face added to the strangeness of his appearance to me. The broad-brimmed Shaker hat sat squarely on his head, and from under it his eyes were, as they always were now, stern and judging, unlit by any peace. Only in Meeting did they now brighten with joy. In Meeting he could be abandoned, sing and go forth with rejoicing, come under the spell of the spirit. Daily, there was no laughter or lightness in his soul. "Richard," I said suddenly, "let's go away from here. Before everything we ever had together is wholly lost, let's go away. Life is good outside this place . . . let's go back to it."

He stared at me. "Have you lost your mind?"

"No. It's you who have lost yours—and your heart and your soul . . ."

"Be quiet," he said. "My soul is safe, which is more than yours is. I shall never leave this place, and you know that. I would no more consider leaving here with you than I would with any other woman. There is nothing between us any more, save your stubbornness about the property."

"That still grieves you?"

"It will never cease to grieve me, and I will never cease to pray that you may be led to see the light."

My own heart hardened. "I am not more stubborn than you."

"I do not like, either," he went on, "this teaching of yours. Learning is a dangerous thing. It would have been better had you never had any."

I swept my skirts around me and stood. "But that is nothing to you, now. It doesn't matter what you think, for there is nothing between us save my stubbornness. I am glad I had learning, and I am glad I am teaching."

His lips set in a thin, straight line. "You are full of pride, Rebecca, and pride is sinful." In spite of his Shakerism, at that moment I am sure he would have been glad for the power of a husband, to compel his wife.

"You sound like Prissy," I said.

He turned on his heel and walked away. I found my books and went toward the house. I wished I had not asked him to go away with me. What had prompted me, beyond impulse, I did not know. But that it would do no good, I might have been certain. I would never do it again, I vowed.

The house was in turmoil when I reached it. I knew it the moment I walked in. There was a stir and busyness not usual at that time of day. Sister Susan was distracted, walking about, her hands picking at her skirts, and Brother Samuel was looking exceedingly stern, standing in the hall, waiting. Prissy was bustling about, setting a few things together in one corner of the hall . . . a basket of poor dishes, a few badly worn quilts, a table that had only three legs. I went to our bedroom and Lacey was there, weeping, trying to bundle together her clothing. "What's the matter?" I asked. "What has happened?"

"Henry is takin' us away," she said, wiping her eyes and her nose on her apron tail.

"Taking you away? All of you—the children, you?"

"All of us," she sniffed, "ever' last one of us. Oh, Becky, we never had it so plentiful an' good, but he's bound to go, an' says we got to go with him."

"He's already told Brother Samuel, then?"

"Done an' told him, an' aimin' to leave out soon as I c'n git ready. He's went fer the younguns, now."

"Here," I said, "let me fold these and tie them. You get hold of yourself." I tried to comfort her. "Maybe it won't be so bad, Lacey. You'll have your own place to keep again. You can do as you please. No Prissy," I said, trying to make her laugh, "to be forever telling you what to do."

"That's so," she cheered a little, "hit'll be right nice not havin' Prissy over me ever' minnit." But she became mournful again almost immediately. "But hit'll be the same old thing. Not enough to eat, nothin' handy, jist gittin' by, same as allus."

"Maybe not. Maybe Henry will work harder now."

I tied her bundle and went with her down the stairs. Henry had come and the children were huddled about him, not understanding what was happening, with that anxious look children have when there is an upheaval which they do not fathom. "Hurry up," Henry told Lacey.

Brother Samuel checked off a list. "We are returning to you what you brought with you, Brother Henry. And in addition we are giving you fifty dollars in cash to get a start, and a horse."

"I'm beholden to you," Henry said.

"We do the same for anyone who leaves. No thanks are due us. Are you certain you want to do this thing?"

"Sart'n sure," Henry said, grinning. "I'm sick to death of bein' told do this an' do that, an' forever pickin' up an' cleanin' up an' bein' so nicey nice. What I want is the leave to throw a cob of corn through the chinkin' of my cabin again, an' nobody to tell me pick it up."

Frostily Brother Samuel said, "You'll have to get the corn, first, Henry. Very well. The Society gives you full freedom to go and wishes you well."

"I don't need yer freedom to go—I'm goin', free or not. An' I c'n do without yer good wishes." He herded the children out the door, placed his hand on Lacey's back and shoved her through. "I ain't ever in my time been so hedged in as here. I got to breathe my own way."

Man's mind and spirit and soul must be free . . . I thought of Stephen's words. Even so poor a spirit as Henry Akins felt it.

Prissy did not stay to say goodbye, but Sister Susan wept as the big family of children pathetically followed their parents, and as Lacey turned once to look back and wave. "They'll go hungry," she said. "Henry can't provide for them."

Brother Samuel turned from the door. "They'll be back," he said. "Come winter, they'll be back. They'll make out during the season, but come the first cold spell and they'll be back, wanting a warm place and plenty to eat. They," he said bitterly, "are good winter Shakers."

But he was wrong. Henry and Lacey did not come back. And for all I know Henry got his pleasure of throwing cobs through the chinking of his cabin, with no one to say him nay. And I knew exactly how he felt.

We missed Lacey in our room that night. She had been fat and lazy, but she had also been good-natured and one of us. Her bed looked oddly

empty. "Reckon they'll put somebody else in with us?" Permilla asked.
"Not till someone new comes, I'd think," Amanda said.

"Well, I hope it's a time afore somebody new comes in, fer it would misput us all, gittin' used to 'em. Seems like the best thing we got here is all of us used to one another in our room. Hit'd be terrible, wouldn't it, if we got somebody we couldn't git along with." She flopped on her bed to rest. "My sakes, but I'm tard."

"What have you been doing today?" I asked.

"Plantin' squash an' corn. I got the garden duty this month. But I ain't complainin'. Hit goes good to be on the outside fer a change. I jist wish I could draw it ever' month fer the summer. This is good ground, Becky. An' the men broke it good. Hit's a pleasure to be workin' in it." She folded her arms under her head and lay still, eyes closed, and soon she had dropped off to sleep.

The bell for Family Meeting rang. It had a mellow tone, the bell atop Center House, and the sound of it was one of the things I liked most about the village. It marked off the time more beautifully than a clock.

We went upstairs and seated ourselves about the meeting room. We were surprised to find Brother Benjamin in charge. He had a folded newspaper in his hand, and as soon as prayers and one hymn were over, he paced to the middle of the floor and unfolded the paper. "It is not often," he said, "that we have need to be concerned with the happenings in the world, but something has occurred which the entire Society needs to know." He put on his spectacles and began to read. Three days before, he read, the Legislature had enacted a law which made membership in the Society of Believers grounds for divorce by the dissenting party in a marriage. The law said that any person, wanting such a divorce, had only to file for it, and it would be granted, together with fair property rights, and custody of minor children.

Astonished looks passed between us all as we took it in. We had been legally pointed out now, as a shame and an abomination. Brother Benjamin's voice broke as he finished the reading, and he struck the paper with the flat of his hand. "Ah, Kentucky! Noble Kentucky! How low hast thou fallen!"

There was a buzz of comment . . . nothing could have kept us from stirring and talking at that moment and Brother Benjamin allowed it for a few minutes. Then he asked for quiet again. "This is but another persecution, and we should welcome it, for in persecution are we strengthened. Go forth in your labors tonight with joy, with faith and zeal. Give thanks that in Mother's name you are persecuted. Rejoice that we are her children, and we can bear all things in her name." He left, then, to take his paper and his news, I guessed, to the other Families.

Brother Samuel rose to lead us forth in the dance, but before he had had time to signal us, Richard stood. "There is one among us," he said, "who has need for humiliation. I accuse Sister Rebecca of pride and arrogance of spirit, of lack of faith and zeal . . ." He paused, and I thought he would go on and accuse me of tempting him. But, white-faced and suddenly wavering on his feet, as if ill, he stopped and sat down.

Beside me, Permilla gasped, "Well, I never!"

Every eye was turned on me and in Sister Priscilla's there was certainly a triumphant gleam. Brother Samuel asked me to stand. "In what way, Brother Richard, has Sister Rebecca been guilty of pride and arrogance?"

Richard's eyes, also, were fixed on me, stonily. "In steadfastly refusing to entreat for full membership, for complete dedication. In holding material things more important than the salvation of her soul."

It was Prissy who cried "Woe," first, but it was taken up by many others within a few moments, and the cries of "Woe, woe, woe" echoed round and round the room. If you have not stood in the center of a room, ringed about by people who have suddenly become your judges, and listened to their cries of shame and contempt, there is no way you can know the feeling. It is a shriveling experience, all the more shriveling for me because my own husband had brought it about. I would not have believed he could do it, that he so wanted to become a full member that he would take this way of forcing it.

Nothing he could have done, however, could have hardened my stubbornness more. The cries, at first piercing me and hurting, slowly became simply a sound, a concert of sound, which beat on my ears, but no longer entered my soul. I stood, alone, through it all, knowing that now I was truly guilty of pride and arrogance. For it was pride which came to my rescue, pride that refused to be humbled. Publicly humiliated and stoned with words, I determined during the humiliation itself that this one thing would forever be denied Richard. If there was vindictiveness in it, perhaps I may be pardoned. I had been much hurt, and this was an ultimate hurt, deliberately planned and done. "I would never wish to hurt you," he had said. But he *had* wished to hurt me, and in my mind it seemed to me Richard's sin of pride was greater than my own. Perhaps I was wrong. Perhaps he had simply become such a zealot that there was no longer any feeling in him, only the wish or the need to be fully dedicated, to secure and save himself.

Standing, listening, it came to me that zealots were always cruel—that they were self-centered and self-seeking, even if it was spiritual grace they were seeking. I thought how, in the end, there was little difference between Richard and any other man wishing to obtain some great good for himself. One man seeks good for himself in trade or politics. Another seeks good for himself in the realm of the spirit. Where lies the difference?

Brother Samuel was kind. He called for the cries to cease, and said, "We are all equally guilty. Let us kneel and pray." Then he led us forth in the dance, and Richard was the most abandoned of all, whirling time and again into a single dance, leaving the circle, spinning, as if under some spell. His gift was respected, but if a vision had come to him he did not speak of it. At the end he was as white and shaken as when he had accused me, and only sorrow showed on his face. Purity of purpose is well-nigh impossible, so long as human feelings and human griefs can be felt.

Downstairs in our room again, there was a gathering about me, a commiserating with me. "They warn't a one from this room opened their mouths, Becky," Permilla told me. "Not a one. None of them 'woes' come from us. Hit was a shame an' a pity. I'd like," she said, brindling with indignation, "to git my hands on that man of yore'n!"

It had been a shame, and it was a pity.

CHAPTER XVII

TROUBLES never come singly. It was the next day as I walked to the Schoolhouse that Cassie stepped out from behind a hedge of bushes and stopped me. "Jency," she said abruptly, "is fixin' to have a youngun."

"But I told her to let me know . . ." I said.

I had forgotten Jency, too. I should have known she would never tell me. I should have gone, myself, to see about her. Cassie's eyes were big and mournful. "You knowed, Miss Becky?"

I told her what had happened in December, then, and I left out nothing. "I hoped," I said, "nothing would come of it. I told her to let me know."

Cassie's shoulders were sagged. "Hit wouldn't of done no good, I reckon. She's too flighty to know or to keer, mostly. Whut'll we do, Miss Becky? Whut you reckon *they'll* do?"

I had no idea what they would do, but as to what we could do, there was very little. "Just say nothing about it, Cassie, for the present. Let me think for a few days. Is she showing yet?"

"Some. Enough that I taken notice. But ain't nobody else, fur as I know. Miss Becky, I wish we ain't ever come to the Shakers. Ain't nothin' but trouble come of it, like I said. I wish we wuz back on our place, like we used to be. Hit was a happy time, then."

In the way that almost an entire lifetime can pass in a few moments before one's eyes, I remembered our home, its order, the peace and the goodness that had filled it before the Believers came. It *had* been a happy time. There was in me the same aching wish that Cassie had voiced, that we had never come to the Shakers. But there is no turning back, and almost as quickly as I felt the wish, it passed. This, right now, the present, was what we had to deal with. I put my arm about Cassie's shoulder. "This is done, Cassie. In my own opinion nothing will come of it except that Jency may be humiliated in Meeting. I doubt if even that will be done, for I think they will not wish to call attention to such a sin. As long as she and Clayton are not married, do not live openly together, I don't think they will do anything."

Cassie wiped her eyes. "You think they won't send her away? That was what I was most skeered of, an' whur the pore little thing could go I had no idee. I never seen but whut I'd have to go to take the keer of her."

"Just say nothing, now. Let it become evident as it will. If they do send her away, you can go with her, and I promise you that I will see to it you are cared for. My mother, or Miss Bethia will take you."

Her burden shifted, she smiled at me, her big mouth quivering at the corners. "I knowed you'd think of somethin', Miss Becky. I knowed you wouldn't fergit us."

"I will," I promised again, "I'll try to think of something."

After school I went to find Jency. She was rocking Annie's baby. "Is he ailing?" I asked.

"No'm. He be fine. But Miss Annie is a weanin' him, an' he's jist fretful. Don't like his milk from a cup, this 'un don't." She grinned at me and went on rocking the child.

Annie's baby was a fat, healthy child, already more than two years old, but women often nursed their children to three or past. "Give him to me," I said.

Jency handed him to me. "Ain't he hefty?"

She stood there before me and with my own eyes I saw the slight swelling of her body. "You didn't tell me, Jency."

Her eyes widened. "Whut didn't I tell you, Miss Becky?"

"That you are going to have a baby."

She giggled and smoothed her dress. "Whut wuz the use, Miss Becky? You git a youngun, you gits it, an' that's all. No use a tellin'."

"What are you going to do?"

"Have me a youngun . . . one of my own. I loves younguns, Miss Becky."

"Have you been seeing Clayton all along?"

Unabashed she looked at me. "Yessum. I likes Clayton, too."

"Why don't you get married, then, and both of you leave here?"

"Why, Miss Becky, we ain't studyin' on leavin' here. We likes it all right."

"Wouldn't you like to be married to Clayton, though, and have you a little house of your own, and all the children you want?"

She twiddled with a stiff braid of hair, then she giggled. "I kin have me all the younguns I wants 'thout leavin', I reckon."

I handed her Annie's baby. To save my life I couldn't help laughing. Moral ideas sat very lightly on Jency. I could foresee a new little black baby every year, a steady procession of them, year in and year out. What amused me most was the look I could also foresee on Shaker faces, as they strove and struggled to imbue Jency with some notion of sin—and failed—and what they would do with all those babies of hers. But I thought she and Clayton should be married and leave the village and I said so again. "That's what you should do, Jency."

"Well, even did we want to, Miss Becky, they ain't no way to. Clayton ain't free."

"But I thought he was! I thought Mr. Steel had freed all his people!"

"No'm. Miss Amanda wouldn't let him. Clayton cain't leave here 'thout Mister Steel say so, an' I don't reckon he could say so 'thout Miss Amanda say so too."

That, of course, put the whole thing in a different light. But I felt more lighthearted than when I had come. I should have known, I reasoned, that not only would Jency feel no sense of shame, she would feel pleasure and excitement over having her own child. I loves younguns—I had heard her say it a thousand times—I loves younguns. Oh, I did too, I did too. I could still feel Annie's baby, fat and soft and baby-smelling, in my arms. And my life was wasting away. I was teaching the children of others, in the certain knowledge I would never teach one of my own.

But it was better than the dryness in East House, I told myself . . . it was infinitely better. At least I was now doing something which refilled me each day as I emptied myself. I looked at the new book Stephen had given me just that day.

"Here," he said, thrusting the book at me, "read this Greek history. Read the story of the Lacedemonians at Thermopylae. Perhaps it will compensate for last night."

"You know?"

"Everyone knows everything in this small a place, Rebecca. I'm very sorry."

I smiled, a little wryly. "Well, it wasn't pleasant, but it's over."

"Yes. This will make your heart sing, however."

"Is it sad?"

"No. It is glorious. The Greeks knew how to die."

"How did they die?"

"Without whimpering."

"Is this to be a lesson for me?"

He shook his head. "You need no lesson. It is to remind you that all men share a common fate."

As I passed by the garden Permilla called to me. "Come look at the onions and the corn and the spring greens."

The whole garden was showing green, the corn spiking up, the thick leaves of the mustard already curling, the darker green of the onion blades standing stiff and proud. I admired it all, and even took a hoe and worked for a few minutes in the crumbly, rich earth, loosening it around a row of beans just breaking through the crust. Permilla followed with her own hoe.

Having come to the end of the row, I handed her the hoe. "I've got to go. I have some studying to do. Jency's having a baby," I added.

Permilla rounded her eyes at me, then laughed. "Now, what do you say! Ain't she the foxy one, though?"

I had never told Permilla what I had seen in December, but I did so now. She listened, chuckling. "Fancy them two, now, streakin' off to that old lean-to! I reckon they warn't *too* skeered at that."

"Evidently not," I agreed, laughing myself.

"What are you aimin' to do about it?"

"I don't know yet."

"You aimin' on tellin' Richard?"

"No."

"You're a gittin' over Richard, ain't you, Becky?"

"The way he is now, Permilla, there's nothing to *get* over. He's like someone I never knew before. Memories are about all that's left."

She nodded. "An' a body cain't live on remembrances."

"No." I picked up the book I had laid on the grass at the end of the row, dusted a bit of dirt off its cover. "I'm not going to try to. I'm studying and learning."

Permilla poked a finger at the book. "That's a pore makeshift fer a man, though."

The sudden remembered feeling of Richard's arms about me made me wince. That's what hurts most about memories . . . the touch, the feeling, the smell, the texture. They flock in, and one's skin is again sensitive to them. But a body can't live on remembrances. Permilla had just said it, and I knew it. "In some ways it's a poor makeshift," I said. "But it has its merits."

"Not in bed, though." Permilla's voice was dry.

"No," I laughed. "Get on with your hoeing, Permilla, and I'll take my book out of your way."

She gave me an affectionate spank as I passed her. "Don't go strainin' yer eyes, now."

"I'll not."

I saw Amanda after supper. "Is it true," I asked her, "that you and William didn't set your blacks free?"

"It's true. William wanted to, but I wouldn't," she said.

"Why?"

She shrugged her bony shoulders. "We might have a use for them."

"You're still hoping, then?"

She set her mouth firmly. "I'm doing more than hoping, now."

I didn't know what she meant and it was none of my business. I had only wanted to know whether Clayton was free, so I asked no questions.

There had been a whispered rumor for several weeks that a new kind of meeting was to be tried—a conversational meeting, in which three or four sisters would be chosen to visit the same number of men in their rooms, with one of the leaders of course, for singing and praying and for whatever talk they wanted to exchange. Brother Benjamin, it was said, thought it would solve the problem of husbands and wives forever slipping aside to talk together.

In our room after supper there was considerable excitement. The experiment was to be tried that night and Annie was one of the women chosen. By that, I thought the leaders had some inkling of the way she and Robert slipped to be together.

Annie was in a state because she had to have a clean handkerchief. "Yore kerchief is fresh enough," Permilla told her. "You jist put it on this mornin'."

"I have to have one to put in my lap," Annie said.

We all stared at her. "In yer lap?" Permilla said, finally. "Fer goodness' sake what are they aimin' fer you to do with a kerchief in yer lap?"

"I don't know." Annie was putting up her back hair, having trouble with the short lengths. "They didn't say. They just said we had to have a clean kerchief to lay our hands on in our laps. What's the reason for *anything* they take a notion for?"

"Are they aimin' to let the men an' women mix?" Viney asked.

"No," Annie said, "you know better than that. Sister Susan said we would sit in our chairs, facing the men, five feet across from them. And we all, men and women both, have to lay our hands on a fresh kerchief in our laps."

Permilla threw back her head and shouted with laughter. "At five foot, I'd like to know what they think a body's hands could do that would amount to anything!"

"Sh-sh-sh," Annie begged her. "Be quiet, Permilla. If Prissy comes in here and commences preaching at me now, I'll lose my wits." She had her hair up, now, and her cap on. "I've *got* to have a kerchief."

"You can have my fresh one," I told her. "I'll rinse the other one out tonight."

"Oh, Becky, you're awful good. Likely you could wear it tomorrow, though. I don't know as it'll be dirtied the least bit."

"Well, where's yore extry one?" Permilla asked. "I bet you ain't washed it."

Annie made a face at her. She was careless about her things, often wore a kerchief two days old, and many times bathed sketchily. She loved pretty things, but she didn't care too much if her neck was dirty, or her body not clean. The discipline of order and cleanliness was hard on her.

I found my kerchief and gave it to her. She folded it four times, in a square. "That's the way we have to have them. Is everything to suit them, you reckon?"

We looked her over. I pinned up a stray lock of hair, Permilla settled a fold in her kerchief, Viney tweaked her skirt and even Amanda lent a hand, retying her apron knot. She sat down, then, on the edge of her chair. "Sister Susan's coming for me."

I laughed. "You'd think we were getting her ready for a party."

Permilla sniffed. "Hit ain't my notion of a party."

"Nor mine," Annie said, "but it's something different to do, and I don't want to miss out on it."

Annie suddenly turned white and swayed in her chair, her hand over her mouth. "What is it?" I asked. She looked very ill.

She gulped. "Something I eat, I reckon. It's about to come back up on me."

The others clustered around. "Lie down," Permilla told her, "an' I'll put a wet cloth on yer throat."

Annie shook her head. "There ain't time. I don't want to miss the conversation meeting. Anyway, it'll pass."

But she did lie down, retching, throwing her head back as if wanting air. I felt of her forehead, but it was cool, though beads of sweat had broken out on it. "You've got no fever," I said. We were ever afraid of the cholera.

"No. It's just my stummick, heaving. It'll pass."

Permilla eyed her shrewdly, then she started laughing. "I'll *wager* yore stummick's heavin'. You're in the family way, ain't you?"

Annie raised her head and looked at Permilla. "Well, it was you give me the idea. Yes, I'm in the family way. I weaned little Robert so's my health would come back on me—and if it don't get Robert away from this place, the Shakers'll just have another youngun on their hands!"

"Sh," Viney hissed, "someone's comin'."

We scurried for our chairs and Annie flew as fast as any of us, though her face was still pale and her throat corded with nausea. Sister Susan opened the door. "Are you ready, Annie?"

Butter would have melted in Annie's mouth. "Yes, ma'am."

"Come with me, then."

As demurely as a girl going to meet her first beau Annie followed Sister Susan into the hall. Softly the door closed behind her, and immediately the rest of us broke from our chairs, giggling and whispering, gathering around my bed. "Well, what do you know!" Permilla said, then, chuckling. "She's a smart one, that Annie. Reckon what Robert'll do?"

"He's a fool if he don't leave with her," Amanda snapped.

Most of us were of the opinion he would, and for my own part I hoped fervently Annie would get her way. They were too young to be thus sealed off from life and their happiness together.

"How many did they take tonight?" Permilla asked, then.

"Three," Amanda said. "I heared Prissy sayin' it."

"Wonder what Prissy thinks of it?"

"I c'n imagine," Permilla said.

Amanda laughed. "She don't approve, I can tell you."

"I jist hope it ain't her duty when my time comes," Permilla said.

"Oh, it will always be either Sister Susan or Brother Samuel," Amanda told her. "Prissy has nothing to do with it. It comes," she went on, "under the *spiritual* side."

"A little *too* spiritual to suit me," Permilla said, and we all laughed. We all knew it would never do what it was supposed to do. How could it, under the watchful eyes of the leaders? What man or woman would talk normally with them hearing every word?

"Have we got to take a turn at it?" I asked. I was out of touch with many things which happened in the Family then, knowing them only by hearsay.

Amanda shook her head. "No. Nobody is to be forced. But it's open to those that want it."

"Well, I'm not going to take any turn, then," I said, making a sudden decision.

"Why ain't you?" Viney asked. But Permilla looked at me understandingly.

"I'd rather read," I said.

"I'm not going to take any turn, either," Amanda said.

"You ain't aimin' to read, too, are you?" Viney asked.

"No. But I'm not going visiting no menfolks. I've got nothing to say . . . not to any of 'em *here*, leastways."

Permilla started undressing. "Well, I'll take my turn, jist fer the change of it an' the curiosity. But right now I'm aimin' to git to bed. Garden work wears a body down."

The others went to their own beds, too. I drew the candle table near my own. We could keep a light till nine-thirty, and while in the beginning I had often been afraid the light bothered the others, they had assured me it didn't, and they had now grown accustomed to my habit of reading until that hour. In a few moments each woman had knelt, said her prayers, and was in bed.

This was an hour to which I looked forward each day. It was a time of quiet, undisturbed, when only the book in my hands was real to me—when, in my mind at least, I quit the Shaker house, went exploring and adventuring into other lands and other times. For one hour, or if I was lucky, for a little longer, I could escape South Union, and gradually it had come to be the best hour of the day for me.

I opened Stephen's book—or rather, like most of his books, it fell open of its own accord, at a page which he had read over and over again. Often as I read his books I had the feeling of his own voice saying the words to me, or of his mind leading me.

Under my hand was the epitaph of the Spartans at Thermopylae . . . "O passer-by, tell the Lacedemonians that we lie here, in obedience to their laws." This was what Stephen had said would make my heart sing?

It did not. But then I did not know yet what lay back of it. I turned the page to the beginning of the story.

Little by little the Persian War came to life for me, Xerxes, the Persian commander, landing with a tremendous army, marching toward the narrow pass which was the only route into the peninsula. The story grew enormous in my imagination. Leonidas, with his three hundred Spartans and his small army of only eight thousand men in all, were frighteningly threatened. Then came the betrayal, and I felt shame for the Greek who could so betray his countrymen. And the decision of Leonidas, knowing he would be trapped, knowing every man would be killed, seemed noble beyond words to me. He told his small army that any man who wished to leave was free to do so, and only two thousand remained with him, but of them, three hundred were Spartans . . . all of the Spartans. And they died, as they had known they would die, in the pass of Thermopylae. I read the epitaph again . . . "tell the Lacedemonians that we lie here in obedience to their laws." That was all. And I felt rebellion that they had not been more honored.

I told Stephen so the next day.

"They died," he said, "as Sparta required them to die, in obedience. That was their real epitaph."

But my woman's mind refused to agree. "They might have mentioned their courage on the stone. They might have told of their bravery, honored it."

"It was honored. It was told. Don't you see, Rebecca? What are the words again?"

" 'Tell the Lacedemonians that we lie here in obedience to their laws.' "

I slowly repeated the words, and I saw what he meant. They died—all three hundred of them, as they had known they would, been required to do. The courage and the bravery were implicit in the deed. The deed was their epitaph.

"One additional word," Stephen said softly, "would have been to whimper."

They did know how to die, those Greeks, without whimpering. And it came to me that one ought to live without whimpering, too. And it also came to me that I had done a considerable amount of whimpering in the last few years—almost since Richard and I had been married. Crying out for myself against the blows of life, pitying myself, being sorry for myself, saying over and over again, why, why, why, must these things happen to me? I determined to try very, very hard never again to give way to the muling and puling cries of a hurt child. I was no Spartan, but neither was I threatened with death. I had, however, to live, and I wanted, now, to live with courage and without whimpering.

That was why, I think, when Amanda came to the Schoolhouse late that morning, during the period when the children were free for exercise and play, I made no argument. She was such a plain woman, with dry lips, sharp nose and chin, and a discontented look on her face, ever . . . and it is true I never had any great liking for her, but I felt pity for her because of the separation from her child. "I'd like," she said, "to talk a minute with Silas, Becky, if you'd agree."

The boy had been ailing for about a week, with chills and fever. On the days when he chilled he hadn't been able to be in school. It had been my duty to tell Amanda, and it had caught her so hard she had had to sit down suddenly. "Is he bad off?"

"No," I had said, "he's just feverish and chilling. Sister Drucie is dosing him and she thinks he'll be all right in a day or two."

"Sister Drucie!" she had said contemptuously. "He's *my* boy and it's my place to nurse him." She wrung her hands pathetically. "I don't know, Becky, if I can leave him to her care. He's the only one left to us. If anything happened to him . . ."

I put my hand on her shoulder. "Sister Drucie is a good nurse."

"But she ain't his mother! She don't have the least idea how a little one feels when he's sick, or how a woman feels that's a mother."

She and William had been overly protective of the boy, but it was easy to understand why they would be. In their place I would have been, too. I felt terribly sorry for her as the days passed. She fretted constantly and had no peace of mind. She asked to be allowed to nurse him, but the Shakers made light of his illness and both Amanda and William were kept at their regular duties.

He was still chilling every third day when she came to the Schoolhouse and asked to see him. "Of course," I said, without hesitation. "I'll ask Brother Stephen to send him to you."

"I'm obliged," she said.

Stephen sent the boy over and she took him off a little distance, stood talking with him, then took him farther, disappearing from sight. Sister Drucie was inside, it being my turn on the schoolyard. Stephen wandered over, leaving the boys. "What did she want with him?"

"I have no idea. But he has been sick, is still sick, and she shall see him when she pleases as long as it is in my power."

"You are fast becoming a rebel, Rebecca," he said, smiling at me.

His hair, which was a very light color, almost as pale a yellow as a child's, grayed a little at the temples, had a way of curling over his ears, and he had a way of twisting at a lock there. Often when he was studying I had seen him, absent-mindedly pulling at it, twisting it between his fingers, thrusting it awry so that it stood like small feathers, on end. He had been twisting it now, and it was ruffled as if by the wind. "You've been tormenting those poor locks," I said, "haven't you?"

He grinned, smoothed at them. "Have I?"

"You'll have them all pulled out if you don't stop."

"I can't," he said. "I've tried. I even wear a cap when I read at night to keep me from tugging at them, and the cap only ends up perched on one ear or the other."

The picture of him, a cap clinging to an ear, the graying locks sticking up in all directions, made me laugh. The creaking noise of a wagon passing on the road made both of us turn to look. A cloud of dust was boiling up. In its fog we made out the wagon, drawn by a team of oxen, a man walking beside them, prodding them, whistling as he walked. The wagon was sheeted and printed in bold letters on the canvas were the words "Missouri Territory or Bust!"

"That," I said, "is the fourth wagon that has passed here this month headed for the Missouri Territory. Where is it, Stephen, and why are people going there in such numbers?"

Stephen watched the wagon a moment, smiled at the man's whistle. "The Missouri Territory," he said, then, "is part of that vast tract which your President Jefferson purchased from Napoleon some years ago—the one called the Louisiana Purchase. It lies west of the Mississippi, and the answer to why so many people are going there is simple. It is west . . . it is new, open, free and wild. Some day," he went on, his hand reaching for a lock of hair, his eyes thoughtful, "when the history of this country is written, its greatest romance will lie in its ever-westward movement—the urge to push on toward the last known land, to the water's edge . . . from Virginia through the Gap to Kentucky, from Kentucky across the Mississippi to the Missouri Territory, and from Missouri, who knows where? To the utmost limits of the land."

My imagination was seized and stirred by the westward movement he had spoken of, and in my mind I saw the surge of people through the Cumberland Gap. I had heard my father and mother tell of it. I, myself, I realized, was witnessing the continuing surge, to the Missouri Territory. Like a pageant acted before my eyes I saw the men and women, the wagons rolling on, the wilderness tamed, the rivers crossed, the homes springing up, the children being born to new heritages. With wonder I knew I was seeing history being made, and I wondered further that it had not occurred to me before.

Suddenly I felt an urge to be a part of it, an almost overpowering wish to be sitting in one of those wagons, Richard walking beside a team of horses or oxen, heading for the Missouri Territory. Without thinking I said it, passionately, "Oh, I *wish* I could go, I wish I could see that new country!"

Stephen was still watching the wagon, which now had passed, its cloud of dust settling behind it. "I *am* going," he said softly, "some day."

"Men," I said hotly, "men can always do as they please! A woman is bound, hand and foot she is tied, to whatever her man wants."

Stephen looked at me, and then he smiled. "Would you be a man, then, Rebecca?"

"At this moment, yes!" Then I had to laugh. "But most of the time, no.

Other things are given to a woman to make up to her. I would not really be a man. But I would like to go to the Missouri Territory."

"Perhaps you will."

I turned back to the schoolyard. "No. I'll never see that country and I may as well put it from my mind."

Stephen's eyes wandered over the schoolyard also. "They're gone again," he said, then.

"Who?" I asked.

"Sabrina and Lucien. Didn't you know? They're in love."

"Oh, no!"

"Why not? It's very beautiful, I think."

"But nothing must happen to Sabrina!" I said it as passionately as I felt it. "She is too fine to be made unhappy."

"Will marriage with Lucien make her unhappy do you think?"

I thought of Lucien Brown, so open and frank a boy, so handsome and manly. I thought of Sabrina, lovely, intelligent, plump and rosy. I shook my head. "They won't be allowed to marry. They are too young, yet."

"Then perhaps they will wait."

"What if they don't?"

"Then I hope they will take me into their confidence, and I will help them get away. See, they are back now. Lucien is with the boys again. Sabrina is coming from the . . . the . . ." She was coming from the out-house, but we had no good name for such a building that could be used indiscriminately. "They are very discreet," Stephen said. "They never leave at the same time, nor come back together. One of them wanders off . . . a few moments later the other goes, in a different direction. They never stay more than a few minutes. What I am afraid of is that it will not long suffice. Right now they are only beginning to love. Soon they will want to be together longer and longer, and the time may come when either they will become indiscreet and get into trouble, or someone must help them get away. I will help them, if possible."

I was glad he wanted to help them, but I was a little worried on his account. "You yourself may get into trouble if you aren't careful."

"I may," he said calmly, "but what could harm me in that? I could only be asked to leave."

"But that is exactly what mustn't happen," I said. "You are needed here!"

He shrugged. "I have no intention of going, unless I am asked to go. But neither do I intend to fail any person in need of my help."

"Don't die at Thermopylae, Stephen," I said, laughing.

"Oh, no," he said, laughing with me, "the Trojan horse is much more suited to me. It's time for books," he said.

"Amanda hasn't come back yet," I reminded him.

Stephen looked up the path.

"It's all right. Sister Drucie won't know."

We rounded up the children and marched them into the Schoolhouse. We did not know until suppertime that Amanda had taken her boy and had left the Shaker village with him.

CHAPTER XVIII

WE ALL MISSED her at the same time, of course. But an empty chair at meals could mean several things. It could mean the person was ill. It could mean he was called away to one of the other houses, or was on some duty which temporarily kept him through a mealtime. It rarely happened among the women, though, and when it did the leaders always knew of it. Prissy did not know where Amanda was, however, for she gave it away by looking puzzled when she saw Amanda's chair. Of course she did not ask any questions. Silence was the rule, and she kept silent, but she also kept looking at Amanda's empty chair.

We had all become adept at whispering with the least possible movement of our lips. We had become equally adept at hearing the slightest whisper. So I had no trouble understanding when Permilla said, "Where you reckon she is?"

I had a premonition, but this was not the time to go into it. So I said, "No idea."

We ate quietly as usual, but all of us kept glancing at each other, at Amanda's chair, at Prissy and the other leaders. Excitement mounted in us and was evident in the haste in which we ate, and by a fidgeting and twiddling with our forks, the bread, and many hurried gulps of milk too often. I remember that we had wild greens for supper, and how, ordinarily, they would have tasted so good, but how I barely knew what I was eating with Amanda's empty chair across the table from me.

She had not brought the boy back before school was out, but I had supposed she would certainly have him in the School House for supper. I wondered what was happening there. Stephen would handle it, I thought. He would know what to do.

As soon as we had finished the meal, we all saw Prissy hurry to Sister Susan's side and begin a whispered conference with her, then both women approached Brother Samuel. That was all we saw, for we were filing out of the dining room at the time. In our room we all stared at each other. "What duty was she on?" I asked, finally,

Annie answered. "She was in the chicken yard and the garden."

I looked at Permilla. "You saw her leave, then?"

Permilla nodded. "I seen her, yes."

I confessed then. "She came to the Schoolhouse and got the boy."

"She's often went down there jist to look at him," Permilla said.

"She took him off with her. She asked if she could speak to him a little while and Brother Stephen and I let him go. At first she went a little way down the path and talked with him, but the next thing we knew she was out of sight. She hadn't brought him back when school was out."

"She's left out then," Permilla said, positively. "She's done an' lit a shuck with him."

"But where would she go?" I asked, wondering.

Viney spoke up. "She's allus been close-mouthed, but the last day or two she's been broody and thinkin' of somethin'. Likely she's been plottin' it out."

Annie looked at me. "I reckon you know you'll be in trouble yourself, letting her see the youngun."

I nodded. Both Stephen and I would be questioned, no doubt about it, but it didn't bother me at all. My thoughts were all with Amanda, wondering where she was, what she intended to do, hoping that whatever it was wouldn't go awry for her, get her into trouble.

We had Meeting of some sort every night, but Prissy came before the hour to tell us there would be none that night, and to tell me I was wanted at Center House. She looked smug and satisfied. She didn't volunteer any other information, just said I was to report to Sister Molly, but the way she said it foretold unpleasantness. "Don't you let 'em badger you, now," Permilla said sympathetically as I made ready to go.

I shook my head. "All I can do is tell the truth."

At Center House all the leaders were gathered—those from our Family, those from the North Family, Stephen and Sister Drucie from the School Family, and of course those from Center House. William Steel was seated among them, looking stubborn and determined. I was asked to be seated. Stephen smiled at me across the room. It surprised me that I was not at all frightened or confused. I had only to tell the truth. I knew no more than anyone else, and I was glad Amanda had been close-lipped about her plans. Whatever I was asked, I knew only that Amanda had come to the Schoolhouse, asked to speak to Silas, and Stephen and I had allowed it. That was all.

But for a time no one questioned me. Brother Benjamin was talking to William. "She needn't have taken the boy and run off with him this way, William."

"She was afeared, I reckon," William said, "Afeared you'd stop her."

"Do you know where she has gone? Did you plan this together?"

William shook his head. "No. She never said a word to me, but there ain't but one place she *could* go . . . back to the farm." He lifted his head. "And I'll be going there, too, Brother Benjamin. I've been steadfast in the faith. I've tried to live in the light, thinking to save my soul. It like to killed me and Amanda both to live apart from the boy, but we done so, thinking you had the right of it. But it's a hard way of living, parting young ones from their folks."

"It was Mother Ann's way, for their salvation as well as for their parents'."

William stood. "It may have been Mother Ann's way, but I've had my fill of it. Silas is all we've got left out of five, and when he was sick in the bed with chills and fever we wasn't allowed to see him. We had to leave him to the care of others. It ain't the natural way. Folks has got feelings, Brother Benjamin, that won't be downed. Amanda has just took the only way out, that she could see. She never talked to me, but I don't hold it against her. She, maybe, was afeared I'd be set against it, too. But I ain't. I'm going to leave out of here, and we'll raise our boy ourselves. When you've got but one he's bigger to you than anything else."

"Even your immortal soul, William?"

William bowed his head. "Even my immortal soul, Brother Benjamin. I don't feel hardly toward you, but it appears to me you're misguided on this raising up younguns apart from their folks."

Brother Benjamin sighed. "The path of righteousness is a hard one to follow, William. But if you are determined, let it be so. We will make a settlement with you in the morning."

William strode out of the room.

Stephen looked at me again, and smiled, and I smiled to see that one of his hands had sought the locks over his left ear. He was tugging at them, as usual. He looked quiet enough, otherwise. Brother Benjamin turned to me, then. Of course he already knew what had happened at the School House. Stephen, it seemed, had told him. "Brother Stephen has told us that he allowed Amanda to speak to Silas. Sister Drucie knows nothing of it. Do you?"

"Yes," I said, "and it was not Brother Stephen entirely. I allowed Amanda to see the boy." Stephen had tried to take all the blame, then.

Brother Benjamin looked at me reproachfully. "You know that you shouldn't have allowed her to speak to the child, don't you?"

"I know that you think we shouldn't have."

He bit his lower lip, looked at the floor, then looked at me directly. "Then why did you do it?"

"Because he was her child, he was sick, and I thought she should be allowed to see him, talk with him, satisfy herself he was all right."

"We decide what the relationship shall be between parents and children, and for very good reasons," he reminded me.

"Yes, sir. But I think you are wrong about it."

"We do not ask you to think," he said sharply. "Every person who enters the village knows what the rules are, everyone among us is expected to abide by them."

"That," I said boldly, "is a thing you may expect, but abiding is a different thing."

"We cannot have discontent among us, Rebecca," he said. "Your rebelliousness has now caused trouble. It was not yours to decide. Neither you nor Brother Stephen had any right. He, of course, bears the burden of responsibility, for he is the leader of the School group. But you must answer for your own disobedience. The school," he said, turning back to Stephen, "is closed for this term. And whether either of you may teach again will be a matter we shall have to consider long and prayerfully."

Sister Susan and Brother Samuel both looked at me, sorrowfully. They were truly hurt by my rebelliousness, it was plain to see, feeling, it may be, they had somehow failed in their own duty. They were good people, devout, dedicated to their duties, but unable to understand any of the problems of those of us who had come into the fold as converts. Both had been born in Shakerism. They were unable to feel any resentment, or difference, or rebellion, or to fathom it in others. They knew nothing of what the world was like. They had never been married or had children. All their lives they had lived in the sheltered world of a Shaker village. Neither had grown up with any knowledge of any other life. How could they possibly understand?

Brother Benjamin dismissed Stephen and me. I left the room first, but I lingered outside. It was dark, no moon, and the sky was full of stars. The air was heavy with the smell of the orchard, and down by the creek hundreds of frogs were croaking. I remembered my father telling me that they asked a question of the water, "How deep? How deep?" And they answered their own question, "Knee deep or a little deeper. Knee deep or a little deeper." And that then the bass rumbles of the biggest frogs advised, "Go 'round. Go 'round. Go 'round." I smiled, remembering. All my life, hearing the frogs in springtime, their voices had asked the question, given the answer, rumbled the advice. They were never merely frogs to me. They were sentient and conscious, querulous, speaking to each other. And in my mind I could always envision the knee deep water, the frog's anxiety over it, the need for going around. I was very literal about it.

I waited in the quiet night, determined to speak to Stephen. Apparently he had lingered to say something more, and I thought I knew he would be making another effort to absolve me of blame. I stood beside a briary rose, the smell of the sweet yellow blooms mixing and mingling with the shine of the stars, the sound of the frogs, the touch of a small wind. Oh, the world was so fair, I thought, so full of beauty, so meant to be loved and lived in. It seemed to me as I waited there were new places inside me eager to live, to be filled up and satisfied. And there was a deep sadness that they must dry up, like springs in a droughty season.

Stephen came, finally, and blinded from coming out of the light into the darkness, he would have passed me unseeing, except that I grasped his sleeve. "Stephen?"

"Becky?"

"Yes. What are you going to do?"

[163]

"Nothing."

"Are they going to send you away?"

"I think not. They say I am to help with the new sawmill they are building up the creek."

"Do you think they will let us teach again?"

"I think so. There is no one else."

"They could bring on someone from the East."

"Yes, but I think they will not. This will die down."

We stood there for what seemed like a long, long time, then Stephen moved. "Good night, Rebecca," he said.

"Wait," I said, catching at his sleeve. "When do you go to the sawmill?"

"Tomorrow."

"I feel I am to blame, Stephen," I said, hesitantly. "I'm sorry I got you into trouble."

He laughed. "Don't give it another thought. I am a grown man and I am responsible for my own actions. Who says it's trouble? Amanda and William have their boy again, don't they?"

"Yes." I thought of Amanda, back at her farm, with Silas, William loyally standing by her, and I was fiercely glad for her. "Take care at the mill, Stephen."

"Yes. Keep well, Rebecca."

"I will."

And then he was gone, and the night was suddenly darker, as if the stars had dimmed, and the voices of the frogs were threatening instead of friendly. I hurried along the path back to East House, each bush a fearful shadow, my heart beating up into my throat. I was frightened. Everything seemed queerly new and confused to me. There was no comfort in the familiar stones under my feet, no comfort in the candlelight gleaming through the windows of East House. Even the ground felt oddly quivery, as if a quake were threatening again. And for some reason I did not understand, I wanted to weep. Nothing had happened to make me weep . . . and I brushed impatiently at the sting of tears in my eyes. Nothing had been said to warrant tears. Nothing was threatening me, I told myself. The school was closed, but it would have closed for the summer in another three weeks anyhow. I would then have taken up my duties in East Family again. What was there to cry about? But the tears came anyhow and I had to stop and give them their way, let them overflow until they had run their course, before going in the house. I laughed at myself, shakily, thinking how often a woman cries without knowing why, and how invariably tears are a sort of relief to her, ridding her of anxieties and griefs. I felt better when I could finally wipe my face, knowing they were done and over with for the present.

It was with some triumph that Prissy assigned me to the garden the next day. The weather was uncommonly hot for May, and the work was tedious and wearisome. For a woman of as much astuteness as she believed herself to be, I have often wondered how she could have been so blind. The garden work was exactly what I would have asked for, had I been allowed my way. Not only was it good, hard physical labor, which I felt the need of, but it was outside, free of her, and alongside of Permilla.

Richard's chair was empty at the noon meal. Back in the garden, later, I mentioned it to Permilla. "Ain't you heared," she said, "he's been sent up the creek to help build the sawmill. He asked to go."

Stephen, I thought—and Richard, both at the sawmill. "Who else?" I asked.

"Brother Rankin, an' most of the men in the North Family."

We worked silently the rest of the afternoon. My own thoughts shifted restlessly about, to Richard at the sawmill, where they inevitably turned, then to Stephen—from them to William and Amanda, who, now, with their blacks had gone from us, and to Sabrina. But all the time my hands moved the hoe in and out between the bean plants, cutting down the weeds, loosening the soil around them.

The sun beat down hot on my shoulders and gradually my dress became soaked with sweat and a little coolness accumulated under it where the wetness touched my skin. How peaceful this village looked to anyone passing, I thought, the brothers and sisters going so quietly about their work, so modestly and sedately dressed, so busy with their tasks. How little that passing person could have known of the seething and boiling emotions that stirred it, roiled and bubbled in it, steamed and threatened to erupt.

I thought of Stephen, with his bony scholar's face, with the ancient dream in his eyes, and I thought how it belied his strong convictions of freedom.

I thought of Annie's demure manners, her pretty downcast lashes, covering the never-forgotten remembrance of their heavy lifting under the weight of a man's gaze. I thought of Sabrina's round sweetness and innocence. I thought of my own longings and yearnings. Did we ever know another person, I wondered. Did we not all go our own ways, hidden behind the masks of our faces, unable to reveal ourselves, lonely and haunted by our own dreams?

CHAPTER XIX

THE ENTRY in my Journal for June 6, 1812, reads: "Annie and Robert have left the village this day."

Annie was all smiles as she told us they were leaving. "Did you tell Robert about the new baby?" I asked her.

She nodded. "I reckon that was what decided him, too. Though he was terrible discontented anyhow. He's kept thinking of his own land and crops. It ain't too late to plant yet. Seems like every time I've talked with him of late he's been yearning for it. Spoke often of how the land lay, and how pretty the creek was, and how the fish would rise and jump of an evening. Said he hadn't had a fishing pole in his hand this whole spring. Robert," she finished, "has always liked to fish."

"An' I don't reckon you recollected to him," Permilla said, "how good a mess of fish tasted along this time of year, with a mess of wild greens an' corn pones."

"He didn't need me to recollect it to him. Last time I talked with him, he'd cut a cane pole and he kept rubbing it and handling it the whole time. 'A man,' he said, 'likes to do his work his own way, know it's his, take time off when he wants, fish a little, hunt, follow his own ways.'"

"What did you say?"

"I said that was the way I'd always seen it, that a body couldn't ask better than to live free. And then I told him about the new little youngun coming. He made up his mind right then. Said we'd get out." She nodded briskly. "He's already talked to Brother Benjamin, and we're leaving in the morning."

We did not watch them go, for we were busy at our duties. We told Annie goodbye the next morning, each of us glad for her, wishing her well. With strict honesty the Shakers returned to them everything they had brought, and returned to them their agreement which gave the Shakers the use of their land, their house, their stock and equipment. We heard later that Annie had quarreled with Brother Benjamin over a new foal and a calf that had been born while they were in the village, but how much truth there was in it, we did not know. The Shakers would have considered the foal and calf theirs. No more than the corn grown on Robert's land would the foal and the calf be considered his.

Annie wore her Shaker dress away, for she had no other. But as she shook it down around her feet that last morning she laughed. "It won't take me long to get shut of this drab thing, I can tell you! First thing I aim to do when we get home is to buy me something nice to wear, something gay and ruffly, with ribbons and lace. I'm that hungry for pretty things I don't know that I'll ever get over it."

"Come to see us in yer finery," Permilla said.

Annie shook her head. "I'm not ever aiming to set foot inside this place again. You want to see my ribbons and lace, you'll have to do the coming."

Prissy went around all that day with her mouth thin and tight. "When the flames of hell are licking at those two," she said once, "they'll regret turning their backs on the way of salvation."

"Maybe," I said boldly, "there are more ways to salvation than one."

She looked at me angrily. "There is *only* Mother Ann's way, Sister Rebecca."

But I had never been convinced of it, and I was less and less inclined to be pleased with Mother Ann's way. I thought of what Stephen had said, and it made a lot of sense to me. I wondered if perhaps she had not been a little crazy, given to the kind of fits some children have. "The Lord requires only that we should walk humbly and do justly," I said.

"Don't quote the Scriptures to *me!*" Prissy said. "I know the Bible back and forth and by heart."

If she did, I thought, she rarely acted like it. Prissy was not an eldress, and I doubted if she would ever be one, for all her zeal and management. Shakers were slow to make appointments to the posts of elder and eldress, for it was a post ended only by death or misbehavior. Brother Benjamin and Sister Molly had only that year received their appointments. One had to serve a long time for such recognition, and to give them their due, those appointed to such responsible positions were usually humble, good, and charitable as well as earnest. I felt certain Mother Lucy would look a long time at Prissy's record before appointing her, and she would see beneath the record of good management, even the record of ecstasies and visions, the almost constant friction at East House, the petty complaints, the turmoil of reported infractions and punishments. No, Sister Priscilla would never be an eldress, I was sure, however much she wanted it and worked for it.

It was a few days later that Jency ran away.

As always it was Cassie who came to bring me the news. She came to the garden, bringing fresh water, brought me a gourdful. "Jency has went off, Miss Becky," she said, waiting for me to drink. "She's went to that yaller boy, I reckon." There was a note of sadness in her voice, but not grief. "Hit's best, mebbe."

I threw the last of the water on the ground, handed her the gourd. "She's free, Cassie. She can go with Clayton if that's what she wants to do. No one can stop her, and I think it is best for her now. Did she tell you she was going?"

"No'm. That wouldn't be Jency's way. She jist went, in the night."

"Well, we'd better make certain she has gone to Clayton. And then Mister Richard can give her the papers. I'll see to it, Cassie."

"Yessum. I knowed you would. Reckon Miss Amanda'll be good to her?"

Amanda would be a very different person than I, there was no denying. She would have little patience with Jency's flightiness, would require much hard work of her, but I thought she would be just and humane. Amanda had too good a sense of values. She would not mistreat her blacks because it would not pay her to. I doubted if Jency would ever be ill-treated, and I said so.

Cassie went away sighing. She sighed a lot these days, as if life had gradually grown very heavy for her to bear. I was sorry for that, for in the old days she had been a happy woman, singing as she went about her work.

I was happy about Jency, though. She would be married and settled now, and maybe with Clayton and a long succession of babies, she would round out her life happily. The Shaker village was no place for her, and no good could come of it. I was glad she had gone to Clayton.

I must write Amanda a letter, I thought, and tell her Jency was free, ask her to allow the marriage and let Jency and Clayton be together. I had no doubt she would agree, for she would be getting an extra hand at no cost to herself, and the children of the union would, in time, be valuable to her also.

Richard must be seen first, though. Jency's papers must be put in order. He was at the sawmill all week, but the men came home for worship on Sunday. I could ask for a conference with him, then.

So I ordered it in my mind, thinking it over, deciding, pleased with the turn Jency's life had taken.

But Richard would not give Jency her papers. I thought it would only be a matter of form. I asked for the conference with him and Brother Benjamin granted it for the interval between morning worship and the men's return to the sawmill. We met in Brother Benjamin's presence, of course. "Jency," I told Richard, "has gone to be with Clayton, and she needs her papers of manumission."

In no way did Richard now look like the man who had been my husband. He had grown steadily thinner until he was now gaunt, and out of his bearded, lean face his eyes blazed almost fanatically. A nervous tic had developed at the corner of his mouth which kept it twitching almost constantly. I think he was entirely unaware of it, for he either could not or did not make any effort to control it.

He stared at me so long without answering that I wondered where his mind was, if he had heard me. "Jency . . ." I began again, but he interrupted me, brushing at the air with his hand. "I heard you. She has left the village?"

"Yes. She and Clayton love each other and she wants to be with him at Amanda and William's."

"She must be brought back," he said abruptly.

"But why? She's free. You gave her her papers!"

"I gave them to her and she tore them up. She is not free until other papers are prepared, and I will not prepare them for her to go and live in sin. I will not set her free to live with a man in sin. I will never set her free for that. She must be brought back."

He meant it . . . and there would be no swerving him. There never was, on anything he felt strongly about. I was stunned. I had not been prepared for this. Innocently I had supposed he would remember his promise, to make new papers any time she wanted them. I appealed to Brother Benjamin. "Richard promised Jency she could be free when she chose. It is not right for him not to keep his word."

Brother Benjamin looked at his folded hands. "This is Richard's decision, Rebecca. I am afraid I agree with him."

Anger flared in me, then, the same kind of anger I had felt when Richard had first told me he intended to join the Shakers, the kind that makes one shake in its grip, as with a chill. I turned on Richard. "You cannot keep Jency from living in sin, as you call it! She has already been with Clayton. She is carrying a child, even now! Let her go, Richard. Let her go. It will do no good to bring her back. She will only run away again, again and again and again. You know Jency's ways as well as I do. You know she cannot be forced. Nothing but trouble will come of bringing her back."

Richard's eyes blazed, then dulled. "You cannot be forced, either, can you?" The tic jerked at the corner of his mouth in a spasm of movement. "You are as wayward as Jency!" He bent forward and spat the words at me.

I stared at him, then I answered him. "You cannot hurt me, Richard. Nothing you can say to me can hurt any more. If I am wayward, then I am wayward, and that's an end to it. But do not take out your spleen on Jency. You can do her a great wrong. Forget me, but remember your promise to Jency."

He shrugged. "I remember it—but the conditions have changed. If she has already sinned, there is all the more reason for her to be brought back and kept safe from further sinning."

"Do you think," I said hotly, "you can watch Jency every second of the day and night?"

"No. But she can be chained."

I could not believe I had heard him. "You would do that?"

"If necessary," he said. "For the good of her soul."

"For the good of nothing," I said, yelling the words at him, "for the good of nothing but your own vanity . . . your own selfishness. You have not the right . . . you are not God!"

[169]

"I am not God, but I own Jency. I will decide what is best for her."

If it would have accomplished anything I would have pled with him, but I knew all too well he could not be moved. I asked Brother Benjamin for permission to end the conference. He granted it, saying gently, "It will be all right, Rebecca. God looks after His own." Oh, the evil that is done in the name of piety!

"Then he'd better get to work," I said, bitterly.

Richard rode to William's farm and brought a weeping Jency back with him. Permilla, who had found a way to meet Seth even on Sundays, told me, when she came in. "The pore little thing is cryin' her eyes out."

"I'll go see her when Richard has left," I said.

"You reckon he'll actually chain her up?"

"I don't know," I said wearily. "I don't know what to expect of him any more. He might. But chains can be broken."

"I'll go with you," she offered. "You mought need some help."

"No. I'll come for you if I do."

Viney was watching at the window. "He's a leavin', Becky," she said. "I jist seen him goin' over to Center House."

I went to the window and looked, myself. When he was safely inside the house I would go. The Black House was at the very edge of the village, near the woods, and taking my eyes off Richard for a moment I saw Cassie stealing toward it and knew she had heard and was going to her child. I also saw the figure of a man, crouching in the bushes at the edge of the woods, saw him stand suddenly, look around and then make a dash for the door. Clayton, too, was going to Jency. I smiled. Chains would never keep Clayton and Jency apart.

The three were alone, all moaning, when I got there, sitting on the floor in front of the empty fireplace, Cassie holding Jency in her arms, rocking her back and forth, Clayton bent with his face on his knees, rocking himself. But Jency was not tied. She looked up when I entered the room, her face swollen from crying, and she broke into fresh tears when she saw me, pulled herself loose from Cassie and flung herself on her knees at my feet, clasping me around the waist. "Oh, Miss Becky, he ain't gonna let me stay with Clayton! He say I got to stay here. Say I ain't free. Say do I run off any more he gonna chain me up! Miss Becky, save me! Miss Becky, he'p me!"

"All of you hush, now," I said, lifting Jency to her feet. "It does no good to moan and weep. I'll think of something, I promise you."

"Whut?" Cassie asked, stopping her sobs and looking at me. "Whut is they you *kin* think of?"

"I don't know yet. But I'll think of something. There *has* to be a way, and I'll find it."

"He right, Miss Becky," Cassie reminded me sadly. "He don't have to make new papers out. Miss Bethia give her to him same as me an' Sampson. He doan have to let her go."

Bethia! A little glimmer of light flickered in my mind. David and Bethia had indeed given Cassie and Sampson and Jency to us, but if they had ever made out legal papers on the transfer, I had not seen them. Maybe none had ever been made out. Maybe Richard had nothing to show for his ownership, save David's word. Maybe that was the way out. "I think I know what to do," I said, "but I'll have to see about it first. Clayton, you go on back to Miss Amanda's. Don't come back over here again. Stay away. Jency, you stay right here. Be as good as gold. Do what you're told to do, so you won't be tied up. Don't try to run off and see Clayton. You hear me?"

"Yessum . . . I hears you. I stays here. I be's good. How long you think, 'fore I kin get away?"

"I don't know. Maybe two or three weeks. But I believe I see the way. However long it takes, though, you stay right here. No matter how bad you get to feeling about being here, don't run off. You'll have to be here when I learn whether this will work or not."

Clayton was standing. "You wants me to go right now, Miss Becky?"

"Right now, before anyone learns you've been here."

"Yessum." He laid his hand on Jency's shoulder. "You do whut Miss Becky say, now, Jency. Mebbe she fix it so's we kin be together." Then he was gone.

The other blacks began to come back into the room, singly, entering quietly, almost slipping in. Richard had frightened them all, I guessed, and like shadows they had fluttered and faded. They could be trusted, though, I knew. Like one mass of black flesh they would feel and think and act with Jency. I asked them to be good to her . . . to help her. Dumbly they nodded their heads. "Send word to me every day," I said. "I can't come each day, but I want to have word of her. And watch her. Don't let her run away."

Jency giggled. "I ain't gonna run off, Miss Becky."

But I knew too well what Jency's promises meant. She could chase a butterfly into the woods and be gone to Amanda's before we knew it, without conscious thought on her own part, following, blindly, an urge known only to her.

When I left the cabin I walked slowly across the pasture, and something directed my steps down the path past the Schoolhouse. As blindly as Jency I followed an urge. I had missed the children, and the school room, and without thinking, for I was thinking of Jency, I found myself on the path leading by the Schoolhouse. When I noticed where I was I decided to go inside. I wanted only to go into my classroom again, feel its walls about me, listen to the echoes of the children's voices saying their lessons, be comforted a little by something which had been my own.

I climbed the stairs slowly to my room, feeling tired, feeling beset and miserably alone. The door of the room was closed and I laid my hand on the wooden knob, carefully turned and polished as were all things made by Shakers. There were never better craftsmen in the world than Shakers. Though they gave no thought to beauty, each thing they made so carefully, so practically, had its own beauty in its simplicity and attention to detail.

A sense of desolation overcame me as I felt the wood under my hand and almost I turned away. But the knob slid easily and the door swung open.

Stephen was sitting at my table, a book open before him, his elbows propped on either side of it, but hearing someone coming he had turned to face the door. "Becky!" he said, shoving his chair back and coming to meet me, his hands outstretched.

I put my own in them and such a tremendous wave of relief flooded me that I could have wept. His slender scholar's hands were warm, held mine closely. Here was strength to stand beside me! "Stephen, Stephen," I said, "if I had prayed the sight of you could not be more an answer to prayer. I need your help."

He drew up a chair for me, seated himself again behind my table. "Tell me," he said simply.

So I told him the whole bitter story, and then I told him what was in my mind to do. "If David and Bethia did not actually make out papers giving them to Richard, I am almost certain I can get them to give them to me, now. Then I can set Jency free without Richard's permission."

He nodded. "You will need someone to go—immediately. The post is too slow. I'll get a horse ready and start at once." He stood.

"Can you? How can you get a horse?"

He smiled. "You forget I am not a Shaker. I have my own horse. He's in the pasture with the others, but the Shakers have no claim on him. I can be there in a day and night, and back in another twenty-four hours."

I thought about it. "They will know," I said, then. "They will know what you have done."

"Yes. They will know. I will tell them myself, when I return."

"Then they will dismiss you—send you away."

Unconsciously his hand reached for the locks of hair over his ear, then, seeing my eyes follow the hand, seeing me smile at the old, habitual gesture, he dropped it, smiled back at me. "Does that matter to you, Rebecca?"

"For you to leave? Of course it matters! What would we do about the school? Who would teach? Who would lead us?"

The smile left his face and he looked past me, out the window. "There are other teachers . . . and other leaders. No one is indispensable."

"You are," I said swiftly. "We cannot do without you. I can go myself, Stephen! Lend me your horse and I can go, as quickly as you."

"Then you might be sent away."

I shook my head. "There is no danger of that. As long as Richard is here and I am willing to stay, they cannot send me away. I must be the one to go, Stephen. Now, right now! Get the horse and bring him here. I won't even go back to the house."

Stephen laughed. "I have no sidesaddle."

"Do you think I learned to ride a horse with a sidesaddle? Get the horse, now, Stephen."

"Let's be serious, Becky. It's a long ride, and there are no taverns or inns along the way."

"I won't need them. I can hold out to ride it all the way without stopping. There are farms. I can get something to eat from them. I can manage it, Stephen."

He pondered it a long time, and I waited, saying nothing to interrupt his thinking. Finally he said, "No. There are too many hazards for a woman alone, and the ride is too hard. I've been thinking. Becky, I have a friend in town . . . a lawyer. The bond between us has been our mutual love of books. I have borrowed his, he has borrowed mine. Would you be willing to trust him?"

"Do you trust him?"

"Yes. I think he is to be trusted. He could find someone to send, or he might even go himself. If you are willing, I will see him immediately."

"Oh, I'm willing. I was just afraid you would be stubborn about going yourself."

"No. It will be better if neither of us go. We would be missed. Richard might be alerted. And then, I do not wish to leave South Union yet. There are things . . . there are reasons . . ." he motioned with his hand, "but they do not matter. Write a note to your people while I get the horse. I'll give it to Jackson and I am certain it will be on its way before the sun is down."

Abruptly he left the room, and drawing paper out of the table drawer and a pen and our homemade ink, I wrote a full explanation to Bethia. I was conscious of a feeling that all would be well, and conscious at the same time of relief that Stephen had found a way which did not involve him in trouble with the Shakers.

CHAPTER XX

FOUR DAYS LATER there was a reply. David and Bethia had signed papers making Cassie, Sampson and Jency my personal property. It was with relief that I tucked the papers into the bosom of my dress. But the courier also brought a note from Mama. "Janie's man died of a stroke the twelfth day of April. She has been here to spend a few weeks, but she has went back to the city to settle up her affairs. Where she aims to live she never said, but I have hopes she'll come home."

So Mr. Leavitt had died and Janie was a widow. It did not surprise me. He had looked too ill the last time I had seen him. But I had little hopes that Janie would return to the Hanging Fork to live. I thought it likely that Mr. Leavitt would have left his affairs in good order and that Janie would have plenty to continue living according to her custom.

I wished I could have been with her, could anyway have known he was gone. I wondered what path her life would take now, and briefly I thought of Johnnie. But I remembered, too, her saying, "What would a senator's wife have to do with a freighter?" She wasn't a senator's wife now, though. She was a judge's widow. I hoped she was not too lonely.

So that he would not be away when Mr. Jackson's courier returned, Stephen had complained of feeling ill and he had not gone to the sawmill with the other men that Sunday evening. "Something may go awry," he had said, "and you may have need of further help. Once we know, I can recover very quickly."

I sent a note by Cassie, and she brought me his reply. "Good!" was all he said. I studied his writing. I had seen it before, of course, many times, but somehow the bold, slanting letters of that one word looked different and new to me. He had made the letters very large, as if for emphasis. He did write such a fine hand, so clear and easily read. Good, he had said. And it *was* good, and a goodness between us.

There was neither fuss nor bother when I handed the legal papers for Cassie, Sampson and Jency to Brother Benjamin. He received me in the small office recently built for the new trustees, with, of course, another person present. The other person was Seth Arnold, Sabrina's father. As Brother Benjamin adjusted his spectacles and read the papers I studied Seth. He went on about his business, which was making up accounts for the various packages of seed each Family had provided thus far to be sold. He was a quiet man, moving quietly, with no unnecessary motion and I guessed he would be patient, calm and deliberate in everything he did. I knew he was one of those chosen to be a trustee, and that he was one of the first who would travel the country with our seeds and straw hats to sell.

Brother Benjamin cleared his throat. "Sister Rebecca, I see that these papers are dated only last week. Are there papers of a previous date making Richard the owner of these blacks? They would supersede these, you know, making them invalid."

"No, sir," I said. "Richard's father and mother gave us the blacks, but no papers of transfer were ever made out. They simply assigned them to us."

"I see." He bent over the papers again. He did not ask me how I had got them. He read a little further, then folded them and handed them back to me. "Now, what is it you wish to have done with them?"

"Has Richard ever given you papers of manumission for Cassie and Sampson?" I asked.

He shook his head. It did not much surprise me. Richard had been willing to set them free, had made out their papers, but once within the Shaker community he had evidently changed his mind. I thought I knew why. Without their papers they could be held in the village, and he had wanted them held there. Of course he thought he knew what was best for them. But no man ever knows what is best for another. "I wish," I said, "to have papers of manumission made out for all three blacks. It would be proper, then, I suppose, for you to hold the papers of Cassie and Sampson, so long as they are here. But it is my intention to give Jency hers so that she may leave the village. She and Clayton wish to be together, as you know. If she is free, nothing can stand in her way to follow her wish."

"Does Richard know of this?"

"It is no longer any concern of Richard's. The blacks are my personal property. The papers are made out to me, not to Richard and me. I can dispose of them as I please."

"Yes," he said, "of course. Very well, Sister. The papers will be ready for your signature tonight. But I warn you, this may upset Richard."

"It is better for Richard to be upset than for Jency's life to be made unhappy."

"Perhaps . . . perhaps." He took off his spectacles, wiped them, slid them into the hard black case in which he carried them and sighed. "I wish we had less friction here. I wish we could all live together in the grace of Mother and in her spirit of humility."

"Mother," I said tartly, "dispensed with her husband quite expertly. Was that humility?"

Brother Benjamin stared at me, aghast. "Mother never failed to live in humility of spirit. Her husband was a worthless man, who fell from grace. She was right to cut him out of her life."

"Then let us remember," I said, "that I am doing this thing in humility and love. Jency is my responsibility and her happiness and welfare are in my hands. I am not acting pridefully. I am reluctant to go against Richard's wishes. I have taken these steps because I had to, not because I wished to. Richard himself made them necessary."

Brother Benjamin rose and told me I could go. "The matter," he said, "will be attended to."

He kept his word, Brother Benjamin, and the next day I signed papers for all three of the Negroes. I took notice that Brother Benjamin placed the papers for Cassie and Sampson in the letter folder. "I would not wish anything to happen to those," I said. "Should Cassie and Sampson ever want to leave, they must be available to them."

"Nothing will happen to them, Sister Rebecca," he promised. "We give a good accounting of all things entrusted to us." He handed me Jency's papers.

I went directly to find her at the Black House. She was moping over washing up the dinner dishes, but she brightened when she saw me. "Miss Becky!"

"Sit down, Jency," I said, "I want to talk to you."

She wiped her hands on her dress tail. "Yessum," she said, her eyes widening in sudden fright.

"Don't be afraid," I told her. "Everything is all right." I unfolded the papers. "Now, listen to me, Jency, while I read this. Try to understand what this paper says." I read it slowly, stopping to explain any words which she could not understand, and when I had finished I folded the two pages and opening her hand laid them there. "You are free . . . no one can ever again own you, or order your life for you. You can go to Clayton when you please. But do *not*, and this is very important, Jency, do *not* lose these papers. Don't braid them into your hair. Don't make buttons out of them, or butterflies. Give these papers to Clayton just as soon as you see him, tell him to keep them safe. Do you hear? Do you understand?"

"Yessum," she said quickly. "I unnderstan's a heap better'n I done before when Mister Richard made 'em out. I ain't aimin' to tear these up. I'll keep 'em, Miss Becky. Kin I go whur Clayton is at right now?" She was eager, excited.

She was very bulky now, being within two months of her time, and I smiled at the figure she made. She had not fattened and broadened, as most white women do, all over. She had stayed slender across the back and through her shoulders. The child she carried looked exactly like an apple dropped midway into a long, black stocking, bulging knottily. "Why don't you let me send for Clayton to come for you?" I said. "Miss Amanda would let him bring a horse for you to ride."

"I ain't got the time," she said, giggling happily, "I kin be there 'fore then. I cuts acrost the woods." I didn't doubt it, and I didn't doubt she had cut across the woods even since Richard had brought her back.

"All right," I said, laughing with her, "go ahead. Tell the people here, though, that you are going."

"You tell 'em," she said, darting to the door, "I'se goin' this minnit."

"Jency!" I called to her. She stopped, looking frightened again. She had so little hold on safety, I thought. The least barrier scares her. "I only wanted to tell you to be happy. Be a good wife to Clayton. Do your work well."

"Yessum. I aims to."

"And Jency," I added, "when the baby comes, bring him to see me."

A broad grin spread over her face and she nodded her head vigorously, making her pigtails fly. "Yessum. Kin I go, now?"

I nodded, and without so much as a backward glance, her freedom papers clutched in her hands, not burdened with any belongings, taking just herself, flighty, child-loving, butterfly-chasing, song-raising Jency, she was gone.

My hands felt empty without the papers. I looked at them, empty-palmed, turned them over, then folded them across my apron front. I wished that somewhere I could find some freedom papers for myself.

Even as the wish rose within me, though, I knew it was a misted, only half-formed wish. What did I mean by freedom? Did I want freedom *from* something? The Shakers, Richard, my present life? Or did I want freedom *for* something? Where would I go? What would I do? Freedom, by itself, is no answer, I told myself. It can be aimless and wandering, no more rewarding than the deadening chains of prison. To be meaningful, it had to have a purpose.

It came to me then, that what every soul wants and longs for is the home of his innocence—that in every heart there is a yearning homesickness for the only bliss it ever knows, the safety of childhood and the circle of parents and brothers and sisters. Growing up means losing that bliss, that innocence, and it can never be recovered. There is no substitute for its loss in the strange world which we inherit as adults, and we drift through life ever seeking the misty, lost, young bliss. Richard was seeking it in religion. Janie was seeking it in love. Mama had sought it in the four walls of her home. Those people going west to Missouri were seeking it in new horizons, beyond new rivers and mountains. The Shakers sought it in ecstasy and withdrawal from the world. It seemed to me, at that moment, as if I saw all the long processions of men, moving in a long line, each alien from the other by his own loneliness, joined only in the mutual yearning of hearts, the mutual search for something forever lost and unrecoverable.

And I . . . where was I to search?

CHAPTER XXI

THERE HAD now gone from our sleeping room Amanda, Lacey and Annie. But that was the spring when Brother Benjamin was especially zealous in his preaching to the world and many converts were made. Before July had ended we had not only three new women in our room, but two other beds were added, and we were very crowded. The other sleeping rooms were just as full.

If I look in my Journal I can find the names of the women who came into our room, but there is no point in doing so. They made little impression on me, beyond a feeling of pity for them in the beginning. They felt, as we had done, bewildered and unhappy. We tried to be kind to them, explained the ways of the house to them, helped them in every way we could, knowing what they were feeling. But Permilla, Viney and I were the ones bound together by our long sharing, our tested friendship, our mutual knowledge of each other, and we found that the new women could not enter into this tight, closed circle with us. There were things we knew which they could only learn with experience. There were anxieties and thoughts we shared which were not yet theirs. So, while there was a surface accord, there was no deep regard among us for them.

The summer passed in a haze of heat and work. The garden bore bountifully and every woman's hand in East Family was turned, when her other duties were done, to gathering, drying, sorting and preserving. Prissy was everywhere at once, her skirts flying, planning, ordering, overseeing. She was determined that East House should make a good showing in the final accounting of the season. The big kettles in the kitchen were hot from early morning until night, and we often went to Meeting so exhausted from the long day's work that the exercises and the dance were almost beyond our energies.

The School Family did not have its own garden and orchards. They were provided for from the community larder, so the women of the Family, and the older girls and boys, were parceled out to the other houses to help with the work. Sabrina, old enough to be counted a woman, was sent to us.

She was a good hand, and it was a joy to me to see her in the kitchen. Sometimes we drew the same task, peeling, or stirring, or drying, and then we could talk together. It was almost like being in the classroom again, then. For Sabrina kept up her studies and as we stood or sat side by side she would recite her lessons to me. "I'm afraid I'll forget before the school term takes up again," she said, one day. "I'd love to say my lessons to you."

I was glad to hear them. A memory which pierces me to this day is one of Sabrina, stirring applesauce at the big kettle in the back yard, waving the smoke of the fire aside, her paddle going round and round, her sweet face red from the heat, reciting the lines of the Spartan poet, Tyrtaeus:

> The youth's fair form is fairest when he dies.
> Even in his death the boy is beautiful,
> The hero boy who dies in his life's bloom.
> He lives in men's regret and women's tears.
> More sacred than in life, more beautiful by far,
> Because he perished on the battlefield.

They were from a book I had loaned her the week before. "Why," I asked, curious, "have you learned those lines by heart?"

"They're beautiful," she said, her paddle slowly moving the thickening batch of applesauce, her eyes dropping to the slow-bubbling mass.

"Remember," I warned her, "that is a Spartan poem. They thought war was the noblest adventure of man's life. They thought it was an honor to die young on the battlefield. They forgot that it was just as honorable to live nobly."

"I know," she said, smiling at me. "But the lines are beautiful, just the same."

"Here," I said, taking the paddle from her hand, "let me stir a while. Your arm must be numb. And you'd better leave off studying the Spartans for a time, Sabrina. Read some Latin for a change. Or read Shakespeare. But read the comedies, not the tragedies. You're too young to be tragic."

She laughed. "I'll get some more wood."

I watched her cross the yard to the woodpile. She wasn't as plump as she had been, I thought. She was slimming up, leaving her childish roundness behind her. I wondered about her and Lucien—wondered if they ever met, saw each other. But she never said, and with Stephen at the sawmill I had no way of knowing if Lucien ever talked to him. There wasn't much chance that he did, for Lucien was in the fields all day. Only on Sundays when the men came from the mill to Meeting could he have seen Stephen.

Sabrina did her work willingly, cheerfully, but as the summer passed there was no denying she was a more sober girl than she had been before. Often as she worked her hands moved mechanically, and her eyes looked into some distant place which only she knew. She's unhappy, I thought. She loves Lucien and wants to be with him. I wished she would tell me, talk about it. And I have wished many, many times I had done what I so often wanted to do, brought it up myself. I would nerve myself to do it, to ask her, casually, how Lucien was, if she ever saw him. But always, just as my tongue was ready to speak, some feeling of reserve kept the words back. She did not know I knew about Lucien. How could I bring it up? There are places in every person's heart no one else has a right to enter, to push into and probe and pry. But I have wished I had.

We had an especially fine harvest of grapes that summer and there was much excitement as we began to lay down the new wine. There is something about making wine which seems almost religious to me . . . gathering the swollen, purple globes, still cool and wet from dew so early in the morning, squeezing and pulping them, the red juice running thickly over one's hands, then putting it to ferment.

We wanted, in East House, to put down the best wine in the village. Entering into the spirit and the excitement, Brother Benjamin had promised a picnic outing for the whole village, with the Family having the best wine honored as guests. "We'll take a day," he said, "the entire village, and we'll take our dinner to the river. We'll have a holiday, and we'll have the men come from the sawmill to join us."

Oh, but we worked! There would be no difference in the grapes themselves, for there was only the one variety, which Brother Rankin had set out many years before. But we could make certain that we picked only the fully ripened ones, those sweetened by the sun, and we could make certain they were perfect and full of juice. We made only the red, sweet wine in which the skins and seeds were left. We left the must, then, to ferment, and we watched it carefully. Was the weather too hot? Would it ferment too rapidly? Would it turn cool suddenly and slow it up?

None of us but Brother Samuel had had any experience making wine in such quantities. It was he who decided we should ferment ours in small vats. "It will stir and yeast more actively," he told us, "if there isn't too much in one vat."

I can tell you that we hovered over those first vats like a mother hen brooding a nest of eggs! A dozen times a day we went to the cellars, looked at the brew, tasted it, tested its temperature. Brother Samuel kept an almost constant vigil beside them, and in ten days he came triumphantly to the kitchen and announced the wine was ready to draw.

We made a ceremony of the drawing, standing in line with cups to receive the first to be drawn off. We tasted, then, almost apprehensively. Had it fermented too rapidly? Would it be a little sour? But it was as sweet as the grapes themselves. We could not believe another house could possibly surpass it. Brother Samuel took the last cup for himself. We watched him as he lifted it to his lips. We knew he had been tasting constantly, that he had decided it was ready—but what would he say, now, drinking down a whole cup? We saw him take the first mouthful, watched him mull it in the heat of his mouth, over his tongue, then he nodded. "If there is another wine better than this, it deserves to win. But I do not think there will be another better."

We were so pleased that we did as small children do in their pleasure and joy—we shouted and sang and danced, until Brother Samuel, fearful that our pride might become arrogance, reproved us gently, reminding us that pride goeth before a fall. Humbled we restrained ourselves, but the Shakers never frowned upon these small contests in which pride of work was the spur and some small pleasure the reward. The men had contests in braiding the straw for the hats we sold, and each house had vied with the others in getting the gardens planted first, in reaping the first fruits thereof, in weighing the fattest calves. The contests added a small excitement to the work, and the honors of the rewards made a little glow when we won. It was but human to enjoy them.

North Family drew their vats four days after ours had been drawn, but it was a full three weeks before Center House drew theirs. We were uneasy during the time of waiting, for we felt perhaps the aging would make their wine sweeter and milder.

When the time came for Brother Benjamin to test all the wine, we were as edgy as new blades, keyed up and trembly with excitement. He was to make the tests at Meeting that night, in the Assembly room at Center House.

When we gathered we could not keep our eyes from the clear glass flasks which held the three vintages. A table had been placed in the center of the room and the flasks and cups were set there. To insure full and separate flavor a cup had been provided for each wine, so no impurity of one would taint another.

We followed our usual procedure of prayer and song, and then Brother Benjamin, stepping forward, read the words of a new song to us, one he had written especially for the occasion . . . a song of praise for the fruit and the vine, for the hands that had labored to make the wine. After reading it, he sang it for us and we quickly learned the notes and sang it all together. It was a beautiful song, and as we sang Brother Benjamin led us in a march and countermarch about the table on which the flasks rested. It was one of the virtues of the Shakers that they could make of the simplest things a ceremony and a rite.

When we were seated again, we were out of breath from the marching and from anticipation. We did not know which flask contained our wine for the labels were all turned away from us. We watched as Brother Benjamin poured from the first flask and tasted—from the second, and then from the third. Then he repeated the order, rinsing the cups with water before pouring the wine again. He placed his hand upon the flask which was third in the row on the table. "It is all good wine," he said, "none of it has any cause to shame its makers, but this wine here has the fullest body, the best aroma and the sweetest flavor." He turned the flask, looked at the label, then smiled. "This is the wine made by East Family."

We could not help crying aloud with joy, and Brother Samuel whirled onto the floor, signaling his permission for us to join in a free dance, each whirling and singing as he pleased. The other Families appeared to have no feeling of envy or jealousy, for they joined with us in the dance, and every face wore a smile, every voice was lifted in song.

Prissy put a damper on our enthusiasm when she had a gift of trance and tongues, which we were compelled to recognize. And I think even Brother Benjamin felt a little impatience, for before he could control his face I saw a small frown appear on his forehead. I know I wondered how real the gift was. Prissy had them very often, it seemed to me. We had to be seated, of course, to honor the gift. She spoke rapidly and in a strained voice for some time, crying out once or twice, loudly, and taking with the shakes. Then the trance was broken and she came out of it with a white face, and her voice croaking with hoarseness. "The vision . . ." she said, "the vision . . ." She put her hands about her throat as if it hurt her.

"Yes, Sister Priscilla," Brother Benjamin said.

Prissy shuddered. "I saw Death, riding a white horse—Death in black robes, and he rode through the gates of the village, and he gathered up on his white horse, one of us . . . and he rode off with that person."

"We are prepared for death, Sister Priscilla," Brother Benjamin said. "Death has no horror for us."

"But he was laughing . . . I could not tell whether it was a man or a woman he took—the vision was dim . . . only Death was plain, laughing. But he said, 'This one came easy into my hands.' Then he laughed again and rode off, with the person clutched before him on his horse."

This was so strange a vision that we were all troubled by it. And there was no longer any doubt that Prissy had seen it. She was too white, too shaken, and her voice was too hoarse with her fear. She seemed visibly to shrink before us and she looked about as if trying to recognize the one marked by Death. I felt my own tremor of fear as her eyes sought mine, but she continued to shake her head, searching each face, continued to clutch her throat, passing over us all . . . then as if worn beyond standing any longer, she slumped to the floor and kindly Brother Benjamin asked Sister Molly and Sister Susan to take her home.

He preached briefly on the subject of death, then, trying to comfort our troubled feelings. "Believers," he said, "welcome death when it comes, though we do not seek it. We do not fear it, nor do we abhor it. We welcome it as the door into a world much better than any we have ever known, a world of pure spirit and new life."

But whatever a religion teaches about death, human beings *do* fear it, *do* abhor it, *do* grieve over its necessity—and while we took a little comfort from Brother Benjamin's sermon, we were not entirely freed of our feelings of threat and prophecy. Who, we wondered, and when?

But when Brother Benjamin had ended his sermon and announced that the picnic would take place on Friday, we recovered something of our anticipation in the pleasure of the outing, though we could not entirely shake off our gloom.

In our room, after Meeting, we were all quiet, until Permilla laughed and said, "Well, there's no use wearyin' about it. There's better than two hundred of us in the village, now, an' there was jist one in Prissy's vision. Ain't no need of frettin' till the time comes. Drat Prissy, anyway!"

I think we all felt the same way—drat Prissy for spoiling our evening. Viney laughed, too, and said, "I'm aimin' to enjoy that picnic, fer it mought be my last 'un."

Laughter was more successful at ridding us of the threat of Prissy's vision than Brother Benjamin's sermon had been, and we began joking among ourselves, saying what we wished done at our funerals did it turn out to be one of us, what songs we wished sung, who we wanted to preach the sermon, and "Cover Me with Lilocks," Viney sang in her quavery old voice. In this rather gruesome manner we exorcised our fears.

Friday was a beautiful day with clear skies, no threat of rain, the heat tempered by a breeze which seemed to come straight from the waters of the river. The men had come from the sawmill the night before.

We did our chores quickly, those which always had to be done, and then we bustled about packing our dinner into baskets. The men brought three wagons, bedded thickly with straw, to the back door, and we loaded into them, our women's tongues chattering happily and gaily over the small excursion. The men were either riding horseback or walking.

Richard did not come. I searched for him among the men when we had reached the river, but he was not present. Fearing lest he be ill, for the habit of concern for a man dies hard in a wife, I sought out Brother Rankin and asked about him. "Is Richard ill?"

"No," Brother Rankin said, shaking his head. "He is not ill. He asked to be allowed to remain at the mill."

"Why?"

"He said there was work he needed to do. Richard is very zealous, Rebecca."

"He is overly zealous," I said sharply. "He did not approve of our plans today, did he? He did not approve of our gaiety."

"He did not say so."

"He did not *have* to say so, but he has shown it, nevertheless. He has become a very different man, Brother Rankin."

"He has become a very dedicated man."

"For which he has paid a terrible cost."

Brother Rankin looked at me sadly. "I would that you could pay the same cost," he said. "You are a heavy burden on Richard's heart."

"And he," I said bitterly, "is a heavy burden on mine." I walked away from him.

Was it, I thought, my stubbornness which was causing Richard's leanness and gauntness, or was it his own fanaticism? I shook off the thought, determined not to allow Richard's absence to spoil the day for me. Indeed, certain that he was not ill, I am not sure that his absence did not contribute to the pleasure for me. It was difficult for me to feel very happy any more when Richard's troubled face was near to remind me of the quarrel between us. I set myself to enjoy the day, and I did. We all did.

We were so unaccustomed to idleness that at first we hardly knew how to occupy ourselves. We wandered up and down the riverbank, plucking flowers, searching for shells and pretty stones. We sat together and talked, our hands in our laps, though Sister Molly had brought her knitting and she kept her needles flashing all the time. Prissy seemed ailing and withdrawn, and I think she was haunted by the fear that, having seen the vision of Death herself, it was she who was marked to go. We tried to draw her into our talk, but we were not very successful.

After our dinner the men had races, both foot and horse races, and we made lines to watch them, cheered them, and acted altogether unlike our usual sober Shaker selves.

Stephen won the horse race, his fair hair flying in the wind, his beautiful bay easily outdistancing all the other horses. He was brown from his work in the sun, and I thought his face seemed a little fuller. I was glad, for he had been too lean and pale during the winter.

Lucien Brown won the foot race, his heels flashing in the sun, his legs moving incredibly fast. He, too, was brown from the summer work, and I thought again what a handsome lad he was. Our leaders had been increasingly troubled about our young single men in the last few months. War had finally come between our country and the British, and there was some danger our lads would be taken into service. Shakers did not believe in violence, and Brother Benjamin had written many letters to Washington so reminding the President. So far none had been drafted, but one or two had wandered off to enlist. When they went of their own volition, they were, of course, outside the jurisdiction of the Society. Watching Lucien's legs driving him so rapidly down the racecourse, I wondered if he felt any duty to fight, was ever tempted to enlist. I thought not . . . not with Sabrina so near.

I had seen his look on Sabrina, had seen her high color in her joy of the day, in being in Lucien's presence, though separated from by the presence of others. She had managed to serve him his dinner, and I had no doubt they had found it possible to exchange a brief message—of love? Hope? Promise? It made me sad to think of them thwarted, but they themselves seemed far from sad this day.

After the races the men wandered off up the stream and, left to ourselves, we women did a most undignified thing. We took off our shoes and stockings and waded in the clear, shallow water. Not for years had I waded or swam in a creek, and the coolness of the water on my feet and ankles gave me a surprisingly happy feeling. We even splashed each other, gently so as not to get too wet. We were laughing, calling out to each other, throwing stones across the creek, more released, more free than we had been at any time since the village was gathered into order. It was gay and such innocent fun.

Then Sabrina slipped on a mossy rock which turned under her foot, and she fell heavily into the water, wetting herself all over. We laughed at her predicament, for all her garments were soaking, and even her hair hung dripping about her face. When we had laughed at her, however, Sister Susan said, "Sabrina, you must return to the village and change your clothing. You'll get a chill. And besides it wouldn't be proper, before the men."

Sister Molly spoke up. "Let her take one of the horses. Can you ride, Sabrina?"

"Yes, ma'am." She was still giggling from her ducking. She bent to examine her ankle, and I looked at it, too, to make certain she had not injured it. I pressed it with my fingers. "Does it pain you anywhere, Sabrina?"

"No, ma'am. It just creened under me."

"You probably fell and took the weight off before any harm was done."

"Yes, ma'am."

"Which horse would you like?" I asked her.

We walked toward the horses and she looked at them. "You reckon Brother Stephen would care if I rode his?"

"Of course not," I assured her. I knew how she felt. Stephen's was a blooded horse and it had a fine pace. I knew I would have enjoyed riding him myself. "He would be glad for you to borrow him."

We bridled and saddled the horse, who stood for us without temper or impatience, then we sidled him to a stump for her to mount. In the saddle which, properly, she did not bestride, she gathered up the reins. "Be careful, Sabrina," Sister Molly called to her. "And you need not return. We shall be coming home before long."

"Yes, ma'am," Sabrina said. Then she arranged her wet skirts as best she could, laughed again, and said to me, a little uncertainly, "Well, thank you, Sister Rebecca."

I laughed up at her. "Oh, you're welcome. All I've done is help get you a horse."

She smiled, touched the horse with her heel, he pranced a little, straightened out, then flew across the field to the road. I frowned, watching her go so fast. It was reckless of her, but then I smiled. She was young. She wanted to feel the horse's speed and strength. At her age, in her place, I should have wanted to do the same.

We were quiet on the way home, tired, as one always is after an outdoor holiday, our energy drained, our pleasure spent. When we had unloaded the wagons each of us went immediately to his chores. I had the duty in the fowl yard. The heat of the day had waned, but at that hour, just after sunset, the air is always very still and some lingering warmth lies close over the earth as if reluctant to be chilled by the oncoming night. My dress was damp with perspiration and I loosened my kerchief about the neck, to let the air reach my throat. I fed the chickens and gathered up the eggs. I was glad when the supper bell rang.

Sabrina was not at supper. Because she had been assigned to us for the summer's work she had been living with us at East House, taking her meals there and sleeping in the house, though not in the room I occupied. Her empty chair was quite noticeable, and I knew at once what had happened. She had gone, and she had tried to thank me for all I had ever done for her. I had no doubt that Lucien was gone, also.

It was always at mealtimes that those who slipped away were missed. In a community of over two hundred persons the hours of the day could pass and it would not be noticed, for we were all busy at our various tasks. But an empty chair at table was not to be hidden.

Apparently, however, I was the only one this time who suspected what had happened. The young people's secret had been too carefully kept. Sabrina was not at supper, true—but no one seemed troubled about it. We could not talk at table, of course, but presumably everyone was thinking that someone else knew where she was. She had fallen in the creek. Perhaps she had hurt her ankle more badly than had been thought. Perhaps she had taken with a chill and was in her room. Perhaps she had returned to the School Family for the night. I can only guess at what was being thought, for all I actually know is that no one seemed disturbed by her absence. Noting it, I felt relief.

My thoughts were busy. Had they missed Lucien yet? Where was Stephen? Had he known? Had he helped them? Had Sabrina actually turned her ankle, or had the whole thing been planned? It didn't matter. What was important was that Sabrina and Lucien had finally taken things into their own hands. I prayed they might get clean away—beyond reach of the Shakers. They were minors and they could be brought back.

Then I remembered that Sabrina's father, Seth, was away on the selling trip, gone to Tennessee, and that he would not return for several weeks. I remembered this with horror, for the responsibility for Sabrina would lie with Brother Benjamin and the other leaders. Seth might have had some pity, a fatherly feeling wanting Sabrina's happiness, and he might have argued to let them go. Brother Benjamin, having to answer to Seth for his daughter, would be compelled to search her out. Let them, I prayed, please let them get far away and not be found.

The long meal was finally over and we went to our rooms. I rested on my own bed, thinking of Sabrina, hoping her absence would not be discovered until morning.

It was a vain hope, however. Permilla wakened when the Meeting bell rang.

We gathered in the meeting room upstairs, but we had no more than seated ourselves when Sister Molly bustled in, whispered to Sister Susan and both of them turned to look down the line of women. "Where is Sabrina?" Sister Molly asked.

"Ain't she in her room?" Permilla asked innocently.

Sister Molly looked inquiringly at the women who shared Sabrina's room. Each of them shook her head. One of them spoke up. "Ain't she at the School Family? We thought maybe she'd gone there to take the night. We thought likely she'd taken a chill after falling in the creek and had maybe gone home till she got better."

"She is not at the School House," Sister Molly said. And she left the meeting room without saying anything more.

Permilla nudged me. "Has she flew the coop?"

"Hush," I said, "keep still."

She glared at me, as if I had insulted her. But I was too worried to care. We had no Meeting that night. Instead we were dismissed, and both Brother Samuel and Sister Susan went hurrying off to Center House. We were told nothing, but by now everyone was guessing . . . not that Sabrina had left with Lucien, for only Stephen and I knew of their attachment, but that Sabrina had left, for some reason or another.

There was some talk about it in our room, but I would not discuss it. I simply said, "I don't know," or "I've no idea," when asked directly what I thought. Finally, with nothing to feed it, the talk died down. The women went to bed and soon they were all asleep, even Permilla. But I lay awake for a long time that night, thinking of Sabrina and Lucien, wondering where they had gone, hoping they had got a good start. Thinking of them, so young, so much in love, my thoughts turned to Richard. In my memory I went back even to our childhood, remembered the goodness of that time, wept a little that it was gone. I remembered *our* marriage and the first blissful year together, the babies buried behind Bethia's house. I remembered the first restlessness in Richard, the first unhappiness and dissatisfaction. I remembered my own fears, my wild hope which had been so ill-founded, and I traced the long road down which we had come. I could not see that ever could I have done differently, nor did I see what I could do differently now. The trap was closed, and that was all. Hopelessness is a very terrible and lonely thing.

CHAPTER XXII

SLOWLY, THE NEXT DAY, through gossip and rumor we learned that what had given the alarm was Stephen's innocent search for his horse. He knew, of course, that Sabrina had borrowed it to return to the village, so he had returned in a wagon with some of the other men. At the village he had gone to the pasture for his horse, for he had to go back to the sawmill that evening. The horse was not to be found. "Why did you mention it?" I asked him, when late the next afternoon I saw him.

Troubled, worried about Sabrina, anxious for her, I had stolen away to seek the quiet of my classroom. It had become a kind of refuge for me, and I often went there, to read, to think, to be alone. The need for solitude can become very urgent in a community such as ours, where privacy is something never encountered.

Stephen was in his own classroom, sorting over some books to take back to the mill with him. I had thought him gone already. We talked of Sabrina and Lucien. And he told me, sorrowfully, how he, himself, had been the instrument of their being missed. "Why did you mention your horse being gone?" I asked.

"I didn't think—I just didn't think. It did not occur to me Sabrina had taken it. I knew she had borrowed it, but without any suspicion I went to the pasture—and David Brown went with me, to see to some colts. There was no way, once I had gone to the pasture with him, of keeping it from him. No way of asking a man like David not to mention it."

"What did he do?"

"He went immediately to check the other horses—to see if any others were missing. One of his own was gone. Then he hurried to report it. I guessed what had happened, but it was too late. David and the others thought the horses had been stolen by some pestering farmer. It wasn't until Lucien didn't turn up for supper that David began to suspect he had taken the horse. And then when Sabrina was missed, too . . . well, it all fell into one piece." His shoulders drooped. "And I meant to help them if I could. Instead I have been the one to hinder."

"You couldn't know," I said. "No one could have guessed. Lucien should have told you. And Sabrina did try to tell me." I told him of the way she had said thank you and of how I had misunderstood. "I was too witless to understand. What will happen now?"

"With such a search as Brother Benjamin has organized, it will be a miracle if they are not found. He feels his responsibility for Sabrina very deeply. He is determined to overtake them before . . . before . . ."

"Before they can be married," I finished for him.

"Yes."

We stood silently, thinking of the two young people, each of us feeling guilt, each of us unable to say much to comfort the other, each of us hoping they might not be found. "They are too young," Stephen said, then, voicing my own fear, "to take enough care. They will simply rush headlong, depending on speed. An older man than Lucien would know to cover his tracks, to hide some place. But Lucien will only think of riding hard toward whatever destination he has set for them. They will be overtaken, almost certainly."

And they were. Three days later the search party returned, Lucien and Sabrina with them. They were very tired, the children were, Sabrina as pale as a sheet, swaying in the saddle with weariness and hopelessness. "She has no mother and she is my pupil," I told Sister Priscilla, when I saw them ride in the gate. "I am going to her."

I did not wait for permission. I flew toward the gathering group and it was I who helped Sabrina from the horse, and held her tightly in my arms. She did not weep. She only leaned her head on my shoulder and shuddered. "I'm so tired, Sister . . . so tired."

"Of course you are, love. Come with me. You can rest in my bed, and I will take care of you."

We were not prevented, though Sister Molly came to us as we began to walk away. "You will see to her?" she said.

"In the place of her mother," I answered.

She nodded. "We will question her tomorrow. Let her sleep, now."

Anger rose in me. If Sabrina did not feel like being questioned tomorrow I determined no one should bother her. She should have peace, for as long a time as I could manage it.

Lucien was taken, by his father, to Center House.

I bathed Sabrina, tenderly. She was covered with scratches, as if she had been through rough, woodsy places. She moaned a little when the water made the scratches smart and I was as gentle as I could be, salving them when they were clean. I asked her no questions, and she did not talk. There was a white, set look on her face, and her eyes seemed fixed in her head. I thought it was because she had been without sleep for so long. I covered her, finally, and told her to sleep. "I will sit here beside you," I promised her, "and no one shall bother you."

She turned on her side, her face away from me, and drew a long sigh, almost a sob, then a deep shudder ran through her and she said, "I am cold."

I brought a blanket and laid it over her. She pulled it around her shoulders and even over her head. Then she was still. She slept all night, and most of the next day, barely moving in her sleep to turn.

Sister Molly came the next day, but she was a merciful woman and when she saw that Sabrina still slept she forebore to waken her. "She is but a child," she said. "No great harm has been done, Sister Rebecca. Lucien has vowed he did not touch her."

"Where were they found?" I asked.

"Near the Tennessee line. They were going to Lucien's grandfather's. David Brown's parents live in Tennessee."

I set my lips. I wished with all my heart they had got there. With his grandparents to stand behind them, they might not have been compelled to return. I did not know the law of it, though, and as a minor, David and Nancy might have been able to bring Lucien back. But I wished they could have got there, been married. There should have been some way they could have got free.

We never heard, from Sabrina's own lips, any word of their flight, their capture, or their return. When she awakened she made no effort to talk, seemed to wish to be left alone. She was taken to Center House, and we heard that even there she would answer no questions, nor talk at all about the entire thing. "She jist set there," Permilla told me, who had it from Prissy, "like a stone statue. She wouldn't open her mouth. Jist set there, an' stared at 'em. Once she said somethin', but once was all. She asked where Lucien was at."

"Did they tell her?"

"Yes. They told her. He's been sent to the sawmill to git him away from the village. David has went with him."

"Oh, I wish Seth was here!" I cried. "Her father *ought* to be here. They should send for him!"

"Well, I wish he was here, too," Permilla said, laughing. "I'd like real well to see him myself. But they ain't goin' to send for him, I c'n tell you that. They got their eyes on them sales he's makin'."

It is true that the Shakers always liked to turn a fair profit on their ventures. Thrift and shrewdness were virtues in their sight, and they gave a certain scriptural passage a far different meaning than was intended by it. Money to them meant "the one thing needful." They had considerable realism, our leaders, for of course it is true that money is the great necessity. Money won't buy happiness, but try being happy without it. Money won't buy health, but it will go pretty far toward making illness more bearable. Money won't fill your head with learning, but it can provide the books to learn from. No, it wasn't likely Brother Benjamin would recall Seth Arnold from this first selling trip.

I was on my way to the Schoolhouse. School was to open the next Monday and Sister Drucie and I meant to clean the rooms. Stephen would return from the sawmill on Sunday, and he would not go back then. We had been informed the week before. There had been no further talk of our not being allowed to teach . . . at least not to us. Nor had we been told whether there had been discussion, how much of it, or how a decision had been arrived at. We had simply been told that school would start and that we would resume our duties there. The bulk of the summer work was over, and while the older boys would have to be spared to help gather the corn in October, school could begin the first week in September.

Even with my sorrow over Sabrina, I was happy that day, scrubbing, cleaning, shining the floors, the windows, the walls, the tables and chairs. I sang as I worked, thinking how soon I would be spending most of my time in this room, the children in their places, the books open, the lessons being said. This was where I belonged, I felt, this was where I was happy. And I hoped that back in school Sabrina would recover some of her own happiness.

I was pleased, also, because during the summer a new room had been added to the School House, and I was to move there. On Sunday I would take my few possessions and leave East House—forever, I hoped. I had looked at the room.

It was a long room, running the whole length of the house, on the second floor. It was spacious, sweet-smelling from the new lumber, and as brightly clean as a new penny. I counted the beds. There were seventeen. Sister Drucie would sleep, she said, at the far end of the room. I would sleep next the door, and fifteen little girls would occupy the beds in between us.

There were three more rooms as large as this, for the girls of the school, and while Drucie and I were the only women teachers, each room would have at least two sisters or older girls in charge. Across the hall, on the other side of the house, were the boys' rooms, where Stephen and several other men, all unmarried, had care of the boys.

I looked forward to living in this new home. I had only one regret at leaving East House. I would be separated entirely from Permilla now. Richard was no longer there and would never be again, I knew. He had asked for permanent duty at the sawmill, and little by little he had been given responsibility until he was now in full charge. Brother Rankin had the duty of the farm at the sawmill, and I had been told that Richard was not required to do any work except that of keeping the mill running.

The sawmill was a highly profitable enterprise. It had been successful beyond all hope, the farmers for miles about bringing their logs there to be sawed. And, I judged from what I heard, credit was due mostly to Richard, who had ever been shrewd with machinery of any kind.

But even had he been living at East House again, I could have taken no joy in it. The wall between us was too high, and his presence would have been more a sorrow than a pleasure. I could not have looked across the dining room at his stern face and taken any happiness in the sight. It would only have wounded me afresh.

I looked forward, too, to being with Sabrina more. She had been sent back to the School Family instead of to East House. She had asked, I had heard, to go back, and since the summer work was nearly finished, it had been allowed. I asked Drucie if she would be in our room. "No. She's old enough to help with the little ones. She's in the Old Room."

I was sorry. I would have liked to have her near. I thought how we might have read together, talked, and how perhaps in time I might have helped bring consolation to her. It troubled me that she did not wish to return to East House. She had given no reason, they said, beyond expressing a wish she might be allowed to go "home." At Meeting the next Sunday night I had seen her, her eyes circled darkly, her face sad and still white, her eyes looking much too large and much too bewildered. She had not entered into the exercises or the dance, and she had been allowed to sit undisturbed. After looking briefly around the room she had fixed her eyes on her hands, folded in her lap, and not once had she lifted them again. She had seemed listless and withdrawn, hurt beyond recovery, helpless to make any effort to recover. I wished to be with her, to try, clumsily perhaps, but with all my heart, to help her.

It was not to be. When we gathered at Meeting the following Sunday morning, the day before school was open, I missed her at once. I asked Drucie where she was. She told me Sabrina was not well. "She said her head hurt. So I told her to stay in bed, and I gave her some herb tea to drink."

I nodded. There was no time to say anything beyond, "I'll go see her when Meeting is over."

But Sunday is the day all Shakers live for. It is the best day of the week. It is the day when ecstasy, in song and dance and worship, runs high and runs long. All week our house meetings prepared us for it. We rehearsed our new dances, learned new songs in readiness for it. The Sabbath meetings were open to the world, and we took pride in presenting ourselves, perfect in order and going forth in good manner. Our services on Sunday always lasted three or four hours, and sometimes went on for five or six. On this Sunday, it was well up in the afternoon before I could slip away to the School House.

I sought Sabrina in the Old Room, so-called because it was the bedroom, enlarged by the removal of a partition, of the original home. Her bed was empty and neatly made. Her head is better, I thought, and she has gone outside to walk, or to do some chore. I was sorry to miss her, but glad she was feeling better.

It was William Steel who found the little heap of her clothing on the bank of the river. The colts had made a gap in the fence and had strayed in that direction. He came upon the clothing, folded in orderly fashion, her dress, apron, bonnet and kerchief. Her shift was not among her clothes. A little note was tucked into the folds of the bonnet, on top. William opened it, saw that it was addressed to Lucien, and hurried with it to Center House.

I have the note now, open before me. I found it, near the walk from Center House, where Lucien dropped it. I would have returned it to him, but there was never the opportunity. So I have kept it. I have not felt guilty about keeping it, for I felt it was in some way also addressed to me. It was I who loaned her the book in which she found the words of the Spartan poet she quoted in the note.

It was very short. It read: "Dear Lucien . . . I do not want to live without you, and they will never let us be together. 'The youth's fair form is fairest when he dies.' Do not grieve . . . but never forget that I love you."

Her body was found on the Monday school began. Instead of Sabrina's sweet face lifted to mine as I taught that morning, it was cold and wet and lifeless, somewhere in the long stretches of the river. Men were dragging for it, now, as I mechanically read words which were as lifeless to me as Sabrina's body. I did not think I could bear it, when Stephen had told me school would open as if nothing had happened. "I cannot," I said, tears flowing, "I cannot go into that room, knowing she has not been found. I must go to the river, too."

He took my hands and held them tightly. "The other children must be guarded from too much sadness," he said. "You loved Sabrina. But they need your love, also, and you must stay with them. You must hold your classes as if Sabrina were there."

"I cannot," I said, twisting my hands free, but I knew I could, and that I must.

All that day, though, I taught in a daze of alternating heat and cold, not knowing, actually, what I taught, nor even caring. I only wanted to get through the hours in some fashion, to hold myself steady, not giving way before the other children. They knew nothing, yet, and in the way of children they accepted Sabrina's absence without curiosity.

When the long day was finally over, I went first to my room and put on my bonnet before starting to the river. Stephen caught up with me as I left the house. "They have found her," he said.

I brushed his hand, stretched out to stay me, aside. "I want to see her."

"They are taking her to Center House."

"Has Lucien been told?"

"He has been told. He was with them when they found her. The note was addressed to him, and they agreed he should be given it."

"They agreed!" I said bitterly. "They have driven her to her death! We, you and I, have helped to drive her to her death!"

"Rebecca . . ." Stephen's voice was quiet, gentle.

"We have!" I cried, angry and hurt beyond caring if I now hurt him. "We knew. We were the only ones who knew. We should have done something. We should have spoken to them, helped them, made them trust us. We sat there all summer, idle, forgetful, and let them drift. Why couldn't they let them go, Stephen? Why did they have to bring them back?" I wept stormily, leaning against the fence, bent over it, holding to its support. "Oh, Stephen, Stephen, this is so cruel and bitter a thing."

He did not try to comfort me. He uttered no mild, scriptural platitudes. He simply stood there, sharing some part of my misery and grief, perhaps all of it, until the worst of the storm was over and I recovered. I wiped my eyes and straightened my shoulders. "I am going to see her," I said.

"Of course," he answered. "I shall help with the grave."

"But they won't bury her until Seth returns, will they? They've sent for him, *now*, haven't they?"

"I don't know. I was not told. But certainly they must have." Then he reminded me gently of a cruel fact. "The weather is very warm, Rebecca."

Of course . . . I had forgotten. Sabrina's sweet, young, lovely body was dead. The weather was too warm. Burial could not wait on her father. I held my mouth to keep it from trembling, and hurried on to Center House.

Lucien was there, sitting beside the couch on which they had laid her. He was stony-faced, white with grief, seeming stunned and dazed. He did not look up when I went into the room, nor speak to me, and I did not speak to him. I did not think he would hear me.

She looked cold and lonely and very young lying there. Water dripped from her hair and from under the blanket covering her. Someone, Lucien or another, had turned the blanket down from her face. Her eyes were weighted and the bandage binding her mouth shut was in place. I dropped beside the couch, on my knees, and the pool of water from her hair wet them through my dress. I touched the dripping hair, the water-cold young face, serene now and untroubled. I did not weep again, but I felt as if my heart would break in two. I tried, bending my forehead against the couch, to pray, but I could only think of the waste, the tragic waste of so young a life snuffed out, and the evil of it. I could not pray, because I could not forgive, either the Shakers or myself.

Sister Molly touched my shoulder. "It will be better if you leave, now," she said.

Startled, I looked up at her. "Why?"

"We must prepare her for burial."

"I will do it," I said, pushing myself up on my feet. "Let me do it. I loved her."

"We all loved her." Sister Molly looked at me thoughtfully. "Very well . . . if that is what you want, you may help."

We were alone in the room, now. Lucien had gone, but I had not heard him go. I hoped Stephen would find him, or that his father and mother were with him.

Tenderly Sister Molly and I washed Sabrina's body. Much of its childish roundness had gone in the past months, and it grieved me anew to see the thinness of her ribs and thighs. We had hurt this child in every way she could be hurt, I thought. We, so smug and so complacent, so certain of our righteousness and goodness. We had done evil to this child, in the name of goodness. We had failed her in every way human beings can fail another. And she had taken her life rather than live among us.

Because she had taken her own life she was not buried in the place set apart for Believers. In her last conscious act she had violated the final law, and she could not lie among the saved. But some of us, Permilla, Stephen, David and Nancy, made her grave sweet, lined it with branches from the trees, heaped late-blooming flowers on it when it was mounded over.

That night, after the funeral, Lucien left us, and we never saw him again. He enlisted in the army and went off to the war. He was killed in the Battle of the Raisin. So ended the brief, sweet love of two innocent children. So Prissy's vision came true, and Death, on a pale horse, entered our gates and snatched one from among us, rode off, laughing, saying, "This one came easy to my hands."

CHAPTER XXIII

HER FATHER, Seth Arnold, returned four days after we had buried Sabrina. David Brown had been sent to find him, finish the selling trip for him, and he rode home on David's horse.

What he said, what he felt, I had only secondhand, from Permilla. "He put the blame square on Brother Benjamin," she told me, "an' they've had a terrible quarrel. He said they ortent to went after her an' Lucien without him knowin'. Said they ort to've sent fer him, right off. Said he would of given his permission fer 'em to leave, had he knowed. Said he had a idee she warn't satisfied here, an' it'd been troublin' his mind fer a right smart time. He blames hisself, too, for ever bringin' her here. Said he done wrong. He's went."

"I don't blame him," I said.

"Nor do I," she promptly agreed. "In his place hit's what I'd of done too."

I stared at the solid, unshakable Shaker buildings about us and thought how much heartache and grief they had looked down on, bounded and confined within them. "This village," I said, "it was never meant to be."

Permilla laughed. "Oh, I don't know, Becky. Hit ain't sich a bad place for them that likes it. They's little to weary a body an' a heap to comfort one. We got plenty to eat, a stout roof over our heads, work that's to be done. I don't know as I ever had it so good. An' I ain't got the younguns to see to, to weary whether they eat or not, an' they're gittin' schoolin'. Hit could be a sight worse fer sich as me."

I could understand what she meant—but then Permilla was unlearned, easygoing, quickly satisfied when life quit pressing her. For me it had become a prison. For her it held the best she'd ever had. The difference lay within us. Permilla would never, I knew, hold firmly to the Shaker beliefs. But it would never trouble her at all. She was beautiful, good, hearty and fine, but the simplest things of life were sufficient for her. She was shut of Thomas, there was food and warmth and shelter, there were no worries. That was enough for Permilla.

Stephen and I were discussing it a few days later. "It's a pity," I said, "that Permilla couldn't have married a man nearer her own years."

"She seems happy enough," he said.

"Yes, but she might have been so much happier."

"Have you been?"

His question stopped me, for of course Richard's age, his vigor, our life together, had been what had led to my greatest hurt. "Marriage," Stephen went on musingly. "I have never had much wish to settle down. I've been a rolling stone, pulled by whatever new thing lay over the mountain. But of late I have seen some virtue in it."

"Ah, then," I said, "you regret never marrying?"

His mouth twisted wryly. "No. No, I don't regret never marrying. But . . . oh, never mind."

I mused on what he had said. "There comes an age, I suppose," I said, "and probably you are reaching it, when companionship seems very attractive. It is all very well to be a rolling stone in one's youth. There is the whole of life ahead. In middle age a fireside, a wife, a good companion, seem somehow more suitable. One doesn't roll so easily when bones begin to creak." I said this last slyly, meaning only to tease.

Stephen threw his head back to laugh. "Becky, Becky! My bones do *not* creak, and neither do I admit to middle age. I am young yet."

"Young enough," I admitted, "to wed and have a family yet. Why don't you, Stephen?"

"I thought you had an idea the school would go to rack and ruin if I left."

"That was selfish of me. We could survive. Perhaps it is time you were moving on, while you have this feeling strong in you."

He shrugged. "Perhaps . . . but not for a while."

"You may become too set in your ways to wed, later. If you have a wish, now, for your own home, your own wife and family, you should not wait."

He kept his eyes on the ground, idly tracing a pattern in the dust with his toe. "There is no danger that I shall lose this feeling. I almost wish there were. It might be better so." Then he rubbed out the pattern he had been drawing in the dust, shifted his books and laughed. "But a feeling isn't enough, Becky. There has to be the right woman."

"You'll never find her in a Shaker village," I said, laughing with him. "Well, Stephen, perhaps you're meant to adventure longer anyhow. There's the Missouri Territory, you know."

"There's the Missouri Territory," he agreed.

The weeks of the autumn passed. In late October the first frosts came and the trees turned scarlet, gold, crimson and yellow, and the leaves blew dryly in the wind and pulled loose, came drifting down. The persimmons ripened, the nuts fell, the grass in the pastures browned. Wood for fires was cut and stacked. Pumpkins were piled in the storehouses and the turnips were dug and the sweet potatoes. We changed into woolen clothing, and wishing to throw off the gloom of the sad weeks which had gone before, I dyed my new dresses crimson. "It is your color," Stephen said, when he saw me in it the first time. "With your dark hair and eyes, red is your color."

"It reminds me of Annie," I said, laughing. "She loved pretty things."

"So should all women," he said.

The corn was gathered and we had a husking bee. In the old days when a red ear was found by a man, he could claim a kiss from the girl of his choice. Among the Believers, a red ear meant an added five points to the score for a Family. We did, though, enjoy the husking bee. We had a little wine, we sang, there were cheers for the various Families as the men shucked faster and faster, and when finally the young men of North Family won, we congratulated them happily.

In November there was ice for the first time, a skim of it on the pools made by the rain overnight, and a few weeks later, just before Christmas, there was a heavy snow. Winter had set in, now, in earnest. Each day I walked across the small patch of dried grass from the School House to my classroom, the sun barely showing, and each evening I walked back, the sun already set, so short were the days. Added now to my usual chores of study and preparing lessons was the necessity of knitting stockings for the little girls. The village continued to grow, for Brother Benjamin went out on a round of meetings in the fall and made many converts. We were swelling at the seams in the School Family, and it was said that East House could no longer hold the men and women flocking in. "Winter Shakers," Sister Drucie said contemptuously. "They come like crows to a cornfield when the weather turns cold. All they want is a warm place to sleep and plenty to eat."

There were always those, of course . . . and the next spring would see them flocking away as fast as they had come. It was getting to be one of the worst problems for the leaders.

It was decided that a new house for the School Family must be built the next year, and one for the East Family. Both were to be built of brick, and all the men who could be spared were set to work in the brickyard and the kilns.

Christmas came and went. Shakers do not make much of it, except to hold sacramental Meeting, and to hear public confessions. I could not attend Meeting that day, for a dozen children were down with the cold plague and I, along with others, had to attend them. It was just as well. I no longer had any heart for the virtue or the necessity of confession. In truth I no longer had any heart for Meeting.

I knitted a pair of warm mittens for Richard, having seen his hands red and chapped with cold at Meeting. Nothing ever kept him or Brother Rankin from coming the twelve miles from the mill to the village for Meeting on Sunday. They came when it was pouring rain, or sleeting, blowing or snowing. Sometimes they continued to shiver for an hour after arriving, losing their ague only in the exercises and the dance. They were exalted by Brother Benjamin and the other leaders, held up as models of righteousness and virtue.

I did not agree. I thought it foolish of them, and I was not surprised when Brother Rankin came down with the lung fever and almost died. I expected it, and I expected to hear, too, that Richard was ill, any day. For all his gauntness, though, his strength must have been very great. It may have been that in wearing off his flesh, he had been pared down to bare nerve and muscle, which served him better than flesh. He, of us all, was not ill that winter.

I knitted blue mittens for Richard, the color the Shakers loved best. For Stephen I knitted red ones. Stephen was pleased with his, wore them constantly. Richard left his on the bench in the Meetinghouse and I do not know who removed them or if any use of them was ever made.

It was a raw, cold winter, with much rain, and the cold plague ran through the village from house to house so that we all came down with it at one time or another. We went about as long as we could, waiting on each other, with runny noses, sore throats, coughs, chills, and fever. Five of our school children died in spite of all we could do, but none of the five were under my direct care. Their chills went into lung fever, they choked and struggled for breath, and died. It was sad to bury them, so little and defenseless, but we had so little time to grieve for them. There were the living, ill and needing our attention.

Among them, in February, just as the plague was abating a little, was Prissy. Word came from Center House. "Pray for Sister Priscilla. She is dreadfully ill."

That was all we could do, pray. For we had twenty children still weak from their sickness, requiring much of our time, and because the plague was passing, school had been resumed the week before. News of Prissy came several times each day. "Her throat is swollen shut." "Her fever is so high that she burns to the touch." "She is out of her head, delirious."

They said that in her delirium she was searching for her caps . . . crying that they had been stolen. That her hands kept pulling at her hair, disordering it, that she whimpered like a child, asking for her caps, pleading that they be found and restored to her. Sadly I thought how deeply Permilla's careless joke had stabbed and hurt. We had thought it was soon over, never dreaming that through the long months the shame had continued to eat away at her. But her unconscious mind revealed how bitter it had been to her, how dreadful a thing had been done to her. I never thought to feel pity for Prissy, but when I heard how she begged for her caps to be found, I felt more than pity . . . I felt sorrow for our pettiness and heedlessness, and I thought how little we know what we do to others, how carelessly we may maim and cripple another heart.

It came to me how Prissy might be soothed, and I asked to be allowed to see her. I would hardly have known her, her sickness had so changed her. She seemed to have shriveled and dried, and the veins at her temples were blue and distended. Her hands kept plucking at her hair, and she moaned and turned restlessly. Her white net cap was in place, of course. She had been told, over and over, that her caps were not lost. She had been told that she was wearing one, but nothing that was said to her could penetrate her sick mind. I asked that her other cap be brought and Sister Susan hurried to get it. Then I took off the one she was wearing, combed her thin, straggling hair down around her forehead and face. I wanted her to feel it, uncombed, uncapped. She pushed at it, moaning, "My caps . . . my caps . . . they are lost. Find my caps, someone . . . please find my caps."

I put the comb down, spoke to her. "We have found your caps, Sister Priscilla. Here they are, both of them. Take them in your hands."

I pressed the caps into her hands. She clutched them, felt of them, ran her fingers over them, then a peaceful look came over her face and she smiled. I bound up her hair and took the cap from my own hair, pinned it in place. "Let her keep the caps in her hands, Sister Susan," I said. "So long as she can feel them she will be satisfied, I think."

It was the only atonement I could make for my share in the joke which had so wounded her, for my laughter at her, for my dislike of her. She died, clutching the caps, never recovering consciousness, but at peace somewhere in her soul because they had been found.

She had her faults, Prissy . . . and her ways were not my ways, but she was flesh and blood, mortal, as are we all, and during the long funeral service, during all the eulogies and speeches of praise, it came to me that whatever drove Prissy, made work a passion with her, made authority unbending with her, made nature proud and dominating in her, made her also a good leader, though we could not see it when we were the led. In petty ways she had irked us, but East House had been well run, its daily routine as smooth as oiled machinery, its organization tight and well-knit.

It came to me, too, that any leader in a Shaker community had many frustrations and irksome things to bear—the frictions of human souls thrown too closely together, the minor upheavals, the gossip and quarrels, the general cantankerousness of people. Prissy must often have felt as irked as we, must often have wished never to see us again, or hear our troubles and dissatisfactions. She must often have felt as distracted as a mother hen with a brood of unruly chickens. But with iron will she had kept East House in order, and her only reward was her knowledge of duty well done. For here she now lay, in death, and she could not hear the eulogies and the words of praise. I forgave her much when I looked on her face as we filed past her casket for a last look at her, and I hoped that her heavenly rewards would be greater than her earthly ones had been.

I thought the winter would never end, but it always does, it always has, and I presume it always will. Even in February the men were plowing deep furrows, to lie fallow until time to harrow and plant. In April the willows by the creek showed a veil of green, and the dogwood offered up its white blooms, starred with the mark of the cross. The redbud trees turned pink and we gathered armloads of them to bring into the schoolrooms. We were hungry for growing, living things, for brightness and cheer after the long cold and sickness of the winter.

In April the peepers began to croak by the waterside, and the first calves were dropped. The gardens were laid off and potatoes planted and early peas. We gathered wild greens, mustard, lettuce, cress and dock, and we ate heartily of them, needing the fresh green stuff. We dug sassafras roots and made pots of tea, drank it down greedily. We felt as if even our blood had thickened during the winter, and sassafras tea and wild greens would thin it and bring the spring into our bodies.

In April, too, the sawmill burned.

CHAPTER XXIV

THE NEWS OF IT was brought by a young man, riding hard into the village. He was not one of us, but he lived on a farm near the mill and he had ridden to bring the word. "The mill is burning," he cried, riding through the gates, pulling up in front of the office, his horse lathered with sweat and heaving. Brother Benjamin and the other men in the office ran out at his cry, "The sawmill is burning!"

Quickly they had the bell atop Center House rung, long and clamorously, to bring every man in the village running. I heard it, wondered at what new crisis was at hand. Stephen came to my door. "I must see what the bell means."

The children were curious and in spite of me flocked to the windows to look. "Is it something afire?" they asked, looking for smoke and flames. But there was nothing to see and when they had satisfied themselves on that score they went obediently back to their places. Whatever it was, I knew Stephen would bring the word when he came.

Within moments he was back, beckoned me to the hall. "The sawmill is burning, Rebecca. All the men are going to help. Take charge of the school."

I thought how sick at heart this would make Richard, who had worked so hard over the mill, taken such pride in it, run it so profitably—what a blow to him it would be. I hoped they might save something of it. "How did it start?"

"They say it was set. This boy that brought the word . . . he saw the fire, ran to help, and Brother Rankin asked him to bring the word here. I have to go. Every man is needed."

"Of course. Whom did you leave with your boys?"

"James Haywood. He can manage, but look in on him occasionally."

James Haywood was an older boy, lately come with his parents to the village. Stephen had spoken of him before, saying how dependable and responsible he was, and how bright to learn. "We'll manage," I said.

He turned to go. I called after him. "Take care, Stephen."

He looked back at me and smiled, waved his hand. "I'll be careful."

As I went back to the classroom I thought what a cruel thing it had been . . . to set the sawmill. When there was persecution from the people of the region, they always hit hard at some vital spot. The mill had prospered. We depended on it for much of our ready cash. The people about were envious, I suppose. But it was a cruel and unkind thing to do.

That was early in the morning. School had barely taken up. All morning I taught, thinking of the fire, knowing how frantically the men were working to put it out, trying to salvage something of the machinery, probably moving piles of lumber, carrying water from the creek, the flames licking high and hot all the while. It was a long morning.

Shortly after noon a blackened and smoke-smudged procession of weary men began to wend its way through the gates. From the schoolyard I saw that the first of them carried a litter. Someone had been hurt. Stephen! My heart gave a great lurch, and not thinking at all what I was doing I caught up my skirts and started running toward Center House. I didn't say a word to Sister Drucie, and as I passed her, running, I saw her mouth drop open in amazement. It was Stephen, I knew. He would be heedless of himself. A flaming timber had caught him. The boiler had exploded and he had been scalded. A stack of new lumber, resinous and hot-burning, had trapped him. As I flew down the path every possibility entered my mind, and as each horrible thing grew vivid before my eyes, passed and a newer and more horrible one took its place, I could not run fast enough. My feet felt clumsy and my skirts were in the way. My bonnet fell off, the knot of my hair came loose, but I did not stop. Hair flowing, skirts about my knees, my feet almost tripping in their haste, I ran on, urged faster and faster by this great fear.

I reached Center House just as they were carrying the litter in the door. Brother Benjamin looked at me, placed his hand on my arm. "He is dead?" I asked, gasping for breath, but still trying to get past the men in the door.

Brother Benjamin shook his head, restrained me. "No, he is not fatally injured, Rebecca. He is burned, on his face and arms, but mostly he is overcome with exhaustion and breathing so much smoke."

My mind was stupid and dull, but I felt an immense relief. He was not dead, then. Dazedly I looked about, and then I saw Stephen himself coming through the gate. I took two steps toward him, in gladness, eager to touch him and reassure myself, then Brother Benjamin's words recalled me. "I never saw a man fight so hard," he was saying. "Time and again he went into the building. He refused to give up until it actually fell in— collapsed. And it is because of him that so much of the equipment was saved."

Not until that moment did it occur to me that Brother Benjamin was speaking of Richard—and that it was Richard who was on the litter, burned, being borne into Center House.

And it was in that moment that I knew how much I loved Stephen, and for how long a time, all these months, I had been loving him unawares—for I had not once thought of Richard. All my thought had been of Stephen, all my fear had been for him, and my strongest feeling was one of relief that he was safe. I looked at him. His face was smoke-smudged, his eyes were red-rimmed, his hair was awry. His shirt was torn at the shoulder and a long bleeding gash showed through. My heart melted, seeing him so. He smiled crookedly at me, lifted his hand and went out the gate toward the Schoolhouse.

I followed the litter into Center House.

I would have nursed Richard but he would not allow it. He preferred the men of the Church Family. I saw him, briefly, when they had laid him on the couch, and I felt a great pity for him. He was in terrible pain but no sound escaped him. He kept biting his lips to hold back the moans. He opened his eyes and saw me standing there. I reached toward him, but he motioned me away. Brother Benjamin touched my arm. "We shall care for him, Rebecca."

"Yes."

"And we shall keep you informed."

"If you will, please."

I turned to go and Brother Benjamin and Sister Molly followed me to the door. They spoke of Richard—of his devotion, his dedication, of how they leaned on him. I thought, ironically, of how, in order for them to lean, it had become necessary for me to stand alone. But bitterness would not serve me now. I had a new problem to face. So I left him there, with the brethren he preferred to me.

Straight from Center House I went to the School Family House. Stephen was there, washing the smoke and the blood from himself. He grinned ruefully at me when I came upon him at the wash bench. He was stripped to the waist, trying to wash with one hand. Evidently the torn shoulder was beginning to stiffen on him. He tried to reach for his shirt to make himself more presentable, but I stayed him. I took the cloth from his hand. "Sit there," I said, pointing to the end of the bench, "and let me finish this for you."

"I'm not a very pretty sight," he said.

"This wound needs cleaning and salving," I replied, and I bathed it as gently as I could. He winced occasionally as the water made it smart, but he remained docile under my touch. It was not a very deep gash, but it was long and it followed the muscle. "How did you do it?" I asked.

"A piece of timber fell."

We were silent as I tended the wound. As my hands moved over Stephen's shoulder I thought of Richard, and of how in the old days I had rubbed knots from his shoulders. I had loved him devotedly, with all my heart. He had been my whole life—all my love, my care, my thoughts, had been centered on him. I had followed where his convictions led him, and though it had brought me deep unhappiness, I had kept faithful to him. To what purpose, I wondered. So that my hands could now deal gently with Stephen's shoulder? It came over me, then, that any woman who ever loves more than one man must carry forever with her, in her heart, a ghost. There is no new thing for her to learn. It has all been done before.

When I bandaged the wound Stephen stood up and looked at me. Without a word I went into his arms, felt them tighten about me, lifted my mouth to his. I held him close, and then I cried. "I thought it was you . . . I was so frightened I couldn't think . . . when I saw the litter I was certain it was you!"

Stephen's arms tightened. "And you cared!" He laid his cheek against mine. "Ah, Rebecca, Rebecca . . . for this I've hoped. For this I've waited, and thought it might never come."

We held tightly to each other, until I drew away, laughing shakily, and asked a woman's immemorial question. "How long have you known?"

He laughed, too. "From the first, I think . . . the sturdiness of your mind, your steadfastness . . . and you are a very beautiful woman, Rebecca."

"I?" I pushed my unruly hair back. "I have always been the plain one. Janie was the beautiful one."

Stephen caught me to him again. "Never . . . never say you're plain. Yours is the kind of beauty that will endure a hundred years. When you are an old woman you will still be beautiful."

"Oh," I laughed, "no one lives that long."

"Try to," he said, covering my face with kisses, "try to, Rebecca. I want a hundred years with you."

Startled I drew away, but before I could answer we heard footsteps. Stephen snatched up his shirt, drew it around him, but I fled into the house. I felt too disordered, too shaken, to meet another's eyes just yet.

In my room I flung myself on the bed, quivering, disturbed, happy, despairing, hopeful, hopeless. He wanted a hundred years with me! And I wanted them with him. But I was married to Richard! And marriage was till death. How could anything come of our love? Remembering his mouth on mine I thought I would rather die than give him up. Remembering my marriage vows, I saw nothing else ahead.

I lay for long hours awake that night, thinking. In the way of a woman I went back through the months I had known Stephen, remembering every word, seeing all too plainly now where every meeting between us had been leading, and at the same time cherishing every word, cherishing even the path they had led to. To be loved—to love, it is life to a woman. Without it she dies in some part of her, shrivels away, becomes sterile and brittle. I felt every pulse of my blood, every beat of my heart, new and more living than they had been in years. I felt alive again. But each time this ecstasy rose in me the thought of Richard came. I had a husband already. Where was any hope for me? What could the end be but a barrier as solid as a stone wall? I slept finally, restlessly, fitfully, and in the morning, tired, unrefreshed, I returned to the schoolroom.

They said Richard suffered much for a few days but that he had great strength of body, and of will, and that slowly, then, he began to mend. He was kept abed two weeks, however.

During that two weeks, slowly, painfully, I reached a decision. There were no more opportunities for Stephen and me to be alone, and I made none. I think he knew I must have that time to myself, for he made none either. Across the dining room, at meals, he smiled at me. In my classroom I found once a great spray of locust blossoms, heavy with scent, sweet and drowsy. On my desk, once, I found a new book. But, reticently, he brought no pressure to bear on me. Each time I saw him, though, there was that sweet softening and melting, that surging desire to be with him, in his arms, to feel his kiss. Just the sight of him walking across the schoolyard made my heart beat fast. I had to fight it very hard.

Then when word came that Richard was being allowed to leave his bed, to sit in a chair, I knew what I had to do. I sought Stephen, in his classroom, to tell him. Deliberately I closed the door behind me when I entered. Hearing the sound he turned, and seeing my face, he rose, but he took no step toward me. "You have decided," he said.

"Yes." This was so hard a thing to do that my head bent under it and I prayed I might keep my courage. I managed, finally, to look at him directly. "You must believe me, Stephen. This is a thing I *have* to do. I am going to ask Richard once more to leave the village with me. He is my husband, and if he is willing to leave the community and take up life with me again, it is the right thing for us, and what I must do."

The light in Stephen's eyes died, but his look was steadfast on me, and he even smiled a little. The silence grew very long until he finally said, "Yes . . . yes, I can see that is how you would think. Very well, my darling."

His face was a little pale, but his smile remained and it nearly broke my heart. From my apron pocket I brought forth a gift I had made for him. During the time of my decision, the remembrance of John Donne's poem had somehow come to me and stayed with me. From my own hair I had cut enough to braid a bracelet for Stephen's wrist. I reached for his hand and bound it on his arm. He knew immediately what it meant, and he quoted the words, "A bracelet of bright hair . . . Our hands ne'er touched the seals, which nature, injured by late law, sets free . . ."

"If this is the last time," I said, touching the braid around his wrist, "this is for remembrance."

He caught my hands, lifted them, turned them and bent his head to kiss each palm, laid his cheek against them, and, leaving him, I folded the touch of his mouth, the warmth of his cheek, into the flesh of my hands.

I was allowed to see Richard that evening. Brother Benjamin was present, since of course a third person was necessary. Richard looked well, more fleshed than before. I judged that resting, eating well, had helped him greatly. There were bandages still on his face, but out of them his eyes watched me. "You are mending?" I asked.

He nodded. "Under Brother Benjamin's care, yes. I have wanted for nothing."

"I am glad."

"I should be able to return to the mill in another week or two."

Brother Benjamin smiled benignly. "In due time, Richard—in due time."

They talked on a little while, about the equipment Richard had been able to save, what they must order from the east, how soon the mill could be rebuilt. When they had finished I plunged, without preface, into what had brought me. "I have come, Richard," I told him, "to ask you, once more, to leave South Union with me and return to the farm."

He stared at me, as if not believing what he had heard. "I am not happy here, Richard, and I want to go away. I can never become a real Shaker. I can never become a Believer. I want you to go with me, to take up life again with me to be . . ." I stammered but it had to be said "to be my husband again."

He found his tongue, then. "Never! You don't know what you're saying, what you're asking! I *have* no home but South Union. I have no life outside, in the world. This is my home and here I intend to stay. You will have to make the best you can of it."

I rose. "Then," I said, very slowly, so that neither he nor Brother Benjamin could misunderstand me, "I shall leave alone."

They both gaped at me. Then Brother Benjamin said, "Your life is here, Rebecca, where Richard is."

"My life," I said, "is where I want it to be, and it is not here. Richard is no longer a part of living humanity. I am. Richard is dead to the world. I am not. I can, and I will be free of this way of living."

"But you are my wife!" Richard shouted at me.

"I have not been your wife for a good many years, Richard, except in the eyes of the law. And the law itself has provided me with the instrument to end that."

"What do you mean?"

"A divorce law was enacted this year, Richard. Have you forgotten? Membership in the Society of Believers is grounds for a divorce by the dissenting party in a marriage."

Richard's eyes blazed. "You wouldn't dare!"

"I would . . . and I will."

"But divorce, Rebecca," Brother Benjamin protested, "divorce is a shameful thing. And to hurt Richard and the Society so!"

"Richard and the Society have hurt me. As for divorce . . . we are already divorced, living apart, no marriage bonds recognized. The law will simply make it legal."

Richard turned to Brother Benjamin. "Can she do this thing?"

Brother Benjamin spread his hands. "I'm afraid she can, Richard." He appealed to me. "Have you given this careful thought, Rebecca? Are you certain this is what you want to do?"

"I have given it a great deal of thought, and if Richard will not leave the village, I am entirely certain it is what I must do."

Bitterly Richard eyed me. "I never thought you would do such a thing . . . I never thought . . ."

"You have not cared what I thought," I interrupted him, passionately, "or what I felt, or what I wanted . . . not for a long, long time. It has been what *you* thought, what *you* felt, what *you* wanted! You love this life here in the village, Richard . . . then stay here. But I shall not, and you cannot make me!" I turned to Brother Benjamin. "I am glad you are here. We can settle the affair at once."

There was very little settling to be done. I had no use for the farm. I would go to my mother's for a time. But I had a right to half of the money which had been ours, and Cassie and Sampson still belonged to me. I asked for their papers, and they were brought. Richard signed for my share of the money, one hundred dollars. I signed over my right in the farm to him.

He looked at the paper when I had put my name to it, then looked dully at me, but even as he looked anger flamed in him again. "You are going straight to hell, Rebecca!"

"But *you* will be safe, and that's really all that matters to you."

"Richard . . . Rebecca . . ." Brother Benjamin pled. "When do you wish to leave, Rebecca?"

"The school term ends next week," I told him. "I should like to leave immediately, then."

"We shall arrange it," he promised.

At the door I turned. "Goodbye, Richard."

But he turned aside and refused to speak. The last sight I ever had of him was that of his stiff figure, erect in the chair, head turned to avoid me.

It had grown dark while we talked and I walked back toward the School House in its soft warmth, the stars looking very near and bright overhead. Halfway, Stephen met me, and I went into his arms sobbing. Anger had upheld me until now, but I was deeply shaken. "He will not go," I said.

In the dark I heard Stephen's breath let out on a sigh. "I did not *really* think he would, but there was a chance. I couldn't wait in my room alone. I had to know as soon as possible." He held me and kissed me. "Now, what, Becky?"

"I shall finish the school term, then I want to go to my mother's."

"What will you do there?"

I raised my head from his shoulder. It was very hard for me to say it. I had to swallow several times. "I shall use the new divorce law to free myself. I shall be disgraced, I know, but it is better to bear the shame than to continue a living death. Oh, Stephen, there is all my life before me . . . all ours . . . I am not willing to sacrifice it on Richard's altar!"

He hugged me close. "You will not be disgraced, my darling. As soon as possible you will be my wife." He held me off, laughing exultantly. "When shall I come?"

I thought about it. "At the end of the summer, I think."

"Not before? Wouldn't you like me to be there when the divorce is heard?"

"No. I must do that myself. The end of the summer, Stephen. What will you do? Will you stay on here until then?"

"No, I think not. I shall go into town—take rooms there. It has been in my mind for a long time to try my hand at a long epic poem. The subject has been haunting me for years. I can begin it while I am waiting."

"How will you live? What will you do to earn while you are waiting?"

"I have not told you before . . . it did not matter. There is no real necessity for me to earn my way. I am not a wealthy man, but there is an inheritance which I have made few calls upon. I shall make use of it now."

"Stephen," I said—he had told me he was English—"are you a lord or an earl or something?"

"No," and I felt his head shake. "No, but my father did very well in trade and he left each of his children a tidy sum."

"I'm glad."

"Yes. We shall not need to worry over money."

"I meant I'm glad you are not a titled person."

We laughed comfortably together. "Be a little glad for the money, too, Becky. We can go where we please."

I said teasingly, "To the Missouri Territory?"

Teasingly he replied, "I've given it some thought."

"I'll be bound you have."

We were silent, then, each of us thinking. This time next year, I thought, we shall be there. And so fine a vision of what our life would be came before me that it misted my eyes. Free . . . with Stephen beside me, loving books as I did, writing, traveling, adventuring together . . . it was as if Heaven had bent down and placed in my hands the perfect gift. There was only the necessity of divorce to mar it. I had believed with all my heart that marriage is till death. But Richard's way *was* death to marriage. It was only left for the courts to bury it, preach the funeral sermon.

During the following week I made an opportunity to talk to Cassie and Sampson. I told them what I was going to do. "Do you want to be free, or do you want to go with me?"

It was Cassie, naturally, who answered. "We's goin' whur you goes,

Miss Becky. We shore ain't aimin' to stay in this place no longer, an' we's free enough with you."

To Permilla I told the whole story. She was the first to know about Stephen. She hugged me in her pleasure. "I'm so glad fer you. You know, I used to think it mought happen. But you was allus so stiff-necked about Richard I misdoubted it. When do you aim to have the weddin'?"

"In the late summer."

"I'd not be wishin' to wait so long," she laughed. "Mebbe," she went on, slyly, "you'll have them younguns yit."

I shook my head. "I shan't let myself hope for that." But it was not true. I did hope, and more than that, I yearned, and even prayed.

We were in the garden and when I went to leave I looked at Permilla and saw that her eyes were full of tears. "Hit's been a long time we been friends, ain't it, Becky?"

My own eyes filled. "It's been a long time, and there never was a better friend, Permilla. I'll never forget you, nor ever cease to love you. I hate to leave you."

"Don't," she said fiercely, "you git on out of here whilst you kin. I wouldn't have you to stay fer no amount of money. Hit's yore happiness I'm thinkin' of."

"I wish you could go," I said, wistfully.

"Oh, they ain't nothin' troublin' me, way it's allus troubled you. We do good here an' I don't know as there'd be nothin' better fer us. But you git out of here an' make you a good life with yer Stephen. Ain't it a fine thing fer you, Becky?"

"The finest in the world," I said.

Stephen told me goodbye the night before I left. Holding me close he whispered, "If you need me you have only to send word."

"I will," I promised.

"It's going to be a long summer."

"It will pass before we know it. Work on your poem. Write to me. Come the first of September."

"I'll come riding up on a white charger to carry you away," he vowed.

"Just make sure," I laughed, "he's strong enough to carry us to Missouri."

I accepted a good horse from the Shakers and bought two others, for Cassie and Sampson. At the last, when I was already mounted, Permilla came, a package in her hand. "You mought git hungry," she said, holding it up to me. "I made you some sweet cakes."

I could hardly thank her for the emotion which choked me. No one else saw me off. Brother Benjamin and Sister Molly had been very cool toward me all week, and Sister Drucie had taken her cue from them. But my last memory of South Union is of Permilla, standing beside the gate, one hand lifted in farewell. I never saw her again.

From the village I went to Amanda and William's and stayed one night. I knew that Cassie would be unhappy at leaving Jency and I meant to try to buy Clayton so that he and Jency might go with us.

Amanda was not nearly so thin-lipped or pinch-faced now, and they were doing well on the farm. At first William was reluctant to sell Clayton. "I don't hardly see how I could make out without him," he said. "He's an awfully good hand."

But I offered an excellent price for Clayton. Stephen had told me to. "You could buy two strong blacks for that price," I told William. In the end he agreed and made out the papers.

I went to find Jency to tell her she was to go with us . . . she and Clayton and the baby. It was a round, chubby little chocolate drop of a boy, lighter than Jency, but not as bright as Clayton. Jency went wild with joy and ran in circles, grabbing up one thing after another until Cassie grew stern with her. "Git yore senses to workin', gal. Miss Becky ain't got all day. We got to be movin'. We'se got to leave out of here. Ain't no use you takin' them pots an' kittles. Jist git yore clo'es together."

Clayton was pleased, too. "Miss Amanda and Mister William," he said, "they awful close with vittles an' sich. They don't mistreat nobody, but they ain't ones to hand out extry."

It was quite a procession we made, Jency, Cassie and I riding in an old wagon I had bought cheap in the town, Clayton and Sampson on the horses. But I think it was the happiest group of people I have ever seen. "Oh, happy day!" Cassie sang, when we left Logan county behind. "I'm shore glad to see the last of that country!"

I did not try to deceive my mother. I told her at once what I meant to do. At first she was shocked. Divorce! Only shameless people were divorced. That a daughter of hers should consider it was unthinkable. "Whom God hath joined," she quoted to me, "let no man put asunder."

"But it was Richard's God who put us asunder, Mama," I said. "Richard has not been a husband to me since the Shakers came, in eighteen seven."

I think that shocked her even more. "You mean he ain't lived with you none at all since then?"

"Not at all. He set me aside, put me away, and for more than a year he has barely spoken to me."

I think she had never before entirely realized what Shakers demanded. She shook her head. "That's the unnaturalest thing I ever heared of." She pondered it for a time and then finally she was able to say, "I cain't say that I blame you none, if that was the way it was."

"That was the way it was."

The divorce itself was remarkably simple. I had only to file the petition, the grounds being that my husband had become a Shaker and taken up residence in a Shaker village. Very quickly it was granted. David and

Bethia were as loyal as if they had been my own parents. "You did right," David told me. "Richard is amongst the living dead."

So it was I became the first woman to avail herself of the new Kentucky divorce law . . . I, Rebecca Cooper, who had been as amazed and as astounded as any when it was passed. I could never have foreseen that I would be the first to make use of it.

The summer passed with long, heat-filled days. My brother's wife had a child, now, and it gave me pleasure to have most of the care of her. Mama was not as strong as she had been, and I persuaded her to let me take over most of her chores. The only sorrow I felt as I thought of the new life waiting for me was in leaving her. It grieved Mama, and I dreaded going so far away. But there is something callous in every child, something on-pressing, something pushing it away from home. And I knew that, short of actual illness, I would leave her again.

It was good to shed the Shaker dress, and my own clothing, hand-woven so many years ago but still stout and sturdy, fitted me as if I had never worn any others. Mama looked at my red woolen dresses, at my two white linens. "Is this all yer clothes?" she asked.

"That's all. We were allowed two each season. I think I'll burn them and be shut of them."

She was horrified. "You'll do no sich. This is good stout weavin'. I c'n turn 'em, rip 'em up, stitch 'em to another style fer you."

I nodded, not caring, and she set to work on them.

A letter came from Janie, jubilant that I was away from the Shaker village and, oddly, full of Johnnie Cooper. "When is the wedding?" she wrote. "Johnnie and I are coming."

Mama nodded when I read the letter aloud. "Them two," she said, "will be next."

I was delighted. "I'm so glad! Johnnie has loved her all his life. But I never thought to see Janie loving him."

"Well, she does, I reckon. She don't write about much else *but* him any more. He's doin' good, they say, freightin' an' tradin' everywheres."

I wrote Janie to come the last week of August.

Exactly on the first day of September Stephen came, brown from the summer sun, a little weightier than when I'd left, coming riding up the slope from the creek at a full run in his eagerness. "That young man of yore'n," Mama said, dryly, "will blow his horse if he don't take keer."

But I barely heard her. I was flying down the hill to meet him, and when he flung himself off his horse and hugged me I thought he would crack every rib in my chest. Not caring who saw, he kissed me and kissed me, and held me off to look at me, hugged me tight again, all the while laughing and saying, "Rebecca, Rebecca!" And I . . . I could say nothing.

All I could do was cling, and weep, and laugh, all at the same time. It was so good to see him again.

They liked him, Mama and Johnnie and Janie. Stephen and Johnnie took to each other at once, and they talked endlessly about the Missouri Territory. Johnnie had once traded into St. Louis, and he knew the famous Chouteau brothers there. "It's the land of the future," he said, over and over.

I thought of the wagons painted so gaily with the slogans "Going West!" or "Headed for Missouri!" Our Shaker brethren had disapproved, shaken their heads over the movement, said grimly, "They are foolish people, stirred by restlessness. They'll be glad to come home when they learn what hardships there will be."

But I had watched those wagons with envy. They stood for more than restlessness to me. They stood for the everlasting way of our forefathers, our grandparents who had crossed the waters to a new land, our parents who had risked their lives in a new country. Neither peril, privations, nor hostile Indians had stayed them. Like a tide rushing at its flood they had poured into the land, pushed back the mountains, cleared the forests, peopled the long meadows with their own kind, raised their homes and grown their crops. It was the way of our folk, that was all, and I had watched it and understood it and envied it, and now I was going to be a part of it. I was not Tice and Hannah Fowler's daughter for nothing.

"By George," Johnnie said, interrupting my thoughts, "whyn't we work together on this? Me an' Janie could go to St. Louis, handle the goods and freightin' out of there, deal with the Chouteaus, an' you an' Becky could run a post, say, at Three Forks!"

"Where," I said, "is Three Forks?"

Johnnie drew a map in the dirt near the doorstep, showing how three rivers came together, the Arkansas, the Verdigris and the Grand. "Here," he said, "amongst the Osages. The Chouteaus trade there, too."

Stephen's eyes kindled, and he looked at me. Well, I hadn't bargained for Osage Indians, but if he wanted to go there, so did I. I nodded. "It's a deal," he told Johnnie.

"How," Janie put in spiritedly, "do you know I will like living in St. Louis?"

"St. Louis is not the backwoods, Janie," Johnnie told her. "You ought to see the way the Chouteaus live! You'd have everything you have right now, and more."

"Well," she laughed, "I'm not made of spun sugar, either." She looked at me, her eyes sparkling. "Would you like this to be a double wedding, Becky?"

"Would you?" I asked, delighted, hardly believing her.

"That's what Johnnie and I planned all along." Her hand stole out and Johnnie took it. "We waited, when we heard your news."

[211]

I looked at Stephen and he smiled at me, nodded. It was all I needed to make my cup run over.

Strangely enough, when the four of us stood up together before the preacher, I wore one of the crimson wools Mama had made over. Styled differently it pleased me very much. Stephen liked it, too. And we both felt sentimental about it. The Shakers had truly given us each other and we could not forget it.

That was twenty years ago. The remnants of the dress have been used in many ways . . . as a coverlet for my first-born son and for the three others who followed him; as pieces in a braided rug which still lies before the hearth; as a cover for the cushion of the chair Stephen uses at his desk.

The Missouri Territory has greatly changed since we first came. It has been divided and redivided, and the part in which we settled is now the Indian Territory. For many years there has been a military cantonment at Three Forks . . . Cantonment Gibson, it is called.

We left Kentucky immediately after our marriage, in good order, for Stephen spared no expense to make the journey a comfortable one. We traveled with wagons and teams. Janie and Johnnie went more swiftly, down the Ohio and up the Mississippi to St. Louis.

Ours was a journey I shall never forget. I was prepared for hardships, but there were none. I rode comfortably all the way, and our camps at night were made easy for us by Cassie and Jency, Clayton and Sampson. And it was on that journey that I knew the fullness of Stephen's love, its tenderness, its sweetness and its goodness, and knew that my own heart had found its home. It was on that journey, also, that I conceived and knew, joyously, that there would be a child. From the first knowledge I had no fear for this one. There was, instead, the conviction, never shaken, that it would be a healthy child, would live, would bring delight to us both.

Three Forks, this place Johnnie and Stephen had chosen, was a wilderness, but I was ready for the adventure of the wilderness, delighted by it, excited. We selected a site on which to build. We could not buy it, for this land had all been set aside for the eastern Indians who were being moved west of the Mississippi. But we could build a house upon it, and carry on trade with the Indians.

Our home was built of logs, with a queer hallway between the main rooms called a "dog-trot." But there was nothing crude or unbeautiful about the home. It was as fine, outside of being built of logs, as a home could be, and the furnishings we brought on from St. Louis were rich, elegant, handsome.

The children came, in quick succession, four boys, as fine as any of Permilla's, husky, healthy, fat and happy. They were the delight of us all, Cassie and Jency especially making much over them. Janie loved them dearly, too. She has no children. Two were born to her and Johnnie, but both were stillborn, as my own first two were. Stephen believes, and I agree, that there is some weakness in the Cooper strain which both Richard and Johnnie inherited.

My boys are nearly grown now. Like young bear cubs they wrestle over the floors, eat hugely, ride their fast horses like the wind, handle a gun as my father must have done. The oldest boy, who is the image of Stephen and named for him, has already made two journeys with Johnnie's men, to the Platte and the upper waters of the Missouri. He will leave us, one day, and move on farther west.

Stephen became fascinated with the Indians all about us, the Osages first, and then the Cherokees, moved west from Arkansas. He went among them freely, learned their languages, wrote down their songs and speeches, their traditions and ceremonies. His finest book is one he wrote about them, translated for the most part from their own tongue.

He continues to write. A part of each day is spent at his desk. And on the wrist of the hand which moves his pen is still the bracelet of hair which I placed there so many years ago. No woman ever had a better husband. We have been happy . . . we are still happy.

Janie and Johnnie make their home in St. Louis, though they visit us often. We have all prospered beyond any expectation. The only sorrow we have known since coming to this country has been the death of Mama. We made a journey back to Kentucky when word came to us that she was failing. As far as we could tell it was simply old age, for she lived to be eighty. We felt grief, of course, but we also felt that she had lived out her years in the way she had wanted. She is buried on the hill back of the house, beside my father. I remembered what she had said the day we buried him. "He'll rest easy here, lookin' out over the country he loved." I think Mama rests easy, too.

The Shaker villages, South Union and Pleasant Hill, are still there, the one on Gasper River, the other on Shawnee Run. But Stephen says they are doomed. Not soon, perhaps, but in time, he says, they will die, for you cannot withdraw from life without sickening and fading. You cannot go against nature without becoming sterile, and no zeal can be kept fanned to the white heat of the early times, the revival days. It may be that when the old leaders have passed on, as some of them have and more will do, the younger ones will lack the purity of the vision, the spur of the adventure. This country was established by freedom-loving men, and few with the zeal and the spirit to endure can willingly exchange freedom for safety. That will be the death of the Shakers. It will be sapped from within, by the loss of its own health.

But I wish them no harm. The most devoted of them were good people, as they saw goodness. My quarrel with them was that their conception of goodness made no allowance for any other man's, and that, I felt, was tyranny. It was the tyranny of innocence, but I saw evil come of it, exactly as evil comes of all tyranny, for innocence is no guarantor of goodness. Stephen has laughed at my efforts to put down our Shaker experiences. But it is a gentle and indulgent laughter. I have written the last words now, and I shall burn my Journals. The wind of the spirit, free and unburdened, has blown sweetly into my life, and my years with the Shakers made it even sweeter for me. I have tried to deal justly with the Believers.